Also by Kimberley Freeman

Wildflower Hill
Lighthouse Bay

EMBER ISLAND

Kimberley Freeman

A TOUCHSTONE BOOK
Published by Simon & Schuster
New York London Toronto Sydney New Delhi

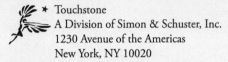

Touchstone
A Division of Simon & Schuster, Inc.
1230 Avenue of the Americas
New York, NY 10020

First Touchstone trade paperback edition April 2014

Originally published in 2013 by Hachette Australia

TOUCHSTONE and colophon are registered trademarks of Simon & Schuster, Inc.

For information about special discounts for bulk purchases, please contact Simon & Schuster Special Sales at 1-866-506-1949 or business@simonandschuster.com.

The Simon & Schuster Speakers Bureau can bring authors to your live event. For more information or to book an event, contact the Simon & Schuster Speakers Bureau at 866-248-3049 or visit our website at www.simonspeakers.com.

Interior design by Aline Pace

Manufactured in the United States of America

10 9 8 7 6 5 4 3 2 1

Library of Congress Cataloging-in-Publication Data
Freeman, Kimberley, 1970–
 Ember Island : a novel / Kimberley Freeman.—First Touchstone edition.
     pages   cm
 1. Women novelists—Fiction. 2. Great-grandmothers—Fiction. 3. Diaries—Fiction. 4. Family secrets—Fiction. 5. Moreton Bay (Qld.)—Fiction. I. Title.
 PR9619.4.F75E48 2014
 823'.92—dc23
                         2013035415

ISBN 978-1-4767-4350-9
ISBN 978-1-4767-4353-0 (ebook)

For Meg Vann, from one big girl to another

PROLOGUE

May 15, 1892

My brain is full of blackbirds! I have heard something this after-noon . . . I scarce believe it. I do not want to believe it. What a burden it is to have such knowledge. Should I tell Papa? I cannot comprehend what she has done, what she yet intends to do. But if Papa knows he will send her away and I have come to love her so dearly.

And I am almost certain Papa has too.

ONE

A Summer Wedding

1891

June sunshine blessed Tilly Kirkland's wedding. Only the luckiest brides married in June, and Tilly could not believe how lucky she had been. Even though her feet were pinched by the white satin shoes, the boned corset under her silk and organza gown made it hard to breathe, and she had been smiling so energetically for so long at all the well-wishers that the muscles in her face ached, she counted herself the luckiest girl in the world. Jasper had come along at precisely the right moment, and one speedy courtship later, here she was married and on her way to a new life.

The garden of Grandpa's house in Dorset was lush and green, flowers bright in the soft sun. Two long tables had been laid out with food, and the guests milled around happily, talking and laughing. The warm breeze lifted her hair and cooled the perspiration at the base of her scalp. The sweet-smelling orange-blossom coronet couldn't contain her wild red curls, and she was constantly pulling strands of hair out of her mouth. A distant and very old aunt related to her in painful detail the unfortunate tale of her old dog's recent illness and death. Tilly was relieved for a chance to frown sympathetically rather than smile, but the story was very long and she couldn't always hear the elderly woman's soft voice clearly over the chatter.

Tilly risked a glance away. Where was Jasper? Where was *her husband*? The thought made her glow a little. Jasper, with his stylish tailcoat and gray cashmere trousers. Ever well dressed, handsome, with a dash of panache other men did not have. She returned her attention to her aunt for a few moments, then tried another stealthy glance around the garden.

There he was. The sun was bright in his golden-brown hair and his neatly trimmed sideburns. His body was lithe and erect, and he seemed to stand outside all the chatter and movement, singular and proud. His gaze roamed over the gathering and his eyes took a moment to find Tilly. In that moment, before he registered that she was regarding him, she saw something that made her stomach prickle with doubt. Was it pity in his expression? Or disdain?

But then he smiled and Tilly smiled in return, warily. Hopefully. She told herself that perhaps she was tired and imagining things. He was now the same Jasper she had always known and the shadow passed like a cloud passing over the sun.

A clumsy crash shook her out of her reverie. Voices rang out in alarm behind her, and Jasper's expression was forgotten.

"Tilly! Tilly!"

Grandpa lay on the grass. Sharp heat speared her heart. Dishes and cups had been knocked off the table in his fall, and anxious guests were running towards him. Time slowed. He looked so pale, so old. When did he become so pale and old?

Then she was at his side, asking people to give him room to breathe, ordering cousin Godfrey to run into the village to fetch a physician.

"Grandpa? Can you hear me?"

His eyelids flickered and his right hand trembled as though he were trying to move it.

"No, no, don't move. Relax. Be still. The physician is coming." She stroked his forehead gently. "Be well, Grandpa, be well," she said under her breath. But she could already feel the ship sailing away from her, pulled on a mighty tide she could neither measure nor control. She grasped Grandpa's hand and waited.

TWO

The Broken Chimney

2012

"I can barely hear you, Nina. You keep breaking up."

I repositioned myself in the very corner of the verandah and leaned out as far as I could. The fresh smell of the sea was laced with the less pleasant scent of seaweed. A quick breeze off the bay shot up my shirt, cooling the sweat on my ribs. Up here on the escarpment I had an uninterrupted view of the pale blue mainland off in the distance, the place where I hoped to entice a mobile phone signal from. "I said, did you already call the builder?"

But my mother was no longer on the line. I checked my phone, saw the *SOS only* signal, and slid it back in my pocket.

No mobile reception. Nobody could phone me. All the knots in my spine loosened.

I turned and went back inside: Starwater House as it had been once called, though I didn't know whether that was an official name or my great-grandmother's romantic appellation. Eleanor Holt had been known for romantic notions. I threw my mobile phone onto the couch and stood by the chimney, poking at the damp wallpaper. Starwater had been the administrative office of a whale-watching business for two years. A whale-watching business that had always been late or light with rent, and which had now failed, packed up, and disappeared without any official notice and owing thousands of dollars in rent to me, their landlady.

It wasn't the lost money I minded. It was that nobody had been here to report the storm damage. October was the heart of storm season on Moreton Bay and the one that had blown in last week was so violent it even made the news in Sydney. I had seen pictures taken over on the mainland: trees crashed through car roofs and powerlines down and floodwater raging down suburban streets. And I thought at the time, I wonder how Starwater held up. It was an old house, built in 1868, and while I'd spent a lot of money on keeping it solid and safe, its position up on the escarpment of Ember Island made it vulnerable to storms. I'd phoned the whale watchers the next morning and got a disconnected notice.

Mum was the one who suggested I pay a visit. Mum was the driving force behind anything to do with Starwater. She had made me buy it six years ago. "You're the only one of us that can afford it at the moment," she'd said, one of the infrequent times she compared my two older sisters unfavorably to me. The engineer and the surgeon usually trumped the novelist. "It should be back in the family."

The damage around the chimney was not as bad as I feared when I'd first arrived to see the blue tarpaulin flapping in the wind on the roof. The tree branch that had split open the roof was still pinned at an awkward angle to the house, the mighty arm of a Moreton Bay fig that had probably been on Ember Island for hundreds of years before white men came here and built the infamous maximum security prison I'd learned about in school. But inside, apart from this large water stain on the wallpaper and a jagged crack opening up in the brickwork of the chimney, there didn't seem much to fix. If the builder could do it in the next few days, I could be back in Sydney by the weekend.

The thought of Sydney made me feel sad and desperate. I didn't want to go back. Not now, not until . . . after. But even then I'd still have to see them, wouldn't I? We couldn't avoid each other.

My train of thought was interrupted by footsteps on the stairs leading up to the front verandah and I hurried out to meet the builder, glad for the distraction.

"Hello," I said. "I'm grateful you could make it so quickly. Come in and have a look."

The builder looked back at me. He seemed startled, but I didn't know why. He was what my mother would have called a "strapping lad" in his thirties, with curling blond hair, broad shoulders, and tanned skin.

"I'm Nina," I said, leading him inside. "I'm the owner."

"Joe," he said, finding his voice. "I put the tarp up. I hope you don't mind. I knew there was nobody here and . . . she's such a beautiful old place."

"Mind? That's really lovely of you. The water damage might have been so much worse. Now you'll see it's mainly a stain on the wallpaper and a cracked chimney."

We stopped in front of the fireplace.

"The walls should dry out okay, though the stain might be hard to get rid of," he said. "But I think the chimney might be cracked up a bit further than this. Somebody would need to get on the roof and look. I don't know how sound the structure would be."

"So can you do that for me? Or do I need to call a roofer? I'm sorry, I don't know much about these things."

Joe blinked back at me. "I guess I could do it. I don't have any other work at the moment."

"That would be great. How quickly can you get it done?"

He tilted his head to the side and scratched just above his ear, surveying the chimney. "I . . . Well, that would depend on the extent of the damage, what supplies you needed, how quickly I could get them from the mainland . . ." His eyes locked on something on the chimney's brickwork. He stepped forward and ran his finger over the jagged crack. It followed precisely the pattern of the brickwork. His finger came to rest on the last line of mortar before the top of the fireplace and he pushed lightly. "Look at this," he said.

I moved close to him and peered at where he was pointing. A mortar-free gap between the bricks had opened up and inside it, there was a thin sheaf of papers.

"What is it?" I asked.

"Let's have a look," he said, pulling out a pocketknife. He gently scraped it into the crack and coaxed out the papers.

I saw and recognized her handwriting before the papers were in my hand. "This is my great-grandmother's handwriting," I breathed as I took it from his fingers.

"How do you know?"

"I've read all her papers. Or at least I thought I had." My eyes fell on the first line on the first page. "It's a diary."

He peered at it. "1891."

"She would have been twelve." Twelve. This could only be a child's nonsense. I'd hoped for something much more substantial. Disappointment sank cold in my veins.

"It's not much of a diary, only a few pages," he said.

"Maybe it's been torn out of a book. I'll read it later."

"The letters are so tiny."

I glanced at the first line. *Papa intends to hire me a governess.* "I'm used to her handwriting. I can decipher it."

Joe was poking other bricks now. "I didn't know this house had a family heritage," he said.

"It doesn't," I replied, folding the pages and sliding them into the back pocket of my jeans. "I bought it a few years ago, for my mother's sake. She'd always hoped it would come on the market one day. My great-grandmother lived here with her father when he was the prison superintendent. When the prison was decommissioned they kept the house. Her name was Eleanor Holt. She's legendary in our family."

Joe folded the knife and pocketed it. "Why?"

"She was a wild nonconformist. Never married, had her son, my grandfather, at thirty-eight, never told anybody who the father was and raised him single-handed. Grandad always spoke so proudly of her. She was a member of the Socialist Party and wrote angry letters to just about everybody. She was fierce."

Joe smiled. "Well, now you'll know if she was fierce as a child too." He glanced at his watch. "I have to go pick up my son shortly, but I haven't answered your question. About how long it would take me to fix your roof."

"Go on, then."

"I'm not a roofer. I'm not even a builder. I'm an okay handyman, I guess."

"Oh, I'm sorry. I assumed you were the builder my mother called." Perhaps that's what Mum had been trying to tell me when the mobile signal fizzled out.

"It's a coincidence that I arrived when you were here." He pulled a set of keys out of his pocket. "I was going to let myself in. I used to work here. For George and Kay."

"I see." George and Kay were the bad tenants who owed me

thousands. I took the keys from him. "If you were going to let yourself in, I presume you needed something."

"I have a locker back in the office with some of my books in it."

"Sure. Go through. Take what you have to."

I remained in the living room while he went through to the office. George and Kay had lived here on the premises, but the furnishings were all mine, left here by the previous owner who couldn't face moving beds and sofas off the island by boat. I unfolded the pages in my pocket and skimmed the first few lines of Eleanor's diary. It was childish but lively. She had always written, it seemed. Not like me. I had come to writing late, reluctantly. That's why I was having so many problems finishing this book, meeting this ever-encroaching deadline. I simply wasn't a born writer.

Joe reemerged with a cardboard box full of books. "Thanks for that. Do you still want me to come back and fix your roof? It might take me a bit longer than a real roofer, but I'm not afraid of hard work and . . . I kind of lost my job when George and Kay shot through."

I pocketed the diary again. "What sort of work did you do for them?"

"I took people on tours. I'm a marine biologist. Or at least I will be once I finish my PhD." He nodded towards the books in the box, and I noted they were thick texts with titles such as *Migratory Cetacean Behaviour*, *Genetic Ecology of Whales,* and *Cyamid Ectoparasites.*

"Wow," I said. "Not light reading, then?" I always felt awed and a little embarrassed around very intelligent people. I'd spent a lifetime in the shadows my terribly bright sisters cast.

"It's been a long time since I sat down with a novel. You're a novelist, right? Kay told me."

"Yeah. Right." I regarded him a moment and tried to think in the straightest line I could. There was something appealing about the way he looked. Sure, he was handsome, but it was more than that. No artifice, no pretension. Just a warm, masculine energy as natural as the sand or the sea. Did I want to give him work so he could do some work for me? Or so I could admire him? Because that wouldn't end well. I had made a very recent vow to be more careful with my heart.

But this man had cared enough about Starwater to put a tarp on the roof; he was strong and capable and he'd recently lost his job. "So," I said, "if you need the money, you can fix my roof."

The slight release of tension in his shoulders was almost imperceptible, but I saw it. "You don't have to be here on the island," he said. "I can do it and send you photos every day so you know I'm not taking advantage."

"I'm certain we can work something out."

He moved towards the door, then turned around and seemed to be about to say something.

"What is it?" I asked.

He laid the box on the battered mahogany coffee table. "I just remembered. My dinghy's in the boat shed."

Not comprehending, I shook my head.

"I have to take a little motorboat across and back to the mainland to pick up Julian, my son. I've been keeping it in your boat shed."

"I have a boat shed?"

"Yeah, it's about a kilometer's walk back down the hill, near the jetty."

I vaguely remembered seeing it on the plans when I'd taken possession of the house.

"Anyway," he continued. "I just gave you back your keys, including the key to the boat shed."

I picked up the keys and offered them to him. "Look, take the boat shed key and hang on to it. You can use it for as long as you like. I'm unlikely to ever have use for it."

"You may want to store your boat in it," he said with a grin, unhooking the key from the ring.

"I don't have a boat."

"George and Kay left theirs behind. Depending on how much rent they owe you, it might be yours now."

"I wouldn't know what to do with a boat," I muttered, but made a mental note to ask my friend Stacy, a solicitor, about it.

He picked up his box again. "I'm going over to the mainland tomorrow to have a meeting at the university. I'll ask around about suppliers and come back in the afternoon with some ideas about how to get this damage fixed. How does that sound?"

"Yes, that would be great."

"Is it okay if I bring my boy with me? I'm a single dad. But he's a good kid. Can entertain himself."

"He'd be very welcome." Now I was bristling with questions. Single dad. Had his wife died or was he just divorced? How old was his child? How young must he have been married? As I was somebody who had married, disastrously, at nineteen, I was always interested to meet a kindred traveler on that path. Luckily for me, there hadn't been children involved. Not for want of trying; but I had a medical condition that meant I wasn't destined to be a mother. Something I thought I'd made my peace with long ago.

I waved Joe off and then stood on the verandah for a while, gazing out over the island. In the south, the big flat grassy areas played host to Ayrshire cattle. To the east, facing the mainland, were miles of mangrove forest: an impenetrable swamp. Behind, where I couldn't see, was the raging Pacific Ocean, crashing against rocks, occasionally withdrawing long enough at low tide to reveal a narrow sandy beach. The afternoon breeze was fresh and tangy, cooling off the moist heat of the day. All across the island, as far as my eyes could see, white and purple crocuses bloomed wild. Over a hundred years ago there had been exactingly maintained English-style gardens around Starwater. Female prisoners had been pressed into service as gardeners to the superintendent. The gardens were long gone, but the crocus seeds had spread everywhere on the gusty sea winds and, year after year, bloomed again, remembering their history.

No traffic noise, no phones ringing to remind me how far behind I was on my work. No running into Cameron and his pregnant girlfriend. Just the sound of the wind in the trees and the ocean.

I went back inside. The lounge furniture was dated, but comfortable. The fridge hummed and the microwave blinked the correct time. I could turn a mattress and put fresh sheets on a bed. George and Kay had even left half-empty bottles of shampoo and body wash in the bathroom.

I decided to stay a few nights.

•

Night came softly and slowly, the blush of pink behind the palms slowly fading to blue-gray. I sat on the front steps of Starwater in the balmy evening warmth, watching the stars come out, reflecting on how little time I spent outside when I was home in Sydney. My apartment, which had cost a small fortune, had views all the way to the honey-colored spires of St. Mary's Cathedral; but they were city views and the stars were dim or invisible against the bright lights of Sydney. In happier times Cameron and I would sip an evening gin and tonic on our penthouse deck. Since the split I'd spent most of my time inside the apartment, locked in my office writing, or trying to.

The first mosquito bite sent me back into the house. I closed the screen and turned on the lamp in the lounge room. I approached the fireplace and ran my finger up the crack as far as I could reach. No more secret stashes of paper with Eleanor's handwriting on them.

I turned, surveyed the room. The original brickwork was hidden beneath plasterboard and wallpaper. Then I remembered the office had one exposed brick wall, so I switched on the lights in there and began a slow walk from one end of the room to the other, carefully scanning the bricks for any unmortared gaps. My fingers traced the patterns on the wall, which was cool and rough. I found nothing. Even if I found something, it would probably be more of Eleanor's childhood diary. But hope had been renewed. I might yet find the papers that I dreamed of finding, the ones that could change everything for me.

Eleanor's writings had come to our family when my grandfather died ten years ago. A great big moldy smelling trunk filled with letters and lists and ramblings and stories and poems. No diaries, which made it odd that she kept one as a child. At the time, my sisters were both too busy to go through the papers and my mother didn't have the patience with the tiny inky scrawl on them. I was twenty-five, recently separated, and between jobs at fruit shops and day-care centers—*again*, as my mother had pointed out—so going through the papers had been my task. I'd read them all. Everything. I'd grown to love Eleanor through this insight into her agile mind, her imaginative turns of phrase, her honesty and sometimes ribald humor.

When I bought Starwater, before the renters moved in, I'd combed the house for more writings and found an old suitcase in the attic. Mostly poems and short stories. And I'd believed then that I must have exhausted all chances of finding anything else she wrote. But tonight I wondered what else might be stashed around the house in nooks and crannies, behind modern renovations, under carpets and floorboards. Eleanor had lived here until her death at the age of seventy-nine. What else might she have written?

Frankly, I was desperate to find it all.

One room after another, I went through the house. Starwater was a rambling T-shaped building: the central column made up of lounge room, dining room, and kitchen; the west wing of three bedrooms and a bathroom; and the east wing of rooms that had been converted to the whale-watching office. The whole house was surrounded by wooden verandahs, open to catch the breezes on hot summer days. I assessed cornices and skirting boards, lifted a loose tile in the bathroom, peeked under lino in the kitchen, knocked the bedroom walls listening for hollows. Then finally admitted I didn't know what I was doing and was unlikely to find anything, and wound up back in the office. I sat at the largest desk. A desk calendar sat open at July the thirty-first. Perhaps that had been the last day George and Kay had been in the office, before hastily packing their things and fleeing their debts. It had also been the date my next book was due. A missed deadline, now ten weeks in the past. I experienced that familiar feeling in my guts of tightening and hardening, and had to breathe through it. "It's writer's block," Mum had said, and Marla and my sisters and Stacy and even Cameron, when he'd come by with a trolley to take the last few things in my apartment that were his. But there was no way such a simplistic name could be applied to the problems I was facing getting the words down.

I went back to the west wing and chose a bedroom. I think it was the guest room. I didn't want to go to bed in George and Kay's room and lie there all night wondering how many conversations they'd had in there about their failing business and mounting debts. I had plenty of anxieties of my own to keep me awake.

THREE

The Deep Quiet

I woke to a deep quiet. It took me a few moments to remember where I was. The only sounds were the distant ocean and the chirp of sparrows in the trees. I rolled over and looked at my phone. The SOS signal was gone and I could see I had one tiny bar of reception. Fearful that my agent, Marla, would call me, I switched it off.

It wasn't the lack of traffic noise and joggers' footfalls that made the morning quiet: it was that there was no way to download e-mail or take a phone call or post cheerful responses on my Twitter stream. I was unreachable. Nobody could expect me to respond to anything.

I hadn't felt this relaxed in years.

And that's when I had the idea: I wouldn't go home. I wouldn't even leave the island. I'd get Stacy to brave my mother's house on the mainland and bring my suitcase over here for me. I had my laptop in my satchel. I could write. The world would go away. It would be me and the story and I would somehow get it done before the new deadline—just two months away—swung around.

I was so excited, so certain, that I practically jumped out of bed and switched my phone back on. One bar of reception became two out on the verandah and I dialed Marla's number. It was ringing before I realized it was six in the morning.

"Hello?" she said, warily.

"I'm so sorry, Marla. Did I wake you?"

"Of course not. I was up at five for a jog." Marla was a ridiculously fit woman of an unguessable age, who seemed to run on coffee and leafy greens. "Why are you calling so early? Do you have good news?"

"I think so. I'm here at Starwater, my great-grandmother's old house. And it's perfect for a writing retreat. I know I can finish the book here." My resolve wavered on the last sentence. I hoped I'd hid it well.

"Hm, really?" Marla sounded skeptical.

"Absolutely. There's nothing at all here to distract me. It will be me and the laptop. Nothing else." Nothing else. Nothing at all else. I gulped a breath.

"Nina, sweetie, I don't want you to push yourself too hard, but you know the publishers are breathing down my neck. There's only so many excuses I can make for you. Are you sure this time? Wouldn't you be better down here in Sydney where I could keep an eye on you? Where I could hold you to some weekly goals?"

And risk seeing them again? No, no, a thousand times no. "I know this is the best decision I could make," I said as forcefully as I could.

She said something but it cut out and cut back in so I didn't quite catch it.

"Sorry, I have really bad reception here," I said.

Then the line dropped out altogether.

"Damn," I said, shaking the phone as if it could help. I grabbed my satchel from behind the door. I'd seen a pay phone down the hill.

The morning was clear and cool, with dew on the grass and damp smells in the air: seaweed, cow dung, muddy fields, the vanilla sweetness of gardenias blooming in front gardens. The unsealed road led down the hill and through pastureland—cows behind wire fences on both sides—and past the old stockade building, which had been converted to shops: a convenience store that doubled as a post office, a craft shop that also sold some tourist wares, and a café. They all stood closed. Only three hundred people lived on Ember Island, most spread out over farms, so trade was slow and sporadic. Six a.m. was far too early to be open.

I found the phone box and pushed the coins into the slot. I couldn't remember the last time I'd used a pay phone. It seemed a practice that belonged to a more innocent time. At the other end the phone rang and Marla picked it up quickly.

"What kind of a place has no mobile signal?" she asked, without saying hello.

"An island in the middle of a bay where I know I'll get some writing done."

"Hm. Well. I was just saying, I've been trying to get hold of you. I had an offer for you to go to Singapore, all expenses, business class. There's some kind of international symposium on Middle Ages in film and literature. They want you to talk about the research you do."

My Widow Wayland books were a series of crime novels set in the 1320s, with a clever widow as the detective. The BBC had adapted two of them for television. I had sold nearly twelve million books. These things should have happened to somebody else, not me. I was incredibly grateful for my success: you've no idea how grateful. But one thing I hated more than anything was being asked to speak about my historical research. "No, I'm too busy."

"It's after your deadline."

"No. I don't want to."

"Fair enough," she said in her usual efficient way. "I'll turn them down nicely. Now, how about you send me what you've written so far?"

My throat tensed. The first half of the book, which I had staggered through somehow, was awful. I kept telling myself I would fix it in the edit, but anybody who had come to love the Widow Wayland would surely be disappointed. I couldn't let Marla read it until I'd fixed it somehow. I wound the phone cord around my fingers, clearing my throat. "As soon as I can access my e-mail I'll send it to you," I promised, knowing it was a promise I wouldn't be fulfilling.

Marla wasn't stupid, but she didn't push the issue. "I'll expect something from you in a few weeks then," she said in a brusque, businesslike tone. Then she softened. "Darling, is this about Cameron and Tegan? Is that why you don't want to come back?"

"No, no, that's not it at all. I wish them well, you know that. I just want to put my head down and finish the book. I'm so far behind, I feel like I'll . . ." I was going to say *I feel like I'll never catch up*, but it wasn't wise to say that to my agent. "I feel like I'll get some good work done here." I leaned my back on the glass and glanced around me, at the shops and the yellow grass and the pale morning sky.

"All right then. You know yourself best, dear. Take care."

I hung up the phone and stood there a while. Cameron and Tegan. I said her name aloud, "Tegan." Yes, that still hurt.

Tegan, who lived two floors below us. Who had been at our dinner parties. Sweet-faced and young, tanned skin and immaculate blow-dry. Everything I wasn't, with my mousy tangle of hair, my limbs freckled by a Queensland childhood, and my furrowed brow from years of being far too serious. Nonetheless, I'd liked Tegan. For all that her rich daddy had bought her apartment for her and she'd never worked a real job in her life, there had been a softness about her, a girlishness that was appealing.

I'd like to be able to say that Cameron and I had had six good years together, but we didn't. We had one good year, one hopeful year, then four fraught years as he tried to convince me to try IVF, adoption, surrogacy, anything. Anything that would make him a father. In my previous marriage, my inability to fall pregnant was suspected, diagnosed, then never mentioned again. I'd stopped having fantasies of chubby-armed babies, and replaced them with reassurances to myself that I would perhaps travel more, or have a couple of big dogs one day. So by the time I got together with Cameron, my emotional pain didn't arise from the idea of ghost children we would never have. It arose from the constant feeling that my body was somehow not right, not good enough for him.

I looked at myself in the reflection of the café window opposite. No curves. Small firm breasts, hips that looked great in skinny jeans. There was nothing womanly about me and I'd never minded before. But those years with Cameron had undermined me. My constant refusal to "investigate possibilities," as he used to say, had eventually become too much. I ended the relationship, telling myself it was for his sake. So he could find somebody else. It was difficult. Cameron was a writer too, we shared a publisher, we would cross paths from time to time and chat brightly across the surface of dark, unspoken feelings. He seemed to find comfort in writing after our split, publishing two collections of poetry within a few months of each other. I was sty-mied, unable to focus, lived in fear and horrible stasis.

And then one day, ten months after he'd moved out, I was com-ing back from the café in the foyer of my apartment building—this was my ritual, one of my only journeys out of the flat: coffee at ten—and the lift doors had opened and inside were Cameron and Tegan. Their hands intertwined. Her belly pushing softly against the silky material of her designer maternity blouse.

"Nina," Cameron had said, surprised. Awkward.

Tegan smiled sweetly, compassion in her eyes. "Nina, I've been meaning to catch up with you."

In that second, I had to decide whether to put my skinny, bar-ren body into the lift next to her juicy roundness. And I couldn't do it. I couldn't ride the fifteen floors up in hot silence with them. So I turned and ran.

I'd ended up on Ember Island just four days later.

•

I had to get serious about my work. I couldn't keep trying to write through this thin fog of remorse and despair. I spent my time choosing a desk in the office. There were two: one with a view into the garden beds and tree branches, and another with a view over the island and out to sea. I sat at one, then the other, then decided the tree view would distract me less and plugged my lap-top in there and made tea while it booted up. This time, this time I was going to write. I was going to do it.

I sat down, opened the file, and looked at it. Black words, white page, just as all the other books had been. This was no different. It would be fine. I could ignore the empty space where my confidence should be. The cursor blinked. I put my hands on the keyboard and wrote, *Eleanor examined the dead man's fingernails.*

Eleanor was the Widow Wayland's name, like my great-grandmother. She had found a body. The Widow Wayland was always finding bodies, often through luck or coincidence; it was a wonder nobody suspected her of murdering them. In this story, the dirt under the dead man's fingernails was the key to discovering which farm he had been snooping on before being struck on the head with a blunt instrument, in a story about a fourteenth-century parish priest who was having a steamy affair with a local wife. This was classic Widow Wayland material: passions, murders, corrupt churchmen, and wily women. It would work, it had to work.

I stopped. I wasn't sure what to write next. I finished my tea. I stared out the window. I remembered I hadn't messaged Stacy yet. My phone had one bar of reception. I quickly tapped out a message. It didn't send. I tried again. Tried again. Waited five minutes. Tried again. Made more tea. Tried again. This time it sent. My phone also told me I had one voice-mail message: they must have called while the reception was down. I dialed into my voice mail to hear a soft female voice.

"Hello, Nina, it's Elizabeth Parrish here from the *Sydney Morning Herald.* Just following up something with you. Can you call me back, please?"

That was the journalist who had come to interview Cameron last year. I remembered her name because she'd written a piece that was as unflattering to me as it was flattering to Cameron. She had actually asked him what a serious, multiaward-winning poet was doing in a relationship with a best-selling hack like me. Well, perhaps not in so many words, but her contempt was between the lines. Cameron had told me I was being too sensitive; his own ego had been polished to such a bright sheen that it blinded him.

Did she want to interview me now? I deleted her message without responding. I didn't like to talk to journalists at the best of times.

Now I was distracted. Where was I? But what was the point of writing? Stacy would get back to me and interrupt my flow. Instead I read through parts of what I'd already written and grew despondent. Maybe I had been angry with Elizabeth Parrish because she revealed the truth: I wasn't an artist. I'd always known that.

I couldn't sit here and feel this way. I needed bread and milk and something for lunch, so I locked the house and walked down the hill to the shops.

The usual noise in my head followed me. *You can't do it. You should pay back the advance and pull out. You can't do it, so why do you keep pretending you can?* Deep breath, steely resolve. Smile for the woman behind the counter, grab a basket and buy eggs and bread and cheese and a tomato and whatever else could be made into easy meals.

"Hello, love," the woman said, wiping work-gnarled hands on her blue apron. She looked at my purchases, piled up on the counter. "You over from the mainland for a few days?"

"Yes, actually. I own Starwater House. I think I'll be here for a couple of months." I took a deep breath. "I'm Nina Jones."

"Nice to meet you, Nina," she said, shaking my hand firmly. "Donna Franks."

Thank God. Thank *God*. She didn't know my name; she wasn't going to ask about my books, about when the next one was due to be published. She ran my purchases through and packed them into bags for me. "We're really just a convenience store for last-minute things," she said. "Most people do their weekly shop over on the mainland. I don't have much beyond the basics, I'm afraid."

"Thanks. I'll remember that." But I was determined not to set foot off this island until the book was done. If that meant living on toasted cheese sandwiches and spaghetti omelettes, that is what I would do.

At home, I cleared the cupboards of George and Kay's things and packed away my groceries. They'd left their crockery and cutlery, and I tidied it all up, made the forks face the same way. Then it was close to lunchtime, so there wasn't much point to get started writing, so I made a sandwich and sat out on the step watching the palms sway in the wind.

By now I knew I was procrastinating and my stomach knotted up. With determination I placed my empty plate in the sink and returned to the desk. But Stacy had finally written back with some questions, so I engaged in an hour of to-and-fro text messaging with her, struggling against the poor reception.

Finally I looked at my work again. Sighed. Shut the laptop. Friday was a bad day to start a new regime of good work habits. Stacy would arrive tomorrow morning and I really should prepare the house for her stay, so it could wait until Monday. On Monday things would be different. Tension slid off my shoulders. I could breathe again.

For now, it was more important to settle in. George and Kay had kept a tidy house, so there was no need for me to scrub out cupboards or knock down spiderwebs, so I settled for rearranging furniture. I was in the process of turning my desk away from the window when there was a knock at the door.

Curious, I went to answer it. Joe stood there, with a skinny dark-eyed boy.

"Joe?" I said. "Is it that late in the day already?" Had I really spent a whole day procrastinating and rearranging furniture? Was time really that easy to lose?

"Sorry, I can come back another time if it's not convenient. I've got my ladder here, though. And my dad's chainsaw." He indicated the equipment he'd left lying across the dirt driveway.

"No, no. It's convenient." I smiled at the boy. "You must be Julian. I'm Nina."

"Pleased to meet you," he said.

"Would you like some afternoon tea? I have milk and biscuits."

Julian glanced at his father for permission and Joe nodded.

"Yes, please, Nina," he said.

"Great manners," I said to Joe.

"He's a good kid," Joe replied.

"Why don't you sit out here on the verandah and wait, and I'll fetch you something to eat," I said to Julian. "That way you can watch your dad while he works."

The boy sat down on the stairs and I went inside to pour him a glass of milk and grab a packet of biscuits. He looked nothing like his father, who was fair-haired and blue-eyed. Even though I'd worked with children, I was not naturally good with them. I was awkward, sure they could tell I was boring or couldn't communicate with them properly. I gave him his afternoon tea and went inside, leaving both of them to it.

I went back to moving furniture, but somehow didn't have the heart for it anymore, so I sat on the sofa and listened to Joe walk around on my roof. I heard the chainsaw start up and logs of sawed-off Moreton Bay fig branch hitting the ground one after another. After about an hour, he was at the door again.

"Knock, knock," he called.

I went out to greet him. I was struck by the smell of him. Soap and washing detergent and light perspiration: a warm, spicy, intoxicating male smell. I took a minute to gather myself. "What's the damage up there?" I managed.

"The tarp should keep you dry unless there's a massive

deluge . . . which, unfortunately, is always possible at this time of year. But I think it's beyond my capacity to fix the damage to the chimney. You should call somebody on the mainland."

"Do you know anyone?"

He nodded slightly. "You want me to take care of it? Find a roofer for you? I can do that."

His willingness to help, his lack of self-interest, struck me strongly. "I would be so grateful."

"Consider it done."

"Look, do you want a cup of tea?"

"Coffee?"

"I don't have any. Sorry."

"I thought all writers drank coffee. And scotch." He smiled. He had a lovely smile, earthy and knowing, and I felt an embarrassing stirring of desire. Luckily, I'm not a blusher.

"I never drink either of those things," I laughed. "I will have to get some coffee."

"Tea will be fine. Julian's outside climbing the tree. I hope that's okay."

"Of course. Is it safe?"

"Yes, the lower branches are all fine. As long as we don't get another storm like the last one, it will still be standing there when we're all dead and gone. And Julian's like a monkey. He climbs everything."

He followed me into the kitchen, and I switched on the kettle. "So, Julian's mother . . ." I started.

"You want the story?"

"I don't mean to be nosy."

"No, it's fine. I have no idea where she is. She skipped out before he turned two. Found another man, went off backpacking around the world. Motherhood wasn't for her."

"That must have been very sad."

"I was just focused on Julian. He cried every night for months . . ." He trailed off and I realized that his eyes were glazed, so I didn't push him further. He collected himself. "But that was six years ago and we're really happy now, and that's all that counts. She contacts me from time to time, but has never asked about seeing us again. And that suits me fine."

I concentrated on making tea, wondering if I'd overstepped politeness by asking him about her, but curious nonetheless. I was intrigued by him. Being in his presence set off all of those deep, primal stirrings I'd been repressing since my split from Cameron. "I wonder why motherhood was not for her. I mean, if she chose to have a child and—"

"She didn't choose. I chose for her. Julian wasn't planned and . . . I talked her into keeping the baby." He went quiet.

"Well," I said, not quite sure what to say.

"I love kids. I would have liked more. I was an only child and I didn't want Julian to be as well. But then she was gone."

I would have liked more. In a way, I was glad he'd said it. Because it reminded me that I had no place trying to form a relationship with Joe, as kind and attractive as he was. I wouldn't put myself through that again.

"This must a lovely place to raise a child," I said breezily.

"It is. My parents live here on the island. They have a farm down at the south point. We live in a converted shed on the farm and we're happy, and I'm nearly finished with my PhD and then things might be different. We won't be struggling so much for money."

I handed him his tea and he leaned his back against the kitchen bench and sipped it carefully. I watched him a few moments, considering the worry on his brow, on his shoulders. And then I said, "I have a proposition for you. While I'm here, the next two months, I want you to work for me a few days a week."

"Doing what?"

"Running errands. Managing the roof and chimney repairs. Getting my shopping from the mainland. I am so far over deadline . . . I can't set foot off this island now." The real world would come rushing back in and crush me. "I'll pay you really well."

He put his mug down and spread his hands. "I accept. I accept, so so gratefully."

Julian slammed the screen door behind him then and called out, "Daddy?"

"In here, champ."

The child entered shyly. He held out his hand. In it was a gecko. I tried not to recoil.

"He's a beauty," Joe said, kneeling to look at the lizard. Its little heart beat visibly beneath its velvet skin. "But you'd better put him back. He probably wants to be near his dad."

Julian ran off, the screen door slammed again. Joe said, "Sorry."

"It's fine. It slams behind me too."

"Okay, well, I'm going to get started in the lounge room pulling off the plasterboard on the chimney wall. That'll save you some time and money when I get the roofer for you. Can I move the furniture out of the way?"

"Yes, thanks."

He took his mug of tea and left me in the kitchen, watching his well-shaped back. Then I told myself that he wasn't for me, and I shut down the machinery in my imagination that was gearing up to make fantasies about him and me together. He wasn't for me; I wasn't for him.

•

Back home in Sydney, I always loved it when evening came. It meant the workday could expect nothing more of me, and I could stop procrastinating or worrying about writing and sit in front of the television for a few hours and forget I had problems. But there was no television here, and after my dinner of instant noodles I sat at the dining table for a while staring into space. What now? I had brought nothing to read except my own painfully wrought manuscript, I had no way to access the Internet and spend a few hours looking up reader reviews of my books and being outraged if they didn't like them, and I'd taken all the games off my phone when I found I spent more hours playing them than I did working on my novel. I felt empty and restless.

Outside, a rumble of thunder sounded in the distance. I went out onto the verandah to lean on the railing and watch the sky. Great gray thunderheads rolled in, bringing the smell of ozone and fat cold rain, breaking the humid grip of the day's heat. But I had a hole in my roof, so even with the tarpaulin, it was probably going to rain in my house as well.

There was nothing I could do. Water had already been in the lounge room and left behind its sour shadow, so I told myself to let go of the worry and get down to the end of the house furthest from it so I wasn't tempted to check on it all night. I had a cool shower and went to bed early to listen to the storm. It was as I was folding my jeans over the brass rail at the end of the bed that I felt something stiff in the back pocket. Eleanor's childhood diary. I pulled out the thin sheaf of papers and climbed between the soft cotton sheets, puffed up a pile of pillows behind me, and started to read.

FOUR

Stories in the Walls

September 28, 1891

Papa intends to hire me a governess. Strictly against my wishes, I might add. I do not need a governess. I was hopeful when Warder Randolph's wife took sick with diphtheria—and had to be moved off the island lest she infect us all—that she might decide not to come back and I could teach myself. I wouldn't have wished her dead, you understand. I simply wished her to realise that she was happier over at Victoria Point with her mother, but Papa said she was recovering well and he expected her back soon.

Then today there was an uproar. The six Randolph children, as you know, diary, have ever been my loathed classmates. Without their very sensible, but quite uninteresting, mother to frown upon them sternly, the eldest two—Anna and Bertie—have been misbehaving most infamously.

There is one rule on this island that I have been told many times I must obey above all things: children are not allowed near the stockade. Certainly I have been curious in the years I have lived here, especially in the early days when the prisoners were punished with the cat-o'-nine-tails and would make a horrific shouting fuss. But Papa banned that punishment and no

*man cries out for his Maker when on shot drill: that is a boring and dif-
ficult punishment, not one that requires the surgeon to attend.*

*So staying away from the stockade has been easy for me. Not so Anna
and Bertie Randolph. Rather than practise forming their cursive letters as I
had chosen to do—because it was two o'clock and that time of day is always
reserved for handwriting—they heard the arrival of new prisoners on the
Oracle, and hid behind the blacksmith's to watch through the window as
the new prisoners were riveted into leg irons.*

*Perhaps they might have been safe and fine. Perhaps their only crime
might have been that they laughed at the lot of those poor souls who have
been confined to Ember Island. Papa is always careful to say that the prisoners are here to be reformed, to be helped to see their mistakes, not to be
judged by us because the Lord is the only Judge.*

*But one prisoner, a hulking man as big as a side of beef, with rotted teeth
and fists like hams (I confess I didn't see him, but the tale is much more co-
lourful with the beef and the ham added), heard the children giggling and
it enraged him. He had already been brought low, I imagine, by his arrest,
his trial, his sentence, his transportation. To hear children laughing at him
was more than he could endure. He went wild. According to Chief Warder
Donaghy, whom I overheard reporting it to Papa afterwards, he roared and
smashed out with his manacled fists, catching the blacksmith on the chin
and sending him crashing to the floor. Then he shuffled to the window of
the blacksmith's shed, dragging the next prisoner on the chain with him, and
reached through the window to pull Bertie Randolph up by his scruff. Anna
had, by this stage, decided the game was no longer any fun and scarpered.
Bertie, legs swimming in the air, screamed for his mama and flooded his
pants; the turnkeys in the shed all pounced on the prisoner and it took six of
them to take him down, none of them daring to fire a shot lest it accidentally
hit Bertie.*

*After which, Warder Randolph came to Papa and demanded to be sent
away from Ember Island because it was too dangerous for his children.*

Papa pointed out (I overheard him . . . I've found that if I sit behind the curtain in the windowsill of the dining room and press my ear against the knothole between that room and the next, I overhear a lot), that if his children had obeyed the first rule, none of this would have happened, and that two of his men were injured in the fray and he held Anna and Bertie solely responsible.

An argument ensued, during which Warder Randolph used the most hideous names for my father, slurring his character, his judgement, and his ability to be satisfactory to women (oh, Papa would be appalled if he knew I had heard, and even more so if he knew I understood! Perhaps he ought not have let me read Chaucer). But Papa did not lose his temper; he was as cool as an autumn breeze. Papa is not the kind of man to rage and shout. He is good and calm in all things. He endured Warder Randolph's tirade, then spoke clearly and slowly.

"You and your children would evidently be happier on the mainland with your wife. I will sign any paper necessary to see you transferred at the earliest opportunity. Good day."

Where does this leave me? The only child on the island, for the first time since we arrived here. Bliss, I thought. I have always held Mrs. Randolph to be a poor teacher. Her knowledge of the medieval period is sketchy and she once spelled "definitely" with an "a," so it is clear she has no idea about Latin roots: there is no "a" in finis.

I told Papa that I would prefer to teach myself. I have sufficient books and a good brain. Papa countered with a threat: either I accept the governess or he will engage the chaplain to take my lessons. It is a clever threat and I admire him for it as much as I am constrained by it. Compared to the chaplain, Mrs. Randolph was a genius.

Papa insists this governess will have to speak French and read either Latin or Greek—both, for preference—have a good brain for figures and have the mythical ability to help teach me to cross-stitch neatly. My hope is that any woman who is accomplished enough to do all those things would not be willing to come to a high-security prison island surrounded by man-grove swamp. My fear is that Papa will then hire whomever is willing, and I will be tied to them for hours every day.

October 2, 1891

It is confirmed. I have a new governess and she will be here within a week. Papa has been across to the mainland to meet her and he says that she can do all the things we need her to do and that I will like her, that she has recently arrived from overseas and her name is Chantelle Lejeune. Oh, and that she is young, perhaps only twenty years. I made a cross face and told him again I do not need a governess, but part of me is excited. A young, clever woman: nothing like Mrs. Randolph or the chaplain. I am telling myself to be cautious, though. Why would any well-educated French woman come here and stay? We are all the way at the bottom of the world and then a little too much further. (That is what the colonial secretary's wife said on the day she visited back in April. "How do you survive," she had asked Papa, "all the way at the bottom of the world and then a little too much further?")

But I have never known any different. I was born across on the mainland and came here when I was very small. Papa had once lived in England, but it seems a distant and cold place to me. And as for Ember Island being "a little too much further"—well, it isn't much further. It is less than an hour on the steamer.

I do hope she is good company.

October 3, 1891

I had the awful dream again last night. I hate it because it leaves me cold and empty inside. Mother is sick in it, just as she was before she died. So sick I cannot recognise her and I am frightened to hold her hand, even though she begs me to hold it, with tears in her eyes. But then when I give her my hand, she crushes it tighter and tighter; her own fingers are bones and her skin is sinking until her cheeks are sharp hollows.

I woke up with my heart thundering, gathered up Pangur Ban, and ran straight to Papa's bed. At first I thought he hadn't noticed I was there, but then he rolled over and put his big warm arm over me and kissed the top of my head and said, "What is it, Nell?"

"Bad dream," I said.

"The same one?"

I nodded, then remembered he couldn't see me in the dark. "Yes," I said.

He stroked my arm with his thumb and I breathed in the warm scent of him.

"Papa," I asked, "did Mama love me?"

"All mothers love their children. Your mother treasured you dearly."

"Why do I keep dreaming that awful dream?"

"I cannot answer, child. Dreams are only nonsense, they are not to be feared, and they do not tell us any hidden truths."

"Did you love Mama?"

He breathed in sharply. I was afraid I'd hurt him. "Yes, I loved her very much. We were happy, in our time. But all times pass."

I burrowed my head into his armpit and closed my eyes. He stroked my hair until I fell asleep. In the morning he was up and dressed and gone to work before I woke.

•

Even though it wasn't the example of Eleanor's writing I hoped to find, I was disappointed when it ran out. Through her writings, I knew Eleanor—Nell as her father called her here—only as an adult. This insight into her childish mind made me feel fondly towards her and I wished, certainly not for the first time, that I had been able to meet her. Mum met her and remembered her as a nice old lady who gave out lollies and wore bright pink earrings; but she died when Mum was a little girl.

I switched off the lamp and lay down to sleep. I thought about Eleanor, once a young girl, now passed away. *All times pass.* Death came for us all and it would come for me. And that wasn't the worst feeling in the world because then nobody could expect anything from me anymore. At length, I slept.

•

Stacy arrived on the first ferry service, a wheelie suitcase in each hand. One was mine, picked up for me from my mother's house.

"Thank you so much," I said, taking the handle of my own suitcase and leading the way down the wooden jetty. The suitcase wheels bump-bumped in a rhythm over the old boards. "Did she ask any questions?"

"Your mother? No. She's used to you being a flake." Stacy smiled at me from behind her big sunglasses. Her lipstick was bright red and her hair was in a tidy bun. She knew the long history of my reputation within my family.

I'd known Stacy since primary school. We'd both started law school together, but I'd dropped out and she'd gone on to become a partner in a property law firm. Unlike my sisters, she never judged me for being flighty; and her pride in my creative achievements was genuine, not puzzled and forced.

"There's no pleasing her, so I've stopped trying," I said.

"I think she's pretty proud of you now. She has your books on the mantelpiece, I noticed."

"She probably put them there because I was back in town."

"How far is it?" Stacy said, eyeing off the hill in front of us.

"Half a kilometer. I should have told you not to wear heels."

"They're wedges. They're the most comfortable shoes I own."

"Should've brought flip-flops."

"Flip-flops? I don't think so."

We bumped up the road with our suitcases, and shortly we were in the shade of the verandah.

"So this is the legendary Starwater House," she said, leaving her suitcase and leaning on the verandah railing. "And what a view. The bay is spectacular, isn't it?"

"One of the most beautiful places in the world," I said. "Coming in on the plane, seeing it there below me . . . it always makes me so glad to be home."

Stacy turned and flipped up her sunglasses. "So this *is* home? You're not a born-again Sydneysider?"

I shook my head. "I don't really know where I belong, Stace. I just know I don't want to be in Sydney for a while. I'm happy here for the next few months."

"As am I. I miss you."

I smiled, probably awkwardly. I'm not great with openly stated affection. Blame my mother for that. "Come in. I'll show you where you're sleeping."

I took Stacy through to the other guest room and showed her where the bathroom was. While she was settling in, I upended the contents of my suitcase onto my bed. Fresh clothes. Toiletries. I gave myself a quick spray of deodorant. And the last four Widow Wayland books.

Stacy was at the door. "I brought morning tea." She held up a packet of chocolate biscuits.

"I'll put the kettle on."

We sat at the kitchen table with tea and biscuits. Stacy was beautiful—china-doll beautiful—with white skin and dark brown hair. I had always felt plain and undignified around her. It had been difficult having a beautiful, accomplished friend in every lecture theater with me at university, but that wasn't the reason I dropped out. It was simply because I couldn't keep up. I only scraped into the program, and there weren't enough hours in the day for the amount of study I had to do to catch up. My sisters were both so clever—both of them had been head of our old high school in their senior years—and I was ordinary by comparison. It frustrated my mother, a fact she didn't try to hide. She noted my lack of achievements, my dropping out, my running away to get married to a jazz musician and live under his parents' house in the outer suburbs of Sydney as a teenager, and she interpreted it all as laziness or lack of motivation. She simply couldn't believe that she and Dad had produced two geniuses and one dud. I had to be a genius who simply didn't work hard enough.

I hadn't even told Mum when the first novel was accepted for publication. But then seven different countries began bidding for it after the Frankfurt Book Fair and long before I'd even seen the first printed copy of it, I had been in the media as the Australian girl made good. In that first newspaper photograph I looked like a deer in the headlights. My success ballooned out of all proportion to my talent. Ridiculous amounts of money began to flow towards me. At first Mum hadn't taken a great deal of notice: Dad was sick and then he died, so her heart and mind were, of course, elsewhere. But when the BBC series went into production and one of her favorite period actors was cast as the Widow Wayland, then she started to talk about my books with grudging admiration.

"It takes a lot of work, I imagine," she said, "to write that many words all in the right order."

Meanwhile, my sisters worked very long hours building bridges

and saving people's lives, and my feelings of being a fraud intensified and intensified. In some ways, becoming a best-selling author
was the worst thing that could have happened to me. Because one
good book wasn't enough. I had to do it again, and again. And,
somehow, again.

But sitting here with Stacy in Starwater's kitchen, eating chocolate biscuits, I didn't feel so singular, so apart from the rest of the
world. I told her all about Cameron and Tegan, and I had a little
cry and she patted my hand, and then she filled me in on gossip
about old school friends and we laughed about the old days and
she told me hilarious stories about her disastrous love life, and the
morning passed sweetly and slowly.

The kettle whistled, and Stacy said, "I can't drink more tea. My
stomach's already sloshing. I packed my bikini. What's the beach
like?"

I was already shaking my head. "Oh, no, no, Stace. It's not that
kind of beach. The sand is only there at low tide and I'm pretty
sure there are sharks. But we can go for a walk down there if you
like. We might see birds. Maybe dolphins."

"I'll get my hat."

•

The Aboriginal name for Moreton Bay was Quandamooka, which
meant bay of dolphins, and Stacy and I both squealed with excitement when we saw a pod swimming past while we were sitting on
the jetty that afternoon. Stacy had her phone out and was taking
pictures within seconds, but none of them captured the glossy
silver of their backs.

"Ah, this is the life, Nina," she said to me, slipping away
her phone and leaning back. "I need more of this. Less of

conveyancing meetings and more of dolphins."

"It's whale season," I said. "Though they pass through on the other side of the island. There's a white one, like Moby Dick."

"Really?"

"Apparently. I had a look through some of George and Kay's whale-watching brochures."

"Ah, George and Kay. I wonder what they're doing now. Probably spending up big on the money they owe you in rent."

I pulled my feet up under me. "I presume not. Things must have gone pretty badly for them to fold right before peak tourist season."

"You want me to find them for you?"

"I don't know. Maybe I should let it go . . . Though, Joe told me they left their boat here and he thought I should take it in lieu of rent."

"Well, you can't do that legally, but I can contact them and see if they'll do a deal if you like. Keep them out of court."

"I wouldn't take them to court."

"You're too kind. And who's Joe?"

"He worked for them. Now he's working for me. Handyman jobs and so on."

"Is he trustworthy?"

I smiled and pushed her shoulder playfully. "You know, I can look after myself. I'm thirty-five."

"And you're worth a small fortune. Be wary of who sniffs about." She sighed, lay back on the warm boards. "With that in mind, can I come back soon? There's nothing as relaxing as an island where my BlackBerry can barely pick up a mobile signal."

"You can come back any time. I'd be happy to have you."

•

Another storm blew in that night, around midnight. The wind rattled at the windows and the rain bucketed down. I couldn't imagine how the tarp could stay in place, and I couldn't sleep worrying about how much water must be pouring into my lounge room. So I rose and turned on the hallway light, hoping it wouldn't wake Stacy, whose door was ajar, and made my way down the corridor.

I switched the light on. A steady drip fell from the ceiling next to the chimney, so I found a bucket in the kitchen to place under it. Joe had stripped the chimney wall back to the bricks and there was a lot of dust and plaster chunks on the floor, mostly caught by the sheet of painter's canvas he had put down. It made it difficult to see if there was any other water seeping down the wall, so I ran my fingers along it. They came away dry. I found a torch in the drawer under the coffee table and shone it carefully on the wall up high, running it along the pattern of the mortar.

Which is when I saw it. I would have missed it if I hadn't already seen the same thing in the fireplace two days ago. A thin sheaf of papers. Standing on the coffee table, I couldn't get my fumbling fingers into the crack to remove it, but with the help of a butter knife I set them free. I scanned the first page. More of her childhood diary; and while I was disappointed, it lit the fire of hope within me. There were a lot of bricks in Starwater, and I would simply get Joe to strip the wallpaper and plaster off them.

If there were stories in the walls, I wanted to find them. I needed to find them all.

FIVE

Waiting on a Letter

1891

The last mail service for the day came and went, and Tilly finally conceded defeat. Another day without a letter from Jasper. That made twenty days in a row now.

She slid away from the window, where she had been watching Mrs. Granger, the housekeeper, greet the postman with the most recent letter Tilly had written. But the postman had nothing to give her in return.

Twenty days. Twenty letters she had sent. And nothing from her husband, nothing at all.

Tilly sat on her bed for a few moments, struggling against her anxiety. In her darkest moments, she imagined Jasper dead, her letters being delivered to a silent house. But she couldn't let Grandpa see her anxiety. He was so ill, hanging by such a fine thread, that if he believed his beloved Tilly was in some kind of distress it might very well kill him in an instant.

She gathered herself, found her smile, and left her bedroom. She crept down the hall, listening for Grandpa's breathing. In the quiet, she heard the turning of a page. He was awake and reading.

Tilly knocked lightly, and Grandpa looked up. His pale face was lined and his cheeks drooped. She smiled at him, and he managed a breathless, "Hello, Tilly."

"Would you like me to read to you?" she asked, indicating the book.

He nodded, and she pulled up a chair next to the bed. The late afternoon sun caught in the filmy white curtains across Grandpa's wide windows, yellow-gold and soft. The night rolled in late at this time of year, which seemed cruel to Grandpa who was so very tired and needed soothing dark to sleep well. Tilly took his book from him—it was Victor Hugo's *Les Travailleurs de la Mer*, one of his favorites—and began to read. Latin and Greek she had learned from the stern governess who taught her in her youth, but her French was from Grandpa. It was a language he adored, and he had taught it to Tilly in the precious, private hours they spent together since he had taken her in, orphaned, at the age of four.

She read as the shadows lengthened outside the window. Grandpa's turn at the wedding had been the start of an alarmingly fast decline. Tilly had made the decision—with Jasper's unequivocal blessing—to stay with Grandpa and nurse him in his last days. Her husband had returned to his home in the Channel Islands, unable to take any further time away from his business.

"I will write to you every day," she'd said.

"As will I, my dear," he replied, and she'd believed him. She'd watched the carriage go and she'd believed him. And when the first week passed with no letter, she presumed the sea between her home and his had slowed it down and his letter would arrive in the second week or the third.

Now she didn't know what to presume. Where had his letters

gone? Where under the stars was her husband and did he know she was worried about him?

"That's enough, Tilly," Grandpa said. His wheeze had become a terrible rattle. "I'm tired now."

"Do you want me to draw the curtains so it's dark enough to sleep?" Tilly said, closing the book.

"No, no. I think a sunset is a beautiful thing. I have only a few left to see. I will lie here and watch the colors in the room change."

"I can stay with you, if you need company."

He waved her away. "You shouldn't even be here now. You should be at your husband's side. In your beautiful house." Here he smiled and that familiar twinkle was briefly in his eye, before fading again to weak dullness.

"I have a lifetime to be at his side, Grandpa," Tilly said. "You didn't turn your back on me when I was alone in need and nor shall I turn my back on you."

"I didn't even turn my back on you through all those tantrums," he said with a smile.

Tilly's cheeks flushed. "Well . . . I did learn to manage my temper eventually. Just."

"You are a good girl." He patted her hand. "I wish things could have been . . . different."

"I know."

"I'm glad you met Jasper when you did."

"So am I."

Grandpa's estate was entailed. His own father had specified only male descendants could inherit it. That meant Tilly's cousin Godfrey could—and would—turn her out quickly and coldly when Grandpa died. The urgency for her to marry had been pressing on Grandpa in the last few years. He had money to offer the right suitor, money that Godfrey would never part with if he had the choice. There had been talk of Tilly marrying a family friend who was old enough to be her father, but Grandpa loved her too well to force her into a lifetime of companionship with a man she did not love.

So yes. Meeting Jasper had been perfectly timed. Now if only Tilly knew if he was still alive. Because without him, when Grandpa died, Tilly had nothing.

She smoothed Grandpa's covers over him and kissed him good night, then let herself out of the room and headed down the stairs. Grandpa kept a small staff, and only Mrs. Granger was on to-night, quietly setting the table for Tilly's supper.

"Good evening, Mrs. Granger," she said.

"How is he?"

"Much the same. Still very tired."

"I'm sure he'll be up and about again soon."

Tilly didn't answer. Mrs. Granger did not want to believe that Grandpa would die; she had worked for him for forty years. Tilly waited for her to finish setting the table, idly picking off the man-telpiece the card that Jasper had given her when they first met. On it was a woodcut engraving of his house, Lumière sur la Mer, on an island in the English Channel. The front path wound up between poplars to a tall house with arched windows. She hadn't seen the inside, but knew it intimately from Jasper's descriptions. The tiled entrance, the sweeping curve of the internal stairs, the ceiling-high bookshelves in the library. On the one hand, she longed to see it. On the other hand, she wanted Grandpa to live forever.

"Will you eat, Miss Kirkland?"

Tilly smiled at Mrs. Granger. "I'm Mrs. Dellafore now, remember?"

"I am so sorry, ma'am," she said with a deferential drop of her head.

"We all have other things on our minds. Thank you. The soup smells delicious." Tilly sat down to eat, but had little appetite. She couldn't blame Mrs. Granger for forgetting she had a husband. He was nowhere to be seen.

•

The weather stayed fine and warm, boldly cheerful in the face of her cheerlessness. Another week passed without a letter, and Tilly spent a good many hours of every day debating with herself in her head about what this lack of correspondence meant. He was dead. He was busy. The letters had all become lost. They had been addressed incorrectly and would arrive in a bundle at the very next mail delivery. She tried not to let her terror seep into the letters she wrote to Jasper. She wrote lightly, gave news about the weather and the village, but always ended with a "please write soon; I long to hear from you, my love."

As always, she found her comfort in the garden. Summer rain had made the flowers riot through the beds, and between taming them and pulling weeds the long afternoons took care of themselves. She returned to the house in the evening, filmed with perspiration and soil, and sank into a perfumed bath to enjoy the dull ache of her muscles. She would go mad without the garden to tend. She didn't know how other women could school themselves to an indoor life of watercolor painting and soft etudes on the pianoforte.

Tilly spent as much time as she could in the mornings and evenings with Grandpa, reading to him and listening to his stories. It seemed the nearer his death drew, the better his memory of his early life became. He told her childhood anecdotes until he was hoarse. Her mind often wandered, but she did her best to listen to every small detail and smiled and laughed in all the right places. She could imagine nothing sadder than Grandpa being without company in his last days, and the gentle squeeze of her hand every time she left told her that he was glad she had stayed.

•

Tilly was in the garden on the Tuesday Godfrey arrived without notice. She sat in the wooden seat she'd had placed between the hawthorn hedges, with a book open on her lap. Sweet jasmine was heavy in the air. A bumblebee buzzed listlessly nearby, and she was almost falling into a doze when the clop of hooves and the rattle of a carriage roused her. She rose and rounded the side of the house to see the arrival of Godfrey's gleaming black and red chaise, drawn by two matching bay horses. They stopped at the entranceway and the footman opened the door to help Pamela down.

Pamela. Godfrey's wife. Tilly's stomach turned over. Why did she have to come? Grandpa despised her. Seeing her would likely make him more ill than he already was. Tilly hurried over to greet them, saying the little mantra in her head she always said when Godfrey and Pamela were around. *Be calm and moderate. A temper serves nobody.* They were words her grandfather had said to her a thousand times.

"I hadn't thought we'd see you," she said quickly, as Godfrey took Pamela's arm. He wore a tall hat and a black coat, and Pamela was in a green traveling coat that rode up over her bustle. With her perfectly rounded blonde curls and big blue eyes, she resembled nothing so much as a porcelain doll.

"I was going to send a letter," Godfrey said, offhandedly. He was as unattractive as his wife was handsome, with mousy hair that always looked dirty and a body like two pillows tied together. "But it was unnecessary. The old man isn't going anywhere and it would be too shocking, I suppose, for you to allow your husband to house and feed you."

Tilly let the jab slide. It had been delivered with Godfrey's customary wry smile, which meant he could say as he pleased and later claim he was jesting if anyone took offense.

"How is the old man?" Godfrey asked.

"He is very tired, but otherwise in good spirits. You must allow me to go ahead and prepare him for your visit. I don't want him to be overwhelmed."

Godfrey was already striding for the front door, nearly bowling Mrs. Granger over to get in the house.

"Granger, we'll have tea in the parlor, thank you," he said.

"Yes, Mr. Kirkland," she answered with a little nod. The slight tightness in the woman's jaw was the only outward sign that she disliked her incoming master.

Tilly smiled at Mrs. Granger. "Do take your time," she said.

Godfrey gave Tilly a frown, but did not push further. Pamela was already in the parlor, inspecting the drapes. "How old are these?" she asked Tilly.

Tilly knew Pamela already saw Grandpa's house as her own, and was so outraged at this obvious and uncouth anticipation of possession that she dared not answer in case she said something everyone would regret. Instead, she tried to stall Godfrey on the stairs. "Please," she said, "let me come with you. He's very frail . . ."

Godfrey took her wrist firmly and set her aside. "Cousin Matilda, I love you dearly, but you have been alone with him for many years, and you will allow me some time alone with him now. Pamela, come along."

Tilly stood back, shaking with unexpressed anger. Just as Grandpa said, Tilly had always been an angry little girl. He had taught her, through punishment as well as reward, that tempers disrupted society and girls especially, with their high voices and pink faces, ought not rage and shout.

But her patience and self-control were all an illusion for Grandpa's benefit. Countless times she had gone home and punched or screamed into her pillows after a disagreement with the postmistress or the greengrocer or the mother who let her child tear around and crush Tilly's foot without a word of admonishment. No matter how hard she tried, she could not stop the fire from igniting in her belly. All she could do was clamp her mouth shut so the fire didn't escape and burn those around her.

Tilly sat on the long, embroidered sofa and waited. This sofa would be Pamela's. Those paintings would be Pamela's. That wallpaper would be Pamela's. The drapes, which she had been regarding with such disdain . . . all of this would be Pamela's, simply because she was married to Godfrey.

Tilly's father and Godfrey's father had been brothers, but not friends. Tilly's father had taken his wife and his young daughter to India, where he had caught typhoid and died. Tilly and her mother made the long journey home, her mother's belly swelling with a pregnancy that eventually resulted in her death and the death of Tilly's unborn sibling. Godfrey's father might have taken Tilly in and raised her and Godfrey like siblings; but Godfrey's mother refused. And so Grandpa had brought Tilly into his home, raised her as he might have raised a daughter, and unwittingly created petty jealousies where there should have been familial love.

A little time passed—no more than fifteen minutes—and Tilly heard the door to Grandpa's bedroom close and footsteps on the stairs. Godfrey and Pamela appeared, and Pamela had tears in her eyes. Tilly felt a pang. Could she have been wrong about Pamela?

"The old man's mind is addled," Godfrey said gruffly. "He gave my wife a dressing-down."

Tilly stifled a laugh. "Oh, dear. He does get very tired. Don't take it badly, Pamela," she said, touching Pamela's cool hand softly. "I'm sure he doesn't mean it."

"Where is that tea?" Godfrey asked.

"Give her a little longer. If we'd known you were coming Mrs. Granger might have made scones. The best she might muster on short notice is sandwiches."

"Yes, yes. You've made your point, Cousin. You're annoyed that we didn't call ahead." Godfrey waved a dismissive hand. "You've made us feel sufficiently unwelcome so we will go."

Tilly immediately regretted not behaving more graciously. "No, no, I didn't mean for you to—"

"And perhaps one day soon, you will know how it feels to be unwelcome in this parlor," Pamela said, with an arch of her fine eyebrows.

And the fire blew hot, hot inside her. "Vulture," she spat.

Pamela put her handkerchief to her mouth in a gesture of shock. Godfrey merely smiled. Then he leaned in close and said, "Cuckoo."

In a few moments, they were gone. Mrs. Granger came in, a tray of watercress sandwiches in her hands. "Where are they?"

"Getting back into their fine carriage and heading home," Tilly said, her heart still thudding guiltily in her throat. "I offended them."

Mrs. Granger pursed her lips, but said nothing. She set down the tray and left Tilly alone in the parlor. Cuckoo. A bird that forces itself upon parents that aren't its own, then starves the other chicks in the nest through its endless demands. That was how Godfrey saw her.

Well, it was nearly time to fly.

•

Tilly woke to the morning sun in her window. She had slept poorly the night before, and had opened the curtains to let an evening breeze into the stuffy room. The sunshine fell onto the bed covers and she folded them back so that the warm light fell instead on her nightgown, across her breasts and belly. Tilly ran her hands along her body, feeling her own curves and hollows. She closed her eyes. The pleasure was sensual, thrilling. How she longed for Jasper to touch her this way. But their wedding night had been spent in the company of physicians and worried relatives, and then he had headed off the following day with promises to see her soon. And that was that. She was married, but still a virgin. A very reluctant virgin.

Jasper had done no more than kiss her, once upon the lips, and quite coolly. But now she replayed that kiss over in her mind, deepening it and warming it, and imagining his hands sliding low to cup her breasts or press the small of her back.

Guilty and a little embarrassed, she stopped. Pulled her bedclothes up again and lay there a while looking at the ceiling.

She had no doubt that Jasper was a passionate man and would reveal that side of himself when they were finally alone together. Theirs had been a courtship closely scrutinized by the village. Jasper had been here visiting an uncle when he and Tilly met outside the tailor's. He had been standing there, looking at his pocket watch, when Tilly emerged with Grandpa's trousers all let out at the waistband.

Jasper glanced up at Tilly and smiled. She smiled in return, eyes greedily taking in his well-shaped jaw, his dark and knowing eyes. "I wonder," he said, "can you tell me where I might find Duck Street? I have an appointment that I don't want to be late for."

"There are two ends to Duck Street," she replied.

"Basil Forster's. The tea merchant."

"I'm going that way, sir. I can take you there."

"I'd be delighted."

They'd set off, exchanged names, and discussed the weather. She'd taken him to Basil Forster's front path and was intending to be on her way home when he said, "I am visiting in the village for a few weeks. May I call on you?"

Tilly willed herself not to blush. "You may, sir. I would welcome that."

Then she'd hurried off, calling herself a fool. Men as handsome as Jasper Dellafore fell in love with queenly blondes, not curvy little redheads. She went home and put it out of her mind.

Until he called. Grandpa sat with them as they had tea in the parlor. Grandpa clearly approved of the young man, who was the descendant of French émigrés living on Guernsey. He worked in trading—tea, silk, shipping materials, anything he could acquire cheaply and sell to a specific clientele—so he traveled a lot. He told them about his beautiful home, which had been in his family for a hundred years. And by the end of his first visit, both Tilly and Grandpa were enamored of him.

"You should marry him," Grandpa had said, after he'd left.

"I barely know him," she'd replied. But secretly she thought she should marry him too.

Within six weeks, she had. Now the wedding was behind her, but the marriage was yet to begin.

•

Tilly went to the post office early, to take her latest letter for Jasper, but also to inquire discreetly, without alarming anyone or subjecting herself to gossip, if any letter had come for her that might have been misaddressed or misdelivered. There were none. She knew there would be none, but the confirmation still stung.

She was surprised, on her return home, to hear voices from the parlor. Even more surprised to recognize one of them as Grandpa's. She quickly hung her bonnet on the stand by the door and hurried to the parlor.

Grandpa sat heavily, legs spread wide, slumped to one side. He had dressed himself but misbuttoned his vest. His cheeks were sunken, so she could see the shape of his skull beneath skin that had taken a yellow-gray hue. It was almost uncanny to see him upright. Almost upright.

"Grandpa!" Tilly exclaimed, moving towards him.

But he held up a frail hand. "No, no, Tilly. I will be fine. This is Mr. Leadbetter, my solicitor."

Tilly turned to see the other man in the room, a rosy-cheeked fellow with a welcoming smile. "How do you do, Mrs. Dellafore?" he said.

She took his hand momentarily, then released it and began to unbutton her gloves. "Forgive me for barging in. I had not thought to see my grandfather up and about."

"I will return to my room soon enough, dear," Grandpa said. "But first I must finish my business with Mr. Leadbetter." He gasped, and took a moment to catch his breath.

"Can I get you water, Grandpa?" Tilly asked.

Again he waved her away. "Business, my dear Matilda. Let the men finish their business."

She squeezed her gloves in her fists. "Of course," she said. "You only need to call if you need me." She gave Mr. Leadbetter a meaningful look, which he returned with a slow nod.

"I will take good care of him," he said.

Tilly backed out of the room and went upstairs to her own bedroom, to hang up her light coat and fold her gloves away in her drawer. She presumed Grandpa's conversation with Mr. Leadbetter was part of his getting his papers in order before he died. She sat heavily on the bed and lay back, fingers tracing lightly over the embroidered bedspread. She closed her eyes. What a special hell she was in. The man who had been the center of her world was dying. Without him, would she not be adrift in the world? The hard, aching sadness gripped her and she felt a tear roll over her cheek and into her hair. She longed to be able to lean on Jasper, for him to catch her tear in the crook of his finger, but now Jasper was a man made of mists and shadows. She couldn't grasp him.

At length she heard Leadbetter's carriage leave and went downstairs to help Grandpa back to bed. She found him, however, shuffling about slowly, making a pile of objects on the tea table. A clock, two gilt picture frames, four silver candlesticks, a crystal vase.

"What are you doing?" she asked, hurrying to him and putting her hand under his arm to steady him.

He shrugged her off. "I've spoken to Leadbetter and there's nothing for it. The wording of my own father's will was clear, and Godfrey and Pamela will take all. Everything. So we need to get some of these things out of here before I die."

Tilly wondered briefly if Godfrey was right and Grandpa's mind was addled. But he had been thinking and conversing lucidly until now. "Where are you going to send them?" she asked.

"To your new home. To Lumière sur la Mer. We'll pack them in a trunk and ship them over."

"We can't do that. Pamela has counted everything with her eyes."

He huffed his way through the next sentence. "We *can* do it . . . and we will . . . I am making you a number of gifts . . . for your marriage. These things are mine until I die."

"You need to be in bed, Grandpa."

He caught his breath. "I understand you will not want to be complicit. Go now. Leave the house and take a walk about the village. I'll get Granger to help. No, wait. I forgot something."

He dragged his feet to the mantel where his cigar box lay, untouched for many months now since he first started feeling ill and breathless.

"I don't want cigars, Grandpa," Tilly said. "I don't want anything. I don't want trouble. Godfrey will give me trouble."

"Hush now and listen." He thrust the cigar box into her hands. "What's in here shouldn't be shipped . . . you must take it with you. Carefully."

She unlatched the box, but he stilled her hand.

"Look later. You will hand it directly back to me if you open it now. I had Leadbetter organize it for you."

Tilly moved the latch back into place with her thumb. She knew she should refuse it, all of it. But she thought of Pamela getting her hands on the silver candlesticks—Tilly had been with Grandpa the day he bought them for her fourteenth birthday dinner—and she hardened her resolve.

"I know nothing," she said.

"Look out for the chest. I don't know if it will get there before . . ." He trailed off, then sat down heavily. "The pain will be over soon." Another fit of breathlessness gripped him and she moved towards him.

"No. Go," he said. "Tell Granger . . . to come . . . The sooner it is done, the sooner . . . I can rest."

Tilly touched his beloved forehead, then turned and left, gathering her bonnet at the door. She tucked the cigar box under her arm to free her hands to tie the ribbons, then headed down through the back garden. She opened the kissing gate that led to the path running beside the stream. Blackbirds and robins sang, and stringy wildflowers lined the way. She kept away from the main village, taking the stream path past the mill and down onto the grasslands that separated the village from the wood.

Here, under a chestnut tree, she sat and opened the cigar box. Banknotes. Lots of banknotes. Tilly gasped, pulling a handful out. Underneath lay a letter. She unfolded it. Grandpa's scrawl was barely legible, blotted and scratchy. But it was only a short message.

This is for you and nobody else. A woman should have at least something in the world.

Tilly refolded the note, placed everything back in the box, and snapped it shut. She pressed it against her chest, heart beating hard. "Thank you, Grandpa," she breathed. "Thank you."

By the time she arrived home, the chest was sent, and Grandpa wouldn't speak of it. "It never happened," he said, once again flat and limp in his bed. "I don't know what you're talking about."

•

Thud, thud, thud.

Tilly swam up through sleep.

Thud, thud. "Miss Kirkland. Tilly."

Tilly sat up, blinking her eyes open. Mrs. Granger's voice at the door. She threw back the covers and moved to the bedroom door to open it. Mrs. Granger stood there, pale, holding a lamp.

"What is it?" she asked.

"It's time. It's his . . . his time."

Grandpa. Tilly grabbed her dressing gown from behind the door and pulled it on. Fast movements, cold heart. She hurried after Mrs. Granger and into Grandpa's bedroom. All the lamps were lit, the nurse from the village who came to sit with him at night was there. It was too bright and noisy.

"Tilly," Grandpa gasped. "I'm sorry to wake you, dear. But I won't be here in the morning."

Tilly sank down next to the bed and grasped his hands. His fingertips were worn smooth by the years. "Hush now, Grandpa. You don't know that."

"I do. I do," he said, touching her hair softly. "I feel life drawing out of me like water runs out of the bath . . ." Deep, shaking breath. Huff. Huff. "Everybody . . . everybody out except Tilly. It is so crowded in here."

Mrs. Granger and the nurse withdrew, the door shut behind them. Grandpa placed his cold fingers gently under Tilly's chin and lifted her face to meet his gaze.

"I haven't . . . been honest . . . with you," he said.

"You have always been the best of men."

"No . . . no, I . . . haven't." The big shuddering breath again, followed by the short series of huffs. "Listen . . . I knew Jasper . . . I already . . . knew Jasper."

Tilly's ears rang faintly. She was overwhelmed by sadness, puzzlement. "What do you mean?"

"You're a . . . proud girl . . . too proud . . . you wouldn't . . . I had to . . ."

"Grandpa, all is well. Whatever you did, all is well."

"Family friend . . . needed you to . . . think . . . it was . . . you who found him. Outside . . . the tailor . . ."

"Shhh, shhh. All is well. I love him, Grandpa, and as soon as you no longer need me, I will go to be with him and . . ." She fought back tears. She absolutely could not let Grandpa guess at the doubt that she felt.

He lifted the back of his hand to her cheek. "I no longer . . . need you . . . my Tilly. My good girl." Breath. Huff. Huff. "My good girl."

With sudden weight, his hand fell and lay on the covers, still and silent.

•

Tilly stood at the dock, her small trunk between her feet, her large trunk already loaded onto the steamer. She had come directly from Grandpa's funeral. Pamela would have allowed her to presume one or two nights' grace, perhaps, but Tilly was aching to go. She didn't care to see Grandpa's house in Godfrey' and Pamela's possession. No doubt they were already tearing down the drapes, moving the furniture, maybe even uprooting her garden beds to put in Godfrey's long-imagined tennis court.

No letters had come. Nearly six weeks after her wedding, no letters had come. She had an address, a ticket across the sea, and a slowly eroding hope in her heart. Travelers bustled about her. A purser rang a bell up and down the dock, calling for the various classes to board. The air smelled of metallic water and coal. Amongst the confusion of sights, sounds, and smells, she tried to find a place of stillness and peace in her heart. Soon the uncertainty would be over. She would find her husband, or she would find that he had never been hers at all. Either way, the journey had begun.

SIX

Lumière sur la Mer

The hackney coach rolled up the hill from farmlands and through the wood that bordered Jasper's estate. Tilly's chest drew tighter and tighter, the closer they drew to Lumière sur la Mer. Jasper had to be there. He had to. Or else . . . there was no alternative. He had to be there. They emerged from the wood, rocking and rattling, onto a smooth dirt road. Ahead, she could see the roof of the house. Her husband's house.

Her house. Lumière sur la Mer. The light on the sea.

She breathed deeply, remembered the cigar box of money in her smaller trunk, and took a little comfort from it. Whatever happened, she would survive. She hoped to find Jasper, alive and well and with a completely reasonable explanation for the lack of correspondence. If he was ill or had . . . she steeled herself . . . simply not bothered to write, she could recover from that, too. But if he was dead or missing, then she feared for herself. Her heart, so recently damaged by the death of her beloved grandfather, could not bear another burden that great. Widowed while still a virgin: that would surely make her the unluckiest woman in the world.

The carriage slowed and stopped. She gathered her courage. The footman came to open her door.

"Please," she said. "Would you wait? I am . . . I am not sure if my husband is home and I have no key of my own." If he wasn't here, she had already planned to go to the local constabulary to ask them to help her, and imagined she would spend her nights boarding somewhere.

The footman nodded, and she stepped out of the coach and into the wild wind, down the little stair, and stood for a moment looking up at the façade of Lumière sur la Mer. It looked familiar from the card. Three storys, conservatory to the south, orchard to the north. But it was also unfamiliar. Those tangled gardens. The peeling blue paint on the door. The curtains all drawn as if ashamed of something.

"Madame?" the footman said.

"Yes, I will go now. Wait for me. Don't unload the trunks . . . yet . . ."

One foot in front of the other, pulse speeding. Her eyes went left and right, noticing the overgrown grass between the poplars, the weeds growing in the urns where flowers should have been. It didn't look as if anybody had lived here for a long time. Her heart caught in her throat. Now she expected the worst, the very very worst.

At the front door she paused for a breath, then raised her hand and knocked hard. Released the knocker and stood back, anxiously checking over her shoulder that the carriage hadn't abandoned her here on the wrong side of the wood. A long silence, unbroken except for the wind and sea. The clattering streets of St. Peter Port, only two miles away, seemed very distant.

She could hear her own pulse.

And footsteps. She could hear footsteps within the house.

The door opened and her heart leapt.

"Jasper!" She launched herself into his arms and he took her firmly against him, his hands spread across her back.

"You're here," he said.

She stood back, beaming at him, all her worries melting away. He smiled in return. She noticed his hair was untidy, his clothes not as sharply pressed as she remembered. But he was still her Jasper, alive and well and here, at the home they were to share together. She turned to the footman and gestured, and soon her trunks were being brought up the path.

"I didn't hear from you," she said to Jasper. "Weeks and weeks. No letters."

"I wrote at least half a dozen!" he protested. "But I had none from you. I thought you'd forgotten me!"

Tilly laughed. All along it had been some miscommunication beyond their control. She should have known it. She pressed herself against him again, and he kissed the top of her head and said, "I'm sorry, my dear, but things might not be as you expected."

She looked up, into his gray eyes, and said, "You are here, alive and well in front of me. That is all I hoped for."

"Your grandfather?"

The leaden sadness tempered her moment of joy. "He's gone. Dead," she said.

He touched her hair. "I am sorry, my dear. Come in," he said. "Welcome to Lumière sur la Mer. Welcome to your home."

While the footman bustled past with her trunks, and Jasper showed him where to leave them and paid him, Tilly removed her bonnet and gloves in the entrance hall to the house. The black and white tiles were as Jasper had described them, the ornate curved stair. But where the chandelier had been there was an iron hook; where the side tables had been were empty spaces; and where the picture frames had hung were discolored squares on the wallpaper. She took it all in. The relief over finding Jasper alive and expecting her was so immense that she was incapable of feeling disappointed that the house wasn't as grand as she'd anticipated.

Finally, her trunks were inside, the door was closed, and just she and Jasper stood alone in the entrance hall.

"My dear Tilly," he said, taking her hand gently. "I have fallen on hard times since last I saw you."

She squeezed his fingers. "I am sorry you were troubled and I wasn't here to offer you comfort. As a wife should have been."

Jasper lifted the smaller trunk, and pulled her close to slide his free arm around her waist. "A business deal went badly. I have had to sell many of my things. But it is temporary, dear. I promise you. Come. I'll show you the house."

The sweet warmth of his body against hers was intoxicating. She barely listened to his words as he took her from room to room—parlor, dining room, conservatory, kitchen—then up the stairs, explaining all the way about his French émigré descendants, how they had fled the Revolution and built Lumière sur la Mer as a haven in the sea, away from the political turmoil of their own country. How he hadn't the temperament of a farmer so had sold off all the stock and struck out on his own import and export business. He showed her the guest rooms on the second floor, and then opened the door to the library she had heard about, dreamed about.

"Oh, my!" she gasped. The shelves were stacked to the ceiling. The smell of old paper and dust was strong.

"You mustn't get too excited. I've had to sell the whole collection to a Scottish fellow living in India. He'll be back for them in six months or so. I promised him I'd have them organized and in crates by then, so do feel free to spend some time in here alphabet-izing them or some such. I'm afraid I'm not particularly interested in books. They sit rather too still for my liking. Here, I'll show you the third floor."

She reluctantly left the library behind, and he took her up one more flight of stairs to the bedrooms.

"Through here," he said, opening a white door on a small but comfortably furnished room with a view out to the water. She could see masts in the distance, the gray churning sea. "This is your room."

"My room?" she asked. "Or do you mean . . . *our* room?"

He smiled. His eyes shifted almost imperceptibly sideways. "I have a room too. But of course, we are . . . husband and wife, and . . . we will . . ." He cleared his throat. Straightened his back. "It is not proper to discuss these things, Tilly. As your husband, I will lead the way, when the time is right."

Tilly's cheeks burned. She was speechless with embarrassment, concerned that Jasper now thought her a woman of scandalous appetites. She made a promise to herself not to make the same mistake twice. What did she know about married life? Perhaps all couples who lived in grand houses had separate chambers.

Jasper laid her trunk carefully on the bed. "I will bring your other trunk up shortly. I had a manservant, but I've had to put him off until our finances improve. I've put off nearly everyone." He frowned, ran his hand through his hair. "I know it's not what you expected," he said again.

He couldn't meet her eye and she ached for his shame and distress. So she went to him, careful not to take his hand or try to hold him again, so he could form a better opinion of her ability to contain her physical desires.

"I expected, Jasper, to find here my husband and start my

married life. I vowed to be with you for richer and for poorer. We will be fine. A few days before Grandpa died, he sent over a trunk of goods from his home. Valuable goods. We can use them to re-place what you have lost."

"Or sell them?" he asked hopefully. "To pay debts?"

Something about his desperate tone sent a niggle of alarm through her blood. "Of course. They are ours to do as we please." She opened her mouth to tell him about the banknotes, but then stopped herself. "Whatever problems we have, we will face them together."

He was much brighter now, more like the sure-eyed, confident Jasper she had married. Tilly felt glad that she had been able to cheer him. "My Tilly. My wife." He kissed her cheek lightly. "I'll go and fetch your other trunk."

And he was gone.

Tilly went to the window. The pane was slightly warped, dis-torting the view. Outside the wind was wild in the trees, but in here she was warm and safe. She smiled. This would be her new home and it wasn't as fine as she'd thought it might be, but then Tilly wasn't a woman who cared overly for fine things. There would be time and comfort here for her to grieve her grandfather, and one day there would be children and bright laughter in the dim corridors of the house.

She turned, flipped open her trunk, and found the cigar box. If he needed it, if he *really* needed it . . .

But no. That would be contrary to Grandpa's wishes, and her memories of him were still sharp enough that she couldn't bear to contradict him. Perhaps what was in the trunk would be enough. She glanced around the room, found the tall wardrobe next to the door, and opened it. Slid the cigar box back as far as she could reach on the highest shelf, then placed her bonnet in front of it for good measure. Then she sat on the bed—hands folded—to await the return of her living, breathing husband.

•

Because they were conserving every penny, there were no lamps lit down the stairs to lead her way to the dining room that evening. Jasper had warned her, before going out for what he promised was no more than an hour's business, to make sure she lit a candle before coming down so she didn't trip on the stairs. So when the supper bell rang, Tilly took the candle she'd been reading by in her room and made her way carefully downstairs.

She arrived to find Jasper pacing, hands clasping and unclasping in front of him.

"You're home, my dear," she said. "Did business go well?" Tilly knew the answer to this without asking. Every muscle in his body flexed against some imagined adversary.

"I . . . uh . . . no. But you're not to worry. I have to go out again."

"But supper?"

"I haven't an appetite. Mrs. Rivard will look after you. Please . . . I wasn't expecting you today and I haven't quite sorted out all my . . ."

He seemed distressed, so Tilly went to him and grasped his hands. "You need explain nothing to me. If you must go to work, then go to work. I will be here, waiting for you when you return. As your wife should be." She squeezed his hands.

Jasper nodded. "Just a few more days of this, and then all will be well. I promise, Tilly." He dropped her hands, ran a hand through his hair to smooth it. "But you are not to wait up for me. You've been traveling all day and you are tired. Sleep well and tomorrow morning we will dine together, I promise you."

Tilly stood back and he brushed past, out of the dining room. She heard his footsteps in the corridor and then the rustle of him pulling on his coat. Her disappointment was acute. She had longed to be with him, to press herself against him and take comfort in his embrace, to explore the special pleasures she understood a husband and wife would share. But she had spent perhaps an hour in his company since her arrival.

"You should have said you were coming." This was Mrs. Rivard, standing in the threshold between kitchen and dining room with a wooden tray. She spoke in a thick French accent.

Tilly had never had a servant speak to her so plainly. Perhaps this was a French custom. "I sent him several letters," Tilly said, then wondered why she was saying it. She didn't answer to this woman.

Mrs. Rivard set the tray down. "Perhaps you should have sent a telegram."

"I sent four."

"Then where are they?" She raised her shoulders theatrically, palms out.

Tilly's blood heated. Was the servant accusing her of lying? It was beneath her dignity to get into an argument with the woman. "Thank you for the food," she said instead, as sharply as she could manage. "I will call you when it's time to clean away."

"I will be gone, madame," Mrs. Rivard said. "My wage covers only a few hours a day. You may clean away after yourself." With that, she untied her apron and left the room.

Tilly sat heavily at the table. The soup was watery and the chicken leg skinny. She ate, alone, as she had so many times at Grandpa's. But this time she was in a big, dark, echoing house on a windy island, with hostile staff and a husband in terrifying financial difficulties.

This wasn't how it was meant to be, but Tilly stopped herself from remembering how she imagined this new life because the comparison would make her ache. She was starving, so she wolfed down the food. She heard Mrs. Rivard leave and realized she was all alone in the house.

Tilly finished her food and left the tray on the dining table for the morning. It was too dark to see properly in the kitchen anyway, and she was worried she would trip or slip. Instead, she picked up her candle and moved into the parlor, shining the dim light around. The only furniture was one small settee, whose stuffing was emerging from the arms. Piles of papers were stacked in the corners of the room. A quick glance told her they were purchase orders and invoices for Jasper's business. Filed horizontally on the floor. Perhaps he had sold the filing cabinets. She sat on the settee for a moment, listening to the panes rattling in the wind. The emptiness in here crawled inside her. She shivered.

Upstairs, then. Tilly had unpacked her things in her bedroom, so it might feel safer and not so strange and hollow. She carefully ascended the staircase, the flickering candlelight reflecting off the austere wood paneling.

Then she paused on the third-floor landing, outside Jasper's bedroom door.

She was his wife, after all. And when things were settled, in the next few days, she would surely be sleeping in this room next to him. Wouldn't she? Was that not how it worked?

Her fingers were around the handle before she could think better of it, and she opened the door.

Tilly placed the candleholder on the writing desk, and looked around. An unmade bed. Clothes strewn about. She had believed Jasper a neat man, a man in control of his belongings and environment. Who was this man who cast his clothes about and stored important paperwork in piles on the floor? In here, there were no decorations either. No clocks or pictures or mirrors or lamps or urns or washing bowls. She itched to tidy the room up, fold his shirts, hang his coat, but then he'd know she'd been in here and, she was loath to admit, she wasn't sure how he might respond. Would he shrug it off? They were married after all. Or would he be angry with her?

Perhaps it was that she hadn't seen him for six weeks—the same length of time as their entire courtship—that made him now a stranger.

Tilly turned to take her candle and leave, take refuge in sleep and then draw comfort from morning light. But she noticed the drawer of his desk was partly open, and overflowing with more papers. Why were these ones up here instead of downstairs in the pile?

If she was very careful . . . There, the first paper was in her hand. What kind of debts did he have? And to whom?

But in her hand was no unpaid invoice or demand notice. In her hand was one of her very own letters. Opened. And, she presumed, read.

> *Dearest Jasper, I still have not heard from you. Do put me out of my misery and send word that you are whole and well . . .*

Tilly's mind was addled. Who had opened this letter, then, if not Jasper? Mrs. Rivard? Is that why she was so cruel about not sending a telegram? Was she trying to hurt Tilly for some reason?

But the letter was here, in Jasper's drawer, in Jasper's desk, in Jasper's room. She carefully eased the drawer open. Saw the edge of another envelope with her handwriting on it, and she also thought she saw a telegram, though it was dark and she didn't want to disturb the papers any further.

Tilly slid the letter back into the drawer, hand shaking. Jasper had lied to her. He had *lied to her*. Why? What reason did he have to pretend he hadn't received the letters?

She scooped up her candle and left Jasper's room for her own. There, she snuffed the little flame and lay flat on her back on top of the covers. Her heartbeat choked her. For a few awful moments, nothing made sense. North was south and up was down.

But then she realized. He had been unable to write from embarrassment. From shame about his reduced circumstances. Perhaps he had intended to write when the money he was expecting came in. Perhaps he would have seen it wrong to write to her, pretending all was well.

Perhaps it wasn't that Jasper was dishonest, but that he was *too* honest. That was it. That had to be it.

Underneath her, remembered waves still rolled. She drifted off, fully dressed, and didn't stir until morning.

·

In the morning light, the house looked quite different. Breakfast waited for her in the sunny conservatory, and she cheered a little. The morning staff was a pretty, oval-faced young woman named Miss Broussard who smiled at her warmly but spoke poor English.

"Has Mr. Dellafore been down for breakfast?" Tilly asked her.

"No, madame."

He must be sleeping late. Tilly remembered the letter in his bureau, and hoped he wouldn't notice the papers had been disturbed. She fought against the feeling again that she didn't know him. She was in a new place, in a new life, still grieving for her beloved grandfather: the only parent she had known. It was to be expected that she would feel displaced for a while.

After breakfast, Tilly decided some fresh air would make her feel better, so she tied on her bonnet and went outside into the overgrown garden. The bracing sea air cleared her lungs of the dusty heaviness of the house, and she walked down the slope peering through weeds into the garden beds. There were hedges here in need of pruning: hydrangeas and dark pink impatiens and flowering magnolia trees. Moldering leaves lay in the beds, nearly a year after they fell. She felt the first glimmer of that quiet excitement, thinking of tidying and weeding and pruning to reveal the natural beauty that grew here. She understood that Jasper could not afford a gardener, so surely he wouldn't object to her pulling on a pair of sturdy gloves and tidying the beds herself. Working outside in the sun and sea air would do her good, make her feel she was contributing in some way.

"Good morning, my darling!"

Tilly turned to see Jasper approaching. He was dressed sharply and smiling. The only thing that gave away his late evening the night before were the dark shadows under his eyes. Tilly's heart lifted. "Good morning. I take it business went . . . better."

He waved his hand dismissively. "You aren't to worry about my business. But your trunk has arrived. And I've seen what's in it." He stopped in front of her. His height and bearing gave her the same thrill she'd felt while they were courting. There was something proud and straight about him, like bright steel.

Her ribs expanded proudly. "The candlesticks will look lovely in the parlor. It is very bare and empty at the moment."

"Well, now . . . perhaps we can keep one or two things. But, Tilly, the value of the items, when I sell them, will entirely erase my debt. Then, when the money I am owed comes in, we will be comfortably wealthy again."

Tilly took a deep breath. "Then the sensible thing to do is to sell it all. The sooner your debt is cleared, the better. I like it better when you smile and are relaxed." Yes, she liked that better than she liked holding on to objects. If anything, there was something pleasant about the idea that Godfrey and Pamela, who had so much, would be helping to pay out Jasper's debt.

Jasper took her hand and raised it to his lips, kissed it gently. Then turned it over and kissed the inside of her wrist, closing his eyes. His mouth was warm, and it lingered on the sensitive skin there. Tilly flushed hot.

"I am so glad you came, my love," he said, then dropped her hand, leaving her longing for more and closer physical intimacy. A shiver of cool ran over her skin.

Jasper gestured around the garden. "I'm afraid the gardener was the first to go. A month ago. But next spring, it will be back to its former glory."

Tilly knew he was lying. There had been no gardener here for much longer than a month, but she understood now that he was embarrassed about his circumstances.

"I wonder," she ventured, "if you'd let me do a little work in the garden. I feel at home with soil and leaves."

"You may do as you please, my dear. If that is what your heart desires, then by all means make this place your own. Here." He fished in his pocket for his keys, and carefully removed one from the chain. "This is the key for the gardener's shed. Use it as you see fit. Now, I have a gentleman coming in an hour to go through the trunk with me and give me some money for it. It's not women's business, so do stay well away."

Tilly was about to say she wanted to see some of the things one last time. The clock from the old parlor at Grandpa's house, for example. But then she realized it would probably make her melancholy. "Of course, Jasper." She smiled. "I am glad that you are happy."

"I feel as though a weight has lifted off me." He touched her chin lightly with his index finger. "Good girl." And then he walked away.

Tilly spied the gardener's shed at the bottom of the garden, between two birch trees. She made her way down, fitted the key into the lock, and swung the door in. A small window let in a little light, filtered through branches. Rakes, brooms, pruning shears, secateurs, pitchforks, watering cans, trowels . . . Jasper must never have been in here, for surely he would have sold the lot if he'd known how much there was. There were shelves along one wall, with boxes full of seed packets, rolls of wire, nails, and spikes. Tilly found a pair of sturdy gloves and took them down from their box to give to Miss Broussard to wash. Once they were clean, she could make a start on the weeds.

The garden shed smelled musty, and she was tempted to leave the door open to let the sea air in. But Jasper might see inside and sell everything and then she could do no gardening at all. So she locked it, strangely pleased that she had a key to somewhere Jasper couldn't go.

•

Tilly sat in her room, waiting for the meeting downstairs to finish. The gentleman, the buyer of all their goods, was taking a long time to agree on a price with Jasper. She hadn't seen him, but he had a Spanish accent and when he raised his voice and Jasper raised his own, Tilly had closed the door so she couldn't hear.

She tried to read, struggling to concentrate on the words in front of her, but they swam about and refused to make sense. Her mind was bent on the situation downstairs, on the uncertainty of what had happened. Jasper, when she'd met him, had been a rich businessman on his way to sell tea to the village tea merchant. Grandpa had known him. There was no question he was wealthy enough to look after Tilly. And yet, the garden had been neglected since last autumn at least, and some rooms in the house had stood empty long enough for the dust to gather in drifts over the floorboards. She knew, too, that Grandpa had paid him a good sum of money upon their engagement, so that must have gone directly into debts as well. So how deep in financial trouble was he? And how could she find out when he refused to talk about his business with her?

Footsteps outside and a frantic knock at her door. Without waiting for an invitation, Jasper burst in. His eyes glittered wildly. "Do you have anything else, Tilly? Anything? Jewelry? Money?"

She hesitated. The banknotes. *This is for you and nobody else.* Maybe Grandpa had suspected Jasper was not all he seemed.

"I have pearls," Tilly said, going to her chest of drawers. "Grandpa gave them to me when I turned twenty-one. They used to belong to my mother."

"Pearls. Pearls would be good."

She retrieved the box from her top drawer, hesitating before handing them over.

Jasper clicked his fingers. "Come now. There can be no senti- ment where money is concerned." He leaned in close, whispered harshly in her ear. "I fear for my life."

Her heart spiked in alarm. "What?"

"The Spaniard. I have owed him too much for too long. His patience has worn thin." She saw his eyes flick to her wedding band.

Tilly lightly slid her left hand behind her back. "I have a neck- lace of jet as well."

"Give it to me. Anything you have, give it to me and all our problems will go away." He stalked to her wardrobe and threw it open, seized her favorite coat with its sable trim.

"This might be worth something?" he asked.

"I . . . take it. If you can get something for it . . . I have other coats." She had to be reasonable. Saving the house would keep her warmer than saving the coat.

And, with her jewels in his hands, he went downstairs to deal with the Spaniard. Tilly's eyes went to the wardrobe where the cigar box was hidden. What wouldn't he do? What would stop him from coming in here, whether she was in the room or not, and going through her drawers, her shelves, to look for something else to sell? Her dresses next? The precious inlaid writing box Grandpa had made her when she was a child? He would find the cigar box and he would take the banknotes.

He said his life was in danger. She wrung her hands together, caught between wanting to keep him safe and not trusting him. Oh, the disappointed sadness. Not trusting him at all.

Tilly knew what she must do.

•

This time she was glad when he went out for supper, for more business, to stay away from her bed one more night. When Miss Broussard left for the evening and Tilly was all alone again, she took a candle and the cigar box and headed to the gardener's shed. The brisk sea wind extinguished her candle, but the moon was high and full enough to provide thin pale light. She unlocked the shed and found a box full of seeds. Emptied it, slid the cigar box in, then covered it again with seed packets. Pansies and sweet peas.

A woman should have at least something in the world.

Grandpa was very wise. Tilly would be wise, too, as long as she could.

SEVEN

Imagining Things

Tilly woke late in the night, eyes blinking open in the dark. A sound. She was still getting used to the sounds here, so she listened carefully. Rattling panes, squally rain. No, it was more than that.

Somebody was thumping on the front door.

She threw back the covers then stood, bare feet on the floorboards, hesitating. If Jasper were home, should he not answer the door? There was no butler, so it had to be either one or the other of them.

Thump, thump, thump.

Tilly pulled on her dressing gown, and lit a candle with shaking hands. She stopped at Jasper's door to knock sharply, but he didn't answer.

He wasn't back? Then she was alone in the house. A rainstorm raged outside. It could be any desperate fellow, looking for shelter.

Thump, thump, thump. "Tilly! Tilly!"

The penny dropped. The desperate fellow out in the storm was her husband.

She hurried down the stairs and pulled the latch. The door flew in, a gust of rainy cold behind it, and he landed in a heap on the doormat. Even by the dim candlelight, she could see his clothes were torn and there was blood on his face.

"Jasper! Good Lord, what happened to you?" She closed the door and knelt, pushing his wet hair off his brow.

"I've lost my keys," he gasped. "I didn't want you to see me like this."

"Come to the kitchen. I'll boil water." She helped him to his feet and he leaned heavily on her. She felt the full weight of his masculine body. His wet clothes pressed themselves on her dressing gown.

In the kitchen she lit every candle she could find and lit the stove to boil water. While he waited, he breathed heavily, resting his elbows on the table in a deep slump.

"Who did this to you?" she asked, while the water heated. But he didn't answer, lost in some subterranean misery.

When the water was boiled, she poured it into a pail and mixed it with cold water, then pulled up a chair in front of Jasper and gently lifted his chin to study his face carefully. He met her eyes darkly, sorrowfully. "I'm sorry," he said.

She dipped a flannel into the pail, squeezed off the excess, and began to sponge the blood from his face.

"Who did this to you?" she asked again.

"The Spaniard," he replied, at length. "But it's over now. I am finished with him. I owe nothing more."

"Then why did he hit you?" She could see now that some of the blood was from his nose and some from a jagged cut on his cheek, perhaps from being struck by a fist wearing a ring. She dabbed the wound gingerly and he winced.

"Because I insulted him." He smiled wryly. "It happens that the Spanish are easily insulted."

"Are you wounded anywhere else?"

"I'm sore and stiff. It was quite a brawl. My knee isn't carrying me properly."

"You'll have to strip out of these wet clothes."

"Will you help me?" he asked. "I can barely stand."

And so she helped him, in the thin glow of the candlelight. Unbuttoning his vest and shirt and putting them carefully aside, then helping him lift his arms to pull off his undershirt and reveal his lean, muscular torso. Tilly's blood warmed at the sight of him. Her fingers ached to trace the pattern of the hair across his chest. She had to remind herself that this was very serious business.

"Come," she said. "Up."

With a harsh sigh he stood, leaning on her, and unbuckled his own trousers and let them fall to the floor, so he stood only in his wool flannel drawers. It was immediately apparent that his knee had ballooned with angry swelling. He could take no weight on it.

"My dear," she said, "I will get you dry, but then you must go to bed and you must stay off that knee. I will call you a physician in the morning."

"No," he said. "I cannot afford a physician."

"I thought you had cleared all your debts?"

"Yes, and so I must incur no new ones."

"A physician, Jasper, may save you from becoming lame." She thought of her money, stashed away from his eyes, and felt a stab of guilt so acute that she almost gasped.

But he said nothing more about a physician. Goose bumps

stood out on his skin, so Tilly slipped off her robe and put it about his shoulders. "Now, let me get you to bed."

Slowly, slowly, they made their way up the stairs. The candle made grim shadows of them on the wall. He grunted and gasped every time he had to bear himself on his injured knee, but finally they arrived at his bedroom. She opened the door and lit the candles from her own, then turned back his covers for him.

"My drawers are wet," he said. "I'll need dry bedclothes." He indicated the wardrobe. Tilly opened the doors. None of the clothes were hung, and nothing was folded. She had to sort through a pile of clothing to find drawers and an undershirt. How had it ever been possible that Jasper had given her the impression of some-body smartly dressed? Was it simply that without servants he had no capacity to mind his own clothing? When she turned back, he stood naked in front of her, his hands modestly crossed over his private parts. The sight was so profoundly arousing that she almost dropped the clothes she held. In the flickering candlelight, she could see the dark crown of his pubic hair. A searing, secret yearn-ing to move his hands away and see all of him gripped her. With a shuddering breath she handed him the drawers and undershirt and he indicated she should turn around while he dressed. She did as he asked, disappointment cooling her skin.

"Thank you, Tilly," he said, when he was done.

She turned to see he was in bed, lying flat on his back. "What do you need? What can I do for you?"

"Nothing. Go to bed."

But there was no chance that she would do as he asked. It was wrong that they should sleep apart, especially tonight when he was injured and needed her comfort. "No. I will stay with you until morning." Without waiting for his approval, she slid into the bed next to him, tucked her body against his.

He braced himself, almost as if expecting another blow. "You should return to your own bedroom."

"Jasper, I want nothing of you. I want only to take care of you," she said, puzzled and hurt. "I am your wife. My proper place is by your side."

"I'm sorry, my dear," he sighed. "This evening has been . . . difficult. I mean to sleep now for a good long time."

"I will sleep next to you and be here for you should you need me." She kissed his cheek and took his hand in her own. Ah, the bliss of finally lying by his side, only their thin nightclothes separating them. Finally falling asleep in Jasper's bed, just as she had imagined it would be.

Or rather, *almost* as she had imagined it would be.

•

The swelling on Jasper's knee had almost gone by the morning, but Tilly cautioned him to stay in bed and delighted in running up and down the stairs with food and tea for him before Mrs. Rivard arrived for the day. Pale bruises were appearing on his face and shoulders, and Tilly didn't dare think about the intensity of rage and violence that had been directed towards him. The world of men seemed such a frightening, exposed place. For once, she was glad her life was sheltered by the comforts of a home and hearth.

With Mrs. Rivard's arrival, she was banished from the staircase. Tilly spent the day in the library. No system of organizing the books had ever been employed, so she had the delight of running her hands along spines, occasionally finding unexpected gems—a first edition of Pepys, a leather-bound, illustrated *Faerie Queene*— and slowly rearranging the books so they made sense. She made piles on the floor, sneezing on dust, readying them to be packed into crates and shipped to Scotland. By nightfall she had created a section for the Greeks, another for the Romans, another for Chaucer, another for Arthurian stories, and hoped to make a Shakespeare section next time she had some hours free. It pained her to think they wouldn't be keeping this marvelous collection of books, but at least she had several months to browse through them.

The evening deepened, and she and Jasper were once again alone in the house. He didn't call for her; most likely he didn't need her at all. But she longed to spend the night lying next to his warm body again. She longed to make their marriage real and not a translucent wish or memory.

So she took her time, unpinning her red curls and brushing them loose around her shoulders. Wiping down her milky white shoulders and arms with rose-scented water. Sliding into a loose cotton, sleeveless chemise. Then taking a deep breath and padding barefoot down the hallway to his bedroom.

Tilly knocked lightly.

"Come in."

She opened the door. Jasper lay where she had last seen him, the covers pushed to one side. His knee was bandaged and elevated on a pile of pillows. He had a wooden dinner tray across his lap, but instead of food on it there was an ink well and an accounts ledger.

"Is it not time for sleep now, my love?" she said.

Jasper sighed and indicated she could take away the tray. "You are probably right. The numbers are swimming before my eyes. But by my reckoning, I am now out of debt. The payment due to me when my next shipment of paving stones is ready from the quarry will mean we can spend some money again."

Tilly's heart felt light. "And are you happy, my dear?"

"I would be, were my poor knee not quite so sore. But it will be fine in a few days, if I rest it." He smiled up at her. "It has been a tumultuous time since your arrival. Perhaps if you'd come a week later."

"Then I wouldn't have been able to give you my jewels. The trunk of goods."

"Ah, yes. Well, the first thing I shall buy with my next sum of money will be a string of pearls to recompense you for the ones you sacrificed." He couldn't quite meet her eye.

"Now, you're not to feel guilty," she said, moving to the bed and sitting beside him. "We are husband and wife now. We share . . . all things." She tried to hold his gaze, to let the full meaning of her words sink in. A moment passed, another.

Then he said, "You should go to bed now."

"I would lie with you again, my husband."

"No. You will disturb my sleep. You will bump my knee."

"Jasper, we are married. When will we—"

His hand went to her mouth, two fingers blocking it firmly. "Do not speak to me of these things. I am recovering from an injury and a humiliation. Let not these base appetites of yours control you, Tilly. It is so unbecoming in a woman."

"But I—"

His voice rode over the top of hers. "When I am well again. When I am rich again, for it is nothing but folly to bring a child into a household that can barely support the two of us. When I know you again, for you insisted on staying in England and letting in this sea of estrangement between us. But above all, Tilly, when I allow it. Not when you desire it. You speak of how a marriage should be: then you will see that you must follow my command. Now go. You have embarrassed both of us and brought us low."

Complex feelings traversed her. Shame, sadness, but above all, anger. Tilly's fuse had been lit and she had to smother it fast.

"I apologize," she mumbled and hurried from the room as quickly as she could. She took to her own bedroom and paced furiously, squeezing her palms tight against each other. She must not—*must not*—return to Jasper's room and open her mouth and let out the stream of words and accusations that were stopping up her throat. *I have brought us low? When you presented yourself as a wealthy man to my grandfather and married me with promises of a grand house full of grand things? When you have sold my jewelery and returned to the house after a common brawl? When you did not write to me for six weeks?*

Gradually, slowly, the fire burned lower. Lower. But didn't extinguish altogether. That was the problem with Tilly's anger; a little always remained, an ember that, kindled carelessly, might rage into life again.

•

Jasper was up and about within five days. He was kindly, as though he had never admonished her so hotly. But also remote, as though he was fending off any warmth from her before she expressed it.

At breakfast they sat across the table from each other, over boiled eggs and toast, while Mrs. Rivard cheerlessly refilled their teacups. Jasper suddenly looked up from his food and said, "Mrs. Rivard, is it Saturday?"

"Yes, sir," she said.

He turned his attention to Tilly. "Ralph and Laura Mornington are hosting a party tonight, down in St. Peter Port. We have to go."

"We do?"

"Ralph is one of my most reliable business contacts, and my closest friend. Do you have something to wear?"

"Yes, I have a number of good gowns."

"Mrs. Rivard," he called back towards the kitchen, "find me my cashmere trousers and gold-brocade waistcoat and have them pressed and ready for seven."

She responded with a grunt of assent and Tilly ventured, "Mrs. Rivard isn't a pleasant woman."

"She certainly isn't. But she is cheap."

Tilly said nothing more about Mrs. Rivard's rudeness. She didn't want to gainsay him. "It will be nice, Jasper, don't you think?" she ventured. "Dinner with friends. The two of us dressed in our best. Rather like our courtship. Perhaps it will give us a chance to become familiar again."

He gave her a noncommittal smile. "I will be very busy in my room today, Tilly. Don't disturb me. And be ready for seven."

He pushed his chair back and walked away, still limping slightly. Tilly finished her breakfast. What would she do with her day? Back home with Grandpa she would have spent her time reading with him, cutting flowers, stitching on her embroidery ring, walking to the village, working in the garden . . . anything she pleased, really. At Grandpa's she felt settled and free. Here, she felt restless and circumscribed by the dim wood-paneled walls, and beyond that by the gray sea that bounded the island. Perhaps that was the reason she felt so hemmed in. Islands were places in between; places neither here nor there, but rather places on the way somewhere. That was how she felt. Not settled.

Where was she on her way to?

Tilly decided the best thing for her restlessness was some time outdoors. She found the gardening gloves, clean and scented of lemon soap, in her drawer where Miss Broussard had put them. She tied on an apron. It was time to tackle the garden.

Outside, the sun was high and clear in the sky, but a cool breeze lifted her hair and rustled in the tops of the bristlewood pines. She laid down an old tablecloth, folded over once, in front of the garden bed she meant to attack first. Then she went to the garden shed, unlocked it, and gathered a pail, a trowel, and a pair of secateurs.

Tilly went to work. She pulled weeds and cut the deadheads from rosebushes. She turned over soil and straightened border stones. Rather than finding the work tiring—it certainly wasn't what she was bred to do—she found it exhilarating. It wasn't the joy of seeing the garden bed transformed from overgrown chaos into tidy serenity; it was the joy of proximity to the natural world of seasons and growth. She sat back and carefully removed her muddy gloves, and looked up at the sky, smiling. Now all she needed was some rain. She had let in light and air, so all would grow well next spring.

She tried to imagine what life would be like next spring. By then, Jasper's finances would be right again, he would find that doe-eyed love for her she'd seen back in England, perhaps they would even be with child. There was much to look forward to when these roses bloomed.

But first she had to get through this evening.

She opened up the old tablecloth and threw the garden rubbish onto it, then dragged it down to a grassless area near the garden shed to make a bonfire.

Tilly sat by the light of the fire, arms around her knees. Her dress and hands were dirty and her arms ached from the physical labor. She watched the flames flicker and shiver in the lengthening afternoon. The blue smoke stung her eyes, but it smelled warm and woody. She thought about Grandpa, about what he would say to her about her growing despondence. To be patient, to be sensible, to expect a little less out of life.

He might also remind her she was dirty and needed to clean up before going out for dinner.

She left the bonfire to burn itself down and put away her gardening things. Surreptitiously, she ensured that the cigar box was still hidden, then locked the shed and returned to the house to wash and dress.

At seven, she waited at the bottom of the stairs, in her pale blue silk chiffon gown with the scooped neck and the navy-blue satin ribbons. Opera toe slippers, long white gloves, beads in the high-piled hairstyle Mrs. Rivard had grudgingly helped her with, a ribboned fan. But no dangling earrings, no turquoise necklace. All her jewels were gone.

She waited. Half an hour passed. Mrs. Rivard walked past her on her way out.

"Have you seen Mr. Dellafore?" Tilly asked her.

"No," the older woman replied. "But the clothes I prepared for him are no longer hanging in his room."

A little dart of shock to her heart. "Might he have left without me?"

"How am I to know?" Mrs. Rivard closed the door behind her.

Tilly ascended the stairs to the third floor and opened the door to Jasper's room. It had been tidied, all his clothes folded and hung. But he was nowhere to be seen. She went to the window, looked down through the warped glass that filled every window frame on the third floor. She could see out to the front path and the road. And there was Jasper, walking up the path with determination, in his waistcoat and wingtip collar. Returning from somewhere.

Tilly opened his wardrobe and removed the tailcoat he would need, and met him halfway up the stairs.

"Where have you been?"

"On business," he said.

"In your party clothes?" She handed him his coat.

He narrowed his eyes. "Don't go into my room without my permission," he said. "And how I dress to do my business is not your concern."

Tilly swallowed hard, tried to keep the mood light. "I meant no harm, my love. Come, let us have a good evening."

He slipped into his tailcoat and she put her hand over his arm. It was a lovely evening for the walk down through the wood to town, and Jasper found it in him to relax and be forgiving.

"I am sorry I snapped, dear," he said, at length, as the trees thinned and the path widened into a road. "Only I would prefer you to stay out of my room simply because that is where I do my journal keeping and correspondence. I once had a study on the second floor, but when I sold all but my desk it made me so depressed sitting in an empty room that I could barely add up my figures."

And there it was . . . an opportunity to ask him about the letters. To have it all in the clear. Perhaps unwisely, she said, "I did see you have a lot of correspondence in your drawers."

"Hm," he said, not really listening, kicking a stone off the path.

"I saw one of my own letters."

"No you didn't."

"I understand if you didn't want to alarm me by writing in response. I know times were difficult for you."

"I received none of your letters, Tilly. What are you talking about?"

"But I saw . . ." She trailed off.

He was regarding her kindly, with a puzzled expression. This was not an angry denial. "Tilly, my dear. If I had received your letters, I would tell you. Just as, I hope, you would not lie about receiving none of mine."

And the self-doubt crept in. Perhaps she *had* imagined it. She'd been tired that day, the light had been dim. Perhaps she had mistaken somebody else's handwriting for her own.

The roofscape of chimney pots, the winding streets, the bristling masts in the harbor came into view.

"I'll show you if you like," he said. "When we go home, I will show you everything that's in my desk."

"No, no. I wouldn't presume . . ." She forced a smile. "I feel a bit of a fool."

"Put it out of your mind," he said.

"Yes, yes," she said. "I'll put it out of my mind."

•

The Morningtons' house on Le Paradis was as grand as Jasper's, but with well-lit stairs, fresh paint, and brilliantly clean tiles. Le Paradis was where the richest of the English lived on the island, a steep street where the watercolored houses faced each other across the worn cobbles. Tilly and Jasper walked up the broad white stairs and knocked on the front door, then waited under the light of the lantern for somebody to answer. A brisk westerly and the smell of damp chrysanthemums.

Then Jasper leaned close to Tilly and said in a harsh whisper, "Do not mention our financial troubles to anyone, least of all Ralph and Laura."

"I wouldn't dream of it," Tilly said.

He glanced around, a bitter frown pulling down the corners of his mouth as he took in the brass door knocker, the stained fan-light. "My house looked like this once."

"And it will again." She squeezed his hand. "I trust you."

Then a stout man with a thick mustache and slick black hair was there, pumping Jasper's hand in a greeting and laughing merrily.

"Dellafore! You made it! After that bout with the Spaniard we thought you might stay in a little longer to lick your wounds."

Jasper smiled. "Perhaps he will think twice before insulting my honor again. I always pay my debts on time, Ralph. I hope you didn't listen to his nonsense."

Ralph chuckled, gesturing them inside. "I rather think you walked away the worse of the two of you, but no matter. At least you walked away and he has returned to Spain, and you'll know better than to do business with him again." His attention turned to Tilly. "And this is the lovely Matilda?" he said, taking Tilly's hand and kissing the air two inches above it.

"Tilly," she said. "Nobody ever calls me anything else. Unless I'm in some kind of trouble."

The man smiled a smile that reached all the way to his eyes and made them sparkle kindly. "And is that often?"

"Less often as I grow older, sir."

He took their coats and handed them to a butler. "Welcome to my home, Tilly, and welcome to the island. Come and let me introduce you to my wife." He turned, and Jasper took Tilly's arm to follow him.

"He's lovely," she said softly to Jasper.

"If he drinks too much he gets silly. Do not take all he says as serious, my dear."

Ralph led them into a parlor where a dozen or so people sat on sofas or in windowsills or stood leaning on the mantel or spilled out onto the terrace beyond the French doors to smoke cigars. The good lighting showed up the fine velvet brocade on the sofas, the gold flocking in the wallpaper, the spotless brass lamps, giving the impression of a room that glowed like precious jewels; and Tilly fought a pang of envy. This was the life she thought she had been coming to, not the dim and empty Lumière sur la Mer. Light on the sea? It barely cast a light on their garden at night.

But then she admonished herself for being petty. She was alive, she was well, she was with the man she loved. They were at the start of their life together and things would improve. Besides, living a simple life was no less noble or worthy than living a life surrounded by fine things. She would get used to it if she had to.

She met a whirl of people, including the soft-voiced, pink-cheeked Laura and the Morningtons' visiting eldest daughter, Maria. Maria had the nurse bring her baby daughter down, a little girl just starting to walk, and all the ladies cooed over her chubby-armed beauty while the men smiled indulgently. Tilly thought about a little girl of her own, and the thought infused her with warmth and light, so that she smiled at Jasper more fondly all evening—not that he noticed.

"Are you happy here?" Laura asked Tilly, when the child had returned to her room and they had a moment alone.

"I am still settling," Tilly said honestly. "But I do believe I will be happy."

An expression crossed Laura's brow that Tilly couldn't read. But it was followed by a quick smile. "You may always call on me," she said. "Ralph and Jasper are good friends. I hope to see more of you."

A meal was served, and Tilly found herself sitting between Ralph and another, much older man who was not interested in her at all and spent the entire meal with his shoulder turned away from her, talking to his other neighbor. Ralph took it upon himself to make her feel welcome, chatting to her, asking questions about her grandfather, touching her shoulder lightly when her eyes grew teary describing his last days. He was a friend to her, a good friend, and she found herself warming to him very easily.

The food was a menu of traditional Guernsey fare—floured ormers with pork belly, whiting pie, *Gâche Mêlée*—created for the evening by Ralph and Laura's cook whom they introduced at the behest of their delighted dinner guests. Tilly was surprised when the cook who emerged was a woman perhaps only of twenty-five, with thick strawberry blonde hair piled up loosely, and a sloe-eyed beauty about her that belied her hours working in a steaming kitchen.

"May I introduce Chantelle Lejeune," Laura said, elbow-prompting Chantelle to curtsy. "Her English isn't very good, but we have been so glad to have her in our employ this last year." Laura smiled kindly.

Chantelle nodded, her eyes found each woman at the table one by one. When her gaze came to rest on Tilly, she assessed her with a proud flare of her nostrils, then looked away. What open arrogance. Between her and Mrs. Rivard, Tilly was starting to wonder why any good English folk would press the French into service if they couldn't keep their manners. She pushed her plate away. The spicy apples in her dessert didn't taste so good anymore. She looked around for Jasper, who was deep in conversation with a man near the end of the table. Laughter and talking started again, as plates were cleared away. Ralph had turned to talk to his other neighbor, so Tilly found herself in the middle of it but all alone. She folded her hands in her lap and tried to look as though she was enjoying her own company. People were moving about now, chairs scraping back, men speaking of retiring to the library with brandy.

Laura was at Tilly's elbow. "Come, Tilly. The other ladies and I will take the southern parlor for tea."

Tilly gratefully took her arm and the five ladies present took their places in the parlor. It had been a long time since she'd been in company and it was good to find herself chatting and laughing. How long since she had laughed? Really laughed? Certainly before Grandpa got sick. In fact, this was the first time since Grandpa's death that the weight of all that had happened wasn't sitting heavy across her shoulders. Perhaps that was the glass of wine she had drunk with dinner, but perhaps it was the company of other women.

Talk turned to the cook.

"I don't know why you have her in the house, Laura," sniffed one woman, a dowager in her fifties with an elaborate hairstyle of ringlets.

"When we met her, she was being treated abominably by a family across on Alderney. She has such a way with food and we felt as though we were rescuing her. She's an orphan, she has always worked for a living and she's very good at what she does. Ralph and I have tried to be family to her."

The other opinions started to spill out. "She's arrogant."

"I think that's just her face. It's a haughty face."

"There's no haughty face without a haughty personality."

"She's very pretty," Tilly offered.

One of the women smiled tightly. "Yes. But pretty isn't everything."

"She has a lovely spirit, really," Laura said emphatically.

At that moment, Jasper appeared at the door. "Tilly, we are going home."

"So soon?" Laura asked, rising and standing between them. "I hope all is well, Mr. Dellafore. Your wife is delightful company."

Jasper nodded at Laura politely, but his gaze returned immediately to Tilly. He snapped his fingers. "Come along. My knee is causing me some pain and I need to rest it."

Tilly climbed to her feet, setting aside her teacup and bidding her new companions good evening.

"I'm sorry you're not feeling well," she said to Jasper in the hall, as the servants helped them into their coats.

He didn't respond, but she thought nothing of it. They began the walk home in silence. Jasper hurrying a little too fast for Tilly to keep up.

"Jasper," she said, "may we go a little slower, please? These shoes aren't meant for walking fast along country tracks."

He didn't answer, nor did he slow. In fact, he gave no indication he had even heard her. Now a cold puzzlement set in. Why was he behaving this way? Had she said something to upset him? But they had been in separate rooms; he would have no knowledge of what silly chatter she had indulged in. Nonetheless, she sifted through her conversations in her memory. What could he have misheard from the other room? Or perhaps she had somehow insulted Ralph, their host, over dinner. That was it. Ralph had had words with Jasper about her behavior. Now she retraced her dealings with Ralph, but could remember nothing. He had turned away from her towards the end of dinner . . . maybe he'd inferred an insult. Her brain whirled as she tried to work backwards, to identify her failing.

"Jasper," she called, hurrying after him breathlessly, finally catching his arm at the start of the path up to the house. "Have I said something to upset Ralph? Because if I have, it was in no way intended. He is a lovely gentleman and—"

He whirled around to glare at her. "You couldn't even make it to our door without mentioning him, I see."

"I . . ." Tilly struggled with her bewilderment. "I merely mean that . . . You are angry with me and I couldn't think of anything I'd done, so I assumed I'd said something . . ." But now Tilly wasn't so sure.

"Oh, heaven forfend that you should have said something that made Ralph dislike you." His tone was unctuous with scorn, and Tilly's frustration began to bubble and steam.

"I can see I've upset you," she said, her voice thick with distress, "so if you'll please simply tell me what it is, then I will make amends."

"You know what you did," he huffed.

"No. No, I don't."

"Then you are a liar."

"I'm not a . . ." She swallowed down her anger. Swallowed it down hard. His anger and offense were genuine. This must be somehow her fault and she mustn't, *mustn't* lose her temper now. "I promise you, Jasper . . ."

But he was already walking away. "The promise of a liar is worth little. Of a woman with faithless eyes, even less."

Faithless eyes?

He stormed up the path and opened the door, and she slid in behind him before he slammed it firmly and stalked up the stairs.

"Jasper, please."

"Don't speak to me."

She sat heavily on the bottom step, heard his door close firmly. Carefully, she went over every detail of the argument, examining them all one by one, then in groups and sequences, forcing her reason to override her passions. Jasper thought she had behaved inappropriately with Ralph, and somehow Jasper had cemented this opinion when in conversation with the men. For all her efforts, she could not remember a single thing she had done to invite this opinion, but she accepted nonetheless that this was why Jasper was angry.

The only solution was to air it out with Jasper, but in the morning. When he had cooled off a little. She cheered herself with the thought. A silly tiff that would all blow over with love and openness.

•

But he wouldn't speak to her in the morning. He wouldn't meet her eye over breakfast and he behaved as if she wasn't there, sitting across from him, begging with angry tears for him to answer her questions, believe her denials. And when she tried to grasp his arm and stop him leaving the house, he shook her off with enough force to frighten her but not hurt her.

By the fourth day of Jasper's silence, Tilly was mad with an angry misery she had never known before. She came down for supper, expecting more of his stony-faced silence. Instead, she found the table set for one.

"Mrs. Rivard?" she asked, as the tray of oxtail soup, braised ham, and vegetables was put in front of her. "Has Mr. Dellafore gone out?"

"He says he will eat in his room for all meals from now on," Mrs. Rivard answered with a subdued delight that twisted her mouth into a faint smile.

The cauldron inside her spat with heat and all at once boiled over. She sprang to her feet, flinging out her arm to send the soup bowl sailing across the room to smash against the wall and fall into sopping fragments on the floor.

"Temper," said Mrs. Rivard, very quietly but unmistakably.

Tilly dashed away from the dining table and up the stairs, slamming open Jasper's bedroom door before her fury dissipated and made her timid again. "I will not have this, I will *not*!" she shouted.

Jasper, at his writing desk, sat back and regarded her mutely.

"This must end. You are my husband and I am your wife. We cannot spend the rest of our lives this way. What will it take to make you talk to me?"

Jasper put down his pen, adjusted it so it was parallel with his paper, and then returned his attention to her and said, "Admit it."

"Admit what?"

"Admit that you desired Ralph Mornington, that you couldn't keep that desire off your face or out of your fluttering eyes, and that the moment you thought it might draw his pity, you told him of our financial problems."

"I . . . I did none of that . . ."

"Then why did Ralph take me aside in the library and say, 'How are things, really, old boy? Those debts all cleared?'"

"I don't know. Because you had a fight with the Spaniard."

"Not about money. About honor. You know nothing of the world of men."

"Jasper, I said nothing to Ralph about our finances, and I certainly didn't—"

He held up his hand in a stop gesture. "Then I have nothing else to say to you. Ever."

The pressure of rage inside her made her ribs and muscles grind. She wondered if holding it in would actually cause her injury. Her mouth opened and closed but no words came out.

Finally she managed, "So if I admit to making eyes at Ralph, you will speak to me again?"

He didn't answer.

"But will you not admonish me? Call me a flirt? A liar? A spiller of all your secrets? For I am not those things, Jasper Dellafore."

Again, no answer.

Tilly slammed out of the room.

•

Sleep would not come. Regret, the gone-cold feeling that always followed her losing her temper, coiled sickly in her stomach. At midnight she was downstairs in the dining room, cleaning up the spilled soup and broken bowl by the light of a candle. At two in the morning she was crying softly into her pillow, her self-righteous rage now wilting into self-blame. There were always two sides to an argument, and perhaps she had been overly warm with Ralph Mornington for a first acquaintance. She hoped Laura didn't think ill of her too. And had she perhaps said something that made Ralph think they weren't doing well? A sad smile and a "we'll get by" might have been all it took, and while she couldn't remember saying such a thing, nor could she remember not saying it.

And did it matter if she was right anyway? They couldn't go on not speaking to each other.

She slept a little, just before dawn, then knocked on Jasper's door when the birds were singing in the garden.

"I'm sorry to wake you," she said softly, kneeling next to his bed and touching his warm forehead. "But I admit it. I admit to everything. Just please, please can we go back to how we were? Back in Dorset? You never wanted to leave my side." Here came the tears. "I felt so loved then, and now I feel empty and cold."

Jasper sat up, leaned over, and kissed her forehead. This small show of favor and fondness flooded her with gratitude. "Go back to bed, Tilly," he said. "It's too early to be up."

She nearly asked to sleep next to him, but feared another rebuff. Instead, she returned to her room and, at last, slept.

•

Jasper was like a completely different person then. For a week, another week, he was kind, considerate, held her hand, visited her as she worked in the garden, made promises of things he would buy her as soon as he had money. Still, there was no invitation for her to share his bed and she began to grow used to it. What did Tilly know about married life, really? Perhaps this was how everyone did it, and Jasper was right: a baby when their financial lot was precarious was a bad idea.

So she slept in her own bed every night, window open an inch to let in the sound of the sea, even on cooler nights, and she came to feel at home at Lumière sur la Mer.

It was approaching autumn when Tilly was roused from her sleep late. She wasn't sure how late, as she couldn't see her clock in the dark, but it felt past midnight. There was a creeping cold in the air that belonged only to the early morning.

She heard a sound. A soft thump. A low laugh. Voices—a man and a woman—talking outside. She went to the window and opened it, strained her ears. But there were no more voices. From here, she looked down on the conservatorium. Was somebody walking past? Taking a shortcut through their grounds?

Then the thump again, and for a moment it sounded as though it came from in the house. Frowning in the dark, she went to the door of her bedroom and tried to open it, intending to listen into the hallway for other noises.

But it wouldn't open. The handle wouldn't turn. She tried again, harder. Rattled it softly.

Then realized: she had been locked in.

The laughter and voices again. This time definitely from near the conservatory. She returned to the window, heard the voices recede into the distance. Nothing to worry about. Far more concerning was who had locked her in and why? Mrs. Rivard? Jasper? Please, not Jasper. She thought of banging on the door and calling for him, but it was so late and he would be asleep; and things had been so good between them. Perhaps Mrs. Rivard had locked her in. It was time she asked Jasper to let the woman go; Tilly was growing afraid of her.

Though she had to admit, it was more likely Jasper had locked her in. He had shown himself capable of jealousy, the will to control her.

She slipped back between the covers, telling herself that all would be well but sliding into a sleep full of dreams about long sunless corridors, locked doors, and great distances between her and comfort.

•

In the morning she tried the door and it opened without effort. In her head she chose her words carefully, so that they were ready for Jasper at breakfast. But he had already gone out for the morning, according to Miss Broussard.

"You might catch him at the post office," she said.

Tilly had not been to town often. Jasper wasn't keen for her to venture beyond the wood by herself, but today she needed to prove to herself she was free. So she put on her walking shoes and a light coat and headed down the front path and into the woods.

The leaves looked tired, skittered down and scattered across the path. The first chill of autumn was in the sea air and she longed for her sable-trimmed coat. She wondered who wore it now? And who wore her necklace of jet or her pearls? The lack of leaves let more light into the wood, a chill pale light that silvered the fallen leaves. She heard footsteps in the wood and looked up to see Jasper approaching.

"Tilly? What are you doing?"

"Coming to look for you. To ask you about something important," she said, forcing her voice to be easy. She ought not always be afraid of trouble; but Jasper's unpredictable moods made her so.

"Well, I am returned. With good news." He took her hand. "But first . . . What is your something important?"

She considered him in the morning light. He looked older than when she'd met him. His brow was furrowed, and lines ran from his nose to the corners of his mouth. And she almost said nothing, not wanting to trouble him more.

"Go on," he said.

"Did you lock me in my room last night?"

His mouth turned down in disdain. "Why do you ask me such a ridiculous question?"

Fool. You should have said nothing. "Because I tried to open my bedroom door late last night and it was locked. If it wasn't you, it was Mrs. Rivard. I know she doesn't like me and—"

"Mrs. Rivard? The servant who is in our employ? Matilda, have you been reading too many fanciful novels?" He pulled her hand. "Come, I want to show you something."

She allowed herself to be pulled back up the path, all the while half apologies and rationalizations fell from her lips. *Sorry. I felt trapped. I was frightened. Don't be cross.* But he simply pulled her along, at speed into the house, up the stairs and stood her outside her bedroom. The door was closed.

"Now look," he said.

"What do you mean?"

He pointed at the door. "Look."

She looked.

"Do you see a keyhole?" he asked.

And she had to admit she didn't.

"Do you see any kind of lock?"

"No," she managed, her mind whirling. "But I tried the door handle. It wouldn't budge. As though locked."

"And yet, as you see, it is unlockable."

The ground fell away from beneath her feet. Where she was once so certain, now cobwebs drifted.

Jasper turned her to face him, his eyes serious. "This is not the first time you have imagined something, Tilly."

"I would have sworn . . ."

"What kind of a man do you think I am?" he asked. He lifted her hand and pressed it against his heart. "What kind of a *husband* do you think I am?"

Shame flushed her face. "Oh, Jasper. I'm sorry. I'm so, so sorry."

He dropped her hand, stood back. "You are lucky. Today I am full of good news and not in a mood to hold a grudge. I have a letter from a man in Dublin who wants to meet with me. A fellow there wants to buy the paving stones I've ordered on the cheap. As soon as the samples are ready, I'll be off to see him and then I will return a wealthy man." He smiled, that smile she remembered so well from their courtship. All charm and sparkling dark eyes. "And then, my dear Tilly, we can start the life we were meant to start. You have been patient. Apart from a few wild imaginings." He chuckled merrily and she threw herself into his arms and tried to take comfort from his warm, male body.

"You'll never forgive my foolishness," she said. "I can barely forgive it myself."

"All I advise you is to stay in the house and rest. You are clearly still not finished grieving for your grandfather and our financial troubles have caused you anxiety. That is why your mind is making up stories. Stay in bed. Relax. I can send the physician if you think it would help. I believe we can afford it now."

"No, no," she said. "I will be fine."

That night, she woke late again. No voices or thuds. Woken by curiosity. Was the door unmovable again? She rose, made it half-way across the room, and changed her mind. This was madness. The door had no lock. She was not locked in. Her husband was a trustworthy man.

Instead, she went to the window and opened it. Evening cold gushed in, but she didn't mind. A clear night; so many stars. The roar of the wind in the redwoods, the distant crash of the sea. Below her window was the conservatory and if she needed to . . . if she had to escape and the door wasn't able to be opened . . . she could plot a course down from ledge, to tree branch, to ledge, to the roof of the conservatory and then to the ground.

If she needed to.

EIGHT

Figures in the Distance

Tilly and Jasper shared a calm few days. They ate their meals together, then he went off to wrestle with numbers at his desk and she returned to either of her projects. The garden if it was fine, the library if it rained. Tilly worked hard to infer love and warmth from Jasper's words and actions: *my dear, Tilly my love,* a soft touch on her shoulder or hair. She also worked hard not to overwhelm him with her own love and warmth. She understood now that such displays of passion unsettled him. So she learned to be judicious with her smiles, temperate with her expressions of regard, and to keep her hands to herself. Only at nighttime, as they parted at the top of the stairs, did she insist on offering up her lips for a kiss. On every occasion, she longed for passion, his arms crushing her, his mouth hot and open to hers. On every occasion, he pressed his mouth against hers coolly, lips firmly drawn together, then said, "Good night, Tilly."

And each retired to their own room, their own cold, empty bed.

Sometimes Tilly cried hot tears, pounded the pillow, screamed silently about how unfair it was that this marriage was such an enormous disappointment. But sometimes she managed to compress all those wild feelings into a hard kernel inside her and let her brain take charge. He did not want children yet. His financial difficulties probably shook him to the very core of his sense of himself as a man. Their long separation between the wedding and her arrival had filled him with doubts, which he was slowly and patiently working through. Just because Tilly could not be slow and patient didn't mean Jasper could not also.

But it wasn't that Tilly was madly keen for sex: she was curious about it certainly, and she desired Jasper. It was that she needed comfort, physical comfort. She and Grandpa hadn't lived a day together that didn't involve a long hug, a stroke of the hair, a walk holding hands. Losing him was one kind of pain, but losing human touch was another, keener pain. She needed Jasper to hold her, not because she was an intemperate woman whose virginity irked her; but because she felt isolated and surrounded by cold. An island. A place in between.

Tilly was in the garden, wondering if it were the last day of the year warm enough to be outside all day. The sea wind was rough this morning, and the sun had not yet lain upon the grass long enough to lift the dew. She knelt on her old tablecloth, tidying the lavender beds. The sky was a great blue arch above her, pale and barely warmed by the sun. She tried not to think about how they would stay warm this autumn, this winter. Jasper hadn't earned a penny in months. All rested on his sale of granite pavers to the Dublin merchant, and the quarrier who had promised him such a good deal had been out of contact for a week.

"Tilly! Tilly!" This was Jasper, calling from the house. She rose, peeled off her gardening gloves and waited. He ran towards her, excited happiness in his face.

A weight lifted off her heart. "They are here?" she asked.

"They are here! Four granite pavers, beveled, cleaned, and ready to be waxed, finally offered up by that wretched man at the quarry," he said. "The price was low and I had nothing to buy them with. But I am not averse to risk. I took a beating from the Spaniard and I took your jewels from you, and I am ashamed of both. But it is all worth it. My man in Dublin will pay three times what I did for them. I leave this afternoon to take him the samples, to sign paperwork." He shook his head sadly. "And to take the down payment that will let us breathe again. I am sorry. I am so sorry."

"I seem to remember vowing to stand by you for better and for worse," Tilly said. "Well done, my love. My husband."

He leaned down and kissed her forehead with such tenderness that her heart lurched. She closed her eyes and leaned in to him. A wild wind whirled around them and then was gone. She turned her face up to him.

And saw it. An expression between expressions, something he felt before he covered what he really felt. The same expression she had seen at the wedding—she had forgotten about it in the chaos after Grandpa's collapse. But now she had seen it again. An expression of pity and . . . condescension? Disdain? Surely not . . . contempt?

"Jasper?"

"The wind," he said. "It's too cold out here."

Should she admit it? That her heart thumped with uncertainty? That she had seen an expression cross his brow—a tenth of a moment in length—that made her fear he didn't love her? She could not admit it. He already thought her prone to fits of wild imagination, and she was already doubting herself. Yes, the wind was cold. He didn't like being outside, at his own admission. Why should she assume that the look of scorn was for her and not the weather?

Simply because she'd seen it before.

Tilly wondered if Jasper was right. Grief over Grandpa's death, the move to this strange new place, the anxiety over money . . . perhaps they had weighed upon her thoughts until the point that those thoughts had started to warp and crook.

Back inside the house she made a vow to herself never to mention these thoughts to Jasper. To rest and keep her heart calm, and to call the physician if they continued. It wasn't right to be so fearful of her husband. That was not how marriage was meant to be.

•

Jasper left as a cold front moved in, bringing leaden skies and chill rain. Tilly was all but trapped inside. The one time she tried to walk down to St. Peter Port, her umbrella blew inside out and she was sodden in seconds. Her dealings with Mrs. Rivard were monosyllabic, and Jasper had sent Miss Broussard on leave while he was away. Two servants were too much for one person, he explained. So for days, she spoke to nobody. The house was silent and grim. The leaden clouds made the dark come earlier and it felt as though she lived her whole life by candlelight.

With the garden awash, Tilly returned to her other task, organizing the books in the library. One by one, she pulled them down, sneezing from dust, collecting them on the floor with their brothers and sisters; then one by one she reshelved them. Even with the curtains drawn wide, the daylight was dim. She went at a leisurely pace, often stopping and sitting on the wooden step-up to read a poem or remember a favorite part of an old story. Rain pounded at the windows and wind danced eerily around the eaves. She wondered how Jasper was getting on, when she might see him again. Sometimes, as she took down books and stacked them, she imagined a change in fortune for them. She imagined having a party like the one the Morningtons had held. The house would be full of cut flowers and rich ornaments, all the lamps lit, the great chandelier restored in the entrance hall. It made her smile and long for him to return so that this future could rush upon them in an instant, rather than being beyond her fingertips.

Then eight days later, the rain stopped. Tilly woke to a fine, clear morning, the sun low in the sky but a cheerful yellow.

And she knew she couldn't stay inside.

Directly after breakfast, she pulled on her sturdiest walking shoes, her gloves and scarf, and her walking coat. She thought about calling out to Mrs. Rivard that she was heading out, but the servant would neither care nor bother with a heartfelt *adieu*, so Tilly let herself out, pocketed the front door key, and set off down the path.

Ten feet into the wood, she realized she could go no further. The path was deep, sticky mud. But she knew there was another way off Jasper's estate—further, and much more dramatic—via the cliff road behind the house. She returned to the grounds of Lumière sur la Mer, crossed the garden, then went through the gate that bordered the neighbor's apple orchard. Miss Broussard had told her about this route, but she had never walked it so she carefully followed the fence, climbed over the stile and then down. From here she could look down over the rolling headland and down to the beach. A stony track led north to St. Peter Port, and south down the hill and to the water.

On a whim, she went south. She had lived here five weeks

without ever having seen the beach, and after all the rain and bad weather, all kinds of interesting things might have washed up on the sand.

Tilly trod carefully. There was no mud here, but some of the stones were mossy. She was very exposed. No trees grew here. The distant sun was warm on her shoulders. She loosened her bonnet and took it off, enjoying the warmth in her hair. She knew she should be careful in the sun or she would freckle, but after days cooped up inside while it rained, a few freckles would be a small price to pay.

The sea breeze was soft, almost still. The hush and pull of the waves soothing. She glanced down and saw two figures on the beach: a man and a woman. He sat on a rock, she stood in front of him, facing the sea. His arms encircled her hips. She smiled at this expression of love. No doubt many folk would be heading outside today, to enjoy the autumn sunshine, many fond lovers like these two.

Her heart knew before her eyes did.

One of those figures was Jasper.

She stopped, skin frosting over. Was this her imagination again? She pinched herself, looked again. Her eyes tried to make him not Jasper. He sat with his back to her after all. Jasper was in Ireland. Jasper wasn't here on the beach with another woman's hips between his firm hands. He stood, his hands sliding up around her waist and embracing her. Both of them, facing out to sea. Two hundred feet down from where Tilly stood.

Two hundred feet. Too far to see clearly.

The woman stepped away from the man and they began to walk along the beach. Tilly moved again, walking fast, sliding and slipping on the stones, desperate to catch them. Because she had seen it, clearly with her own eyes: the woman wore her coat, her treasured sable-trimmed coat. Long red-gold hair spilled over its collar and was caught by the wind. Jasper had her hand. Oh, yes, it was Jasper. The closer she drew to them the more certain she was. Running now, desperate to get to the beach before they disappeared around the cove and out of sight.

But Tilly's feet were in too much haste to be careful. A stone punched into her toe, the slippery moss under her other foot could not hold her. Over she went, landing heavily on her left wrist. The fall itself seemed slow, almost as though it were happening to somebody else. But the pain in her wrist brought her back to herself: hard and sharp.

And just as she was trapped in her body with this horrible pain, so she was trapped in this marriage, on this island, with the hard, sharp fear that her husband didn't love her. He loved somebody else.

•

She lay for a long time in the damp grass, heart thudding in her ears, dreading to look at her wrist. Finally, she lifted it up in front of her, wiggled each finger in turn. Then she tried to bend her wrist. It moved too freely. Searing pain. She let out a little cry.

Keep it still, then. Keep it still. She maneuvered herself into a sitting position, then slowly climbed to her feet, nursing her wrist defensively against her chest. The figures down on the beach had gone, of course, and she looked back up the hill, wrist throbbing. And started trudging up and up, much more carefully than she'd gone down.

In her head she began composing the dignified, cold lecture she would give her husband when he got home. About marriage vows and how God would judge him. To think that Jasper wouldn't touch Tilly, wouldn't take her to his bed, but had raced to meet with this other woman and put his hands on her body so . . . comfortably. She realized she was crying, open-mouthed crying like a tiny child, with tears and mucus running over her face. She stopped, took a few deep shuddering breaths, and applied her handkerchief to her damp cheeks and mouth. Her heart was thudding from the walk, her wrist filled with a dragging pain, her head crowded with thoughts and phrases. *How could you? Who is she? My coat!*

Tilly continued up the path. She needed to get home, to her bed and rest her wrist, and wait for Jasper to finish with his lover and come home to Tilly's fury.

•

He didn't come. The hours passed in agony. He didn't come. When had he stepped off the ship? How long did it take to . . . service that woman? Why wasn't he returning home to his wife?

Mrs. Rivard rang the bell for dinner and supper and Tilly stayed in her room. She had no appetite and her wrist hurt too much to lift a fork. She watched in horror as it swelled to nearly twice its normal width. She found a clean pillow slip and folded it to a narrow strip, then using her good hand and her teeth, wrapped her wrist tightly. She needed a doctor, but she wouldn't call one. Let Jasper get home, late and guilty, and find her here injured and in pain. Then perhaps he would regret his actions.

Night came, but still he didn't arrive. A darker, sharper thought: what if he had never been away at all? What if it had all been a story so he could spend time with the other woman? Tilly heard Mrs. Rivard leaving. The house settled into the grim, dark quiet she had become used to the last week. She lit no candle, she barely moved, she prayed for sleep but it would not come. A dozing fit here, a long period of quiet in her head there, but mostly the night passed in whirling thoughts and hot pain and the knowledge that he was not in his own bed because he was in somebody else's.

Just before dawn, she startled awake, surprised that she had slept at all. Her curtain was still open, and she could see the sky was losing its inky darkness. Footsteps on the stairs, but it was too early for Mrs. Rivard to be here. That meant Jasper was home.

Tilly leapt out of bed, ignoring the hot throb in her wrist, ran out onto the landing, and caught him at the bottom of the stairs.

"What happened to your wrist?" he said, indicating the pillow slip.

"Where have you been?" she shrieked. Red fog had built up behind her eyeballs and her fury poured out of her. "What hour do you call this to come home?"

Jasper gaped at her, seemed about to answer, but she cut him off with her tirade.

"Who is she? Do you think me a fool? Do you think I will put up with *any* kind of foul treatment? When I think about the times I have pressed myself upon you for physical affection only to be rebuffed and judged—*judged*—by you! And all the time, you were—"

Both his hands went in the air. "Stop it!" he roared, and Tilly could have sworn the whole staircase, the whole house, shook from the force of his words. "Stop it, you foul creature. What on earth are you saying to me?"

"I saw you!" she cried, tears flowing. "I saw you with that other woman. She was wearing my coat, the one you said you needed to sell! I saw you down at the beach yesterday afternoon."

"Tilly, I am twenty minutes off the steamer from Dublin." And his face was a completely open book: he looked bewildered, offended. He looked innocent.

Tilly gulped back a sob. Her chest jumped with the effort of trying to get breath in her lungs. The anger was retreating along her veins now, leaving them cool and frightened. "What?" she said quietly.

"The steamer. I have been on it all night. I barely slept a wink and I had to walk miles to my own door and . . . what *is* this? What are you saying to me?"

"I saw you," she said. *Two hundred feet is a long way.* "At least . . . I thought I did."

He ran his eyes over her clothes. "And here you are, covered in mud and grass stains. Are these yesterday's clothes? Is this what I am to expect as a greeting from my wife, when I have been away so long, putting a roof over your head?" With one swift movement, Jasper reached for her, picked her up as easily as if she were a wooden doll, and put her over his shoulder.

"Put me down!" she shouted.

"You have clearly lost your mind," he said, as he carried her to her room. He dropped her on her bed, making her cry out in pain as her wrist bumped against the mattress.

He held up a cautionary finger. "Sleep. Think about what you have said to me."

He stalked out, slamming the door behind him. She gingerly picked up her wrist, retightened where the pillow slip bandage had become loosened. Then heard a strange noise in the corridor, a light thud at her door.

Tilly went to the door and tried to open it. She couldn't move the handle. But she knew there was no lock. Reality swam. Was she really losing her mind? How had he locked her in without a key?

She dropped to the floor, peered under the gap between door and carpet. She could see the legs of a chair. So he had barred her in. The door handle didn't move, just as last time. And he had done it swiftly and easily. As though he had done it before.

He had lied about locking her in the first time. He was a liar.

Or was this more of her temper getting the better of her? *Girls ought not rage and shout.*

Tilly returned to her bed, lay on her side, and gazed at the window with aching eyes. She tried to recall what she had seen yesterday in better detail, but already the figures were dissolving at the edges, turning to sand. A flash of golden hair, a man who touched the woman's waist with knowing tenderness. That was all she could be sure of. And had she really run after them down a rain-slick hill, over stones, and not expected to hurt herself? Tilly closed her eyes, desperate and desolate, realizing she no longer knew what was real and what was a product of her own troubled mind.

•

She woke a few hours later when the door opened gently. She turned, hoping to see Jasper, concerned and kind. The face she saw was concerned and kind, but it wasn't Jasper's.

"Mrs. Dellafore?" he said. "I am Dr. Hunt."

She sat up, nursing her sore wrist. He put his big leather bag down next to the bed.

"Sit on the edge of the bed for me."

"Who called you?" she asked, moving into place.

"Your husband, of course. He's worried about you."

"He is?"

Dr. Hunt didn't answer. Instead he gently unwrapped the pillow-slip bandage. Even though the swelling was a little better, Tilly was shocked to see her wrist was almost black with bruising.

"Can you still move it?" he said.

She nodded. "Please don't make me show you."

"I believe you." He smiled up at her through a thick gray mustache, and she was put in mind of Father Christmas.

"All your fingers work?"

"They do."

"Does it hurt if you hold it still? Or all the time?"

Tilly held her wrist very still. "No, it only hurts if I move it."

He reached out and gently bumped her forearm. "Did that make it hurt?"

"A little. Not much."

"I don't think it's broken or even fractured. I think you've sprained it badly. I'm going to bandage it up properly and I insist on complete rest for at least a week."

"So I can't use it at all?"

"It's your left wrist, so you can eat soup and bread. I hear Mrs. Rivard makes a capital *vichyssoise*." He opened his case wide and pulled out a silver hip flask, which he offered to her. "Brandy," he said. "For the pain."

Tilly took a swig. It burned the back of her throat and made her eyes water. She coughed.

"But I didn't mean to rest only your wrist," Dr. Hunt continued, pulling out a bandage roll and beginning to wrap her wrist very firmly. She winced. "I demand that you rest completely. In your bed. For at least one week. I will come and visit next week to see how you are. Your husband told me how you acquired this injury. I have seen it before. Women aren't prepared for the isolation here on the island, and you are recovering from the shock of your grandfather's death. Now, more brandy."

Tilly gingerly sipped it again. Dr. Hunt put a gentle finger under the flask and tipped it up so the fiery liquid filled her mouth. She swallowed, nearly choking. The heat spread down into her belly.

"Come on, and another."

She bravely swigged again. Her head began to swim.

He took it from her and screwed the lid back on. "You'll feel better soon," he said, placing the flask on the bedside table. "Have a belt of that every so often. That will keep you calm. I'll make sure Mr. Dellafore refills it for you."

Dr. Hunt moved to get up, but she caught his wrist with her good hand. "Please," she said. "Jasper locks me in. I can't bear it."

He frowned. Unhappy Father Christmas. "I'll talk to him."

"I'm afraid . . ." she said, her voice trailing off to a whisper.

"Of what?"

"He's not the man . . . I don't know if he's the man I thought he was."

"Nonsense," he said, buckling up his case. "You see, this is the reason you need to rest. In a week's time you'll feel better. Mark my words."

Then he was gone, leaving the door open behind him. She heard him creak down the stairs and went to the threshold to listen, very unsteady on her feet. He was right; all her pains dulled with the brandy.

"Complete rest for a week. Make sure her meals are brought to her. And for heaven's sake, man, don't lock the girl's door. She's anxious enough as it is."

"Of course," Jasper answered smoothly. "I'll take good care of her."

Then the door opened and closed, leaving her alone in the house with Jasper.

•

Days passed and fog moved in outside her window. Tilly lay in her bed and spent long hours of every day crying for the life she had left behind, for the loss of her grandfather, and for the nerve-loosening uncertainty of her new world. Jasper, still angry with her outburst, came to see her only once a day, to bring her evening brandy. He treated her the same, silent way the last time she had upset him. She grew used to the fiery liquid and it helped her to sleep every night; but she could not grow used to his stony refusal to speak or answer her questions. Tears and rages achieved nothing, except to give her a hot, flushed face and a sobbing heart.

Apart from Jasper, she only saw Mrs. Rivard when she brought her meals, also wordlessly. But the judgment was all over her face: she thought Tilly hysterical, a troublesome burden. Tilly was always glad to hear her leave at the end of the evening—with a cheerful good-bye that was always returned by Jasper. Every night, she and Jasper were alone in the dark house. She was confined to bed on Dr. Hunt's orders and Jasper saw no reason to call on her. It was as though the house was an island, and they plotted different courses around it, navigating around one another.

So it was a surprise one morning when Jasper burst into her room, without knocking, and stood there beside the door glowering at her. His knuckles were white around a letter.

His expression frightened the curiosity out of her. She opened her mouth to ask what was wrong, but he threw the letter on her bed. It had already been opened.

"You have received something in the post," he spat.

She was too baffled in that instant to ask precisely why he had opened her mail. The return address was her old address: it was from Godfrey. She unfolded it to read it. The paper whispered against itself. Meanwhile, Jasper had thrown open her wardrobe and was pulling out dresses and flinging them onto the end of the bed.

"What are you doing?" she asked, fearful and indignant all at once.

"Where is it?" he demanded.

Her pulse thudded guiltily in her throat. "Where is what?"

He began to scoop items off the top shelf of the cupboard. Boxes full of old cards and letters and even a few photographs she kept to remember Grandpa by. They spilled out of their boxes and onto the floor. Tilly scrambled out of bed and began to gather them up with her good hand, but now he was into her chest of drawers, pulling out stockings and corsets and brushes and hairpins.

"Stop it!" she cried.

"Read the letter," he returned, gruffly, continuing his ransacking of her things.

So she read the letter:

> *Cousin Matilda, do not think me a fool. Pamela and I spent*
> *many hours in the old man's house, cataloguing everything*
> *within. The number of items missing astonishes me. Did*
> *you really think I would not notice?*

And here, he listed all of the items Grandpa had put in the trunk, the ones that she and Jasper had already sold. She felt no guilt: they were gifts, when they were still Grandpa's to give freely and she would write and tell him that. But then why was Jasper still jumbling through her things? She returned to the letter.

> *There is also the matter of two hundred and thirty-three*
> *pounds in banknotes, which Pamela saw in a cigar box*
> *on the old man's mantelpiece last time we were there. You*
> *can imagine how she felt when she saw you had stolen*
> *this too.*

Tilly's mind reeled. Pamela knew how much money was in the box; Tilly had never even bothered to count it. What kind of people were they, to comb through an old man's belongings in the weeks before he died?

Now, at least, she understood why Jasper was pillaging her room.

"Jasper, stop," she said, in a quiet but firm voice. "I presume you are searching for the money?"

"Of course I'm searching for the money. We are a partnership. I have debts, you have money. You cannot keep it from me."

"It isn't here," she said. Then more forcefully, "He gave me no money. Everything he gave me we have already received and sold."

Jasper stopped, turned to her with a shoe in one hand. "Then why does Godfrey think you have it?"

"Because that is the kind of man he is. And he is married to that awful woman . . ." Tilly could have choked on her anger, that they were living in Grandpa's old house, making paths over her old familiar ones, along the corridors, through the rooms. "If Grandpa had banknotes, perhaps he intended to spend them. Or give them to somebody else like poor Granger, who Godfrey no doubt has turned out on her ear already."

Jasper dropped the shoe and, without a word of apology, turned to leave.

"Jasper," she said, climbing out of bed. "I can't pick all this up. I'm supposed to rest my wrist. You must help me."

But the silence had returned. He left her, closing the door behind him.

Tilly surveyed the mess, then decided to return to bed as the doctor had said. She took a swig of brandy. She was growing used to it now. Godfrey's letter lay on the bed and she picked it up to read the rest of it.

In short, we both feel your dishonesty a terrible betrayal of
us, and a terrible ingratitude shown to our grandfather,
who had already paid twelve hundred pounds to Dellafore
as a wedding gift. Pamela has been urging me to call the
constabulary, but the solicitor has advised against it. So I
suppose you may feel proud of yourself that you got away
with it; but know this: you are never welcome back in this
house ever again.

Tilly folded the letter. She hadn't known Grandpa had paid
Jasper such a large sum, though she knew, of course, he had
given her new husband something. What had happened to the
twelve hundred pounds? She got out of bed, intending to go
to Jasper and ask him, then changed her mind. He wouldn't
answer. She would have to wait until he was speaking with her
again.

As she surveyed her belongings, all over the room, she entertained the idea of simply packing them all back in her trunk and
leaving. Walking away from this mess. But no, she had made marriage vows in the eyes of God, and she took them seriously.

Tilly lay on her back. She was heartily sick of the view of the
inside of her bed canopy, and yet this was where she fixed her eyes
as she thought it all through. Grandpa had confessed he had found
Jasper for her, but made it appear as though they had met by chance.
What negotiations had taken place? Had Grandpa offered Jasper
money to marry her? Surely not; surely Grandpa would know that
was a recipe for misery. Or had Jasper charmed Grandpa with his
smooth ways, his well-turned outfits, and made himself appear a
much more suitable husband than he actually was?

She sighed. None of this was material at the moment. She simply needed to get her husband to speak to her again, to be kind

and warm enough towards her that she could talk to him about her doubts. And at the moment, kindness and warmth from him did not seem remotely possible.

•

It took Jasper six days to start talking to her again. Out of nowhere, as far as she could see. He brought her an evening brandy and said, "Dr. Hunt's very pleased with how your injury is mending."

Tilly tried not to express astonishment. Instead, she rotated her wrist. "So am I."

"We've been asked to the Morningtons' for dinner this evening, but I have already made apologies for you. Until you are well again, you should stay precisely where you are. I shall go, though."

"I'm well enough to go," she said. "Please let me go. I'm so tired of being here in my room."

"I note that since you've been in your room, you've had no more hysterical fits and imagined no more nonsense," he said archly, the corners of his mouth turning down beneath his mustache. "This suggests to me that it would be better that you stay here."

Tilly sipped her brandy. The liquid over her tongue burned away the angry retort that was always waiting there.

"Now your wrist is getting better, I'm going to have to let Mrs. Rivard go. We've run out of money to pay her," he said. "You'll have to take over the household chores and meals for a while."

"Run out of . . . but your trip to Ireland?"

"I'm still waiting on that payment. It won't be long."

She studied his face, wished she could tell if he were lying or not.

"Why do you look at me so?" he said.

She forced a smile. "Cannot a wife look upon the beloved face of her husband?"

His mouth actually twitched as though he might smile in return. For a few hopeful moments, her heart lifted. She remembered their courtship, his kindness, his loving face. Was that man still there, inside her increasingly angry and desperate husband? Or had he always been angry and desperate, but knew how to smooth over those feelings to trick an old man into paying for his granddaughter to be married off?

Surely there wasn't a man alive capable of such an ambitious deception.

"Jasper," she said, "tell me truly. The day you and I met: was it really by chance? I often suspected Grandpa had arranged it somehow. He knew how resistant I was to the potential husbands he touted."

"Of course it was by chance," he said, face all open and honest and sincere.

My, what a good liar.

"And we fell in love and married quickly. Too quickly. Like a couple of fools." His eyes darted away. "If you want to know why my affection is dimmed, you need only look to your behavior of the last few weeks."

Tilly bit her tongue.

"But we must make the best of it," he continued, "and that means getting by without servants for a little while."

Tilly thought about the money in the garden shed. If she gave it to him, how long would it last?

"But for now, rest." He indicated the glass of brandy he'd brought. "And don't forget your medicine. I'll give Mrs. Rivard notice."

Tilly gulped the brandy as he left, then went to sit at the

window and watch the myrtle trees along the side fence sway in the wind. Dr. Hunt had been quite clear with her on all his visits: she was given to hysterics and she needed to stop imagining terrible things or her health would continue to suffer. To believe her husband had married her for money while all the time carrying on an affair was the kind of hysterical imagining he would discourage in her.

And yet, Tilly suspected strongly that it was true.

•

Late in the night, Tilly woke. Her head thudded. Too much brandy. She no longer needed it for the pain in her wrist, but had found it a good medicine for the pain in her heart and Jasper was happy to supply her with a little every night. He never drank it. He was completely sober. Perhaps if he was a rough drunk she might find it easier to believe him a liar and a womanizer. But Jasper was nothing if not clinically, almost cruelly, rational.

She heard a light thump outside her door, as though somebody were trying to walk very quietly past. It was probably Jasper, tiptoeing by and hoping she didn't wake and start shrieking at him like a harpy again. But the thump was followed by the sound of something being softly dragged across the carpet runner. She sat up and listened. Her doorhandle rattled, there was a scrape and a thud, and then the footsteps retreated.

Her heart fell. She went to the door. The handle wouldn't budge. He had barred her in again.

But why?

She crouched down, hands flat on the ground, and looked under the door. All was in darkness. She stayed there a little while, straining her ears. Heard Jasper's voice, muffled by the wooden walls. So he had company. Now all her senses and skin were alert.

She waited.

Then the confirmation. The light, high laugh of a woman.

Jasper's lover, in the house with him. While his wife was barred in her room.

The rage that began to seethe and simmer in her stomach terrified her. Before, she had been able to doubt herself, she could argue away her worst fears, believe Jasper's lies. But this . . . this was confirmation.

Every nerve and sinew in her body struggled to hold in the rage that threatened to split her apart. She wanted to punch holes in walls, tear up her bedding, pull the door off its hinges, scream at him in one long, hot, deafening shriek until he fell down dead. Instead, she lowered herself completely to the floor, facedown, and clenched her teeth so they wouldn't hear her sob.

NINE

The Sable-trimmed Coat

Tilly had spent too much time inside. She had rested enough. She had drunk enough brandy. She had lived enough in the confines of her head. After a fitful night's sleep, she found the door to her bedroom unbarred and wondered when he had come to move the chair. When had the woman gone home?

She washed her hands and face, dressed, and went downstairs. Jasper was nowhere in sight. Mrs. Rivard had put out her breakfast, but she ignored it, going for the front door instead.

"Where are you going?" Mrs. Rivard asked.

"I don't know," Tilly said.

"Mr. Dellafore was clear that you were to stay in your room."

Tilly ignored her, slamming the door shut behind her.

She walked. Down the front path, through the gate, down the little gravelly slope, and into the wood. She walked and felt her body move, her blood pumping, and it eased her troubled mind a little. One foot, the other foot, moving through the world, down to the granite cliffs of St. Peter Port where there were other human beings and noise and activity in the gully-like winding streets. She found herself on Le Paradis, the corner block where the Morningtons' house stood, and she stopped for a moment and thought.

Ralph and Laura had been so kind and welcoming of her. Laura had said Tilly could always call on her. And at this moment, she needed very badly to speak to somebody about what to do.

She hesitated. If word got back to Jasper . . .

She didn't care. She couldn't care. Jasper had let her down so very badly. The love inside her had curdled, turned into sour resentment. She no longer knew what the future held, she no longer knew what Jasper wanted from her or expected of their life together. Except that she should take over the unending list of household chores and be barred in her room when she was inconvenient. That wasn't a marriage: it was a terrible fairy story. All that was missing was a locked room full of dead wives.

Tilly headed towards the Morningtons' house, climbed the shallow stone steps, then knocked hard.

A maid answered. They had staff. Tilly remembered having staff. "Yes, madame?" the woman said.

"I'm here to call upon Mrs. Mornington. Is she available? It's Matilda Dellafore."

The maid nodded, recognized the name. "One moment, madame."

Tilly waited, straightening the cuffs of her gloves and glancing around her. The Morningtons' house was in good repair. This was supposed to be how her life looked. This was what she had always known, what she had been bred for. Not the grim existence she had been plunged into.

Laura Mornington emerged a few moments later, sliding her

hand under Tilly's elbow. "Tilly! I'm so pleased to see you, but so surprised. Jasper said you were still very ill."

"I am not ill. I was not ill. I had a sprained wrist. I am tired of being inside." Tilly realized the words were spilling out without her consent. "I am desperate. I . . ." Her breath hitched.

Laura's face crumpled. She pulled Tilly close, and called out over her shoulder, "Myra, lemonade in the garden. As quickly as you can, please." She leaned back, looked in Tilly's eyes. "We will sit in the sunshine, and we will have some fresh air, and I will listen to your heart."

Tilly was so grateful that her knees became weak. "Thank you," she whispered. "Thank you."

Laura led her around through the house and outside onto a broad stretch of grass, bordered by hedges and a high fence. A tall iron gate stood in the corner of the fence, between veronica and lavender bushes. Through its bars, Tilly could see another narrow street with high granite walls overgrown with vines. It was barely wide enough for more than one person to walk at a time. Laura sat Tilly down at a wrought iron table-and-chair set, then sat opposite. The sun was white and bright on Laura's face and hair, picking up snowy highlights. "You must tell me all, my dear," she said.

Tilly drew a deep breath. "Jasper . . . is . . ." She didn't know the words to use to talk about something so private. "Jasper has a lover."

Laura showed no sign of shock. "I know," she said.

And it was a relief, such a relief, to have somebody believe her, and not deny it, and not offer her brandy and tell her she was hysterical.

"Many wives find themselves in your situation," Laura said. "Many choose to ignore it."

"I thought he loved me."

"Perhaps he loves you both."

Tilly's heart shrank at the idea. "He bars me in my room. He never speaks kindly to me. I fear he married me for the money my grandpa promised him."

Laura nodded, her kind eyes fixed on Tilly's. "We have known Jasper a long time. He is a charming and clever man, and I have always found him to be well mannered and entertaining. When he told us he had married you, we were delighted for him. As long as I've known him—and it has been several years—his money ebbs and flows unexpectedly. I doubt that he married you for money. He has never been so desperate that he would use somebody so cruelly." Laura leaned across and patted Tilly on the knee. "I have faith that his finances will come good again. They always do."

Laura's kindness prompted tears. "But how can I bear it, knowing he is loving somebody else? Who is she? Why her?"

Laura turned her head and looked behind her, and gestured at one of the windows on the lower floor of the house. Then she turned back and dropped her voice. "For two years Jasper has paid us a small amount of rent money to ensure one of our staff has her own private room."

"What? He hasn't any money, though."

"He is many months in arrears."

"Who is she?" Tilly said, thinking of the maid who answered the door. But then it became blindingly clear. The long red-gold hair. "Chantelle?"

"Ah, here's our lemonade."

While the maid laid out the jug of lemonade, Tilly studied the window Laura had indicated. The second last one from the end, with an empty windowbox. Perhaps no flowers could grow in the windowbox because Jasper had been climbing in and out over them. Her stomach heaved. She felt she might be sick. She shot out of her chair, but Laura caught her, brought her back to the table. The maid considered her, puzzled.

"Thank you, Myra, that will be all," Laura said smoothly.

Laura returned Tilly to her seat and poured her a glass of lemonade. "Here," she said, "a drink will make you feel better."

A cold, sea-borne wind sussurated along the tops of the hedges. Tilly gulped the drink. Sour and sweet all at once. It made her feel no better.

Laura sipped hers politely, then put it aside and took Tilly's hand. "Tilly, a life without a husband is no life. The shame of leaving a marriage . . . what would you do? You have no relatives to return to, Jasper told me that. Perhaps you can learn to turn a blind eye? I know that in this moment you feel awful, but perhaps you can get used to it. When Jasper has some money again and Lumière sur la Mer is more like a home to you, you may feel more comfortable."

"Is life not meant to be happier than that? I could have married one of the elderly donkeys my grandfather introduced me to and felt 'comfortable.' I expected to feel happy."

"Expectations are the enemy of happiness," Laura said, her cool fingers leaving Tilly's hand. The magnolia trees moving in the wind made the sun flicker. "If you need me, I am here. You may always call, even if it is just to cry. I will listen." Laura's voice dropped to a whisper. "I know some of your pain."

Tilly's eyebrows shot up. "Ralph?"

Laura pressed her lips together, but smiled. Tilly noticed a deepening in the lines around her eyes and mouth. "Well," she said. "It was a long time ago."

"Go on. Please." Tilly was desperate to hear that she wasn't the only person who had suffered this way.

"Our children were small. I never said anything. To do so would have invited an argument, perhaps even seen me thrown out of my home. If I was to leave him, I wanted to control how and when." She shrugged. "Twelve years have passed and I find that I am not angry anymore. Ralph and I are very happy. Their mistresses can never keep them. Their wives always can."

But all Tilly's body and blood resisted it, wanted to cling to the ideal that she had believed in all these months: that Jasper loved her and she loved him and their life in the beautiful house would unfold lovingly. The pain was horrifying, worse than anything she had felt in her injured wrist.

"Don't be angry. The anger simply makes it worse. Chantelle knows no better and I worry for her when the affair is ended. I know you would not relish hearing that, but she has far less power than you in the world. Jasper is your husband. As long as he is discreet, you should aim to be comfortable in the knowledge that she has no real claim on him."

Sympathy for Jasper's mistress? Tilly carefully hid how infuriating she found Laura's words.

"So, do you think you can be comfortable, Tilly?" Laura asked.

Tilly forced a smile. She said yes, but she didn't mean it.

Because it wasn't fair and, more than anything, Tilly wanted to stand before her husband and tell him, in a fiery rage, that it wasn't fair. But she feared him too much to do so. And with so much anger in her belly, she could never be comfortable again.

•

That night, a storm blew in. Tilly was reading in the library, by the dim light of a candle, when she heard the first rumble of thunder in the distance. She went to the window and lifted the sash to look out. The stars were being obliterated as thick clouds rolled in, lightning flashing between them. The first gust of stormy wind jumped down her throat, and she slid the window shut and watched the treetops torn this way and that through the glass.

The storm was so loud, she didn't hear Jasper's footsteps at the door.

"Tilly?" he said, making her jump.

She turned. He stood in the threshold with a candlestick, which threw cruel shadows on his face. Tilly realized her heart had sped a little.

"Shouldn't you be resting?" he said.

"I feel quite well."

"I think you should be in your bedroom. Rivard will bring you some food before she goes for the evening."

"I could eat downstairs with you."

"Dr. Hunt has been very clear that you—"

"You certainly believe me well enough to take over keeping this enormous house clean soon." She gestured around.

"I do not like your hot tone."

Tilly said nothing.

"You were so sweet-lipped when I met you."

"I think it fair to say that we were both quite different when we met," she said boldly.

"To bed," he said. "Your sharp tongue doesn't change anything. I am your husband and I demand you return to your room."

Tilly collected an armful of books and went ahead of him. She was not surprised, after the door was closed, to hear the chair being moved into place. By her bedside table was a glass of brandy. She gulped it, hoping it might put out the fire inside her. Then laughed at herself: throwing brandy on a fire only made it worse.

Her candle sputtered and burned out, and she sat on her bed in the dark, listening to the storm rattle overhead and move on. Nobody brought her any food and she supposed Jasper was punishing her. She wondered if Chantelle had arrived in the rain, whether her clothes hung drying in the kitchen while she lay naked in Jasper's arms. She wondered if the sable-trimmed coat was among those clothes, the one that she had chosen while out shopping with Grandpa one cool autumn morning. From the moment she slid it on, she had known she wanted it. Not heavy enough for the snow-silent winter, but lovely for a windy October afternoon, with deep pockets to hide her hands in if they grew cold. How she had loved that coat.

How she had loved that life.

The misery fed her anger. How dare he? She wanted her coat back. She would get her coat back.

She went first to the door, jiggled the handle roughly. It would not turn. She kicked the door, but succeeded only in hurting her toe. So she went to the window and pulled up the sash.

The rain had eased to a soft drizzle. The clouds had shredded apart to reveal a few lonely stars. Tilly looked down. She remembered planning this route. Over the windowsill, the ledge, tree branch, ledge, conservatory roof, and ground. Her fear was no match for her anger. One leg out the window, then the other, and onto the narrow ledge. She kept her fingers on the windowsill. Vertigo rolled up through her and a hot flash of fear crossed her heart. But then it passed and she edged along the ledge and put one hand down, then the other, on the sturdy branch between her window and the next. Pulled her knees behind her, then her feet. Waited, dreading the branch creaking or breaking.

Then slowly inched along it and down. Arms around the branch, rough bark getting caught on her sleeves and stripping her hands of skin. She swung her legs down, reaching out with the tips of her toes. Then half stepped, half jumped, steadying herself on the windowsill.

Tilly took a moment to breathe. The roof of the conservatory was made of glass so she had to be careful to let herself down onto one of the thick parallel roof beams that joined it to the house. She almost lost her nerve. If she landed too hard in the wrong place, she would go through the glass and be cut to ribbons. The rainy cold had cooled her temper, too. This seemed a bad idea. It was all very well to plan an escape route for fire or other emergency, but to use it simply to reclaim a coat? It was madness.

Well, her husband and physician already thought her mad. Conveniently so.

Tilly pressed her back against the stone wall and slid down so she was sitting on the ledge. Her feet were still several inches from the roof beam. She reached out, slid forward.

And landed. She wasn't prepared for the roof of the conservatory to be so slippery, so she got down on all fours and crawled along the beam. It sloped downwards then left a space of about eight feet to jump. It was too far. She nearly sobbed, to have come all this way and not realize she couldn't get down from the roof of the conservatory . . .

The problem was, she didn't dare step off this roof beam to find a better place to land. But she knew there was a hawthorn hedge growing beside the conservatory near the front of the house; it would be enough to break up the jump.

Tilly crouched on the roof beam, and reached her hands out gingerly for the glass. It was wet and slippery. She tested her weight, slid off the beam and onto her stomach. Before she was only damp, but now she was wet and cold through the front of her blouse and skirt. She slithered, snake-like, over the glass conservatory roof. At each roof beam she had to get on all fours to climb over it, wincing as one knee, then the next, connected with the glass; always expecting the glass to crack. It didn't.

And finally she was on the last roof beam, looking down at the hawthorn hedge in the dark. It had once been carefully kept, so had thick, stiff branches that would support her weight. But it was also overgrown, with long, wild, scratching stems reaching out of it. She braced herself, pressed her injured wrist hard against her body, and jumped.

Only it wasn't so much a jump as a controlled fall. The hawthorn caught her weight a little and then collapsed. Thorns tore at her clothes and skin.

But then she was down, on the grass. She panted. The rain intensified. Tilly ran around to the kitchen entrance and pushed the door open.

It was as she thought. A woman's wet clothes hung in front of the fireplace. But there was no sable-trimmed coat. And they were not upstairs in Jasper's room. Almost immediately, she realized their voices were coming from the parlor.

Tilly looked down at herself by firelight. Torn wet clothes, blood seeping from thorn scratches on her arm and thigh. Her hair, too, was loose and errant around her shoulders. She did not want to confront Jasper's lover like this.

But her curiosity was aroused. On the tips of her toes, she crossed the kitchen and into the corridor, slipped into the dining room and listened against the wall. Nothing. Somebody had once told her if she held a glass against the wall she could hear conversations in the next room. She took a glass down from the sideboard, but still could hear nothing.

So instead, she went back to the corridor and sat on the floor beside the closed sitting room door. Soft candlelight glowed underneath it. Chantelle's soft voice. Jasper's hard breathing. They were saying no sentences. They simply moaned words such as, "yes" and "please"; and fragments such as, "just there" and "oh, my love."

She wondered if Laura Mornington had ever had to listen to her husband betray her. She put her head on her knees and listened until the end. All of those things she had imagined learning with Jasper. Now the closest she would ever get was to hear him doing them with somebody else.

They turned to conversation. They laughed softly, made reference to things she didn't understand: no doubt little pieces of intimate shared knowledge. Tilly thought about leaving. Her dress was wet and she was cold, but then Chantelle asked him, "How long now?"

Tilly wanted to know what the question meant, so she leaned a little closer to the door and listened sharply.

"The money will be in my hands at the end of the month. All my debtors have agreed to wait. The worst of this awful mess is over."

Tilly was at once relieved to hear this news, and sad that he hadn't chosen to tell her, his wife, the truth.

"You know I didn't mean the money. How long?"

A silence. Tilly wished she understood them.

"You know how long. Two years. But if I can just crack her so she leaves me be . . ."

A hot chill over her skin. Were they talking about her?

"You don't need to crack her. Just rid yourself of her somehow. She's of no more use to you, you've said that yourself."

"I didn't realize her grandfather had told the wretched cousin about our agreement."

Tilly's skin prickled. Were they talking about Godfrey?

"You promised you would be with me. I don't want to be your

lover forever. I want to be your wife." Chantelle's tone was petulant; Jasper's much more measured.

"And I want to be your husband. But we must take things slowly."

Tilly remembered what Laura had said, that their mistresses can never keep them but their wives always can. She believed it. Jasper would no more leave Tilly and marry a cook than he would give up this house and live in a mud hut. He had a place in society and he cared what people thought of him. But there was something about her questions that unsettled Tilly.

Yes, it was the word choice. *Rid yourself of her somehow.*

Was she in danger? What did he mean by "cracking" her? Making things so awful that she left of her own accord? Or . . . something worse?

"It's too slow for my liking," Chantelle said, but then she was quiet and Tilly realized Jasper had silenced her with kisses. The kisses Tilly had always longed for herself.

She was growing too cold, too sad. She climbed silently to her feet and crept up the stairs to her landing. Here was the chair, balanced on its back two legs against the door. She could see now why her door handle had appeared to be locked: it was one of their dining room chairs, which were carved with a deep U-shape on the back beam. He had positioned it so that the U-shape was jammed into place around the handle: it was almost a perfect fit. She moved the chair, turned it gently on its side so it would look as though it had fallen, and went inside to change into a warm nightgown.

Tomorrow she would leave him. That was the only solution.

•

In her bed, lying on her side, she watched the stars appear behind the clouds and cried all the tears she had to cry. For the loss of her grandfather, for the loss of her love, for the loss of her dreams. But the tears were hot, angry tears. It wasn't fair; she had done nothing to invite this. She had simply been a woman. One who wasn't bred to earn money or look after herself. One who had had to presume upon the generosity of a series of men—her grandfather, Godfrey, Jasper—who had each treated her unevenly. Yes, even Grandpa, who had lied about Jasper and left her exposed. She thought, not for the first time in her life, that if she only had control of her own fate, she would be so much better off. Now she was married, she was inextricably tied to lifelong problems. Divorces were expensive, impossible. She would have to prove Jasper's adultery, spend money she didn't have, endure the stigma. The path she had chosen, to run and pretend she had never married, was easier, but meant she could never fall in love and marry again. Her future was blighted.

So the angry tears poured out of her and eventually she slept, dreaming of stormy seas.

•

Tilly knew that she had to plan it carefully. The steamer to St. Malo in the north of France left early in the morning, before sunrise, but she may very well be barred in her room at that time. But if she left in the afternoon, Jasper may grow suspicious and come looking for her. So she decided she would leave directly after supper: make it look as though she was going up to her bedroom and instead head out the front door while Jasper was lighting the fire in the parlor.

This meant she needed to pack her trunk and stash it outside the house during the day. The garden shed was the obvious place to hide it, with the cigar box full of money that would get her from St. Malo to wherever she went next. She still had the only key to the shed. Her stomach felt hollow at the thought. She had no idea where she would go next, but it had to be far, far away. India. Africa. The other side of the world.

I am not afraid, I am not afraid.

She had breakfast with her husband. He didn't speak to her. She told him she might spend some time in the garden today. He shrugged, and said nothing about the clouds and the weak sunlight and the cold wind.

He went upstairs, as he always did after breakfast, with the post. She went to her own bedroom. There was no way she could pack a trunk and take it fully laden downstairs. He might emerge at any moment and see her. She opened her wardrobe and chose the small, leather trunk she had brought with her. The large one would have to stay here. She pulled the sheets from her bed and wrapped them around the trunk. Her heart was beating so fast it made her feel mildly nauseated. She swallowed hard and went to the door. Crept along the corridor. If he caught her, she would simply say she was taking sheets to Mrs. Rivard to wash. But he didn't emerge. She sneaked through the kitchen door and out into the garden, made it to the garden shed, left the trunk there, then returned to the house.

Mrs. Rivard caught her at the kitchen door with the ball of sheets in her arms.

She tried not to show she was startled. "Oh, there you are, Mrs. Rivard," Tilly said. "I've been looking for you to give you these." She dumped the sheets at the servant's feet. "May I have fresh sheets, please?"

Mrs. Rivard narrowed her eyes, looked at the ball of sheets at her feet. "Mr. Dellafore doesn't pay me enough to wash sheets."

"Then I'll do it. And in the meantime, I'll get my own fresh ones from the linen cupboard." Tilly turned on her heel, pulse thudding. Mrs. Rivard said nothing.

The next things to smuggle out were her clothes. This she achieved by undressing, putting on all her chemises at once, then a housedress over the top. In the garden shed, she peeled it all off, folding and packing the underwear by the dim light through the grimy window and cracks in the wood. Her body remained on high alert; she jumped at the slightest sound. Her dresses next. Back and forth between bedroom and garden, wearing a different dress under her housedress each time. She tried to walk confidently, not to tiptoe and draw attention to the fact she was doing something surreptitious.

Jasper emerged on one of her trips, frowning at her disapprovingly. This time, she was wearing two corsets under her clothes, both loosely fastened. She crossed her arms over her ribs so he wouldn't see her odd shape. "You are moving around a lot today. I thought you were going to the garden."

"It's quite cold out there," she said. "I've been up and back to get my scarf and gloves."

"I'm trying to concentrate. Can you perhaps not do it with the feet of an elephant?"

"I apologize."

His door slammed behind him. She breathed again.

Next, the few other possessions she had left. Hairbrush and hand mirror, her writing box. In small light loads she smuggled them out to the garden shed, hidden in clothes or in a folded coat. Now her trunk was full to overflowing. It only remained to slide the cigar box out of its hiding place and push it down on top of the clothes, close and lock the trunk. She hid it under a low shelf, then placed empty pots all around it so it couldn't be seen.

Tilly went out to the garden and took one last walk around it. She would never see these roses bloom, she would never live in that fantasy of love and children she had imagined.

I am not afraid. She found that being angry made her less afraid, so she cultivated it. How dare Jasper treat her so cruelly? How dare Godfrey make it clear she wasn't welcome? How dare Grandpa arrange such an idiotic marriage for her? There, that was better. The hollow fright turned to hard determination.

Perhaps her temper could be an asset after all.

•

Tilly descended the stairs for dinner, knowing she was leaving the bedroom behind her for the last time. Good. It had become like a prison. Every step she took, every movement she made, was laden with solemn purpose. Her shoulders felt heavy. She could hear her own blood and breath in her skull.

"Good evening, Jasper," she said to him.

To her astonishment, he smiled. "Good evening, Tilly."

Mrs. Rivard moved about, laying their food in front of them. Tilly had no appetite for the muddy-looking fish on her plate. She poked it with her fork, every ounce of her energy bent on seeming as normal as possible. Just because he was being nice to her didn't mean she should forgive him.

"That is all, Mrs. Rivard," he said.

This was new. Tilly's heart hammered. Things weren't meant to be different tonight. They were meant to be the same as always.

Hold your nerve, hold your nerve.

"How did you enjoy your gardening today?" he asked as he buttered his bread.

"I . . . ah." She cleared her throat, reached for water. Admonished herself for appearing anything but natural and smoothly spoken. "I very much enjoy time in the outdoors."

"You'd best be careful with your complexion," he said, and it was kind concern. It wasn't a cruel poke.

Deep down, something stirred. She wanted very much for this to be a new Jasper; or a renewed Jasper. He was speaking to her as he had spoken to her at the start. She tried to recollect the last few weeks of poor treatment to stop that stirring. But had she overreacted? She had always been too quick to anger. She was so busy adding up his sins in her head that she missed his next question.

"I'm sorry?" she said, then forced a smile. "I was away with the fairies."

"I said that all the rest has clearly done you a world of good."

And she reminded herself: at the start, he had treated her kindly because he wanted something from her. If he was being kind to her now, he wanted something. There could be no more self-doubt. The man sitting across from her was a charmer, a liar, an adulterer. Tilly Kirkland would not be taken in by him. She made her guts steely, but her voice smooth.

"I believe you are right. I feel quite differently now about many things. I am sorry if I troubled you."

It was his turn now to look nervous. How had she not noticed his darting eyes when she sat down? Perhaps because she had been too busy protecting her own anxiety. She wondered what it was he was going to ask her to do. If he asked for dresses to sell, she would be exposed. There were only a few drab ones left in the back of her wardrobe.

But he asked for nothing. He continued to make small talk as if the last days of stony silence had never happened. They would visit the Morningtons soon, he said. Money was coming in the next few weeks and she could help him choose new furniture for some of the empty rooms. She nodded and smiled and laughed where she should, aware that they were both playing a game. Only she hoped he didn't know that she was playing too.

Dinner finished, he pushed back his chair. "Well," he said. "Good night." And he came around the corner of the table and he kissed her, full on the lips. She remembered the first time he had kissed her: how her body had responded with warm spreading sensations and giddy delight. But now, she no more wanted to be kissed by him than kissed by the undercooked fish on her plate. It was all she could do not to shudder. Instead, she infused her lips with warmth and, when he stood back, gave him her brightest smile.

"Good night, Jasper," she said and left the room.

Behind her, she heard him go into the parlor and shut the door. This was it, one foot in front of the other, straight down the corridor and to the front door. She had the handle in her hand. She had the door open.

"Tilly? What are you doing?" His voice was sharp.

She turned. He was advancing slowly down the hall, his face a mask of suspicion and disdain. He had a glass of brandy in his hand. Heat spread through her chest. "I . . . I'm . . ."

But he was shaking his head. "Oh, no. No, no, no. You are not leaving. You cannot leave me."

"I am going for a little walk."

"No, you are going upstairs to bed and I am going to bring you an evening brandy and you are going to sleep."

Her skin crawled. Why was he bringing her brandy? It had been over a week since he had done that. She remembered their conversation about ridding themselves of her. "I am not tired. There will be few evenings left in the year that are—"

"Do you think me a fool?" he roared. He was nearly on top of her, reaching across her to bar her way. "You cannot simply leave your husband. We are married. You are mine."

"No, sir. I am my own." She inched away from him, back into the house. Her eye caught on a coat hung along the wall. Her coat. Her sable-trimmed coat. She snatched it down, held it in front of her. "You see? The coat. You lied. You said I had imagined seeing it, yet here it is. Not sold. Your lover left it here last night, didn't she? Did you think the storm outside drowned out the sounds of your adultery? It did not. I heard it all. And I will not stay where I am treated so monstrously."

"Come with me," he said, grabbing her arm with his free hand.

She twisted away from him, shaking him off roughly. The brandy spilled all over the coat. Jasper lunged and picked her up wriggling and shouting, and bodily carried her to the parlor. He threw her down on the sofa. She hit her head on the hard endboard and cried out.

"Weakling," he laughed.

"You cannot treat me this way."

"You will do as you're told," he said, looming over her. "Your grandfather made me certain promises . . ."

"My grandfather had no idea what kind of marriage he had made for me. I assure you if he were alive, he would break every promise he made." She balled the coat in front of her defensively. "You care nothing for me, so let me go."

"No. If I let you go I have to pay Godfrey back the money. I have enough debts."

His confirmation of her true worth to him, his lack of love now or in the past only made her more determined. "Is that so? Then perhaps you had best stop spending money on your lover. How long would I have to stay? I will not stay a day." She stood, he pushed her down, pinned her down. She struggled against him, brought up her foot and kicked him as hard as she could between his legs.

He went over, pulling the brandy-soaked coat with him, knocking over the lantern.

At once the coat was ablaze. Jasper screamed and threw it away from him. It landed on one of the piles of old documents he had stacked on the floor. Tilly was closest to the door and she ran. The flames had already caught on the rug where the lamp oil had spilled. She pulled the door closed behind her, saw a dining room chair, and seized it to bar the door, the way he had barred her door so often.

Then Tilly ran. Ran for her life. She took her flight down the west side of the house, knowing he would climb out the parlor window on the east. Into the garden shed, slamming the door, locking it, and clutching the key in a sweating palm.

Then hunching down in the dark, heart thundering. She crawled across the dirt floor to a crack in the wood and peered through, too fearful to put her face at the window, watching for Jasper. He would go after her in the woods, she knew. Any second she would see his dark figure running down the front path.

But that was not what she saw. Instead she saw orange-bright flame against the dark night sky. Thick smoke. The house was going up. Fire surged out of the windows on the lower floor. Oh, God, she had burned their house down. Whooshing, thundering fire. Now smoke was pouring out of the second-floor windows. She watched in horror, thinking of all the books in the library. Chaucer and Shakespeare and Milton and Wordsworth. All burning to ashes in their tidy rows. The smoke stung her eyes. The house was two hundred feet away, but the blustering wind blew the smoke and embers away from her. Tilly was frozen in that position; her stinging eye against the crack between the boards. Watching for Jasper, not seeing him. The sound of vast flames echoed in her ears, crunching boards and beams collapsing. Where was Jasper? Why hadn't he run?

And then the light of realization flickered to life. The coat. It hadn't been left there the night before. Chantelle had worn it to their home tonight. When Jasper was charming Tilly in the living room, his eyes shifting nervously, it wasn't so that she would drink a poisoned brandy. It was so she wouldn't realize Chantelle was already in the house. So Jasper hadn't gone into the woods to find Tilly because he had gone upstairs to rescue Chantelle.

And neither of them had come out.

TEN

A New Woman

Tilly did not sleep in the musty garden shed. She watched until the fire burned itself out. Nobody came. They were far enough from town that nobody would have seen the flames. Tilly hadn't run down to report it because what was she to say? That she had barred her husband inside with a fire and left him to burn to death? That she had unwittingly caused the deaths of two people? By the time help came, it would be too late: it had already been too late by the time she realized Chantelle was in there with him.

Why had she locked him in? Why? If only . . .

Instead, she had curled herself into a ball on the dirt floor and rocked herself slowly from side to side. The guilt that flooded her stomach was immense: an ocean. She feared that it would inhabit her for the rest of her days. Here was proof of what Grandpa had always said to her, that her temper was a thing to be controlled and regretted. Look what her anger had done. It had burned them to death. Her imagination conjured the morbid details of flames and fear and shrieks. No matter how much she had come to despise Jasper, how much rage she had for Chantelle, she would not wish such a death upon them. Upon anybody. The punishment was immeasurably out of equivalence with the crime. Certainly they had sought to trick her, to make her docile enough to put up with their adultery while they waited out the period set down by Grandpa for the money to be repaid. No doubt, Grandpa had thought there would be a child in the first year, cementing Jasper's obligations to her. And no doubt, that was one of the reasons Jasper wouldn't have her in his bed.

Jasper was dead now, his bed burned to cold embers.

As dawn's first light glimmered thin on the horizon, she got up. She changed into clean clothes and proper shoes, pinned her hair with practiced fingers. Focused on little details—buttoning gloves, pinning on her hat—so she wouldn't think about the big bad thing that had happened.

The big bad thing she had caused.

No, she couldn't think that way. It would undo her and she would be a screaming heap on the floor. She had to move now, she had to walk down to St. Peter Port and take the early service across to St. Malo.

But what if they aren't dead? The thought came to her sudden and unbidden, and already she could feel knots untying all down her spine. Jasper paid for Chantelle to have her own room at the Morningtons' house. Perhaps he had gone out the east window and bolted behind cover, going straight to his lover's arms.

If Tilly left now, she would never know. She would curse herself for a lifetime for her role in their deaths, when perhaps they were safe and well at the Morningtons'.

It was early. Nobody would see her.

Tilly took her trunk and left, turning a shoulder against the sight of the still-smoking house, its white stone scorched, its roof fallen in, its conservatory a heap of glass and burned wood. Down the path and through the woods, hoping and hoping that she would press her face against Chantelle's window and see them there sleeping, curled together like lovers.

On this awful morning, St. Peter Port had a hollow, emptied-out feeling. Without the noise of carriages and people, without the movement at the harbor, it seemed a grim labyrinthine town carved out of unforgiving rock. The cold wind rattled the hanging signs on the bow-windowed inns and chilled her cheeks as she rounded the corner of the Morningtons' block, and into the gully-like street behind it. Vines tickled her shoulders as she walked along, looking for the Morningtons' garden gate. When she found it, she realized it was too high to climb, but she could just slip her fingers through the gap between two bars to unlatch it from the inside. She closed it quietly behind her.

The grass was wet with cold dew. She was outside Chantelle's window before she realized that if Jasper saw her, he would stop her from leaving. He might even want to press criminal charges: she had locked him in a burning room.

Oh, dear Lord, she had locked him in a burning room.

She stood, sick with fear and self-loathing, not knowing what to do. Then stood her trunk up against the window and put a toe on it. Fingers on the windowsill, peering through the glass. Found herself looking at an empty room, a bed unslept in. Her heart fell all the way to her toes.

The window was open a crack. She pushed it up and it slid open easily. She didn't know what she was doing, what she was looking for, but she hoisted herself up and climbed through the window.

The room was small and dingy. A chipped dresser that leaned

to one side, with a mirror so tarnished Tilly could see only a flash of her own hair and little else in it. Chantelle's bed was a narrow mattress on the floor, with a rough gray blanket. Her circumstances were grim, so much grimmer than Tilly's, and she swallowed a bolt of shame that she had begrudged Chantelle the small comfort of a sable-trimmed coat. Weren't all of God's children created equal? A photograph of Jasper was pinned behind the wardrobe door. He wore a boater hat, a white jacket. He smiled at her; a smile of genuine affection. A smile that Tilly had never received.

Inside the wardrobe were Chantelle's dresses. Chantelle's jewelery . . . Tilly recognized her own mother's pearls but couldn't bring herself to take them back, now Chantelle was dead. Here was Chantelle's little suitcase, little more than a box with a lid and a clasp. She flipped it open, saw papers. Unfolded one. A love letter from Jasper. All of the love letters that he didn't send to Tilly, he sent to Chantelle instead, one every two or three days. She sat on the floor for a few moments and skimmed some. *Last night was beautiful. I love you more than I can say,* ma chère. *Nothing will change when she comes, but I will lose the house without her money.* On and on, every letter a condemnation of him. He had duped Grandpa, undermined Tilly—gleefully, according to the letters—and intended to put her aside the moment two years were up. She didn't have Chantelle's letters here to read, to see how complicit the other woman was, but she supposed from Jasper's loving phrases that they were in as deep as each other.

Now they were both dead. And Tilly was alive.

Tilly took a deep breath, was about to put the letters back when she spied a small leather wallet at the bottom of the suitcase. She pulled it out and it fell open, a large sheet of paper folded in it, written all across in French.

It was a passport from the French Foreign Office.

To all it may concern, please allow Miss Chantelle Marie Lejeune to pass freely without hindrance and to afford her assistance and protection should she stand in need. Dated the fifteenth day of March in Paris 1889.

And then underneath, a description.

Stature: 5 feet 3 inches. Eyes: hazel. Hair: red gold. Complexion: fair. Face: small round.

Underneath, Chantelle's signature.

The thundering of the brass knocker reverberated through the house, frightening Tilly to pieces. Her blood jumped in her veins. She remembered where she was, what she intended, and made for the window to climb down. From here, she could look down onto the street. A black carriage waited with the badge of the St. Peter Port police painted on it. Her heart doubled its speed. She pressed herself against the side of the house and sidled up behind the tall hedges, to see if she could hear what was going on.

By the time she caught the conversation, Laura's voice was already distressed.

"What? Both of them?"

"I'm afraid so, ma'am. We found their bodies in the conservatory. They must have tried to jump from an upper-story window."

Tilly's ears began to ring. She pressed her palms against the stone to keep herself from falling.

"That's a devil of a thing," Ralph said. "Laura, calm yourself. Go inside."

Sounds of movement. Tilly froze, but then she realized Ralph had sent Laura back into the house and walked a few paces out with the constable. Tilly could see through the corner of the hedge the shoulder of his blue frock coat, the back of his glazed top hat. She willed herself not to move a muscle, not to make a sound.

"If you have any information that can help with our investigations," he was saying.

"Dellafore was tupping our cook. You can come through and see where she slept if you think it will help."

Then they were gone and Tilly had to somehow find the courage to run while they were inside, in the very room she had been in moments before.

Forcing strength into enervated limbs. Running back for her trunk, then bolting for the garden gate and back into the narrow lane behind, then down to the harbor, to the ships that would take her off this island of nightmares, into an uncertain future.

•

Tilly was not quite five feet three inches, but she could stand tall. Her hair was too dark to be called red gold, but perhaps they would only notice the word red. Her eyes were more green than hazel, but hazel was a color open to interpretation. Her face was more oval than round but her cheeks were full and rosy. She looked nothing like Chantelle, and yet the description on the passport was vague enough not to arouse suspicion. As for the signature, she practiced it a hundred times on a scrap of notepaper while she waited for her ferry. Writing the name over and over—*Chantelle Marie Lejeune*— forced her mind awfully and with stony reality on what had happened, what role she had played. And yet, this was her chance to get away and never look back. The police believed her dead alongside her husband; rather than believing her to be responsible for her husband's death. If she wanted to have any kind of future beyond this moment, she had to allow them to keep believing that.

From St. Peter Port to St. Malo. From St. Malo to Paris, from Paris to Marseilles, she practiced that signature over and over until she could write it as though it were her own, as though she were Chantelle Lejeune. Her French, thanks to Grandpa, was flawless. She changed her banknotes and found her way to the deep port at La Joliette, lined up at the first counter selling accommodation on long-distance steamers, and booked the first berth leaving that day. To Australia; to the other side of the world.

That would do.

ELEVEN

She Is Not My Mother

2012

The storms stayed away for a week. Blue sky after blue sky, sun sparkling on the sea and dazzling off the rough yellow-green grass that grew along the side of the dirt track that led up to Starwater. It gave the roofer a chance to come and seal the roof properly. The three days he was there I found it very difficult to work. I was too distracted. I wasn't sure of the protocol: make him coffee? Check on him from time to time when the roof went quiet to make sure he hadn't fallen? While the roofer worked outside, Joe worked inside. He'd filled my fridge and had set about pulling off the plasterboard. I found I could ignore him more easily because he kept saying, "Ignore me. Do your work."

I tried. I really tried. I applied myself with force to the task. I'd reread the last Widow Wayland book. It bristled with Post-it notes where I'd analyzed and notated what worked well. Then realized I couldn't go any further forward with the new story until I fixed up the problems with the start. So I resigned myself to rewriting huge sections, only to find I got myself mixed up, lost track of time and plot threads, made things a worse mess. I'd done a week's work and I was going backwards. My nerve was failing.

So on the Friday, when Joe quietly slid the mail onto my desk and there was an envelope there forwarded from Marla with my publisher's logo on it, I was overcome with a sense of thickening dread. What was going to be in here? A legal document holding me in breach of contract? A harshly worded letter about their disappointment? A newspaper exposé and a please-explain note?

It was none of these things, of course. My publishers were infinitely patient with me. My editor had told me several times that every author she knew suffered with bouts of writer's block or became convinced they were an impostor or saw their success as random, senseless, a horrible mistake. What made me think I was different from them? I opened the envelope and slid out a mock-up of the cover art for the next book.

I could no longer sit still. I jumped out of my chair and started to pace, the cover in my hands. It was striking: a shadowy picture of the Widow (beautiful, as always), a ruined abbey, some medieval illuminations. My name—Nina Jones—occupied its usual position in its usual font with "the international bestseller" beneath it. In the place where the title should be, they had written *Title Goes Here*, and I remembered I had promised them a title by the end of last month. Or was it the month before? It had completely slipped my mind.

Joe was back, watching me pace. "Are you having a break? Can I make you tea?"

I glanced up, distracted. "Ah . . . no. I should . . . I should keep going."

"Hey," he said, a smile spreading across his face. "Is that your new book cover?"

I held it out to him, trying to appear bright despite the dark whirlpool of fear and self-doubt inside me.

"That's an interesting title," he laughed.

"Yes, I know. I have a few ideas. I just . . . I just can't seem to, um . . ." I ran out of words.

Joe looked at me curiously. "Are you all right?"

"I'm so far from finished. The cover is done, and I'm . . . not."

"But you'll be fine. You've done it before. You just need to get over this writer's block. I really admire you, what you do. I'm not creative at all." He handed the cover back. "You should pin this up. For inspiration. In the meantime, I shouldn't be in here bothering you. Let me know if you want anything."

I almost called him back. I didn't want to be by myself. The inside of my head was a scary place to be on my own. But the last thing I needed was another person in my life offering me consolation and reassurance about my work. Or worse, jollying me along and asking me about daily word counts.

Because the amount I would have to write every day to finish this book on time was more than I was capable of, and I knew it.

I returned to my desk, stared at the black words on the white screen. I felt completely lost, terrified, depressed. Why had I ever signed this contract? Why had I thought I could do it? I'd been lucky the first three times. Why had I believed I could reproduce that luck again? I should have walked away.

I was too sick and frightened for tears. I put my head on my desk and listened to my own breathing for a few minutes. Then, rather than pin it up for inspiration, I screwed the cover into a ball and put it in the bin. If I was going to get this done, I needed to forget there was a vast publishing machine ticking along without my manuscript, hoping like hell I could get it done.

•

I had stopped for lunch—spaghetti on toast, something I never got sick of—when my phone beeped. It was a message from Stacy.

Call me when you get this. Business.

I put the phone back on the table and finished eating. I'd had such good intentions of getting straight back into work after lunch, but maybe some fresh air would be good for me. Get my brain stimulated so it didn't keep trying to rewrite the same hundred words over and over. The phone booth was the only reliable place to make a business call, so I put my plate in the sink and headed down the hill.

I had to wait ten minutes for an elderly woman to finish talking to a young friend or relative who had just had a baby. I tried not to look impatient while I waited, but I knew the afternoon would get away from me if I didn't get back to my desk soon.

Finally, I had Stacy on the line.

"Hello, island girl," she said. "So you finally got my text? I sent it last night, you know."

"I see other people around here with mobile service. I don't know why it avoids me."

"Maybe you should change your carrier."

"I'm not going to stay that long. I hope." But how long was it going to take to finish? I shook my head, clearing my mind. "What's the business?"

"Somebody's trying to get access to your papers."

My papers, the old manuscripts and correspondence for my novels, were all housed at the Fryer Library on the mainland. I'd donated them, along with most of Eleanor's papers, the previous year, but put a restriction on their access so that I could approve who used them. When I'd moved to Sydney, I'd left Stacy in charge of managing their access. "Who is it?"

"A journalist named Elizabeth—"

"Parrish," I finished for her. "Damn it, why won't she leave me be? What does she want from me?"

"I don't know, Nina, but it's easy enough for me to deny her access."

"Please do." I was uncomfortable. A little afraid. "I've told her I won't talk to her. I don't know what she thinks she's going to get from reading my old fan mail."

"You want me to call her? Tell her to leave you alone? I can use some lawyer speak."

I laughed. "No. Just deny her access and let's hope she gives up. And I'll see you in a week?"

"You sure will. I might just have a surprise for you by then."

"What is it?"

"If I told you, it wouldn't be a surprise," she said. "Now get back to work."

"I will," I said. Not sure if I was lying.

•

Around five, I heard voices outside the house and gratefully closed my laptop for the day. I trudged out to the verandah in time to see Joe greeting a round-faced woman in her early sixties with dark hair and eyes. She accompanied Joe's son Julian.

"Mum," Joe said, "this is Nina. Nina, this is my mum."

"Hello, Mrs. . . ." I turned to Joe. "I don't even know your surname."

"McKiernan," she said. "But please call me Lynn."

"It's nice to meet you, Lynn," I said, extending my hand. "And hello, Julian."

Julian was busy climbing up onto the verandah railing and walking along it like a gymnast. I smiled at Joe. "Thanks for all your help this week. The same three days next week?" Joe had worked for me Monday, Wednesday, and Friday. I would have had him stripping walls every day, but he had his thesis to be working on.

"Yes, if that suits you."

"Are you heading back over to the mainland for the weekend?" Lynn asked me.

"No. I'm trying to avoid the mainland," I replied. It was a week before Stacy could get back to see me, and so the weekend beckoned, long and empty.

"You here alone?" Lynn asked, sensing my melancholy.

"I am."

"Come home with us, then. I've made a lasagna. There's more than enough for all of us. Joe's dad would love to meet you."

I was surprised by the invitation and hesitated. I didn't know if it was wise to see Joe outside of work times. There was already a warmth between us that shouldn't be there; and I was determined not to get myself tangled in the same mess I'd been in with Cameron.

Julian piped up. "You should come," he said. "I can show you my *Star Wars* Legos."

His little face was so shiny with excitement that I couldn't refuse. "Okay, then," I said.

"Lovely," Lynn said. "We'll open a nice bottle of wine."

"I'll just slip some shoes on."

We all walked down the hill together in the soft afternoon light. The sun was setting behind clouds and had sent amber-gold rays out across the sky. Our shadows were long. Julian ran ahead and ran back, blowing away the cobwebs that had gathered on him sitting still in school all day. It was as though I could see the sea air freshening his cheeks, invigorating his skin. I thought about what a wonderful place this must be to raise a child. Lynn swung open the gate to their property and we headed up the long driveway.

Julian ran back and pointed out a steel shed. "That's where Dad and I live. Dad, can I show her my Legos? Please?"

"I doubt she's interested in Legos," Joe said.

"No, I'd love to see it," I said. I was curious about how Joe lived in a shed.

"I'll get the lasagna in the oven," Lynn said, giving Joe an affectionate rub on the head. "You take your time."

So Joe, Julian, and I turned off the path and picked our way through the overgrown grass to the shed. It had windows and a door, and boxes of pink and white impatiens sat outside it. Joe unlocked the door and reached around to switch on the light.

Inside was one big space, but very homey. A small kitchenette, carpet squares on the ground with a lot of Legos spread out on them, a saggy couch, two single beds in opposite corners, and a bookshelf made of old bricks and long planks of wood.

"Welcome to my mansion," Joe said with a half smile, and I realized he must feel embarrassed.

"It looks very comfortable."

"We don't have a bathroom."

"We bush-wee!" Julian declared with delight.

"Only in the middle of the night when we don't want to disturb Mum and Dad," Joe clarified, face flushing.

I laughed it off. Julian dragged me over to his Legos and insisted I sit on the ground with him on a big round rug woven with a city streetscape. While Julian showed me his spaceships and figurines, Joe fetched two beers out of the fridge. He opened them both and brought one over to me.

"Cheers," he said, clinking his bottle against mine.

"Cheers," I said.

We looked at each other a few moments and I let the warmth wash over me, all the while berating myself for letting him raise his expectations.

"How long have you lived in the shed?" I asked.

"Four years. Before that we lived over on the mainland for a while but it's hard. Rents are high and I'm living on a scholarship. As brilliant as Julian is at Legos, it's not a big earning profession."

I ruffled Julian's hair. He didn't notice, he was so absorbed with his Legos.

"I had the opportunity to do this PhD and the whale-watching job came up at the same time. It worked really well for a while. I bought the shed and fitted it out, paid Mum and Dad some rent . . . But, as you know, George and Kay lost the business."

I leaned back on the seat of the velour couch. "What were they like?"

"A little clueless." He laughed. "Sweet people, though. You probably don't want to hear that. They owe you a lot of money."

"I don't care much about money," I said.

"Anyway, Julian and I are only here until I've finished my thesis. Then I hope I'll get a great job somewhere and we'll be off. And then we'll buy a house. With a bathroom. No more weeing in the garden."

"An admirable goal," I said with a smile, tilting my bottle to my lips.

We sat with Julian on the round rug, drinking our beer and chatting. Whether it was the beer or Joe's presence, I don't know, but I started to feel relaxed. I started to feel okay, as if things might work out and the world wasn't so bleak. Lynn called us for dinner after a half hour, and I went inside to meet Joe's father, Dougal.

Joe looked nothing like his mother, but even less like Dougal, who was a burly Scotsman with bright ginger hair. He called me "lassie" and gave me a very warm hug, and invited me to sit down. Julian demanded I sit on the long bench seat next to him. Their dining table was so big it took up most of the kitchen, with Lynn having to breathe in to move around us as she set out the lasagna and the salad bowl. It was made of scarred wood, no tablecloth, the cutlery all thrown in the middle for us to help ourselves.

"Och, it's grand to have a guest for dinner," Dougal said.

"It's lovely to be here," I said. "This table is huge."

Lynn slid into her seat. "We love to entertain, but don't get the chance much. Every Christmas we have a big group of extended family that come over from the mainland, but usually it's just the four of us sitting here. Go on, eat up."

I served myself a small portion of lasagna, only to hear Dougal tsk-tsk and tell me I needed to put some meat on my bones. Joe looked pained. Julian was leaning his head on my shoulder. I thought about my family dinners growing up. The carefully laid table, the insistence on using the right fork at the right time, my mother clearing her throat softly every time I put my elbows on the table. Joe's parents argued merrily with their mouths full, Julian ate cherry tomatoes with his fingers, everybody helped themselves to seconds. The wine flowed freely, too. I had never seen my mother touch a drop.

I decided I really liked Joe's family.

"So what are ye doing on Ember Island, lassie?" Dougal boomed during a lull in his good-humored ribbing of his wife. "You working or playing?"

I had just taken a mouthful of food and chewed rapidly to swallow before I spoke, but Joe spoke ahead of me. "Nina's on holidays. She's a . . . journalist."

"Journalist, eh?"

"What paper do you write for?"

I swallowed, not sure what to say. Why had Joe lied about what I did? "Just a local Sydney paper," I said, hoping I sounded convincing. My voice was too small for lies. "Covering dog shows and so on."

"Joe was saying Starwater has always been in your family," Lynn said.

It wasn't entirely true, but I was out there on a limb, going along with Joe though I didn't know why. "Yes, my great-grandmother Eleanor Holt owned it. She was quite a lady." I told them a few Eleanor stories and the topic of what I did for a living moved on and disappeared.

Joe leaned over while Lynn and Dougal were up clearing the table. "Trust me," he whispered. "If they get a whiff that you're famous, they'll drive you mad. Mum will have you guesting at book clubs and Dad will show you his unfinished memoir."

I laughed softly. "Thank you. It's nice to pretend I'm not a writer."

"Well, you do write about those dog shows."

We shared a giggle, and Dougal looked over his shoulder at us fondly. I pulled away a little from Joe then, remembering my vow not to get involved. It was just so nice to feel that spark of initial attraction, to flirt a little. I had so few small pleasures in life that I was clinging to this one.

"Will ye have a pudding with us, Nina?" Dougal said.

"I'd love to."

"Sticky toffee," Lynn said, uncovering an oven pan.

"The sauce will kill ye," Dougal added. "Made with butter, cream, and sugar. Nowt else. A heart attack waiting to happen."

"You'll never die," Lynn said, flicking him playfully with a towel. "You'll stay around to torment me forever, you ratbag."

They were so affectionate with each other, laughing and cuddling and play fighting. It was no wonder that Joe was such a good-hearted man, that his son was so demonstrative.

Lynn placed bowls of sticky, warm deliciousness in front of Julian and me, then scooped frosty vanilla ice cream on top. She turned to Joe and said, "Are you having some, Jonah?"

"Sure," Joe said.

"Jonah?" I asked, smiling at him. "Your name is Jonah? And you work with whales?"

"Ah, that's a tale," said Dougal, refilling my wineglass. After the beer earlier, my head was beginning to swim, but he wouldn't be refused.

Everybody sat down to eat—the most evil dessert I have ever tasted—and Dougal filled me in. "Lynnie and I couldn't have our own child. We tried for years—"

Lynn butted in. "Six years," she said, in a voice so impassioned that I understood just how long those six years had been for her. Heat rose in my solar plexus. I remembered Cameron's face and voice, as he pleaded with me, "Can't we just try? Can't we investigate the possibilities?" Easy for him to say. It wasn't his body that was going to be investigated, its integrity called into question, found faulty.

"Yes, dear, now keep quiet and let me talk," Dougal said. "We tried for six years and then we waited another eight on an adoption register. It was August the first when we got the call. Whale migration season. Lynnie and I were overwhelmed with the news. We walked down to the pier to wait for the boat across to the mainland, to go and pick up our bundle of joy, and a pod of humpback whales was passing. Och, ye've never seen anything like it, lassie. Heavy as trucks, but thrusting themselves out of the water like they weigh as feathers. So I said, let's call our boy Jonah, because of the whales."

"Of course, Dougal here has never read the Bible in his life and tells me Jonah rode whales and was some kind of whale king," Lynn laughed. "After we've named our boy and signed off on the paperwork, I looked it up in an encyclopedia and found he was *eaten* by a whale."

"I *have* read the Bible. The best bits, anyway. I misremembered that part from Sunday school."

"In any case, he was already our little Jonah, though he's all grown up now and prefers Joe." Lynn reached across the enormous table to pat Joe's hand. "And it's no surprise he should be interested in whales. He's watched them come up here every year of his life and they are great, grand creatures."

More gentle ribbing passed between them, more laughter, and Julian shouted "I love whales!" because he was keen to be part of the conversation. Somehow I managed to fit every last sodden crumb of the toffee pudding in, though my stomach was sore. It was hard to feel sorry for myself while half drunk, full bellied and surrounded by warmth and family. Then Dougal turned to me and asked me directly, "So, lassie. Are ye married? Are ye seeing anyone?"

"Dad . . ." Joe protested.

I opened my mouth, hesitated, knowing I had to shut this down. Joe had to know I was unavailable and it wasn't as though I could easily tell him why. I wouldn't be on the island for long; it didn't matter if I lied. "I have a boyfriend," I said, then cleared my throat. "His name's Cameron."

"Then where is he, love?" Lynn asked, puzzled.

"He's back in Sydney. He couldn't come with me, he has . . . work."

I could feel an uncomfortable distance opening up between my shoulder and Joe's. He was disappointed, maybe angry. Perhaps he thought I had led him on. Perhaps I *had* led him on.

A little of the warmth had left Dougal's voice. "What kind of work does he do, then?"

"He's a poet," I said.

Dougal laughed loudly, then realized I was serious and feigned a coughing fit.

"A poet, eh?" said Lynn. "He must be quiet and sensitive."

"Um . . . I guess so." They weren't the first two words that came to mind with Cameron. Obsessive and vain?

"Well, then, it's a shame he had so many poems to write he couldn't be here with ye. I hope you enjoy your holiday, nevertheless," Dougal said, regaining his warmth.

"And you're always welcome to come for dinner. Any time, dear. Any night of the week."

"Come every night," Julian said, hooking his elbow through mine.

"I will certainly come again," I said, heart beating hard as the awkwardness slid past. Joe insisted on walking me home, while Lynn and Dougal wrestled Julian off to have a bath and clean his teeth. The sky was clear and warm, a sea breeze ruffled the palms. We were silent for a while, then I said, "I'm sorry I hadn't mentioned Cameron to you. There hadn't really been a chance." There. That would put an end to it.

"You don't need to be sorry. It was nosy of Dad to ask."

"I . . . I hope that isn't weird for you or anything."

"My parents are always weird for me," he laughed.

"I think they're fantastic," I said.

"So do I. But they've embarrassed me more times than I can count. I'm used to it." We walked on a little further in silence, then he said, "Is he really a poet?"

"Um, yes."

"Does he make a living out of it?"

"He teaches as well. Writes articles for magazines sometimes." But mostly he had lived off me. And now he was sponging off Tegan and her rich daddy. We were at the foot of the pathway up to Starwater now. I cleared my throat, keen for a change of topic. "I'll see you on Monday then?"

"You want me to take you up to your door?"

I think we both felt the awkwardness. "No, I'll be fine," I said. "There are no murderers on the island, right?"

"Not anymore. Not since they closed the prison."

I smiled at him. That thrill was still there and I knew he could feel it too. But that ship had sailed. I told myself over and over it was for the best. Next time I fell in love, it had to be with somebody in his fifties who had had a family and was looking forward to a quiet retirement with a clean house. Maybe with a cat. "Thanks," I said. "Good night."

"Good night."

We parted ways and I trudged up the hill and let myself into the house. I felt a little lost, all on my own after a warm evening of company. But I put myself to bed and decided to read the next little diary entry I had pulled out of the brickwork. This one was dated a year before the last, written when Eleanor was only eleven. It didn't surprise me that she wrote beautifully, even as a child. The deep well of language had always been inside her. If only I had inherited that instead of a box of old papers.

•

October 5, 1890

I have decided to start this diary because my mother is dying and I have nobody else to speak to. My teacher is without much compassion, my classmates are without much brain, and Papa says I need to be strong and not lean so much on him.

The thing that makes me saddest of all is that Mama is the person to whom I would love to tell my troubles. So when she dies I will suffer the double blow of losing her, and losing the person whose lap I would rest my head in to cry. I feel as though I am on a ship in deep water, sinking slowly.

Mama has been sick for two months. At first she would sleep a lot. She was hard to wake in the morning and couldn't wait to get into bed at night. Some nights she went to bed before me. The tiredness grew worse. She couldn't make it through the day without having to put her head down. I heard her making jokes with Papa about getting old, but she's only 36 and I once met a lady who was 80 who could stay awake all day.

Then she started growing thin. She had no appetite, she complained about a constant back ache.

Still, I didn't worry about it because she and Papa didn't seem worried about it. But then one Tuesday, the day the surgeon always came over from the mainland to check on the sick prisoners in the infirmary, Papa called the surgeon to come up to the house and look at Mama. I was playing with my peg dolls on the southern verandah so I didn't hear what he said to Mama, but then he and Papa came out on the eastern verandah and I could hear them quite clearly.

"The lumps under her arm. How long have they been there?"

"She's never mentioned them. I presume she's had them for some time."

"It doesn't look good, Superintendent Holt. That and the back pain. I've seen it before."

His words lit a little fire in my heart, a soft whoosh of flame.

"Should I get her across to the mainland?" Even under these circumstances, Papa sounded perfectly measured.

"It won't make a difference. I don't think she has long."

A silence. I wished I could see Papa's face. My body buzzed with fear.

"What will happen?" Papa asked, in a quiet voice.

"Well, she will simply grow tireder and one day she will lie down and not get up again."

I sobbed out loud, once, then clapped my hand over my mouth. I leapt to my feet and ran down the stairs and into the garden, fearful of being caught eavesdropping (Papa simply hates me eavesdropping), but also feeling shocked and not sure what to do with my body. I climbed the giant fig tree, with its teeming roots, and sat on the rough branch a while and cried.

It was some time later, perhaps half an hour, that Papa found me.

"Come down," he called from the ground. He didn't look too stern.

"Is it true?" I asked. "Will Mama die?"

"Come down."

I did as I was told and clambered down from the tree. I jumped the last three feet and he caught me, and held me close for a moment before lowering me to the ground. He never hugs me usually.

I looked up at him, waiting for my answer.

"Your mama is very sick. You overheard what the doctor said, I gather."

"Not all of it. I ran out here."

"She will grow more and more tired. She won't be able to get out of bed at all. Then she will sleep a lot. She will feel some pain, but the doctor will give us something to help her. She will look very ill. One day she will not wake up from her sleep." He nodded once, decisively, as if he had imparted to me all I needed to know. "This may take a few weeks or a few months. In that time, you are not to ask her to do anything for you. Not so much as read a line of a book. In fact, you will do anything that she asks, without a flicker of defiance. Do you understand all this?"

I felt hollow. "Yes, but . . ." I trailed off into tears.

Papa put his hand on my shoulder. "You must remind yourself that you should not cry because that will upset your mother. You will live on and see many more sunrises and sunsets. She will be watching down on us both from Heaven." On the last word, Papa's voice wavered a little and it fed that little flame of heat in my heart. Papa never wavered. Never. The world was upside down.

That was July. She has been confined to her bed for five weeks now, and I sit with her every day to read to her and chat with her and embroider while she dozes. But lately her smiles do not come as easily, and today . . . Today was the worst day of all.

I had been reading to her—Sir Gawain and the Green Knight, which is my favourite story in the world—and she had fallen asleep just as Lady Bertilak makes her second attempt to undermine Gawain's courtesy. So I closed the book and leaned over to kiss her cheek, and I accidentally leaned on her elbow under the covers.

And her eyes flew open and she roared at me. "You foolish child! Are you trying to torture me? Am I not already in enough pain without you pushing your whole weight onto my aching joints?"

I leapt back and told her how sorry I was and could feel tears brimming but remembered what Papa had told me and sniffed them back. Then Papa, who had heard her shout, came into the room and roared me out. I ran outside and sat heavily on the steps to put my head on my knees and cry.

Papa came out after a few minutes and sat with me.

"I'm sorry," I said. "I didn't mean to hurt her. I didn't know her arm was there."

"Hush," Papa said, quietly. "All is well, child. She is in much pain. You cannot even imagine how much pain she is in. It strips her raw."

"Can I go back in and say sorry again? Has she forgiven me?"

"No, I think it best if you spend less time with her. You should be concentrating on your school work. It may yet be some time before she passes and you are too young to be good company to a dying woman."

I wanted to cry, but she is my mother! But this was the moment that I realised she is no longer my mother. That woman is already gone. She has been dissolved by illness and pain, and in her stead is left this husk who is impatient and angry with me and I cannot bear it. I cannot bear it.

October 15, 1890

Mama looking very unwell. Papa allowed me to sit with her for an hour today. I can see her skull under her skin. She barely speaks. Papa says that is because the medicine that takes away her pain also takes away her ability to know what is going on around her. I am frightened of her. She looks like a monster. She is not my mother.

October 19, 1890

I spent the whole day reading Malory in bed and cuddling Pangur Ban. I could hear Mama in the next room. She breathes strangely now, as though there are razors in her throat. I don't like the sound. I wish I could go to another room. I want my mama back. I don't know the creature in the next room. I want my mama back.

October 27, 1890

Dawn is breaking and I don't know what's happening and nobody will come to me and tell me. Very late last night I woke because there were voices and footsteps rushing about and I went to Mama's room to see. Doctor Groom was there, he's been staying one or two nights to tend to

Mama, and Papa was kneeling at the bed with Mama's hand in his and I think he was crying. I have never seen my papa cry! Why was he crying? Doctor Groom pushed me out, he said, "Go away, child, go back to sleep."

Do they think I am still asleep? Is Mama dead? Surely I would know, wouldn't I? Wouldn't I feel it somehow if my own mother died? Wouldn't the strings that hold the cosmos together quiver, like a spider web when a fly lands in it? I am afraid to go next door in case she is dead, or in case she isn't and she's more horrible to look at than ever, or in case Doctor Groom shouts and says that he told me to go away and why would I bother them all at such a time.

I don't know what else to say or write.

November 1, 1890

Two days ago my mother was buried in the graveyard at the southern end of the island. She passed in her sleep late in the night on October the 27, when she was 36 years and 107 days old. She had only four grey hairs on her head and her hands were still smooth. Papa invited me in to see her body and kiss her cold cheek the next morning, and I did it but then wished I hadn't because I felt as though I had a frost of death on my lips all day and sometimes I still have the feeling and I don't like it.

The day we buried her was very hot. The chaplain, who is a large, doughy man, was sweating furiously as he read from the Bible. The sky burned blue and the sea sang behind us. Every now and again a breeze would rise off the water and rush past, cooling my flushed cheeks and sticky skin. The whole thing seemed over so quickly, considering how long Mama suffered before she died. I rather suspected the chaplain rushed through it because of the heat.

There are two graveyards on this island. One for staff and family, and one for prisoners. The one for prisoners has no names on the headstones. The crosses are bare except for a prison letter and number. The headstones in the family graveyard tell sad stories of people like Mama, who were "much beloved" or "missed for always" or "at rest." Mama's headstone has not been carved yet; it is coming over from the mainland, but Papa has told me it will say, "treasured wife and mother, now at rest with angels." I think that is a lovely epitaph, and asked Papa who thought of it. And was surprised to hear that it was him.

Papa has ever been a stranger to me, but I think that is about to change. At the funeral he held me tightly in his arms while I cried. He stroked my hair, and he kissed the top of my head and told me not to be sad because she is no longer in pain and has gone to a better place. He did not shed a single tear, but something in him has softened, I can feel it.

Now she is in the ground, the next room is very quiet. Sometimes I feel sad about that. I remember the times when I would have a bad dream and run next door, only to press myself against her soft chest and have her shush me back to sleep.

But it has been a very long time since I was able to take any comfort from her, so above all things I am relieved. I can get on with remembering her as she was, before that awful illness took its hold on her body, twisting her all out of shape, and erasing all her loveliness and light.

•

I lay awake for a long time after reading the diary. These were my ancestors. This was my family history. I would be nobody's ancestor. That's what had been too much for Cameron in the end: nobody to carry on his genetic heritage. It had been important to him in a way that I never fully understood, but perhaps it made more sense now, thinking about my link back to Eleanor. Do we honor the past by projecting ourselves forward into the future? By carrying on genes and traits and family stories? I was mulling over these things when my phone beeped. I was used to it going off at odd times, as the signal flickered and flared depending on the weather and the wind. I reached for it in the dark. It was an SMS from a number I didn't recognize.

Nina, please contact Elizabeth Parrish urgently about a piece I am writing. I need urgent information from you. Please do not ignore this message.

I switched the phone off and put it in my bedside drawer. My hands were shaking with anger. Urgent. For whom? Not for me. I wasn't going to talk to her. *Please do not ignore this message.* Why did I find that last part so menacing? It wasn't a threat. Was it?

I tried to put it out of my mind. I needed to spend the week writing, not thinking about nosy journalists and what they might want from me.

TWELVE

This Is the Life

I sat on the shady verandah enjoying watching the morning sunshine on the long grass that covered the hillock and the blue sea beyond the island. Earlier in the week, I'd dragged the kitchen table out on the verandah. I spent a lot of time out there, laptop flipped open, trying to write. This morning, I packed the laptop away and put a jar of water and wild crocuses in its place. Stacy would be arriving soon, and I had a plan that we'd eat takeaway fish and chips for lunch and wash it down with a chilled bottle of Sauvignon Blanc. She'd insisted I didn't need to meet her off the ferry, so I was keeping an eye out for her.

Eventually I saw a figure in the distance with a wheelie suitcase and a huge floppy hat, and I stood and leaned over the verandah railing to wave madly. She waved back, ran-walked the rest of the distance, and was soon pulling her suitcase up the five front stairs.

"I told you I'd find my way," she said.

"I didn't doubt you."

She whipped off her hat. Her hair was in two tight plaits

underneath. "I'm going to drop my suitcase in my room and then I've got business to get out of the way."

"That sounds ominous. Shall I get the wine?"

"It's not ominous, but you should get the wine anyway. It's evening somewhere in the world."

We met back at the verandah table two minutes later, and I poured us a glass of wine each. Stacy handed me a manila envelope. "Congratulations on your new boat."

"My new . . . ?"

"I've been in touch with George and Kay and made arrangements for them to sign the boat over to you in lieu of the rent they owe. Stamp duty and registration are all paid too."

I glanced through the paperwork, holding the sheets down as a warm sea breeze went past. "Wow. I have a boat. What am I going to do with it?"

Stacy leaned back, sipping her wine. "Learn to drive it? Or do you say sail it? Does it have a sail?"

I peered at the description in the papers. "I've no idea. Joe will know."

"Joe!" she said. "See if he'll take us out in the boat. He can drive it."

"I don't have his number."

"There are three hundred people on the island. He won't be hard to find." Then she narrowed her eyes suspiciously. "You *know* where he lives, don't you?"

"Yes, I do."

"Then why the reluctance?"

"No reason. It's just . . . you know, he's my employee." I'd been avoiding Joe all week after the awkwardness of dinner with his parents. When he arrived for work, I hid in my office and didn't come out to chat. He seemed just as happy to get on with stripping plasterboard without having to engage with me.

"Come on, it'll be fun. I'm only here for the weekend. We can have a picnic."

"We'll see," I said, trying to sound light and noncommittal.

"You like him, don't you?"

I laughed. "Are we in high school again?"

She sat back in her chair, looking me up and down with a smug smile, swishing her wine around in her glass. "I can always tell when some man takes your fancy. You go all quiet about him."

I put my palms up reflexively, a stop gesture. "Please. Don't."

"Why? What's wrong? You've been single nearly a year . . ."

"It . . . I never really told you what went wrong with Cameron."

"You didn't need to. He was vain and he sponged off you."

"That's not why we broke up."

"It should have been." Stacy smiled to soften the blow of her words. "Sorry. You know I was never fond of him. Why don't you tell me what really happened then?"

I realized I hadn't spoken this particular pain out loud to anyone. "He wanted children and I . . . well, as you know I can't. I let him go. That's why it hurt so much to see him with Tegan that day."

"Do you still love him?"

"No."

Stacy pressed her lips together for a moment, in thought. "What does this have to do with Joe?"

"I can't put myself in that position again."

"Wait. You're worrying about *children*? You haven't even been on a date with him!"

"He likes kids. He has one. He probably wants more."

Stacy leaned across the table and patted my hand. "I only want you to ask him to take us out on the boat. I promise I won't force you to bear his offspring."

This made me laugh and I finally agreed. We put the wine back in the fridge and made our way down the hill and across the sunny path until we found Joe's shed.

I knocked. It echoed loudly. The door opened and little Julian was peering out.

"Nina!" he said, nearly knocking me over with an enthusiastic hug.

"Julian, this is my friend Stacy. We're looking for your dad." But I'd already seen him, set up with his books at their little round dining table while Julian played a loud game on his PlayStation. "Sorry to disturb you while you're working," I said.

Joe was at the door a moment later, shaking Stacy's hand and brushing away my apology. "It's fine. My brain is starting to hurt and Julian's been blowing up cars for long enough. TV off now, mate." He returned his attention to us. "Can I offer you a cup of something?"

"No, we really didn't want to trouble you . . ." I started.

"But Nina has a new boat," Stacy interjected.

"A boat?" he asked.

"*The* boat," I said. "George and Kay's."

"And we were hoping that you weren't busy tomorrow," Stacy said, flashing her eyelashes. It always worked on everyone: men, women, children.

"You want me to take you out in the boat?" he asked. "Sure, I'd love to."

"Can I come?" Julian asked.

"He's welcome to," I said. "We're going to have a picnic."

"Grandma's taking you across to the mainland to see Aunty Pam," Joe told him.

"Aunty Pam smells funny. Nina smells nice."

"She does, doesn't she?" Joe said, smiling so warmly that parts of me melted.

Stacy kicked my ankle gently, grinning.

"But Aunty Pam still has your birthday present from last month," Joe added.

Julian nodded, all businesslike. "I'm sorry, Nina. I can't come on your picnic after all."

"Never mind," I said. "Maybe next time."

Joe returned his attention to Stacy and me. "I've got a few things to do in the morning, so why don't we meet at the boat shed around midday?"

"Great!" Stacy enthused.

"You know it's whale season," Joe told her. "Not making any promises, but we might see one or two."

"Are they scary?" Stacy asked.

"They are . . . big." Joe chuckled. "You know you're alive when you're cruising alongside one, that's for sure. Keep everything crossed."

I started to wonder if Joe, who seemed to me so close to nature, might be able to make the whales appear with that earthy magic he had.

As we walked back to Starwater, Stacy wore an irrepressible smile.

"What?" I asked.

"You know," she said.

I did know. I absolutely did.

·

I had just slipped between the covers that night, when Stacy knocked lightly on my bedroom door.

"Come in," I called.

The door opened. Stacy wore pale pink pajamas and had her long dark hair in a plait. "Look what I found," she said, holding out some folded sheets of paper.

I sat up, alert. "Where?"

"I dropped my earring and it rolled under the dresser. I had to move it and this was right between two bricks, where the mortar should have been."

I took it from her and opened it, reading the first lines by the lamplight. "*The Secret Confession of Eleanor Holt.* I can't make out the date."

Stacy peered at it. "1869?"

"Well, she wasn't born then, so I think it must be 1889. She was ten."

"Can you read it? Her handwriting is appalling."

"Sure." I flipped back my covers. "Hop in."

Stacy squeezed in next to me and I started to read.

"*To whomever finds this letter, in confidence. On this day, I record that Mr. Burton, our chaplain and some-time scripture teacher, did act in a most inappropriate fashion towards me. This letter shall serve as a record of said actions &c &c.*"

Stacy laughed. "What ten-year-old writes like that?"

"My great-grandmother apparently," I replied.

"I know where you get your writing gene from, then," she said.

I didn't answer, peering at the next line.

"*Mr. Burton took us for religious lessons today, in the chapel. There were only five of us there as two of the Randolph children were ill with the vomits. Mr. Burton made us read proverbs until Bertie fell asleep, and then dismissed us at one so that we could have lunch.*

"*He held me back after the Randolphs had run off and said that he had something to show me. I was curious so I followed him to the back of the chapel, under that dreadful sad carving of poor Jesus. He pulled a chair from the corner of the chapel and placed it beneath a hatch in the ceiling, then stood on it and felt around for a moment. The hatch fell down, and a wooden ladder slid out.*

"'*This was built by the first chaplain on the island,' he told me. 'So that he could light the lantern beside the cross each night. We long ago gave up lighting the lantern.' He ushered me ahead of him. 'Go on, climb up. I'll show you what's up there.'*

"*I was not at all sure that I should go up the ladder, but I reminded myself that this was the chaplain and he was a man of God and so would not willingly put me in danger. I climbed up, while he watched me from below. Then I found myself inside the hot and dusty ceiling of the chapel, having to bend my head because the roof was directly above me. Ahead, I saw a half-size door.*

"'*Keep going,' Mr. Burton said, and I did, finding the door easy enough to open, and then I was on the roof, on a walkway about three feet across that led to the big wooden cross that stood above me.*

"'*You see?' said Mr. Burton, for he was behind me now. 'Is it not a lovely view?'*

"*I believed Mr. Burton misunderstood the best purpose of the walkway. It was not so much a good place to see, but a good place not to be seen. Nobody knew of this place, I was certain. Papa had certainly never mentioned it. I imagined myself slipping away from classes and coming here to write on the walkway, hiding my stories in the warm, dark ceiling. I was quite taken with the idea.*

"*But then, Mr. Burton touched me. He extended his fleshy hand and rubbed the back of his knuckles lightly across my cheek. I flinched and he laughed and said, 'No need to be so precious, Miss Holt. I won't hurt you.' And he looked at me in a way that made me confused and ashamed, and I cursed myself as a ninny for letting him bring me up here.*

"'I would like to go down now,' I said, for he was blocking my way and I didn't want to push past him and have him touch me again.

"'You will be such a beauty when you are sixteen, Nell,' he said, and his voice was thick and I was frightened. But then I remembered that my father was the most strongest man on the island and I said in a big voice, 'Let me past or I will tell my father.'

"Mr. Burton stood aside, but he was laughing, and as I squeezed past him he moved a little so I rubbed against his belly. He thought it terribly funny, but I simply felt embarrassed and hot in my face, and came back here immediately to record all this and now I feel better for having it out. I cannot tell Papa for he already has so much on his mind and I know I shouldn't have gone up there anyway. So if you have found this, you are the only other person to know.

"Yours sincerely, Eleanor Holt."

Stacy took the letter from me and scanned it. "That is super creepy."

"The poor little thing, thinking it was somehow her fault for going up there."

"She's lucky she got away without something worse happening," Stacy said. "The nineteenth century wasn't a great time to be a woman. I wonder, is the chapel she's written about the same little church that's still down near the Stockade?"

"It is. It used to be considered part of Starwater. But there isn't a big wooden cross on it anymore. Just that tacky light-up one on the front."

Stacy yawned and climbed out of bed, handing back the letter. "Thanks for the bedtime story. Good night."

"Good night."

After she left I reread the letter. From my great-grandmother to me. Though she didn't know it would be me who found it. I wished I could reach back through time and take that little girl in my arms and tell her not to worry about wretched Mr. Burton, tell her how incredibly clever she was and what a wonderful writer she would grow up to be. I fell asleep into half dreams about shadowy old churches and shelves full of dusty, empty books.

•

Sunday afternoon, I saw my boat for the first time. It was a seven-meter fiberglass 1979 Shark Cat with near-new twin outboard motors. Or so Joe told me. I just saw a boat. A yellow one. He had backed his van up to the door of the boat shed and unlocked the roller door. Stacy, slathered in nuclear-proof sunscreen and wearing a gigantic straw hat, waited with me on the grass. We had a picnic basket between our feet: Stacy may have been a high-flying property lawyer, but she was also a magnificent baker of savory muffins and lemon curd tarts. The bottle of champagne was my contribution.

Joe hooked up the trailer and tugged the boat out of the shed. I peered into the empty space. Cobwebs and mold. The creeping cold that only stone buildings can harbor.

"Nina! Come on!" This was Stacy calling. She had started down the path after Joe and the boat trailer. I hurried down after her, the picnic basket awkwardly held against my hip.

Joe knew what he was doing, of course. He'd been getting this boat in and out of the water and steering it round the bay for two years. He was confident and comfortable in his body, dressed in cut-off jeans and a long-sleeved T-shirt. Stacy and I did as he said, strapped on our life jackets, and got in when we were told.

Then we were off, powering out into the bay. The boat was in poor repair. The vinyl on the long bench seats was torn and the sponge was falling out; one of the front windows was cracked and taped up with duct tape; and the waterproof carpeting was almost worn through. But Joe assured me that it was safe and that I'd got a good deal.

"Where are we going to go?" I asked.

"Out a little way and then north. We might see a dugong, maybe a few turtles. Heaps of jellyfish. Go look over the side. Relax."

So I did. I leaned over the side and watched as we cut through the water. A flotilla of pale blue jellyfish surrounded us. The sun was warm on my back and I felt a warm sense of being in good company on a good day. I even managed to forget about the book for a while. Stacy opened the picnic basket and pulled out crackers and cheese and a flask of coffee. She poured one for Joe then settled next to me with a plastic cup. "This is the life."

"Thanks for my boat."

"Any time."

We cruised a little further, and Stacy and I chatted and ate and made up stupid jokes. I could see my reflection in her sunglasses and—even though I was thinner than I had been and my hair looked a bit wild—I was surprised to see myself laughing.

Then Joe cut the motors and we were drifting lightly, bobbing on the waves. He went to the other side and beckoned us. "Loggerhead turtle," he said.

"Where?" Stacy cried, leaping to the other side of the boat. Shoulder to shoulder we stood, peering at the water, following Joe's finger.

"I see it!" she said. "Look at that!"

Then I saw it too, its barnacled brown shell and its big black eyes, then it had dived under again.

"Is it time for our picnic?" Stacy asked hopefully.

"Great idea," said Joe.

There wasn't really anywhere to lay out the food, so we sat like three birds on a wire on the long bench, picking what we wanted out of the picnic basket and chatting. Joe didn't have any champagne, but Stacy and I got stuck in. Joe seemed to enjoy our company, laughing good-naturedly at our silly in-jokes, his body close enough to mine that I could feel the heat of his skin and smell the sunshine-and-salt scent of his hair. I needed more of this: more silly joking with old friends, more Joe, more moments in the sunshine. I'd become a hunched creature of the city, turned in on myself, like something out of a Poe story.

But then Joe stood up suddenly, a startled expression on his face as he peered off to the east.

"What is it?" I asked, following the direction of his gaze.

He was back at the engines a second later, starting them up, then returning to the wheel. "I saw a flipper."

"Whales?" Stacy squealed.

"Hang on." He turned the boat and we sped out further into the bay. The speed and motion didn't agree with the champagne and lemon curd tart in my stomach, but I held on.

A few minutes later I saw it myself. A great hump breaking the waves, its flipper raised almost as if it was waving, then disappearing again. I was utterly unprepared for how I would feel. I had seen photographs of whales, I knew what they looked like. But this, here in the wild open sea, thrilled me in a way that was both deep and natural.

Stacy clutched my arm. "It's a whale," she said, "a real one."

"You must have seen so many of these," I called to Joe. "Do you still get excited?"

"Yes, every time," he answered. "You never get used to it. They are magnificent."

He knocked back the speed and we slowly approached the place we'd seen the whale. Then he cut the engine and we waited, holding our breaths.

With a huge watery gasp, a gray-black back cut up through the waves and sprayed water everywhere. Stacy yelped with fright and I found myself laughing and laughing.

"Other side!" called Joe, and I turned to see another one, swimming below the water, close to the other side of the boat.

Now Stacy clung to my arm. "They can't tip the boat, can they?" she asked.

"It's never happened," Joe answered.

The closer one skimmed up through the water and sprayed through its blowhole.

"It's breathing," Stacy gasped. "Just like us."

"Yeah, that's pretty close," Joe said, getting ready to start the engine again.

Then the first whale broke through the water, its huge bulk impossibly airborne in a glorious arc, its white belly visible as it backflipped into the sea and disappeared, showering us in seawater.

My heart thundered as the water dried salty on my skin. Words and meaning failed me. I felt as though I had just seen through all of the artifice of civilization, all the way to the other side where nothing was as important as the pulsing sea and the brazen sky. Stacy's death grip on my arm tightened.

"Oh. My. God," she said.

"Yes," I said, because it was the only word I could think to say.

Joe smiled, as happy as if he had orchestrated the breaching creature himself. "He came to say hello," he laughed. "Lucky you."

•

After our boat trip, Stacy invited Joe up to Starwater to have dinner with us, but he said he'd promised Julian he'd be home by six so he parted company with us on the road home. I was more disappointed than I could understand. I kept thinking about him, his face turned to mine, the sunlight in his hair, telling me the whale had come to say hello. He had become entwined with my memory of that experience, that deep and thrilling moment. Why was I thinking of him like this? Why couldn't I get my head and my heart to agree?

•

I couldn't sleep. I think my blood was still jumping from the encounter with the whale, but it might also have been that these days I didn't sleep that well. Too much on my mind. Tomorrow was Monday, and the moment Stacy got back on the ferry, I had to get back on my computer and write the damn book that I couldn't write.

It was two in the morning when I stopped trying to sleep and got up. I switched on my laptop, thinking I might even write something, but ended up standing in the kitchen staring at the bench while the kettle boiled. Made tea. Stacy, roused by the sounds of my soft clattering, came out.

"What's up?" she said.

"Can't sleep. You want tea?"

She hoisted herself up on the kitchen bench. "Yeah, thanks. You want to talk? Is this about Joe and all the babies you can't give him?" She smiled, expecting me to laugh along with her I suppose. But I was tired and overwrought and my breath began to hitch.

"Oh no, Nina. I'm sorry," she said, reaching for my hand.

"It's not that," I said, forcing a deep breath. "It's the book. The book I can't write. I'm going backwards. I'm going to fail."

"No you're not."

"I promise you, I am. I can't do this. I'll have to pay back my advances: publishers in twenty-three countries have given me advances, and some of them were enormous. I have a mortgage on my Sydney apartment. I'll have to move. I'll have to find another job. I'll have to face my mother, who always knew I'd screw it up eventually."

Stacy waited for her mug of tea, waited for me to sit on the opposite bench, and said, "And if all that happens?"

"It would be awful," I snapped. "It would be the end of everything."

Bless her, she let me snap at her and kept her voice gentle. "No. It would be the end of something, absolutely. But you'd still have so much. You're young, you're healthy, you have friends." She smiled. "You'd still have me anyway. And you'd still have this place: you own it outright. So what if your mother and your publishers and whoever else is disappointed in you? If they abandon you, they weren't worth having."

I frowned. I could see how what she said made some kind of sense, but it didn't bring me any comfort. Stacy didn't have to live my life. I was stuck here in my head with me, and not a single other soul in the world knew what I had done and maybe it would never come out, but I'd still know.

"I've known you for ages, Nina," Stacy continued. "You were always way too critical of yourself. You don't need to be. I think you're great."

"Thanks, Stace," I said, cupping my cool hands around the warm mug. "I'm sorry if I woke you."

"That's okay." She slid down off the bench and tipped her tea in the sink. "Sorry, too many sugars."

"Don't you have two?"

"One."

"Oh, that's right."

"Lack of sleep interferes with your judgment. So don't go getting too depressed. You'll feel better in the morning."

"It is the morning."

"You know what I mean. Good night."

I watched her go, heard her door close quietly. I drank my tea, sitting on the bench, turning her words over in my mind. Then I put my cup in the sink and went down to the living room, where Joe had now removed all the plasterboard. With the torch in my hand, I carefully ran the beam over the mortar. I knew if I found anything, it would just be Eleanor's diary. Still, desperation drove me to keep looking, fantasizing about that moment that my hand would close over the papers that would make everything all right.

•

Monday morning I saw Stacy off, then returned to my office determined—*determined*—to make today different from all the other days. I could hear Joe working at the far end of the house, pulling off plasterboard and throwing it on the pile out the window. I wanted to go down there and sit and watch him. Watch his muscles moving under his sun-kissed skin, breathe in that warm, earthy scent he had. The magic of the weekend would come back; the expectations of the world beyond the island would recede again. But I had obligations, long-overdue obligations, and being near Joe was starting to feel dangerous.

I was desperate enough to try any strategy to get going, so I put aside the new book. It was a complete mess, anyway. In my fear and self-doubt, I'd cut out a huge section of it, and that now seemed like a bad idea. Instead, I opened a copy of the first

Widow Wayland book, and I started typing it out. From the first line. All over again.

I didn't really know what I was hoping to achieve, but I thought that maybe I could trick my brain somehow. If I went through the motions of putting these words on the page, the way I had five years ago when I'd started out, it might awaken a mechanism in me: switch on whatever piece of machinery I needed to write another one.

The best part about this new plan was that it had me sitting at my desk, working in flow, doing *something*. Time flew. When Joe poked his head in and said, "I've got enough of Mum's leftover cottage pie for both of us," I realized I'd worked for three hours straight.

I smiled up at him. "I have had a great morning."

"That's great," he said.

"And I'd love to share your mum's cottage pie."

"It's heating up now," he said.

"I'll be out in a few minutes."

He withdrew and I sat there staring at the words on the screen in front of me. I actually had a sense of accomplishment, even though nothing had been accomplished. Now I was full of confidence, I could go back to the new book that afternoon and get some words down. I knew it. Sort of.

No, dammit, I knew it. I opened up the file of the new book, and I cursored to the front page and I boldly typed in a title: *The Unquiet Field*. Then I cursored to the bottom. I had stopped in midsentence. Gripped with the same bold feeling, I completed it. Hit the full-stop key with a flourish.

Hard return. New paragraph. *Eleanor ran, faster than she had ever run.* Resisting and resisting the feeling that this was a bad sentence. *She sought shelter in the . . .* what was the word for the entrance to a church? And shouldn't I make some kind of witty or philosophical reflection on the role of the church to shelter souls? If only I knew more about the Middle Ages. If only I was more widely read, smarter, more creative. I took a deep breath, forced myself to stop the spiral. *She sought shelter in the {foyer: check this later} of the church, and watched the rain team down.* No, that wasn't right. . . . *teem down.* I sat back. That didn't sound right somehow. Nothing I did sounded right.

"It's ready." This was Joe, in a quiet voice, from the door. "I can put yours in the oven to stay warm if you're working."

I thrust back my chair. "No, I'm coming."

We took our plates out to the verandah table. I sat across from him but my eyes were drawn off into the distance to the restless sea. We ate in silence for a while, then Joe said lightly, "What happened?"

"What do you mean?"

"I mean, when I first came to see you, you were happy and smiling. Then when I came back . . ."

"Oh. Yes. I guess I wasn't as happy with my work as I'd thought. On reflection." I noticed his hair was full of white plaster dust, and resisted the urge to reach across and brush it out with my fingers.

"I suppose that's life for an artist? Sometimes it flows and sometimes it gets all stopped up. And then you drink whiskey." He flashed his warm, sexy smile.

I diverted my gaze to my lunch. "I guess so. I never feel much like an artist."

"No? Not after all those books?"

"There are only three."

"Three more than most people." He finished his meal and pushed away his plate, then said, "And your boyfriend, the poet? Does he get writer's block too?"

I sighed, put down my spoon. "I never saw Cameron with writer's block, no. But I need to be honest with you. He's not my boyfriend anymore."

Joe tipped his head curiously, waited for me to finish.

"Your parents were . . ."

"I know. Overbearing and pushy."

"I should have told you all the truth." I jabbed a finger in his direction. "But I'd like to remind you that it was you who started the lies, telling them I was a journalist."

He chuckled softly. "Yeah. Blame me."

We ate in silence a few more moments, then he said, "So, does that mean you're single?"

"It does. But I'm not . . . it ended badly. I need a lot more time. I . . ."

"Of course . . ."

"It's not that I don't . . ."

"Yes, I understand."

We couldn't look at each other, made awkward by the half-finished overlapping sentences we had spoken. I felt sad, but relieved.

Joe picked up his plate and stood. "I might go . . . um . . ."

"Leave your plate. I'll clean up."

"Thanks."

I watched him go, a pang in my heart, but knowing it was for the best.

•

Mail arrived in a big chunk twice a week. Bills forwarded from my home address, royalty statements from Marla, and the usual helping of junk mail anyone receives. I always opened it immediately. If I let it sit on my desk, wrapped in a rubber band,

I wouldn't be able to work. Today, in amongst the business mail, I had a pretty card from Stacy. Folded neatly inside was the original correspondence about Elizabeth Parrish's attempt to access my papers and a copy of Stacy's refusal letter. I put them aside and pinned the card where I could see it, and got back to work.

It was only after dinner that I came back to the journalist's letter. I intended to glance at it and then throw it away, but once I unfolded it, something caught my eye.

. . . access to the papers of Nina Jones and Eleanor Holt . . .

I went back to the start of the letter and read it carefully. Stacy hadn't mentioned that detail, because she didn't realize how significant it was. Elizabeth Parrish had put in a request to see not only my papers, but my great-grandmother's.

A chill walked up my spine. My worst suspicions were confirmed. Elizabeth Parrish and I were looking for the same thing.

And if she got to it first, I was ruined.

THIRTEEN

Another Island

1891

Tilly sat on the wooden bench inside the dusty church hall, her hands clasped in her lap and her heels lined up neatly. In the last several weeks she had made a study of physical and mental self-control. On and off boats and trains, looking for a place to settle and start a new life. Somewhere warm, because the chill of regret never went away and her bones were aching from it. Mrs. Fraser's women's boardinghouse on the bayside of Brisbane had provided a comfortable if modest new home. Mrs. Fraser herself was solicitous, a little nosy, but had a big hearty laugh and provided a solid meal every night.

Tilly knew her money wouldn't last forever, which is why she had applied for this position. It wasn't the first position she'd applied for. She had been offered a job as a lady's maid at a prosperous cattle station in the west, but decided on the day before she was due to leave that neither the hot dust nor the servility would suit her. It happened that on that day, she saw the little advertisement in the *Courier*: a governess was required for a twelve-year-old girl, and French and embroidery were a must.

She could be a governess; she knew it. She was clever, she liked children, and it meant she wouldn't be a servant.

Now she sat, soberly dressed in a black wool skirt and navy walking jacket, her hands sweating in her brown suede gloves, watching as one by one the other applicants were called. Tilly began to be convinced she could not secure this position. The other women were older, with stern faces and bristling résumés. Tilly had nothing but the letter she had been sent, confirming the place and time for the interview. She pulled it out of her pocket and unfolded it. Sterling Holt, Superintendent, Ember Island Government Facility, Moreton Bay.

Sterling Holt had thus far been a disembodied voice on the other side of a door at the end of the church hall. One by one, the other applicants went through that threshold and returned again, their faces unreadable, and let themselves out of the hall and into the bright daylight. Until only Tilly was left.

"Chantelle Lejeune," came the call from the end of the hall.

Tilly stood. She had become used to being known as Chantelle Lejeune, yet every time she heard the name said aloud, she felt the deep stirrings of guilt. Perhaps it was an appropriate punishment that, in order to escape what she'd done, she had to spend the rest of her life being reminded regularly of the woman whose death she had caused.

She entered the little room at the end of the hall and closed the door softly behind her, turning to catch her first glimpse of Sterling Holt. He was backlit by a small window, a man with a tall, proud back, dark brown curling hair parted on the side, and thick sideburns. He smiled up at her, taking her off guard. There was a kindness about his eyes she hadn't expected from his gruff voice.

"Good morning, Mademoiselle Lejeune," he said.

She pulled off her gloves and laid her hands in her lap. Her wedding ring now lay at the bottom of the ocean. "Good morning, sir," she said.

His eyebrows shot up. "You're not French? I had assumed, with that name . . ."

"My father was French but I barely knew him. I was such a little thing when he died. I grew up in Dorset with my mother's family." The lie came easily; she had rehearsed it in the mirror enough times.

"But you speak French?"

"Oh yes, sir, fluently."

A weary expression crossed his brow. Perhaps he had been subject to a number of false claims of French fluency today, because he then asked her, in French, who her favorite French writer was.

She answered, in French, "Victor Hugo, sir. I often read his books to my grandfather when he was ill and preparing to die. I will treasure those memories forever."

Sterling Holt hid a smile. "*Très bon,*" he said. "Now, Latin and Greek?"

"Both, sir."

"Will I need to test you on those too?"

"You may do as you please, sir. I do not fear any test of reading either."

He leaned back in his chair, steepled his fingers. "No, I trust you." He tilted his head to one side, considering her. "You have no references."

"I have never taught before and I was completely honest with you in that regard in my application letter. But I do love children and I do love learning. And I have a fair hand for embroidery. I would not let you down, sir."

"My daughter is . . . precocious."

"You must be proud."

"I want to let her grow. I do not want to crush her. Some of these other women . . . You do not strike me as a disciplinarian."

"I would be a friend to your daughter. A firm friend."

"Still . . . your lack of experience . . ." He trailed off, looking at the papers in front of him. "I have very qualified applicants here."

Tilly forced herself not to feel the full weight of despair. She was done with the high peaks and low troughs of her past. "As you see fit, sir."

"Tell me something, do you know anything at all about medieval history or literature?"

"Certainly, sir, I've read Chaucer, Malory, some of the French Arthurian romances . . ."

"But do you love them?"

Tilly was taken aback by the question. "Love them?"

"Nell, my daughter, is quite obsessed with the period."

Tilly smiled. "She sounds fascinating. Yes, I love them. I love many books, but I do have a soft space in my heart for *Sir Gawain and the Green Knight*."

Tilly suspected she had said precisely the right thing because Sterling was now smiling at her openly, nodding. He stood and leaned across his desk to extend his hand. "Mademoiselle Lejeune, I am pleased to offer you this position."

Tilly, too surprised to remember to stand up, took his hand. Relief flooded through her. "Really?"

"I think you and Nell will get along beautifully. I will be in touch by letter with details of the passage across to the island."

She stood, feeling light. "Thank you, thank you, sir. I will not let you down."

"I don't expect you will. Now, I don't know if the letter made it clear, but I am the superintendent of a large government facility on the island. There are very strict rules about security, I would urge you to observe them all fully and carefully, and insist that Nell does the same."

"What kind of facility?" Tilly asked.

"It's a high-security prison," he replied, and his casual response was so out of balance with the cold chill it elicited in her that she almost gasped. She had been thinking of a hospital or a manufacturing plant or . . . anything but a prison.

Even though she tried to hide her dread, he must have perceived her discomfort because he said, "Will that suit you?"

"I . . . are there . . . murderers?"

"Yes, of course. But you will be perfectly safe. The prisoners are under lock and key and we run a very tight ship. I wouldn't have Nell on the island with me if I thought there was even the slightest chance of danger to her."

Tilly nodded. "Thank you for your reassurance. I gratefully accept your offer and I look forward to your letter."

Only out in the bright street, with the sea breeze streaming over her, she allowed herself a moment of horrified guilt. For Sterling Holt didn't understand that it wasn't the idea of prisoners escaping that bothered her; it was the idea that somehow she would end up in a prison herself. After all, she wasn't so different from them.

•

Approaching Ember Island on the steamer was similar to her arrival on Guernsey, before all the horror had started. There was a bay, a boat, a trunk, and a heart full of misgivings. But in many ways it was also very different. Rather than gray skies and rain, today was bright and sunny. Indeed, she hadn't seen a dull day since she'd arrived in Australia eight days ago. The colors of everything were different, brighter, reflecting back light until her eyes ached. She stood at the front of the upper deck, with her parasol up, and watched as the island drew closer. It was surrounded by bushy green trees that seemed to live right in the salt water. She could see an escarpment on the island, more trees, the peak of a roof.

A well-dressed, elderly man joined her, gripping the railing in front of him as they bobbed over a wave. "Ember Island," he said.

"Yes," she replied. "That's where I'm stopping. You?"

"I'm the visiting surgeon on all of these islands. Dr. Groom."

"I am most pleased to meet you," she said, extending her hand. "I am Chantelle Lejeune, the new governess for the superintendent's daughter."

"Nell?" His mouth turned down in a frown. "Good luck."

"Superintendent Holt did warn me that she is precocious."

"Uncontrollable would be a better word."

Tilly decided to reserve judgment on Nell until they met. But she was starting to worry: what if the child pushed her so far that she lost her temper? She could never *ever* lose her temper again.

"Nevertheless," Dr. Groom continued, "I am not stopping on Ember Island today. I am traveling on to the leprosorium on another island."

"A leprosorium?"

"For lepers. To keep them apart from the community. Moreton Bay is where all the colony's outcasts finish their journeys, my dear."

The island was drawing closer now and she could clearly see the jetty, a crooked pin stretching out into the water. She could also see a tall chimney, puffing smoke, and numerous brick buildings. "Do you know why it's called Ember Island?" she asked him.

"They say that when Matthew Flinders came through here and discovered this area, he named all the islands Green Island. Green Island one, Green Island two, and so on . . . But this one was on fire at the time. A raging bushfire and he wrote in his diary that from a distance it looked like an ember glowing in the dark sea."

Fire. The thought of it made her stomach turn to ice.

Dr. Groom remained, asking her idle questions about her journey from England and how she had come to be a governess, and she had all her lies ready and they slid off her tongue as easily as the truth.

"Well, I'd best let you go and fetch your belongings," Dr. Groom said as the steamer pulled in at the jetty. "It's been a pleasure to meet you and I know I will see you again, Miss Lejeune. Or may I call you Chantelle?" he asked.

"Tilly," she said on impulse. It wasn't such a stretch, after all, to imagine Tilly was a short form of Chantelle. "Everyone calls me Tilly."

It took several minutes to bring the steamer to a complete stop. Men ran about on the jetty and on the deck, tying thick ropes to bollards and shouting instructions at each other. Tilly fetched her trunk from below the deck and then waited patiently for instruction. The air was warm and damp, and tiny nipping sandflies gathered on the exposed skin between her gloves and sleeves. She flicked them away idly. A purser came to help her with her trunk and she followed him down the gangway and onto the jetty.

"What's that?" she said to the purser, pointing to what looked like a fenced square in the water. Thick metal poles protruded above the waves.

"That is the warders' swimming pool, ma'am," the purser said, over his shoulder. He walked very fast and she had to hurry to keep up with him.

"Why do they need a swimming pool?" she asked. "Can't they swim in the sea?"

"No, ma'am. There are too many sharks."

Sharks. The thought filled her with dread. All those teeth. "Are there many sharks?"

"Oh, yes, the island's surrounded by them. The blood and unwanted offal from the slaughterhouse all gets thrown in the water to encourage them." He gave a cruel chuckle over his shoulder. "Discourages escapees."

Tilly marveled that a place could at once be so beautiful—sunshine and blue skies and shady trees—and so hostile. Saltwater forests and murderers and bushrangers and sharks and even the sandflies, who had left red welts on her wrists. It struck her very plainly that she would have to develop a hardness she didn't already have. Or else she would be on the receiving end of many cruel chuckles.

Sterling Holt was waiting for her at the end of the jetty, with a horse and an open carriage ready. The purser loaded up her trunk as Sterling greeted her.

"Miss Lejeune."

"Superintendent Holt. You should probably call me Tilly."

"Very well, Tilly." He didn't offer his first name to her and she found herself a little disappointed. He simply nodded once, then offered her his arm so she could climb up into the carriage, then climbed in beside her and urged the horse forward.

"I trust you had a comfortable journey over," he said.

"Yes, thank you. I met Dr. Groom."

"What luck. He's a good ally to have."

She didn't tell him the doctor had described his daughter as uncontrollable.

The carriage left the paved run-up to the jetty and began to rattle over uneven ground. He raised his voice a little to be heard over the wheels. "Let me point out a few of the buildings on the island. We are not simply a prison: we are a set of thriving businesses." He lifted his right hand momentarily, then brought it back to the reins. "There's the lime kiln; you would have seen that chimney from the boat. The large building to the west of it is the sugar mill. Coming up here on your right are the workshops. We keep our prisoners very busy: bootmaking, tailoring, tinsmithing, even bookbinding."

Many people were moving around between the buildings, but she couldn't immediately distinguish between warders and prisoners. Then she realized that the men in blue uniforms were well kept, stood up taller. The men in white overalls were rather more stooped, tired, unwashed.

"How many prisoners do you have here?" Tilly asked.

"Two hundred and forty-six men and eight women. The female prisoners have their own cell at the southern end of the stockade. There's the bakery and, over there, is the smith." He kept pointing out buildings, but Tilly couldn't get the idea of those eight women out of her mind. She wanted to ask him what each one had done.

"And that building over there is the stockade. That's where the prisoners eat, sleep, and live their lives when they aren't working. There is no need for you to go there."

"Understood."

"Now," he said, as they clattered up the road, "it's time for you to meet Nell."

As they drew up towards the escarpment, Tilly looked back and could see the wide fields of sugarcane, the cattle dotted about, and beyond that the great gray-green sea that separated them from the mainland, which was a hazy blue blur in the distance.

They crested the hill and the road flattened out. She could see the house now, a sprawling brick and wood dwelling surrounded by wide wooden verandahs and, in front of it, a magnificent flowering garden.

"The garden!" she gasped. Since arriving in Australia she had seen only straggling bush and the occasional brave front garden with parched roses and impatiens. But this was a true English garden with wide stretches of lawn bordered by low hedges and colored flowers, a stone sundial, and a beautiful white statue of a Grecian woman with an urn on her shoulder.

"Yes, it's quite something, isn't it?" he said.

Roses and violets and petunias and peonies, daisies and lavender and columbine and crocuses, shaped boxwood and flowering dogwood, and borders of purple and pink hydrangea. Glorious colors and smells in profusion. Tilly found herself laughing. "And this is your garden?"

"I don't spend much time in it. I'm mostly in my office." He pulled the horse to a halt, his face turned away to the garden. "But Nell likes it out here."

"Is there any chance that . . . I could do some gardening? I have always loved it. It soothes me."

He turned back, a little frown on his lips. "Hm. Well, let me think about that. You see, one of the prisoners tends this garden. She's very good and it keeps her busy and that is good for her."

"A prisoner? In the garden?"

"You're not to worry. She won't offend again and we know that. But while she is here serving her time, I'd like her to make the best of her situation and she's out there most days, being busy and productive. That's the best thing for prisoners like her." He climbed down and came around to help Tilly.

"How do you know she won't . . . offend again?" Tilly asked cautiously as she stepped down from the carriage.

But Sterling didn't answer her properly. He just said again, "You're not to worry," and she sensed that these things weren't for her to know. It was likely that, in his eyes, Tilly was part of the inside world of the household, working not for him but for his daughter. Why would he talk to her about the affairs of men?

"I'll send somebody to fetch your trunk," he said, gesturing to the front stairs. "Let's introduce you to Nell."

Then they were inside. The position of the house up high, the dark brick, and the many large open windows and wooden verandahs, meant that it was cool inside. The floorboards were bare except for rugs and runners. The walls were hung with paintings and brass sconces with candles in them. Sterling indicated a long, padded bench under the front window in the entrance hall and told her to wait. Tilly sat down, pulled off her gloves, and waited while he moved further into the house.

Then Tilly heard her. A girl's voice, but deeper than expected. She said, "But I am occupied at the moment," with defiant force.

Sterling's voice, too quiet to hear any words, but stern and forceful.

Tilly braced herself. Nell didn't want to meet her. Nell didn't want her here at all, by the sounds of it.

Sterling emerged, the girl behind him. She was tiny, slender, with white skin and her father's clear blue eyes. A mop of unruly brown curls and a mouth turned almost upside down with disapproval.

Tilly stood. She decided that it was important not to offer the first smile. If Nell wasn't friendly, then Tilly wouldn't force it.

"Miss Lejeune, this is my daughter, Eleanor. I call her Nell."

"You may not call me Nell," Nell said to Tilly.

"Be respectful, Nell," Sterling cautioned.

"I'm pleased to meet you, Eleanor," Tilly said.

"Why are you Miss Lejeune and not Mademoiselle Lejeune? Why do you have an English accent? I thought you would be French."

"Enough!" Sterling snapped. "Nell, Miss Lejeune is your governess and you will treat her with the respect that is due to her. Now. I have spent long enough away from my desk. Nell, I would like you to show Miss Lejeune around the rest of the house and, in particular, show her to her own room and bathroom. Miss Lejeune, you will ordinarily eat with Nell and me. You have missed lunch, but supper is at six. I won't be joining you this evening as I have a meeting, I do apologize."

"Of course, sir."

"If you are hungry in the meantime, see if you can find the cook or the housekeeper. Try the kitchen, the laundry, or anywhere in the east wing. We don't stand on ceremony here. We are a long way from society, so we don't have a bell to ring for tea or any such method. If you need something, find somebody to help you. My office is through there. I'm best left undisturbed." With that, he gave Nell another cautionary glare, and went off through the door to his office. It closed quietly behind him, leaving Tilly alone with Nell.

They looked at each other. Neither of them smiled. Seconds ticked past. But then Tilly began to see the ridiculous side of the situation. Both of them trying so hard not to be the first to make any kind of concession to politeness and warmth. Here she was, a grown woman, competing with a child. Laughter became trapped behind her lips and it became increasingly hard to hold back her smile. Nell caught it and she, too, struggled to contain her laughter.

So Tilly let it go. She tilted back her head and laughed out loud, and Nell did the same. Then Nell reached for Tilly's hand and said, "Come, let me show you the house."

"Thank you, Eleanor," Tilly replied, taking her hand.

"Nell."

"Tilly."

Hand in hand they moved down the hallway. "Just remember this: the wing to the west is the wing that is best. That's where my room, Papa's room, and your room will be. And the library too, of course, which is where Papa wants our lessons to be. Papa has his own bathroom, but you will share with me. The east wing is where the servants are, where things are stored, and where the kitchen and laundry and lamp room are. I'll fetch you at suppertime to show you the dining room, but it's next to Papa's office. He finishes work at six." Nell opened the door to a small room with books on every wall, a huge gleaming table set up in the middle. "My classroom." She dived onto a wooden cat, about the size of her two fists and painted white, that sat on the desk next to her papers. "And this is Pangur Ban. I've had him since I was four."

"He's very handsome."

"He comes everywhere with me. He watches me when I write."

Tilly glanced around. "Your father has a lot of books."

"Papa is not much interested in books. He likes facts and figures much better. These are all mine. I don't ask for toys. Pangur is all I need. I ask for books." She approached one of the shelves and ran her fingers lovingly over the spines. "What is your favorite book?" she asked.

"I love many books. Your father told me you are partial to Arthurian romance. Is that so?"

"I'm mad for it. Anything from the medieval period."

"I'm very fond of *Sir Gawain and the Green Knight,*" Tilly said, remembering that it was this admission that secured her the job.

Nell turned and squealed. "Oh! It's my favorite! You know, when I was eight or nine, I used to wear a green sash all the time, and pretended it was Gawain's baldric."

"I'm surprised you could read and understand the poem at that age."

"I read before I was three," she said proudly. "I have a good brain and a fair hand and I love to write my own stories. Look." Nell placed Pangur Ban carefully on the desk and picked up a sheaf of papers. "I'm writing an epic poem in the style of *Beowulf* at the moment. There are many monsters." She began to read: "*The creature's jaw dripped vile gobbets of blood and gore; and the hero shuddered all the way into his soul with mortal horror.*"

"That's very . . . colorful," Tilly said.

"I'm very proud of this one. What I am terrible at is embroidery."

"I can help you with that," Tilly said. "And perhaps you can introduce me to a few medieval stories that I don't know."

"Have you read *The Canterbury Tales*?" she asked, with a sly tilt of her head.

"Yes, of course."

Her eyes widened. "Don't ever tell Papa that there are rude ones. He'd take the book away."

"I shan't." Tilly thought about the copy of *The Canterbury Tales* in the library back at Lumière sur la Mer. Ashes now.

"What is it?" Nell asked.

Tilly shook her head, confused. "I don't know what you mean."

"An expression crossed your face. Like a goose had walked over your grave."

Tilly told herself to guard her expression more carefully around the girl: she was very sharp. "I was thinking about the library in a house I once lived. A house on an island, but very different from this one. All the books got burned."

Nell recoiled. "Books all burned? That's utterly tragic. Whose was the house?"

She had said too much. "It was a long time ago. Somebody I knew. The house was called Lumière sur la Mer."

"The light on the sea? That's lovely. We should give this house a similar name. Light on the sea, stars on the water, something like that. What do you think?"

"Stars on the water is nice."

"Come, I'll show you your room. You are probably tired and in need of a rest."

Nell, who had now warmed up considerably, led Tilly down the western corridor and opened up the door to a small but cozy room, with blue flocked wallpaper and a big oak canopied bed. Tilly went to the window and drew the curtain. It looked directly over the garden.

"This is lovely," Tilly said. Through the hedges, she could make out the figure of a woman, all dressed in white. She wondered if this was the female prisoner Sterling had spoken of.

"The bathroom is next door," Nell said, "between your room and mine. I'll leave you be now and come fetch you for supper."

"Thank you, Nell."

Nell left, then a second later was back, before Tilly had had a chance to sit on her bed and ease off her shoes.

"Tilly?"

"Yes?"

"I hope we may be friends."

Tilly smiled. "I'm sure we will be."

•

Tilly often dreamed of fire. Surging fire, running from it, ashes swirling all around her. Nothing more clear or specific than that. This night, her first night on Ember Island, she woke from the dream to the crack of thunder.

It was late. Very late. She had left her window open an inch for the sea breeze—she didn't think she'd ever get used to the sticky nighttime warmth here—and now a cold wet wind was whistling through it. She rose, drew the curtain, and closed the window. She could feel with her toes that there was water on the floor and hoped nobody would find out she had let the rain in on her first night here. Tilly lit a candle and bent down to mop up the water with the dress she had worn that day, then hung the dress on the back of her chair and extinguished the candle. She stood at the closed window, watching the storm. The rain sheeted down with a power and intensity she had never seen. The garden heaved under the weight of the water.

What had the gardening prisoner done? Did she deserve to be locked up in a miserable prison on an island where, as Dr. Groom had said, all the colony's outcasts finished their journeys? Did she deserve it any more than Tilly might, if people knew what she had done?

I got angry and set a house on fire, then I locked my husband and his lover in.

No, that wasn't the whole truth. That was the version of events she tortured herself with on nights as black as these. Yes, she had been angry. A fire had started accidentally. She had locked her husband in a room that was easy to escape from, to give her enough time to run because she feared for her own safety. She had no idea the house would go up, she had no idea that his lover was upstairs. She could not possibly have foreseen the consequences of her actions.

But it didn't matter how many times she had reassured herself, the black feeling hung about her and wouldn't go away.

FOURTEEN

An English Garden

Nell was terrifyingly precocious. Tilly struggled against the feeling that she could not teach the girl anything she didn't already know. The first Latin and Greek exercises Tilly set for her had induced in Nell fits of laughter.

"But, Tilly," she said, pink cheeks shining. "That's far too *easy*."

She had settled when Tilly suggested she do a double translation of parts of Bede's Latin *Ecclesiastical History* and was now quietly working away, her pen clinking on the lip of the ink bottle then scratching at her paper. Nell insisted upon not using a slate and pencil. She loved pen and ink, had developed a tiny, flowery script all her own; and apparently her father indulged her by giving her paper from his own office. A warm sunbeam came in through the tall window, between the heavy drapes, and illuminated their papers and books. Tilly supervised while idly unpicking Nell's stitching from that morning. The problem was Nell didn't have the patience for sewing. She raced ahead, keen for it to be over so she could galvanize her brain again. Tilly couldn't blame her. The girl was clearly formed for more important things than cross-stitch.

"Finished the first one!" Nell declared.

Tilly looked over her work, realizing she was anxious. She needed to find at least one error to prove to the girl that she was worthy of being a teacher and not just a fixer of poor cross-stitch. "Very good," she said, slowly. "But you've mixed up your cases here. Ablative?"

"Ah, yes. You're right." She smiled slowly. "I'm working too fast to try to impress you."

"Impress me? Or intimidate me?"

Nell laughed. "I think the former. Though I have done quite a lot of the latter with past teachers, I must admit."

Tilly hid her smile. "Now translate it back into Latin. Without looking at the original."

"Right." Nell put her head down, flicking through her dictionary and grammar guide. The little wooden cat watched over her.

Tilly read over her shoulder. She had chosen the famous remarks about man's life on earth, likening it to a sparrow flying through a hall on a wintry night: *what follows it or what comes before, we have no way of knowing.* The warmth of the room ebbed away on reading the line. Where was Jasper now? Was he in heaven? Or somewhere else? Was he aware of what had happened to him? Would he hate her for what she had done?

A soft knock at the door made them both look up.

"Papa, my new governess has set me the most difficult task," Nell said with an excited smile.

"Is that so?"

"She is performing it alarmingly well," Tilly added.

"I mixed up my cases," Nell said, and again, she sounded thrilled. Not frustrated or ashamed.

"Then you need to slow down and take more care," Sterling

said. He turned his eyes to Tilly. "I'm pleased that she's enjoying working with you."

"So am I."

He folded his hands behind his back. "I have considered your request from yesterday and decided the answer is yes."

Tilly was baffled. "My request?"

"Yes. About the garden. I'm going to have 135 clear you a spot and you may do what you like with it."

"One-three-five is the prisoner's number," Nell said, sensing Tilly's confusion. "We don't call them by their names."

"I see. And will I have to . . . work with 135?"

"She is perfectly safe and approachable and will show you where everything is. But you need not talk with her or have anything but the barest interaction with her. Prisoner 135 works the garden because she loves it, she's very good at it—we won a government award for our gardens—and her conduct here has been beyond reproach. Prisoners often earn the better jobs around the island for good conduct. The uncontrollable ones end up chained together in the cane fields."

"And does 135 have a real name that I could use when I speak to her?" Tilly asked.

He frowned. "I'd have to look that up, but I'd certainly discourage you from becoming friendly with her, no matter how well behaved she is."

"Prisoners are prisoners for a reason," Nell said, with all the conviction of somebody who had been drilled her whole life to repeat a phrase.

"Yes. Well." Sterling cleared his throat. "In any case, Miss Lejeune . . . Tilly. In any case, I'd be happy for you to spend some of your free time in the garden. I want you to be happy here." He shifted his gaze. "Nell's education means a great deal to me."

"Thank you, Superintendent Holt," Tilly said.

As soon as he left, Nell leaned across to Tilly and said, "Hettie Maythorpe. That is 135's real name."

"How do you know?"

"I see her nearly every day. I was curious. I had a look in Papa's registry. Don't you dare tell him."

Tilly trod cautiously. "It is very improper for you to look at your father's paperwork, Nell. Now back to work."

Nell reddened, chastened, and put her head down to continue working. Secretly Tilly was dying to ask if Nell knew what Hettie had done. She rose and went to the window. The sun was warm on her face and dazzled on the cane fields. She thought about men, chained together out there.

"Finished!" Nell declared.

Tilly turned. "How much sugarcane is on Ember Island?" she asked.

"Forty-five acres of it. You're thinking about what Papa said, aren't you? About the chain gangs? They have to chain them up. The cane gets so high in autumn that escapees could hide in it."

"Has anyone ever escaped?"

Nell shook her head. "Fourteen prisoners have tried. Eight were recovered, six died." She held up her translation. "Are you going to check this?"

Tilly brought her mind back to the present. "Of course," she said. She returned to the desk and reached out to take the paper.

Nell grasped her wrist. "You really mustn't feel sorry for them. Papa is a good superintendent. He is very humane. But we must remember that they are here to be punished and that is good for them and for their souls and for the communities left behind."

"Thank you, Nell. I have much to learn about living in a place like this."

"I've been here since I was three. I know no other life. You can always ask me." Nell gave her a dazzling smile. "I bet you find no errors in that translation."

Nell bet right. Tilly then set her the task of resewing the bad embroidery, with a metronome timing her stitches so she couldn't rush. It ticked on in the dusty library while Tilly sat on a chair pulled up to the window, a book open but unread in her lap. Her mind was out there, in the cane fields, with the prisoners chained, one to another, for their sins. She had chains for her sins too, attaching her forever to things she couldn't run from and no golden plants high enough to hide behind.

•

While Tilly was already growing fond of Nell, her company was exhausting. Her mind ranged from one thing to another with lightning speed; she had an opinion about everything and was certain Tilly wanted to hear it; and she liked to be physically very close, which Tillly found cloying in the sticky humidity. Returning to her company at suppertime after a short break meant Tilly had to hide a sigh of exhaustion. The previous night, her first night, Nell had talked to her as insistently as a steam train for the entire meal. But tonight was different because Sterling had joined them.

"Good evening, Tilly," he said. He had taken off his jacket and was in a white cotton shirt and vest. His sleeves were rolled casually up towards his elbows, revealing a pair of surprisingly strong forearms. Tilly felt the first flush hit her cheeks and had to look away.

"Good evening, Superintendent Holt," Tilly said, sitting down next to Nell.

Nell immediately moved her chair closer. "What are we doing in lessons tomorrow?" she asked.

"Tilly isn't working now," Sterling said gruffly. "Give her a chance to breathe, Nell."

Nell dropped her head and Tilly felt sorry for her, so she rubbed her arm lightly. "I'm sure we'll have a lovely day no matter what we do."

An awkward silence descended. The maid brought out a small roll of roasted pork, bowls of potatoes and peas, and a gravy boat. Sterling stood to carve the meat and they passed the plates around in silence, helping themselves. Then Sterling cleared his throat and said, "Tilly, I wonder if you would join me in the parlor after our meal so I may speak with you alone?" His face was very serious.

"Of course," Tilly said, cursing the guilty ticking of her heart in her throat. She had no reason to assume he wanted to speak to her about her past or that she had somehow offered him some offense that needed pointing out.

Nell pouted. "Why can't I join you?"

"Because you are a child, Nell," he answered, without elaboration.

Nell knew when she was defeated. She ate in sulky silence. The quiet was broken only by the tick of the clock and the clank of their cutlery against their plates.

When they were finished, Sterling urged Nell to go fetch the maid to clear up, then head off to her room to read before bed.

"You will come with me?" Sterling asked, setting down his napkin and pushing his chair back.

"Yes. Please lead the way."

Evening was closing in now, and she followed Sterling into the parlor by the light of a lantern. He lit the other candles in the room and went to the liquor cabinet beside the piano. The floor-boards were partly covered by a thick rug with an intricate Indian design on it. She had the urge to slip off her shoes and sink her bare toes into the pile.

"Please sit," he said. "Can I offer you a drink? Brandy?"

She shuddered. The smell or taste of it would bring back too many dark memories. "No, I . . ."

"Sherry?"

"Yes. That would be lovely."

He set out two small crystal glasses and pulled the stopper from a bottle of sherry, speaking the whole time. "I hope you don't mind me taking you aside, but I need to be able to speak to you freely about Nell."

"I'm happy to do as you wish," she said.

He handed her a glass. "Before I start I need to reassure myself that Nell isn't listening in." He cocked his head and, sure enough, Tilly heard footsteps retreating. He shook his head regretfully, clinking his glass against hers. "Nell is a terrible eavesdropper."

"She has a quick brain and gets bored easily."

"I know. And I am so glad that you know already. Her last teacher, one of the turnkeys' wives, never understood that about Nell. She thought the girl was simply trouble."

Tilly remembered that Dr. Groom had called Nell "uncontrollable." "Well, I like Nell very much."

"And she clearly likes you. I couldn't have wished for a better start for the two of you. But tonight I saw her cozy up to you and I . . . I needed to say something."

Realization dawned. Tilly felt embarrassed that she hadn't understood until now. She had already allowed Nell to be too familiar with her. "I understand," she said, "and I will absolutely keep my distance from now on if—"

"No, no," Sterling said, raising a long hand to stop her. "No, that's not it at all. Our capacity to love is what sets us apart from animals, Tilly. I am happy for Nell to grow to love you, which I am sure she will. You are everything she wants to be one day: clever and graceful."

Tilly willed herself not to blush.

"I simply wanted to say . . ." He paused, struggling for words. "Nell's mother died only a year ago. If she does come to love you, will you promise not to leave too soon? You are a young woman of many accomplishments and some perceive Ember Island to be an unpleasant environment, so isolated, so far from everything. Could you guarantee me a full year at least?"

So isolated, so far from everything. Exactly where Tilly needed to be. "I can absolutely guarantee you that, Superintendent."

He smiled at last and it transformed his face. She could imagine how he might have looked as a boy: with a hairless jaw and freckled nose. "Then you'd better start calling me Sterling," he said.

•

At four o'clock on Friday, when the heat was cooling off the island with the sea breeze and the lengthening shadows, Tilly finished Nell's lessons for the week and changed into a housedress for gardening. She was curious to see the small plot that Sterling had set aside for her and think about what she might do with it. He had told her that Prisoner 135 worked in the afternoons and evenings to avoid the worst of the sun, so Tilly set off down the front steps and into the sprawling garden to find her.

Tilly saw her kneeling at the foot of a row of hydrangeas, pulling weeds. She wore a plain white shirt and white skirt, that were stained with grass and mud. Black writing was printed across the back of her clothes. Tilly paused, watching her for a while, not sure how to approach.

Then the woman stood and turned, almost as though she had heard Tilly coming. She was older than Tilly by fifteen or twenty years. Her dark hair was streaked gray and tied back in an untidy bun; she was sturdy and florid, with dark eyes and heavy eyebrows. She considered Tilly without expression, offering neither welcoming smile nor hostile scowl.

Tilly said, "Hello . . ." She couldn't bring herself to call the woman 135, so she trailed off and waited.

"Are you Miss Lejeune?" the woman said.

"Yes."

"The superintendent said you might come. Let me show you the section of the garden that will be yours." She offered a small smile, and Tilly's shoulders relaxed.

She fell into step beside the prisoner. "Thank you. I would like that. I . . . Look, I know your name is Hettie. But I know I'm supposed to use your number . . ."

"Call me Hettie. Some of the turnkeys do. The chaplain always does."

"Good. Thank you, Hettie."

"The superintendent told me that you are a keen gardener."

"I find putting my hands in soil soothes me," Tilly responded, guardedly, not sure how much small talk was too much. Sterling had been very clear that she oughtn't befriend Hettie.

"I agree," she said, emphatically. "If I didn't have the garden . . . well, I would have sunk into despair by now I am certain."

Tilly said nothing, though she wanted to ask a million things. What did you do? Why are you here? When will you be allowed to go home?

Hettie led Tilly down a long row of rose beds to a back corner. "You'll have to clear it first. I can help."

The plot was ten feet by ten feet, covered in old garden rubbish and weeds. There was enough shade here from a spreading fig tree for her to work in the afternoons without fear of freckling. It was right at the edge of the escarpment, so she could catch the sea breeze and be distracted as often as she pleased by the view of fields and bay. Her heart leapt at the possibility that she might find some happiness here.

"I'm afraid I've used it as a dumping ground for all my cuttings. But we can put those over the other side of that line of bushes and nobody will see them, and this can be your own little corner of the gardens."

"Thank you so much," Tilly said.

"Don't thank me. Thank the superintendent."

Tilly looked back towards the house. From here she could only see the roof past the trees and hedges. It would be a place that she could get some distance from Nell, too, if she needed it. Like Hettie, the work in the garden might keep her from sinking into despair. "I'm grateful for your offer of help," Tilly said, "but I am keen to do this myself. Not to have to talk, just to think . . ."

"I understand," Hettie said with a smile. Her mouth was very small and her smile was little more than a turning up of the corners, but her eyes were kind. "But I am here if you need me. And I can work in silence if needs be." Hettie drifted off, disappearing back amongst the bushes. Tilly stood for a few moments, reflecting on the work that needed doing. She had guaranteed Sterling at least a year. She had plenty of time to clear and turn soil and plant and tend. She wandered back to the house in the afternoon cool, only to collide with Nell coming the other way.

"Oh, there you are!" exclaimed Nell. "I wondered where you'd got to."

"Your father has given me a plot in the garden."

"Can I see?"

"Follow me."

Nell chatted idly as they walked, then stopped to view the plot with a look of concern. "But that will be such a lot of work for you."

"I don't mind it. I'll enjoy it."

"I can help."

Tilly took a deep breath. She had been anticipating this. "Nell, you know when you are reading a truly wonderful book, how you like to imagine the world has gone away and it jars you terribly if somebody speaks to you or interrupts you?"

Nell looked back at her with big, sad eyes. "Oh. I see."

"I will be a better friend to you if I have time on my own at the end of every day."

Nell formed a resolved expression. "You are quite right. And I do need to devote much more time to my epic if I ever want to save Prince Claudio from the maw of the Firebeast."

"Absolutely. I cannot wait to see how he escapes."

"You can always ask 135 to help too," Nell said, then dropped her voice low. "You needn't be afraid of her, I know what—" The wind picked up then, rattling through the treetops and pulling strands of Tilly's hair loose. Nell looked up at the sky. "Another storm coming," she said.

Tilly didn't want to change the topic. "What were you going to say? I know what . . . ?"

Nell put her fingers to her lips. "Perhaps I oughtn't say. Will you be cross and tell Papa?"

Tilly shook her head, leaned in against Nell's ear. "I want to know."

Nell turned her head, met Tilly's eyes. "I know what they say about her. That she won't commit the same crime again. She can't commit the same crime again."

"Why? What did she do?"

Nell held her gaze, didn't blink. Then whispered, "She killed her husband."

FIFTEEN

Evening Conversation

Tilly closed the door of the little stone chapel behind her, shutting out the bright sun and humid heat. In the last two days, the fierceness of the subtropical summer had become apparent. Damp heat clung under her arms and between her breasts, perspiration beaded along her hairline, and she wanted more than anything else to strip down to her chemise and petticoat and sit very still somewhere cool. There hadn't even been the respite of an evening thunderstorm. She hadn't the slightest inclination to work in the garden: the very idea of doing hard physical work in these conditions made her ill. Instead, she had sewn two cotton nightgowns, thin and sleeveless, to wear as she melted into her bed at night. Then she lay, in and out of sleep, on top of the covers. Window open, fighting off the occasional buzzing mosquito that made its way under the net. Nell had reassured her that it wouldn't remain this hot forever; that all that they needed was a change from the southeast that would bring cool ocean air flowing over them. But in the meantime, she sweltered.

So the comparative cool of the chapel was welcome. She made her way down between the rows of wooden pews and slid into the front one. Trapped air and unfinished wood. One little window let in a beam of yellow sun. She bowed her head and clasped her hands and prayed, as she had every day since Nell had told her about Hettie's crime.

Forgive me, Father. Forgive me for what I did to my husband. I didn't know he would die. He wasn't without sin, but it was for you, not me, to decide his punishment. I am sorry. I am sorry. Forgive me.

She raised her head and looked at the icon of Jesus on his cross that hung on the wall behind the lectern. "Forgive me," she said aloud.

A cleared throat behind her made her turn sharply. She had always been alone in here before now, but this time a tall, plump man stood in the aisle, looking at her curiously. His hair was completely white, his skin was the exact color of undercooked pastry, and moist with a slick of perspiration.

"Hello," she said, climbing to her feet, pulse thudding guiltily at her throat. "I didn't know you were there."

"I just came in. You didn't hear me?"

She shook her head. She had been too immersed in the recriminations in her head.

He looked at her, his expression both cocksure and greedy as his eyes roamed from her hair to her waist and back to her face. "I didn't mean to alarm you. I'm the chaplain, Mr. Burton."

"I'm Miss Lejeune. Eleanor's governess."

A light of recognition went on in his eyes. "Ah. The governess. I had wondered when I would meet you." He strode down the aisle and extended his hand. She gave him hers and he lifted it gently to his mouth to kiss it. His lips were too wet, pressed against her fingers for too long. She straightened her shoulders so she wouldn't shudder. As soon as her hand was free, she clasped it against her other hand, safely behind her back.

"May I ask . . . ?"

"Just praying," she answered, hoping he wouldn't prod her further.

"I heard you say, 'Forgive me.'"

"Yes, I . . ." Tilly looked behind her at Jesus, whose eyes were still turned mournfully heavenwards. Had Jasper gone to heaven? Had he thought about heaven before he died, or had he fought, animal-like, until the last moment, against smoke and heat and terrible injuries from his fall through glass?

She turned her attention back to Mr. Burton, hoping her horror wasn't clear on her face. "I have rather a bad temper," she finished. "I got angry when I accidentally stepped on my hairbrush this morning and threw it so hard that I cracked my mirror. It was very childish. I'm praying to improve myself." Tilly cursed herself for the silly, thin fabrication. She certainly didn't want to be known as a thrower of hairbrushes.

If he could tell she was lying, he gave no indication. "It's a good idea to improve oneself. Especially if one is bad tempered. And slovenly enough to have left a hairbrush on the floor."

She bristled at him calling her slovenly, although that made no sense as she had just admitted it to him.

"You're welcome in the chapel at any time. To pray, to think, or to escape the heat." He smiled in a knowing way, that smug surety returning to his countenance. "I would always like to see you here."

Tilly felt uncomfortable and hot-faced, but not because of the weather. Was she imagining the glint in his eye, the obvious sexual interest?

"And will you be coming to the service on Sunday?"

"I expect I will come with Eleanor and her father," she replied.

He nodded, a half smile on his lips. "Good. Now I have matters to attend to, so if you'll forgive me . . ." He offered her his hand again.

Tilly thought about his wet lips, his hungry expression, and she folded her hands behind her back. "Good-bye," she said.

His hand waited, in awkward space for one second, two. Then, with lips so tight they went white, he withdrew it, nodded curtly, and left.

Tilly sank into the pew. She would have to be much more careful about hiding her guilty feelings, if she also wanted to hide what caused them.

•

Late on Saturday night the cool change did come through, as Nell predicted it. Tilly's window was open so she felt and heard it clearly. The clatter of palms growing louder, the rustle of leaves in the monstrous fig trees. Then the gust through the window, fresh and sweet. She rose and went to the window, leaned her upper body out as far as she could to catch the breeze, letting it dry the perspiration on her skin and bring out her bare arms in goose bumps.

A small noise caught her attention. She turned to see Sterling, shirtless and in long johns, walk out onto the verandah steps. Clearly he had woken with the cool change and come out to enjoy it too. Tilly was shocked into immobility at seeing him so undressed. The shape of his shoulder, his arm, the musculature of his back. She flushed warm again, then realized she needed to pull herself inside if she didn't want him to see her in a comparable state of undress.

She withdrew, dropped the sash. Lost control of the window in her haste so that it bounced shut loudly in its frame.

Tilly threw herself facedown on her bed, hiding hot-faced laughter in her soft cotton pillow slip.

•

The Sunday service in the chapel was attended by the prison staff. Prisoners had their service later in the day in the stockade, under lock and key. Tilly sat in the front row with Nell, who held her hand and chatted while the chapel filled up with turnkeys and clerks and storekeepers and trade supervisors. Sterling came in last and sat on the other side of Nell. Tilly hadn't seen him since last night out on the verandah, and she studiously avoided eye contact in case he guessed that she'd witnessed his moment of undress. He was buttoned into a shirt, trousers, and a single-breasted tweed jacket. A faint smell of soap reached her as he sat down. He had bathed this morning. The thought caught in her imagination and wouldn't let go. His skin, the warm water, the soap. She was so distracted that she didn't hear Nell ask her a question.

"What do you think, Tilly?" Nell prompted.

"I . . . I'm sorry, I wasn't listening."

"I said, this chapel used to be the schoolhouse, and I wondered if you would rather work in here over summer as it's quite cool. There's a good view from up on the roof when the whales come and you can only get up if you know the secret ladder in the ceiling."

"Secret ladder? That doesn't sound safe."

"It's perfectly fine. Bertie Randolph and I hid up there for two hours from his mother when she was in a foul mood because I corrected her spelling. It's a good hiding place." She turned to her wooden cat, which was in a little woven bag slung across her shoulders. "Isn't it, Pangur?"

"No, no. I prefer to be near the books, and as long as we keep the windows and door of the library open for the breeze, it's not so bad. And it means you don't have anywhere to hide from embroidery."

"Good. We are of one mind," Nell said with a definitive nod.

Sterling glanced at Tilly over the top of Nell's head and gave her a kind smile. She smiled in return, but was too embarrassed by her errant imagination to hold his gaze. She looked away and was fortunately distracted by Mr. Burton taking his place at the front of the chapel, behind a rickety wooden lectern. He began to speak and Tilly tried very hard to focus, so her imagination wouldn't run away with her again.

It took only a few moments for her to realize that the sermon was about her.

"Today I want to speak about anger," he said. "In particular, the anger that makes us lose control of ourselves and shout or throw things or behave in other imprudent ways. Remember, all of you, that the Proverbs tell us, 'He that hath no rule over his own spirit is like a city that is broken down, and without walls.' Losing one's temper leaves you defenseless. You can never be sure what ill might follow: 'For the wrath of man worketh not the righteousness of God.'"

At first Tilly reasoned that their encounter had inspired him to write the sermon and that this was probably acceptable. But as the sermon went on, the references became more pointed, his tone more contemptuous. "A woman, in particular, must take extra care because petty and trivial things tend to crowd the minds of women. It is often those who reckon themselves clever or well read or have a superior idea of themselves above others, especially men, who are the most given to fits of temper. It is a very grave and unpleasant thing for a woman to give in to violent anger."

Tilly saw Sterling's hand reach for and find Nell's and squeeze it gently. Tilly's stomach flushed with heat. How dare he? There were only two females in the room: herself and Nell. And really, only Tilly could be considered a woman. The sermon was a very public shaming. It was all she could do to sit still on the hard wooden pew, and not jump to her feet and shout at him. A lesson in controlling her temper in itself.

After he had finished, he moved on to leading a group prayer for one of the turnkeys' mothers who was ill. Tilly bowed her head against her clasped hands. The skin on her face was hot to the touch. She kept her head bowed, even when the prayer was finished, so nobody could see her embarrassment.

Finally the morning service was over. Nell climbed to her feet and declared, "Thank goodness," but Sterling stayed where he was.

"You two go on ahead," he said. "I need to speak with Mr. Burton."

Tilly's heart sank. For certainly Sterling would ask Mr. Burton about the sermon and Mr. Burton would then repeat Tilly's ridiculous story about losing her temper over a hairbrush and Sterling would think her a fool.

Nell dragged her out by the hand into the morning sunshine. "Do you think he's right, Tilly?" Nell said as they walked through the long grass and back towards the dirt road. The other staff dissipated in various directions. "Do you think petty and trivial things crowd the minds of women?"

"No, I don't think he's right," Tilly said boldly. "I think he is completely wrong and that a mind for the petty or the trivial can appear in either sex. I do not think men and women so different beneath the skin."

"I agree with you. Completely," Nell said.

Tilly looked over her shoulder. "I suppose I shouldn't speak against him."

Nell dropped her voice low and leaned in close. "Mr. Burton is the stupidest person I know."

Tilly looked at her serious face and her round eyes, and burst into laughter. Nell did the same and they stood there on the road laughing hard enough to take the edge off some of Tilly's worry.

•

Even though it was Sunday and there were no classes, Nell spent the whole day clinging to Tilly, asking her to join in games or to read with her. Tilly complied, wondering though whether she would be consumed every weekend with the girl. She had a need to sit quietly and think and read to herself. Nell, with her quick mind, got bored too easily.

At supper, Sterling sat down with them and Tilly examined his face carefully while he wasn't looking. Did he disdain her now? Had Mr. Burton poisoned his opinion of her? But he gave no indication that anything had changed since last time they spoke.

Until he finished eating and said, "Tilly, I would like to sit and talk with you in the parlor after dinner."

Sit and talk? That sounded ominous.

Nell interjected before Tilly could answer. "No, but Papa, I had wanted to read Tilly what I wrote today and—"

"Eleanor Holt!" Sterling roared, in such a big voice that even Tilly was frightened.

Nell cowered. Tilly had never seen her cower before.

"Miss Lejeune is your governess. She is paid to work with you from eight until four weekdays only. She is not your nanny. She is not your bosom companion. Before she came along you entertained yourself perfectly well and you will continue to do so."

Nell's bottom lip trembled.

"Do not cry," Sterling said gruffly. "You are stronger than that."

Nell got her lip under control, and said, "Yes, Papa."

Tilly reached out to touch Nell's cheek, but Sterling stayed her hand with his own warm fingers, placing her wrist gently back on the table.

"No," he said, but gently. "She is stronger than that."

Tilly felt embarrassed, chastened. She ate her meal, awkward and anxious, while Sterling and Nell put the chastisement behind them and got on with talking about a ship they had seen pass through the bay that day and where its cargo might be headed.

When they were done, Sterling sent Nell to fetch a servant to clear the table as he always did, and then nodded at Tilly. "Come," he said.

Tilly stood, her chair grinding behind her too loudly. Her temples thudded lightly as she followed Sterling into the parlor.

"Sit down. Make yourself comfortable," he said, indicating the plain but plump sofa. "We don't have many comforts on Ember Island, but this parlor is one place I like to retreat and indulge myself." He went to the window and slid it open, and the sea wind tumbled in, bringing damp cool with it. "I have a glass of brandy or a glass of sherry every night—just the one—and I let the day slip off my shoulders. It is something of an evening ritual."

"It sounds like a very clever thing to do."

"Sherry for you?"

"That would be lovely." She watched his back. He wore no jacket or vest, and she could imagine his musculature through his thin shirt. "I had thought to ask you . . . did Mr. Burton, the chaplain, say anything to you about me?"

"He did."

Tilly flushed, cursed that she was flushing. Perhaps the dim lamplight wouldn't reveal it.

Sterling turned, offered her the tiny glass of sherry. "Do you believe in God, Tilly?"

She took a gulp, swallowed down hard so she didn't splutter. "Yes. Of course I do."

"So do I. So do I." He sipped his sherry thoughtfully, and she waited, tense. "I have always felt very strongly that there is something beyond us, some great good machine that drives the cosmos. I cannot say confidently what form He takes, nor what particularly He wants from us. Nonetheless, I do believe in God. But the God I believe in wouldn't say the sorts of things that Mr. Burton says."

"No?"

"Our chaplain is a man who judges. I run a prison. I work with people who have been found guilty in a court of law, but Tilly, I do not judge. I'll leave that to God."

She smiled at him. "So he hasn't lowered your opinion of me?"

"He has only lowered my opinion of himself." He smiled and added, "It was already quite low. I stayed behind to ask him to be careful what he says in front of Nell." He sat down across from her, stretched out his legs, and crossed his ankles. "Before I had a daughter I had not once thought about the relative positions of men and women in the world. I thought the 'new woman' a bit of a joke, the idea of women's suffrage a curiosity. But then Nell came along and . . . is it paternal pride or is she very clever?"

"Spectacularly so."

"And I hear the nonsense that some men say around women and I can't bear it. My daughter is easily more clever than Burton. As are you. He is a dullard who spent a year in an Anglican Bible college before finding it all too hard and coming here to preach to prisoners, people he can be certain he is superior to. Why should he sit in judgment of you or Nell?" He laughed lightly. "Did you really break a mirror with a hairbrush?"

Tilly shook her head vehemently. "No. I lied because I didn't want to tell him what I was really thinking because those thoughts were private. I made something up. I promise you I am not the kind of woman who breaks things in a temper."

"I'm glad to hear it. Another sherry?"

Tilly looked at her empty glass. Had she really drunk it that quickly? "Oh, dear. I'm afraid I was rather anxious coming in here. I thought I may be in trouble."

He rose and brought the sherry back with him, topped up her glass. "Please do not be anxious, my dear. I simply wanted to include you in my evening ritual, and give you some space from my daughter who cannot bear to let you out of her sight."

"She's very sweet."

"Yes, but she is a child, and you are a woman. You need adult conversation." He rested the sherry decanter carefully on the tea table between them.

"It is such a long time since I made conversation with anyone. My grandfather and I were very close, and since his death . . ." She couldn't say more without saying too much. "I left a world behind me, and I feel I haven't arrived in a new one yet. I have often thought an island is the perfect place for me. It's neither here nor there, it's somewhere in between other places."

"Perhaps you are right," he said. "Though I don't know if Ember Island is on the way to anywhere else particularly. It's more as though it's outside of everywhere."

"How long have you lived here?"

"Six or seven years."

"That's a long time to live outside of everywhere."

"I don't know that I can leave now. Rebecca, my wife, she's buried here . . ." He trailed off and Tilly could see the sadness on his brow.

"I'm sorry," she said.

"It will come to all of us, I suppose. The clouds will roll apart and that last mystery will be revealed. It was a relief in many ways when she died. She was not herself towards the end. The pain made her crooked. Poor Nell was terrified of her."

"Was your wife . . . Rebecca . . . was she a learned woman?"

"Not particularly. She was the daughter of my father's closest friend. I'd known her since I was four; she was a dear friend to me. There was never a time when I didn't know I would marry her. I do sometimes wonder whether, had I met her as an adult, I would have fallen in love with her and asked for her hand myself."

"So you married her because your father wanted it?"

"Everyone wanted it. Even Rebecca. Even me. We were good companions. But there was never . . ." Again he trailed off, and his cheeks reddened. "You must forgive me, Tilly. Life on a prison island has made me forget my manners. You are a young woman and I shouldn't speak to you so personally, I imagine."

"I don't mind," Tilly said, but she knew what he had been going to say. Passion. There was never any passion. "And I think I know what you mean, in any case. I turned down all of Grandpa's suggestions for potential husbands. No . . . spark. No light. Some of them were wonderfully pleasant men, with gentle laughs and clean fingernails. I could have made a good life with one of them, perhaps." That was why she had married Jasper. The spark had been there, though only on her side and it had extinguished soon after she'd arrived on Guernsey.

When Jasper was still alive.

She gulped her sherry and slid the empty glass onto the tea table. "As for manners," she said, "I have drunk far too quickly and you mustn't give me any more."

"As you wish." He shook his head. "You must think me a villain to speak ill of my dead wife. Of Nell's mother."

"You spoke no ill of her. You spoke of her being a dear friend and companion, of not wanting to leave her grave here alone. All of your bearing was sad and respectful."

"I must say, you have a reassuring way about you," he said. "You make me realize I have missed company."

"I feel the same," she said. They fell silent. She could hear the rattle of the palms in the distance, the faint sound of the sea.

"Have you had a chance to see your garden plot?" he asked, before the silence became awkward.

"I have. Thank you so much. And I have met Hettie."

"Hettie! That's her name. It always escapes me. Do you want me to send a prison team up there to clear the plot? I understand there is some rubbish on it."

"No, I rather want to do it myself. I thrive on outdoor work, especially gardens." She hesitated, then pushed on. "Is it true Hettie killed her husband?"

"Did Nell tell you that?"

Tilly realized the sherry had skewed her judgment, and she'd unwittingly put Nell in trouble.

"It's no matter. I can see on your face that Nell was the one. I do wish she'd stay out of my paperwork. We have rapists here, men who have done unspeakable things to children. I don't want her to read about such business. I must get the smith to make a proper lock for my office." He shook his head. "For I am not going to be able to stop Nell snooping where she oughtn't."

"Curiosity is a sign of intelligence."

"Yes, yes. It's also a sign of disrespect. In any case, to answer your question, yes, Hettie was convicted of killing her husband, four years ago. The crime was ill considered, but not particularly violent, nor cruel, and I have the highest hopes that over the next fifteen years or so, however long her sentence may be, she will atone for that crime and she will not find herself in trouble with the law again."

"Can one atone for such a crime? A man's life, snuffed out forever. All the potential, all he might have become . . ."

"As I said earlier," he replied, "it is not for me to judge. A force far greater and more intelligent and wise than me knows Hettie Maythorpe's soul." Sterling finished his drink. "Ah, there now. I feel refreshed. I will sleep well and get on with my work tomorrow. As for you, don't let Nell take over your life."

Tilly put her hand to her temple. The sherry had made her headache worse. "I shall do my best. You must forgive me. My head is throbbing."

"Of course. Good night, Tilly."

"Good night, Sterling."

•

Tilly's headache was still throbbing at her temples the next morning, but she dressed and went down to the dining room for breakfast anyway. Nell was waiting, and distracted her with bright-eyed enthusiasm for the new school week. They went straight from the dining room to the library for lessons, but as the day wore on Tilly's throat grew dry and constricted and the headache migrated into her joints.

"It is so warm," she said to Nell, as she tried to concentrate on sums that swam in front of her aching eyes.

"You look pale," Nell said. "Perhaps you need some fresh air."

Yes, that was it. Cooped up in the library all day. She needed to be outside in the sea air. As soon as lessons were over, she stepped outside into the fresh breeze, which cooled the sweat on her skin to ice. She made her way down to her garden plot and stood a moment, considering the mountain of old hedge trimmings that covered it. A wheelbarrow: that's what she needed. Tilly glanced around, looking for Hettie, but believed herself alone amongst the hedges and flowers.

But then Hettie's dark head popped up from behind a hydrangea bush. Tilly hurried over.

"Hettie?" she said tenatively.

Hettie turned. There was that small smile again.

"I thought I might make a start on clearing the plot. Is there a wheelbarrow? And can you show me where I can dump all that rubbish?"

She nodded respectfully. "Certainly. Please, miss, if you wait down near your plot I will join you in a few minutes."

Tilly did as she was told, trying to enjoy the afternoon breeze. But her face and head felt terribly warm and she sat on the grass with her forehead against her knees, listening to her own breathing.

"Miss Lejeune?"

Tilly looked up. Hettie stood there with an old wooden wheelbarrow. "Thank you," Tilly said, climbing to her feet.

"I had wondered if you were coming back," Hettie said. "I haven't seen you for a few days."

"It's been rather too hot to work. But I have lots of ideas about what I might do here."

"I'm almost envious. A brand-new plot to turn into a garden. I remember a number of years ago, back home on the mainland, turning over soil for the first time in the little garden behind my home. The children playing at my feet . . ." She trailed off sadly.

Tilly couldn't speak. Hettie had children. She'd once had a life on the mainland, with a house and garden and children. Where were her children now? Who was looking after them?

"Let me help you with this task," Hettie said, recovering herself. "I understand you want to plant this garden by yourself, but clearing all this rubbish is a big task and you look a little pale this afternoon. We can fill the wheelbarrow together and then I can take it down to the dumping place for you in loads."

Ordinarily, Tilly would have refused, but it was a hard and tedious task and she wasn't feeling well.

"Yes. Thank you. I would appreciate that."

"You need not thank me. It's my job."

"As a human being to another human being," Tilly said forcefully, "thank you. I am not quite myself today and can't manage on my own."

Hettie nodded and together they started throwing garden rubbish into the wheelbarrow.

The sea breeze cooled the perspiration off Tilly's skin and she enjoyed seeing the pile of rubbish diminish. In her mind's eye she imagined beds of lavender and rose, jasmine and magnolias. A garden she could sit in on balmy evenings and be surrounded by sweet mingled scents. Perhaps Hettie could help her find an old garden seat that she could paint.

"Only a few more loads now," Hettie said, returning again with the empty wheelbarrow.

Tilly whirled around, and when she stopped her brain kept whirling. Stars spangled on the periphery of her vision and a low ringing sound blocked her ears. Darkness descended slowly as she dropped to the ground. She felt warm hands on her arms, heard her name repeated three times.

"Miss Lejeune?"

She tried to speak but the dark crushed over her. Just as she passed out, she thought she heard Hettie saying, "Weakling," as Jasper had that night, before she burned him alive.

•

The dreams that came with the fever were the horrors she deserved. In and out of days, she fluttered on the edge of consciousness, the heat in her body mutated into fire in her nightmares. She was running and running from a crushing black monster with hands of charcoal and breath of flame; stuck hard and heavy in her body. Or she was back at Lumière sur la Mer, standing outside the parlor window watching Jasper as he stood unmoving with his mouth open in a silent scream, fire billowing behind him. Or she shivered in the garden shed, flattened against the cold, soft dirt, while Hettie Maythorpe, sitting like a rag doll in the corner, moldered away to brown bones. "Trade places with me," she said, "you belong here as much as I do." She woke periodically to drink a little water, but could hold down no food. Nell was there sometimes, pale-lipped with anxiety in the chair. Sometimes Dr. Groom was there, offering her foul-smelling medicine. But mostly she was alone with her delirium and her guilt, flickering into febrile nightmares and then back to the real world, where her body ached as though she had been punched from crown to toes.

On the fourth night, she woke very late, her sheets and nightgown soaked. The fever had broken. She was weak, but managed to get up and change her linen and clothes, then slept restfully for the first time since she had fallen in the garden. By the time the dawn came, she even had an appetite.

A quiet knock and Nell's little face.

Tilly sat up, tried to smile. "Hello, dear."

"You look better."

"I feel much better."

Nell's face split into a grin. "I'm so relieved." She ran into the room and squashed Tilly into a hug.

Tilly gently pushed her away. "I'm starving, but far too weak to rise."

"I will wake up the cook and get you some breakfast. Lord, I've been so worried. So worried." She stood up and raced to the door. "Papa! Papa, Tilly is better!"

Tilly sank back into the bed and closed her eyes again. No nightmare images pressed themselves into her brain now, but she was alarmed at what the fever dreams had brought in, like a rough tide dredging up the ugliest debris of the ocean. Those images were her story, how she would be defined forever after. She would never be able to put them behind her. She thought of Sterling, what he might say or do if he knew. Even he would find her beyond forgiveness, surely. This thought made her sad. She hadn't realized how important his good opinion of her was.

Nell returned and slid into the bed next to her. She had her wooden cat in her arms, and Tilly could see the underside. Her name, *Nell Holt*, painted in thick, uneven letters on Pangur Ban's bottom.

Tilly stroked Nell's hair softly and said, "Have you been keeping up with your lessons?"

"No, I've been working on a new story. About a girl whose mother gets lost in a magical wilderness—like the Wirral in *Gawain*—and her daughter has to go on a quest to save her."

"It sounds wonderful. I can't wait to read it."

"The mother character is based a little on you. And a little on my own mother." Nell hesitated a moment, then said, "I got the idea when you were sick."

"Really?"

"You seemed lost in a wilderness. I sat with you sometimes and you must have been having terrible dreams because you . . . you said some strange things."

Tilly's skin prickled coldly. "I did?"

"You kept calling for somebody named Jasper. And you said over and over that you were sorry."

Tilly swallowed hard. Nausea rose.

"Who is Jasper?" Nell asked.

"A man I used to know."

"Why are you sorry?"

Tilly forced a smile. "That's the nonsense people talk when they're sick and lost in a fever. I dreamed about all kinds of things."

"Was Jasper a suitor?"

"Jasper was a man my grandfather wanted me to marry, but he wasn't very kind to me."

"So you didn't marry him?"

"As you see," Tilly said, showing Nell her left hand. "I am not married."

Nell considered Tilly in the morning light, and Tilly had the distinct feeling the girl didn't believe her. In fact, Nell's expression was, for a few moments, devoid of its usual love and joy. All that remained was the curiosity, and it looked cold and detached. But then Nell gathered her thoughts, kissed Tilly's forehead, and said, "It's no matter. You are well, and as soon as ever we can, we will start lessons again."

But it took four more days, with a hacking cough, before Tilly was up and about properly. Nell was ecstatic the day Tilly joined her and Sterling for dinner again, finally able to sit up at the table and talk without coughing or wheezing. She had seen Sterling only fleetingly the whole time she had been ill.

"I am pleased to see you are well again," he said, as she took her place at the table.

She smiled at him, and he smiled back and there was a softness in his smile she hadn't seen before. It stirred something inside her; a feeling of vulnerability that was yet somehow sweet. "I am pleased to be well again," she said.

"And will you join me for a glass of sherry in the parlor after dinner? I have a desire for conversation and there aren't many I can talk to as pleasingly as I can talk to you."

Nell hid her smile with her fork.

Tilly nodded. "I would like that very much."

SIXTEEN

The Truth Fixes Everything

"I didn't pull the weeds."

Tilly turned. The warm afternoon sunshine momentarily blinded her, but then the silhouette of Hettie Maythorpe came more clearly into view. It was Tilly's first afternoon back in the garden after her illness. All of the rubbish was gone, cleared away by Hettie.

"I didn't pull the weeds," she said again. "I thought you'd prefer to do it yourself."

Tilly smiled at her. "You're right. There's a special kind of pleasure . . ."

"I know," Hettie said, nodding towards the plot. "And there are plenty to pull."

"There certainly are."

Hettie looked back to Tilly, smiled her tight little smile and said, "I'm glad to see you're well again."

"Thank you." Then memories of the last time she had seen Hettie came back to her. "Hettie," she ventured, "that day I collapsed.

Did you say something to me as I passed out?" *Weakling*. That was the word she remembered. A shiver grew in her belly.

Hettie frowned, concentrating. "I said your name a number of times. And when you tried to get to your feet, I told you that you were too weak to stand."

That was it, then. Her fevered imagination had turned it into that other hated word.

"Is there something the matter?" Hettie said.

Tilly shook her head. "Nothing. I had some rather colorful dreams while ill. Thank you again for your help with the plot. I will get on with the weeding now."

"As you wish, ma'am."

Tilly kneeled on the soft grass. The entire plot was overgrowing with a tangle of weeds. She took her little garden fork in her hand and began, enjoying the task: the spiny resistance of the weeds and then their liberation from the ground. Her mind wandered, off and away. She was in another summer's day, in her childhood in India. Playing at her mother's feet while her mother did exactly this. Was that where she had learned her love of gardening? Was it those deep, humid summers, those long, balmy nights in the garden full of sweet-smelling blossoms that had made her long to be outside with her hands in soil?

She thought about Hettie's children and glanced over her shoulder. Hettie was down near the magnolia trees. Tilly stood and walked over to her, watching her own long shadow proceed her.

"Hettie?"

Hettie looked up. She had a smear of dirt across her forehead. "Do you need some help?"

Tilly sank to the grass next to her. "You said you had children. How old are they?"

Hettie's eyes turned downwards sadly. "My daughter is eight and my son is six."

"Who looks after them now?"

"They are with my mother and my sister. My sister is simple. She's never married, but she is very gentle and sweet with the children. It is the best I could have hoped for them, under the circumstances." Hettie's voice was strained over something else, something more primal and unspeakable.

"You must miss them."

Hettie's lips twisted: she was holding back tears, and Tilly felt terrible for bringing the matter up.

"I'm sorry," Tilly said, rising. "I'm being nosy and I've upset you. I will leave you be."

But Hettie climbed to her feet and blocked Tilly's way, stopping her from leaving. In a raw, guttural voice she said, "I would give anything to hold them against me again. Their little bodies . . ." She gathered herself, stood aside. "I am so sorry, ma'am. I ought not have stopped you."

"It is I who should be sorry," Tilly said. "My curiosity was rude."

"There are few here who care if they are rude to a prisoner," Hettie said, putting her head back down.

Tilly didn't know what to say, so she said nothing. Instead, she returned to her own plot. Hettie's words still burned her brain. Such urgency, such instinct had been in those words. *I would give anything to hold them against me again.* Tilly bent to pluck more weeds from the ground, risked a glance over her shoulder at Hettie. She no longer sat where Tilly had left her. She had disappeared in amongst the hedges.

•

Her illness behind her, Tilly settled in to life on Ember Island. Nell was still the focus of her time and attention, but there were afternoons in the quiet garden for her mind to unwind, and evenings with Sterling in the parlor for long conversations about books and ideas. She didn't return to the chapel, even for the Sunday service. This choice, which she thought would have made her appear to be bold and disobedient, went unnoticed or at least unremarked by all but Nell, who pouted about having to go with no good company. Instead, Tilly prayed in her own way, every night, for forgiveness. She received no answer from God, no sign that the twisting and turning of guilt in her guts would stop, but she continued to pray nevertheless, sending out her thoughts into the mute dark of the cosmos.

Late one night, or perhaps it was early one morning, Tilly woke with the sound of a creaking board out on the verandah. She always slept with the window open now, as the spring warmth intensified towards summer and the only thing that could cool her down was the southeasterly wind off the sea. Tilly fought her way out of the mosquito net and went to the window, hiding behind the curtain to peer out. She saw Sterling, sitting on the top step, his elbows on his knees, gazing out over the island and to the dark sea.

Why was he up? It was past midnight, she was almost certain. She hesitated a moment, then pulled on her dressing gown. Her heart beat hard in her throat, but she opened her door anyway, and went outside.

"Sterling?"

He turned and saw her, smiled, then hid his smile. "It's late. I'm sorry if I woke you. Please go back to bed."

Tilly boldly came to sit beside him instead, and he didn't tell her to go away. "Why are you up?" She breathed in the warm smell of him.

"Nell had a nightmare. She's had the same one, over and over, since Rebecca died. She's asleep in my bed at the moment, spread out like a starfish." He chuckled. "It's hard to sleep with a starfish her size in my bed."

"What happens in her dream?"

"It's about her mother, being cruel or monstrous to her. She always asks me the same thing, when she comes into my bed. She always wants to know whether her mother loved her."

Tilly let the silence linger a few moments, sensing Sterling still had more to say on the matter. The waves pulled and shushed. Possums scrabbled in the trees. The balmy night was soft, lit only by stars, heavy with the scents of damp earth and sea salt. She studied his profile, his strong jaw.

"What do you say to her?" Tilly finally prompted.

"Her mother loved her. Of course. But Rebecca was . . . ambivalent about motherhood. When Nell was first born, Rebecca fell into a dark, deep well of hopelessness. It seemed some days that she tried to ignore the baby. Nell would be left to cry for hours. I could hear her in my office and it always tugged at my heart. I had my budget extended for two nannies for the child and a nurse to tend to Rebecca until she was feeling better. But something was amiss between mother and child from the start. When she had finally climbed out of that miserable abyss, she begged me not to ask her for another child. We were to stop at one."

"You wanted more?"

"I wanted six," he laughed. "I am an only child myself. I longed for siblings. Nell would have been improved by a younger sister or brother to teach her she isn't the center of the world." He sighed. "Rebecca learned a degree of tolerance and patience, but it was always forced. I remember once asking her, when Nell was perhaps four or five, whether she loved the girl. And Rebecca said,

'Yes, but it sometimes feels as though she isn't mine.' Which made no sense at all because Nell grew in her body." Sterling shook his head. "The more Rebecca pulled away, the harder Nell clung. You can imagine."

"I can."

"That cat she still carries around sometimes . . . She wouldn't let it out of her sight. It was so clear to me that she needed Pangur Ban because Rebecca wouldn't give her the affection she craved. It broke my heart." He sighed. "I always knew I loved Nell more than Rebecca did."

"Then she's lucky to have you. Many fathers are indifferent to their children."

"But I am always so busy. I work seven days a week." He ran his hand through the front of his hair, then gathered himself. "I am sorry, Tilly. It is wrong to show such weakness in front of you. Not the least reason being you are my employee, and a young single woman, and neither of us are dressed. Living and working on this island means we all forget our manners, we forget what is respectable and appropriate."

"Please don't apologize. I like to listen to you, and I hope that I am a friend to you, more than I am an employee."

He didn't answer and nor did he move away. She could feel the heat of his shoulder, so close to hers, as they sat on the stairs together in the early morning dark. It was bliss to be so close to him, so intimate. But, on the heels of happiness as always the guilt came. If his feelings were growing for her, as she suspected they were, they were for someone he didn't really know. She was not Chantelle Lejeune. She had a disastrous marriage behind her, a horrific secret. Was it not wrong to allow Sterling to believe she was someone else, some*thing* else all together?

"I should return to bed," she said, her hand covering an

exaggerated yawn. "I need to stay one step ahead of Nell in the classroom and it is already difficult enough." She rose.

"Good night, Tilly," he said, and he brushed his own hand against hers. Sparks flew. Heat suffused her. That touch, a tenth of a moment in length, awoke such liquid warmth in her body that she almost gasped.

She stood, speechless a few moments, then managed to say, "Good night," and returned to her room.

•

The days grew longer and, impossibly, warmer. Some days, trapped in the grip of endless northeasterly conditions, Tilly slept enveloped in a slick of perspiration under her mosquito net. On other days the wind would swing around from the southeast and bring the fresh smell of rain. One week, it poured from Sunday to Sunday, huge fat drops of rain that hammered on the roof of the house as though the great flood was on its way. Then it suddenly stopped and she woke to bright blue skies, blazing sun, the smell of mud, and the raucous burr of cicadas in the bushes that grew on the escarpment.

And somehow, in the midst of all this boiling sun and sickening humidity, she was going to celebrate her first Christmas since Grandpa died. She had never longed so much for the hard ache in her fingers of icy weather, for snow and roast beef and opening presents by the fireplace. Six weeks had passed since her arrival on the island. The same length of time as her courtship with Jasper, as the wait for her grandfather to die, as her doomed marriage itself.

On Christmas morning she entered the chapel for the first time since Mr. Burton's pointed sermon. It was nine o'clock, and the sweat was already collecting under her arms and between her breasts. Nell wore a simple gingham pinafore over a cotton short-sleeved top and Tilly envied her light clothes. She wore petticoats, a corset, a laced dress, and gloves. Sterling was equally well dressed, but she didn't ask him if he was equally uncomfortable in the close heat. While they still kept their evening ritual in the parlor, Sterling had shown more reserve around her since the night he touched her hand. Perhaps he admonished himself for flying too far past politeness. Although Tilly longed for him to touch her again, she knew no good could come of allowing herself to fall for him. She had too many secrets to hide, and secrets were like holes in the foundations of a relationship. Eventually they would sink it. So they talked and talked and talked—each in their own corner of the parlor—about philosophies and stories and history and humanity. Sterling had worked in prisons since his youth; he had strong ideas about justice and how it should be administered humanely. Tilly admired him greatly, she admired him so much that her chest sometimes ached with it. But she assiduously avoided imagining a closer relationship with him. At night, falling asleep, she simply prayed for strength and forgiveness.

The Christmas service was lackluster, as though the chaplain may have written it that morning. When it was done, the congregation stood and filed out noisily. Sterling, Nell, and Tilly waited until last. Tilly found her way out of the chapel blocked by Mr. Burton.

"Miss Lejeune? A word?"

Tilly looked around for Sterling, but he had been swept away in the crowd. She allowed herself to be drawn aside, inside the front door of the chapel. It was quiet in the shadows. The voices outside seemed a long way off. Mr. Burton leaned close and said in a harsh voice, "I know why you haven't been to Sunday service."

"You do?"

"Everybody is talking about you and the superintendent. You can't bear to show your face, can you?" His eyes were flinty with anger.

"Me and . . . what have I done to make you so angry with me?"

"I know your type."

"You know nothing about me." Tilly tried to soften her tone. She did not want to lose her temper, especially not in front of Mr. Burton, who already judged her so harshly.

"You should remove yourself from this facility, from this island. Before you bring shame on a good man."

The last person who had aroused such fury in her was Jasper. Fear prickled along her skin. She didn't know what her anger would do this time; she was afraid of herself. With an enormous effort of will, she stilled her hands and ducked around Mr. Burton and away. He tried to reach for her shoulder to stop her, but she rounded on him and hissed, "Don't you touch me, you unctuous churl!"

He recoiled, but the alarm on his face was soon replaced by a sneer. "I know what you need. I know what would stop up that mouth of yours."

Tilly turned and strode away. Nell was waiting for her, Sterling had gone ahead.

"Tilly?" Nell said.

"Not now," Tilly replied. "I need to go for a walk to cool off."

She took the back way up to the house, through a horse paddock and then up the escarpment from the steeper side. The exercise helped. She breathed through her anger and managed to unball her fists sufficiently to dislodge her fingernails from her palms. She came around the northern side of the house and walked up the long grassy corridor between flower beds until she arrived at her own plot. It had been cleared and she had planted a neat border of marigolds. She sat down on the grass, then sank onto her back and looked at the blue sky, breathing.

A shadow fell nearby, and Tilly sat up. Hettie stood there, looking hesitant.

"Hettie? Are you working on Christmas Day?"

"I asked if I could, instead of Christmas dinner. My cellmates are not good company. And I . . . here." She reached into the inside of her dress and withdrew a slip of paper, handed it to Tilly.

It was a card, made out of an old seed packet. Hettie had slit it neatly and turned it inside out. On it, she had written, "Merry Christmas to Miss Lejeune from Hettie," in a painfully childish hand.

Tilly found her eyes pricking with tears. "Oh," she said. "I haven't anything for you—"

"Of course you don't. I expect nothing. I . . . I made it for you and I was glad to see you here today."

On impulse, Tilly reached out and squeezed Hettie's hand. "Thank you. It means a lot to me."

"Really?"

"Yes, really. It has brightened a day that had become quite . . . dark."

Hettie offered a small smile and then retreated.

Tilly turned the flimsy Christmas card over in her hands. Today, she had been offered both insult and treasure by a chaplain and a prisoner. It seemed more and more clear to Tilly that it wasn't always the right person who ended up behind bars.

•

The chaplain's words preyed on Tilly's mind: everybody talking about her and Sterling, harming his good reputation. That evening after dinner, when he asked her to join him in the parlor, she begged off, claiming she was tired. The following night she did the same.

On the fifth night the question was almost a challenge.

"Tilly?" he said. "Sherry?" Weight in the words. Nothing light or casual, despite his forced tone.

"I would rather not."

He assembled his expression carefully, but in the split second before he did she saw his disappointment. She saw that he felt rejected, bewildered, and it pained her greatly to have been the cause. But she reassured herself it was for the best.

And resigned herself to the miserable relief that he wouldn't ask her again.

•

The old year swung to make way for the new year. Criminal cases held over for the Christmas period began to be processed and new prisoners arrived more numerously. Sterling was busy; he grew distant from her. She was busy too. She had turned down a summer break on the mainland and, much to Nell's great delight, devised a medieval-themed project for summer. They learned some Middle English together, wrote poems in the style of Chaucer, carved their own woodcuts for prints, and designed and sewed a medieval gown for Nell. No matter that the gown turned out rather uneven, with a hem that continually fell down. The girl was hardly out of it through most of January, despite the humid heat.

Tilly saw Sterling in the evenings, of course. They conversed over dinner with no trouble, they even shared jokes and laughed together, but Nell was there to prevent any intimacy. She got to know him better, though, and admire him all the more for his principles, his intelligence, his good heart. She wondered if there were any such things to admire in her own conversation. He never gave any indication either way.

The summer heat made going in the garden impossible until late afternoon, when the sun went over the water and the breeze cleared away the humidity. The balmy early evenings drew her outside, and sometimes she was in the garden until the crickets started to sing and the dew began to fall.

Most afternoons she saw Hettie. They worked around each other, sometimes in close quarters, often in companionable silence. But Tilly didn't let an afternoon go past without offering Hettie some small kindness. An expression of gratitude for help, a compliment on her work: any small thing to make the corners of her little mouth turn up. Affection grew, almost by accident. A mutual love of being bent over the earth, surrounded by the smell of soil and flowers, bound them to each other more strongly than hours of meaningless chatter might.

She didn't return to the chapel. She felt closer to God here in the garden anyway.

Life on Ember Island became simply life. Dorset and Guernsey faded from memory and this warm, sea-swollen place became her home.

•

February steamed. Heavy rain all night, ferocious sun the next day. The air was always moist and warm, the garden grew in mad profusion.

She would never like this weather, but Tilly learned how to live with it. The key was not to leave the shade between ten and four. Then, a quick walk down to the beach with Nell to stand knee-deep in the sea would cool her down sufficiently to start thinking about working in the garden. The mosquito net had to be in perfect repair: not even a tiny tear could be tolerated. And once it was tucked in tightly, her window open to catch the damp breeze and smell of rain, she could sleep on top of her covers almost peacefully.

One afternoon near the end of February, Nell had cried off their walk to the beach because of a stomachache. Tilly wavered between staying to tend to the girl or cool off in the shallow water, but Nell waved her away forcefully.

"I'm just going to lie in my bedroom and moan and groan," she said. "You hardly need to be here."

So she walked down to the small strip of sand, peeled off stockings and shoes, and hoisted her skirts up over her knees to wade in.

The sea was cool, not cold. The waves broke around her, sucking at the sand under her feet, calming her. She closed her eyes and took deep breaths of the briny air. Then opened them again. A ship went by in the distance, heading to the mouth of the river over on the mainland. People moving about the world, just as she was learning to stay here very still. She wriggled her toes into the sand.

"Tilly?"

She turned, saw Sterling, realized her legs were on display, and dropped her skirts directly into the water.

"Nell said you'd be here," he said, advancing as she waded out of the sea, skirts sodden and dragging around her.

"What is it?" she asked, picking up her shoes and stockings. Ordinarily she would sit here on the rock and allow her legs and feet to dry naturally, but she couldn't do that with Sterling here. Nor could she put stockings on wet, sandy feet. Instead, she held them in front of her awkwardly, as she stood in front of Sterling.

"I need to review with you the order for schoolbooks for the new year. I'm afraid I've left it a little late. Nell's always so far ahead anyway, but I don't want her education to slow down because I didn't order her the right resources."

"Ah, I . . . Can we talk about this tomorrow in your office, perhaps?" She began to walk back up towards the path, and Sterling fell into step behind her.

"I need to send the order across in the morning. After dinner tonight?"

"In your office. If you wish."

They came up between the graveyards, and Tilly became aware of warders and prisoners moving about. Men looking at her, shoeless, her wet dress outlining the shape of her calves and ankles. This wouldn't do. Sterling's reputation was at stake.

"Good day, Sterling," she said, moving swiftly ahead of him.

"Wait, Tilly," he said, grasping her arm.

She shook him off. They stood apart a moment. Her heart thudded in her throat.

"I said, good day," she repeated, and redoubled her speed so she was almost running. She was out of breath before she reached the bottom of the slope, then she checked behind her. Sterling had gone. She trudged up the escarpment, her bare feet bruising themselves on stones.

•

An hour later Tilly was planting begonia cuttings when Sterling's tall figure emerged from the house and made his way down, directly towards her. He came to stand in front of her and glanced around as if to check if anybody was watching.

"Sterling?" she asked, curious, nervous.

"I wanted to see what you had done with the plot I granted you."

She climbed to her feet. "I must look a fright," she said.

"No, you do not."

They considered each other a moment in the long afternoon shadows.

"As you can see," she said, waving her hand over the blooming birds of paradise, hibiscus, and daylilies. "It might be another year before I see how it will look when finished, but it is tidy and it is full of potential."

Sterling glanced only momentarily at the garden, then back to her. The question sprang out of him as though he'd been holding it back a long time. "Why did you stop our evening ritual?"

She blinked, not sure how to proceed.

"Did I say or do something to offend you?"

"No, I . . ."

"Today you wouldn't even walk next to me. Have I embarrassed you? Please tell me the truth."

Tilly hesitated. "It may make things . . . awkward."

"The truth fixes everything," he said, his conviction clear on his face. It was just such a statement, delivered without a shred of doubt, that made him the best of men.

"Well, then," Tilly said, not meeting his eye. "It was something Mr. Burton said."

"I've told you my opinion of Mr. Burton."

"He was quite sure that the whole facility is . . . that there is a rumor we . . ." She trailed off.

"Ah," he said, and she didn't know whether he was looking at her, witnessing her burning face.

"He said that the best thing for your reputation would be if I left the island." She lifted her head. Sterling was staring off into the distance. "I am hardly going to do that, so I put some distance between us instead."

"And did he say anything else to you?"

Tilly cringed, thinking of the veiled sexual threat Mr. Burton had made. She wasn't even sure she understood it, but it had been darkly apparent where his intentions lay. "He said . . . something that no woman should have to repeat. Something that no woman should have to hear, said so violently and with such malignance."

He nodded, still not looking at her. A little muscle at his jaw worked. Then, without another word, he returned to the house. Tilly closed her eyes, feeling the pull as he left. "The truth fixes nothing," she muttered under her breath. "The truth is a great burden."

•

Sterling avoided her then for a week. He had other business at dinnertime, she didn't even pass him in the hallway of the house. She wondered if he might be preparing to relieve her of her job. She tried hard to concentrate on lessons with Nell, but one ear was always cocked for the sound of his footsteps.

But then, in the middle of the week, Nell was waiting impatiently in the library when she came from her room, dressed for the day.

"Tilly!" Nell shouted, then remembered herself and dropped her voice. "I have something to tell you."

Tilly went to the window. It was closed, and the room was stuffy. She released the latch. It grinded in the sill, but she got it open. "Oh yes?"

"Come closer. It is extraordinary news."

Tilly frowned, anticipating something bad. She came to sit

with Nell. A stack of Greek texts waited between them. Anything but Greek, while she was feeling so distracted. "Go on then."

"It's Mr. Burton. He's gone."

"Gone?"

"Back to the mainland." Nell held up four fingers. "Four days ago. Shipped off the island by Papa."

"How do you . . . how do you know this?"

"I didn't know it. I only overheard this morning. Papa was talking to the chief warder Mr. Donaghy about it, about how the prisoners will have to do their own Bible studies now. When Mr. Donaghy asked Papa why he'd got rid of Mr. Burton, do you know what Papa said?"

Tilly's throat was constricted by her own heartbeat. "What?"

"He said, 'Because he has been unspeakably rude to somebody dear to me.' I wonder what he meant. Mr. Burton has never been rude to me, though I've always thought him a bonehead. Maybe it was that sermon, where he talked about how silly women are. Though that was a long time ago."

"Maybe you misheard," Tilly said, hiding her smile. "In any case, you oughtn't eavesdrop." She tapped the pile of books. "You need to be getting on with your Greek grammar."

"Greek! Hurrah!" Nell reached for a book and was soon scratching away on her paper. Tilly sat by, eyes turned towards the window, suppressing the smile that tried to force its way onto her lips. *Somebody dear to me. Somebody dear to me.* Just for now, she put all the attendant worries and doubts out of her mind and basked in the warmth of that simple thought: she was dear to him, she was dear to Sterling.

"There!" Nell proclaimed, sliding a sheet of Greek exercises under Tilly's nose.

The letters swam. She tried hard to focus. *I take the torch from*

my father. I give the torch to my brother. It is my mother's torch.
I take my mother's torch from my father and give it to my brother.
"This all looks right," she said. "Good work."

"Too easy."

It is my mother's torch. How would Nell feel if she knew that
Sterling had been speaking of Tilly, that Tilly was the "somebody
dear"? Would she love the idea? Or was it too soon after her own
mother's death? "Do you ever miss your mother, Nell?" she asked.

Nell cocked her head. "What a question. Where did that come
from?"

"We've never spoken about it."

Nell pondered for a moment, her lips tightly drawn. Then she
said, "I think about her every day and when I think about her I
feel hollow somehow. As if a piece has been taken out of me that I
can't get back. I suppose that is missing her. But then I remember
feeling like that sometimes even when she was alive. Even before
she got sick. She was often busy and that meant she got impatient
with me or told me to go away and leave her be. I'd get the hollow
feeling then, too. What about you? Do you miss your mother?"

"I . . . I don't even remember her. She died when I was four."

"Then I suppose I am lucky. I remember my mother well
enough to miss her."

Tilly felt no clearer, but then perhaps she was preempting a
problem that would never arise. Nell may have misheard, perhaps
he didn't say "dear to me" at all. Nonetheless, she made a little
vow to herself that she would seek Sterling out that evening and
boldly insist that they reinstate their evening ritual.

It was in the early afternoon, while Tilly watched Nell stitch
to the metronome, that the door burst open and Sterling himself
stood there.

Tilly smiled up at him, but he didn't even notice her. "Nell," he said urgently. "We need to go to our emergency plan number three. Please explain everything to Tilly. I haven't time."

And then, just as suddenly, he was gone.

Nell had gone pale.

"What was that about?" Tilly asked.

"Papa and I, we have a set of emergency plans, for various things. Fires, storms, and so on."

"So what is plan number three?"

"We have to lock all of the doors and windows," Nell said. "A prisoner has escaped."

SEVENTEEN

A Rescue

The island looked different today. Through the glass—for they were forbidden from opening the windows, despite the cloying heat—Tilly could see out across the fields. No white uniforms moving about. Instead, only blue uniforms, dozens of them, combing every dip and hollow. The two tall watchtowers were manned and a warder with a rifle paced the verandah of their house. The world was strangely quiet up here on the escarpment, without the constant footsteps of people coming to see Sterling in his office. Nor was Hettie in the garden: she was locked down, like every other prisoner.

Well, every other prisoner but one.

Nell came up behind her. "You oughtn't worry, you know."

Tilly turned. Their schoolbooks lay forgotten on the table. There was far too much excitement to work. "Then why are we locked in?"

"It's just a precaution. We've had escapees before. Trust me, they are trying to get away from the turnkeys, not closer to them.

They never come up here. They head for the mangrove forest. That's where most of them get caught."

Tilly raised an eyebrow. "Most of them?"

"The ones that don't die," Nell said, in a matter-of-fact tone.

Tilly glanced back at the window. "It is strange," she said. "We are up here so far from it all. Down there, all must be very tense."

"Yes, and Papa will be running himself ragged. He needn't be down there, you know. He need only give orders then sit back with a pipe." She mimed a man smoking a pipe with a smirk on his face.

Tilly had to laugh. "Your father doesn't smoke a pipe."

"Yes, but he could, you see. He could be one of those men who sits back and smokes a pipe, but he's not. He's something quite different. Whenever there's an escape, he hopes to be there when they catch the prisoner. Because he knows . . . what goes on when the turnkeys catch one. They can be cruel."

"And how do you know 'what goes on'?"

"People shouldn't say things quite so loud if they don't want me to hear," Nell said with a defiant tilt of her lips.

Tilly reached out and stroked Nell's curls. "Your father would be appalled. If you hear too much of this grisly stuff, Nell, you will become hard."

"And so what if I do?"

"Then . . ." Tilly couldn't answer. The first words in her brain were, "Then you'll never find a husband." It was the kind of thing her grandfather had said to her, to encourage her to regulate her behavior. But saying it to Nell seemed all wrong. So what if she never found a husband? With her brain and her strength of character, she would probably get on fine. Perhaps Tilly would have too, if she'd been given a chance. Here she was, working and earning a living without the benefit of inheritances and fancy country houses. In fact, she preferred to be busy with work than to be idle and produce an endless parade of embroidered cushions or watercolor paintings.

"I would rather that you enjoyed the innocence of childhood a little longer," Tilly said instead. "Because the adult world comes rushing upon one so quickly and so unrelentingly. There is time enough to be horrified when you are grown."

"Pish," Nell said. "I'll be thirteen this year. Juliet was married to Romeo at thirteen."

"I think you'll agree that didn't end so well."

Nell laughed, dancing away from the window and back to the table. "Come on, Tilly. Let's pass the time this afternoon by me reading you my new epic. It's almost the same as schoolwork. I think you'll agree that I've used the word 'crepuscular' very well in a sentence, and thus demonstrated both my knowledge of twilight animals *and* extended metaphors."

Tilly took comfort in Nell's complete lack of concern about the situation. She listened as Nell read, impressed as always by the girl's imagination and grasp of idiom and tried to forget about the escapee, and the strange empty feeling of the day.

They didn't see Sterling at dinner. The staff retreated back to the eastern wing of the house, eager to lock themselves in their rooms. Nell and Tilly went to their bedrooms early.

Tilly stood by the window a little while. Lanterns bobbed up and down between rows of sugarcane and she imagined others would be glimmering dimly far out in the mangroves. She longed to open the window and let the cool evening air in, but dared not. Imaginings of a creeping murderer tormented her. Instead, she lay down on top of her covers and tried to sleep, with no success.

She heard Sterling come in, very late, and rose to greet him in the hallway by lamplight.

"Sterling?"

He glanced up. He was muddy and sweaty and looked exhausted. "Why are you up so late, Tilly?"

"It's so hot and I've . . . I've been worried."

He shook his head. "You're not to worry. We found a raft down in the mangrove forest. Old branches and driftwood bound together with rotting string and vines. We're concentrating our search down there. That's where he'll be. A long way from here."

"What did he do, Sterling? I mean, what was the crime that had him sent here?"

"I won't talk about it, Tilly, save to reassure you he wasn't a murderer." He ran a hand through his hair, leaving some of it sticking up at a strange angle. "I'm going to try for a few hours' sleep and get back down there at dawn. I'm sorry. I can't stop to talk."

"Yes, of course. Don't let me hold you up."

Tilly watched as he walked down the corridor to his bedroom. The door closed. She tried to take comfort knowing he was nearby, that the criminal was down in the mangroves, that he wasn't a murderer. She returned to her bed and slept fitfully.

Some time, much later, she woke in the dark with her skin prickling. What had woken her?

She listened into the gloom, tense but not certain why. Then heard it again. A sound on the roof. Not the rough skitter of the possums that sometimes woke her. Creeping footsteps.

Tilly sat up, her pulse so hard in her ears she couldn't hear. She forced her blood to be still, and listened.

One footstep . . . another . . . a pause. Then again . . . trying not to be heard on the roof.

Tilly threw back the covers, jumped to her feet, hastily donned her dressing gown, wrenched open the door, and raced light-footed to Sterling's bedroom in the dark. She stopped herself before she knocked: if she could hear footsteps, then the person on the roof would hear knocking. Instead, she tried the door and found it unlocked.

Sterling lay, half dressed, asleep diagonally across his bed. No doubt the long hours in the fields and mangroves today had taken their toll. He slept like the dead.

Tilly reached for his bare shoulder and shook it lightly. He stirred, blinked open his eyes, startled when he saw her.

She held a finger over her lips, and pointed at the ceiling. His eyes went upwards and together they waited.

And there they were again, the footsteps. Sterling bolted upright, every muscle in his strong chest tensed. He stood, pulled Tilly close. For a brief, almost unbearable moment, her breasts were smashed against his chest through her thin dressing gown.

"Go to Nell," he whispered in her ear. His hot breath tickled her. "Bar the door. Don't move."

Then he released her and rushed off, leaving her reeling with desire and fear. She hurried to Nell's room, opened the door, and slid onto the bed next to her, her hand clamped gently over Nell's mouth.

Nell's eyes flew open. Tilly motioned that she should be quiet and uncovered her mouth. She lay down so her lips were against Nell's ear and said, "There's a man on the roof."

"The prisoner?"

"I don't know. Your father's gone to investigate."

"But they thought he was in the mangroves. Are there any warders outside? What if he attacks Papa?" she said in a desperate whisper.

Tilly held up a cautionary index finger. "We need to be calm. Stay in bed. I'm going to bar the door."

Nell ignored her, grabbed Pangur Ban from the side table, and followed Tilly to the door. Together, they lifted the writing desk and moved it across the door. Nell dropped her end and it thudded against the floorboards. They both froze. Tilly's heart ticked in her ears.

Moments passed. Nothing happened. They relaxed. Tilly went to the window to check the latch was in place.

Nell was right behind her again. "What if he breaks the glass and comes in?" she whispered.

Tilly's eyes had adjusted properly to the dark now, and she could see the girl was pale and shaking. "Perhaps we should hide under the bed."

So they clambered under the bed and lay there, in the heat and dust, waiting.

No more footsteps on the roof. A long, dread silence. Nell started to cry.

"Shhh, Nell. It will be fine."

"Yes, Papa is very strong," she said cheerlessly. "Isn't he?"

"Very strong."

"And he will have taken the rifle."

Then the sudden sound of thudding and bumping, coming from the verandah. A scuffle. No sound of gunshots. Tilly felt helpless and hopeless, here under the bed. And while she recognized it was the safest place for Nell to be, she also had to make certain that Sterling wasn't alone out there. She intended only to listen, hoping to hear the voices of other warders.

"Wait here," she said to Nell.

"Where are you going?"

But Tilly was already out from under the bed, across the room, and carefully positioning herself behind the curtain. She cautiously peeked out, but could see nothing on the verandah.

Carefully, as quietly as she could, she reached out to unlatch the window and lift the sash an inch.

Nell was under her arm. They both listened.

A man moaning. Another man's voice. Nell gripped Tilly's wrist. "That's not Papa's voice," she said.

Tilly's skin ran hot and cold. She was right. The man speaking—snatches came on the wind: "you pig," "you tyrant"—was not Sterling. Which meant the other sound, the moaning sound, was Sterling.

"Did he not take the rifle?" Nell whispered, harsh and frantic. "Why doesn't he shoot him?"

Tilly's skin ran with cold fire. Who would come and save them if something happened to Sterling?

Nobody. Tilly would have to save them.

"Is there more than one rifle?" Tilly asked, closing the window and latching it.

"I'll come with you."

"No, you will not. You will get under that bed with Pangur Ban and you will be as still and silent as him. Where will I find a rifle?" Her heart hammered.

"Papa's office. The cabinet over his desk."

"Wait here. You will put us all in danger if you don't wait precisely here. Get under the bed and do not come out until one of us comes for you."

Nell choked on frightened sobs. "Come back safely. Please."

Tilly crept to the door and dragged the writing desk out of the way. She checked that Nell was back under the bed, then made her way down the hallway to Sterling's office. Then changed her mind. She had no idea how to fire a rifle. Instead, she turned to the parlor, to the cold fireplace, and seized the brass poker. She took it back to her own room, which was on the same verandah as Nell's. From here, she climbed out the window and listened for the voices. They were coming from the north verandah, behind the house. Her body shook with fear, but she couldn't stand by and let Sterling be injured or killed. Where were the warders? Was everybody down at the mangroves? If she screamed into the dark, perhaps they would all come running and she could cower back inside where she wanted to be.

Or perhaps that would prompt the escapee to kill Sterling.

Tilly stopped at the corner of the verandah. She needed to peer around to see exactly what position they were in. Deep breaths. Then she darted her head out and back. In that split second, the scene on the adjoining verandah burned itself into her mind. Sterling, lying facedown as a fair-haired, grubby man crouched over his body, sitting on Sterling's skull, pummeling him with fists and elbows.

How dare he? How dare this low, low creature brutalize a man of such vision and compassion? How dare he hurt Sterling. *Her* Sterling. Fury wound up inside her. The escapee's back was to her.

Tilly gulped another deep breath and dashed round the corner. The escapee turned his face around in time to express surprise at the crazed red-haired woman, right before she smacked into his head with the heavy end of the brass poker. With a sickening intake of breath, he fell off Sterling. She slammed the poker across his face, hearing his nose break under it. Then once more around the head and he lay still, bloody and smashed, his chest heaving, breathing wetly. Still alive.

Tilly panted. Sterling lifted himself up on all fours, spitting blood onto the wooden boards. He reached down off the verandah and retrieved his rifle from the bushes, pointed it at the prisoner. The night held its breath. But then he raised the rifle to the sky instead and squeezed the trigger. It was deafening, a flat smack in the quiet dark.

He leaned on Tilly, dropping the rifle with a clatter. "Thank you," he said.

Lanterns started bobbing from all directions, called by the gunshot.

"He knocked the rifle out of my hands," he said, heaving, hands going to his ribs. "I should have protected you and Nell. I should have stayed awake. The warders on duty probably all thought I was."

"Nobody expected him to come to the house."

"I'm too merciful, Tilly. I had a clear shot. I could have killed him, but I tried to negotiate instead." He indicated the unconscious figure on the ground. "I could have killed him now too. But I can't. I can't do it. I'm weak."

"No. You are strong. So strong. I admire you so greatly, Sterling."

Footsteps ran towards them. Voices shouting and overlapping. Tilly's ears still rang from the gunshot, from the fear. Men in blue uniforms apprehended the prisoner. Their lanterns showed the extent of injuries to his face and head, and Tilly felt sick that she had caused them. Sterling, holding his ribs, barked commands at the warders. One of them—Tilly recognized him as the chief warder, Mr. Donaghy—reached for Sterling's shoulder.

"Go inside, Superintendent," he said. "You're injured. You must rest. Dr. Groom will be here tomorrow. Let us take care of this."

Sterling hesitated, confusion and exhaustion in his face.

Tilly found her voice. "I'll take you in," she said. She became suddenly aware that she stood in front of a group of men while wearing only her dressing gown. What might they think of her? What gossip would it arouse?

But then Mr. Donaghy stepped forward and said, "Yes. Go with Miss Lejeune, Sterling. Miss Lejeune, there is a first-aid kit in the superintendent's office. Do what you can. If you are concerned that his injuries may be life-threatening, come to find me down at the eastern end of the stockade and we will send a boat across to the mainland tonight."

Tilly put her hand under Sterling's elbow and led him inside. Nell sprang on them in an instant. "Papa! Papa!"

"You were supposed to be waiting in your bedroom," Tilly said, all her focus on keeping Nell away from Sterling.

"Please, Nell, leave me be," Sterling said. "I am bruised and shaken up."

"But I want to help, I want to—"

"Nell!" Tilly admonished, hating herself for raising her voice when she saw how the girl cowered. She smoothed out her tone. "Nell, my dear. If you want to help your father, you'll go to bed. I will call you if I need you."

"But it's not fair. You won't call."

"I will."

"The night my mother died, they never called."

Tilly released her grip on Sterling's arm for a moment and bent so she was Nell's height. "I promise you."

Nell nodded wordlessly, eyes brimming, and slipped slowly away down the dark corridor.

Tilly led Sterling into the parlor, where he lowered himself into the sofa and she lit all the lanterns.

"Wait here," she said.

"I can hardly move," he replied with a wry smile.

She went to his study for the first-aid kit, then to the kitchen for water and a cloth. When she returned, she saw that Sterling had stripped off his shirt. There was a bloody laceration near his collarbone and blood on his face. Tilly had a brief, alarming flashback to that night Jasper had come home from the fight with the Spaniard. She stifled a gasp. "I'll have to clean those wounds."

Sterling was turning his ribs towards the lamplight. "I think it's mostly bruising." He took a deep, full breath in. "I can still breathe fine. I don't think any ribs are broken."

"Dr. Groom will be the judge of that, Sterling. Hold still." She cleaned away the blood from his neck to reveal a ragged bite wound. In the first-aid kit was a small white pot labeled in the doctor's handwriting. She gingerly rubbed some of the ointment on the bite wound, then turned to cleaning Sterling's face. The blood had come from his nose and hid no great injury.

Sterling sat still and patient as she tended to him.

"You hit him hard, Tilly," Sterling said.

"I had to," she replied, realizing she sounded defensive.

"And you, such a soft thing." He touched her hand briefly.

She smiled into his eyes. "I was angry."

"You are fearsome when you're angry."

She didn't answer. Couldn't answer.

"There," she said, closing up the first-aid kit and putting it aside. "He bit you?"

"He was like a wild animal. Some of them . . . incarceration plays with their minds. He was in his fourth year of a five-year sentence for theft. This time next year he would have been free. But he got the idea in his head that he was going to punish me as I had punished him."

Tilly shuddered. "And you deal with men like that every day?"

"They're not usually trying to kill me, Tilly." He paused, thoughtfully. Then said, "You do know he would have killed me? It's not a way you want to die, being beaten to death."

She sank onto the sofa next to him. "Don't talk of it, Sterling. It didn't happen. You will be fine."

"Only because you saved my life." He reached out again, brushed her cheek with the back of his hand. She shivered. "I could never have imagined, that day I met you in the church hall, that you would become so important to me."

And as hard and hot as her anger had come before, now came her desire. It roared over her skin, surged up through her core. She was rendered speechless, motionless by it, certain it would kill her.

Sterling took her face in his hands, leaned in, and pressed his lips against hers softly.

But softly was not enough. She pushed herself against him, on top of him. His arms encircled her waist. His hard body was under her fingers, his warm mouth under her lips, her tongue.

"Tilly," he said softly, urgently, pulling away. "Tilly, no."

And here it was, the rebuff she feared. The familiar feeling of having exposed her heart, her desire, too readily. Flames on her cheeks. "I'm sorry," she said, moving off him.

"No." He grasped her hand, smiling in the lamplight. "Not here. Come." He stood, winced, and pulled her to her feet. "Nell might still be snooping about. I rarely lock my bedroom door in case she has nightmares. But tonight I will."

His bedroom. He was inviting her to his bedroom. The thought of it made her knees weak.

In the dark, they softly stepped across the hallway together. All was quiet from Nell's end of the corridor. Sterling ushered Tilly ahead of him, closed the door with a low clunk, and dropped the latch into place. He turned to her, grazing her throat and face with his warm hands, then gently taking the edges of her dressing gown and pushing it off her shoulders, so that only her gauzy nightdress came between his body and hers. His hands gathered her breasts, thumbs brushing her nipples and making her ache hungrily. His eyes met hers, held her gaze a moment, then he pressed his lips against hers.

"Sterling," she murmured against his mouth. "Oh, God."

His hands were on the hem of her nightdress now, pushing it up. She lifted her arms and tore it off, threw it to the floor. He fumbled with the band of his trousers, wriggled half out of them, nearly fell over.

They laughed, stumbled to the bed.

"Be gentle with me," he said in the dim room, indicating the bruising on his ribs.

"I think I'm the one who is supposed to say that," she said with a smile.

"We will be gentle with each other," he said, rolling onto his back and pulling her down astride him. Her breasts fell over his face, his hands reached for her hips, massaging the soft flesh that gathered there. Warm skin on warm skin. She ran gentle fingertips over his ribs, then firm hands over the dense muscles of his arms and shoulders. She closed her mouth over his. As he entered her, she gasped with a brief sharp pain, but his mouth over her breast soon turned pain to pleasure. He cupped her buttocks and they moved together, wild with both desire and heady relief, their bodies molded together as though they had been designed for one another.

•

Sterling led her to her own bedroom afterwards, after she helped him pull his clothes back on. He chuckled about how he had felt no pain during their embrace, but how it was all rushing back now.

"I'm sorry," she said.

"Never apologize for what happened. But, Tilly, we cannot risk Nell finding us sharing a bed . . ."

"I understand. We will talk tomorrow about . . . this."

He leaned down to kiss her. She parted her lips and his mouth lingered, firm and loving. But then he drew back. "Good night."

She smiled. "Good night."

Then she was stripping off again, on her own this time, and sliding into her bed.

She lay there a long time, going over the details of their lovemaking in her mind. What beautiful, fluttering, diving, soaring feelings he had aroused in her. She groaned softly remembering it, ran her hands over her body wondering how she had felt to Sterling. Soft and curvy. She wanted to do it all over again.

But in time the happy thoughts began to dissipate, and gave way to much darker ones. What business did she have falling in love with Sterling? She couldn't love him, and she certainly couldn't allow him to love her. She was living a lie and such a lie could only continue to function if she never grew close to anyone.

The thought kept her awake as surely as pebbles in her bed might. This side, that side, covers on, covers off. Dawn glimmered outside her curtains. Then it occurred to her: she had saved Sterling's life. Surely that went a little way towards canceling out her other, darker deeds.

And suddenly it was clear: the guilt was permeable. It didn't need to crush her forever. She could erase her actions of the past with her actions of the present, she could make herself free to love Sterling.

Her tired brain was shutting down now; she balanced on the edge of sleep. For some reason, Hettie Maythorpe came to mind, so far from her children. She fell asleep as the sun crept over the horizon.

•

The day after was a day of bedlam in the house. A constant stream
of people—warders, administrators, doctors, investigators from
the mainland—came and went. Somehow Tilly and Nell were
supposed to concentrate on schoolwork.

At one point, Nell threw her French grammar book down and
proclaimed theatrically, "Too many footsteps!" It was true, the
sound of feet going up and down the stairs and around the verandah was a constant distraction, but for Tilly, the much greater
distraction was wondering when she'd be alone with Sterling again.

"Come along. Four more exercises and then we'll find something else to do."

Nell put her head down, but then the door opened and Sterling
stood there. Tilly hadn't seen him since last night. He had been
holed up in his office since before breakfast, dealing with the af-
termath of the escape. He looked tired, but his cheeks had good
color under his thick sideburns, and his eyes shone.

"Hello, ladies," he said with an easy smile.

He glanced at Tilly, met her eyes, and she blushed furiously.

Nell didn't notice. She ran to him, threw her arms around him.
"Papa! I've been dying to see you."

"Not so tight, Nell. Here, look at this." He lifted up the corner
of his shirt.

Tilly caught a delicious glimpse of his hard flank and memories
of last night flooded through her. But then he lifted it further, and
she could see what he was showing Nell. His ribs were practically
black with bruising.

"Oh, Papa, you poor thing!" exclaimed Nell. "What a beast he
was to do this to you. I hope you gave him what for."

Sterling tucked his shirt in again. "Ah, well, that's an interesting story. In fact, it was your governess that gave him what for." He smiled up at Tilly. "The turnkeys are all terrified of you now. It's a shame Burton isn't still around to hear what they're saying about you."

Tilly laughed and Nell looked up at her with round eyes. "Tilly, you didn't."

"I did." She remembered last night's vow, to make amends in the present. "And it was unpleasant and that man, no matter what a beast he was being, was badly injured. Has the doctor seen him, Sterling?"

He answered her in the detached tone of an administrator. "The prisoner regained consciousness shortly after he was apprehended. He has a broken nose and multiple bruises and lacerations. He's being returned to the mainland for treatment and then a new trial for assault. He won't be returning to Ember Island as he's considered a danger to me, particularly now. So that's the end of it."

The end of it. And the beginning of something else.

Sterling pulled out his pocket watch and huffed. "I must go. I have more meetings."

"I'm glad you're well, Papa," Nell said, squeezing his hand. Then she reached for Tilly's hand. "And I'm glad you were the one who rescued him."

After he'd left, Tilly turned to Nell and said, "There's no way either of us can concentrate any further. The afternoon is cooler, shall we finish classes in the garden? You can bring your sketching pad and draw some flowers."

Nell practically jumped. "Yes. Oh, yes, yes, yes." She raced off to her room to fetch her sketching pad, and Tilly met her at the front verandah and they walked down into the garden.

Nell, set free, disappeared amongst the hedges and Tilly walked up to her plot and found a shady place to sit down. She put her arms around her knees and dropped her head and listened. The breeze shushed in the fig trees, but rattled in the palms. The sea crashed on the shore in the distance. Birds called: the sweet chirping of sparrows and somewhere far off the hooting call of a kookaburra. She thought about that moment they had all held hands, like a family.

Did she deserve a family?

Tilly raised her head. Off near the far edge of the garden, by the magnolias, Hettie stood.

Without knowing what she was going to say or do, Tilly climbed to her feet and walked across the soft grass towards her. Hettie didn't see her at first, but then she turned and smiled.

"You're out here early today," Hettie said.

"I brought Nell out to sketch flowers." Tilly looked back over her shoulder. Couldn't see Nell, but presumed she was sitting somewhere drawing lavender heads. She turned back to Hettie.

"And are you well?" Hettie asked.

"Why did you do it?" Tilly said, knowing she was pushing past some invisible barrier, but unable to stop herself.

"Beg pardon?"

"Why did you kill your husband?"

Hettie's face reddened deeply. She opened her mouth once, twice, but no sound came out.

Curdling regret. "I'm sorry," Tilly said, palms in the air, backing away. "I shouldn't have said anything."

But Hettie's hand shot out and grabbed Tilly's wrist so hard that she winced. She leaned close, her eyes glittering darkly. "He treated me like dirt. He came home every night drunk and he beat me and I knew it was only a matter of time before he started on the children. I couldn't see any other way out."

Tilly's thundering pulse made it hard for her to swallow.

"But now I regret it, I regret it with all my heart. I loved him once and I have to live with knowing I robbed him of every moment from that awful day onwards. Every morning birdsong, every evening breeze, I took them all from him. I took them all."

Tilly struggled to speak. "Do you feel . . . do you feel that being in prison will erase your debt?"

Hettie released her arm, stood back. "That is what I pray for sometimes. God doesn't answer."

Tilly considered her a moment. Hettie's dark hair was coming loose at the nape of her neck, being whipped across her face by the wind.

Hettie took a deep shuddering breath and said, "But what I pray for the most is to see my children again." Her eyes brimmed and Tilly's heart twinged. She became very aware of Hettie's physical presence, her dense fleshy body, so open and vulnerable and so in need of an embrace. Against any good judgment, she gathered Hettie in her arms and let her sob. She doubted anybody had held Hettie since her arrest because the older woman clung to her with such force that it winded Tilly. Tilly rubbed her back and made soothing noises, but Hettie cried and cried, and Tilly was afraid of what she had unleashed.

"Tilly?" A small voice behind her.

Hettie jumped away immediately, covering her face with her hands. Tilly grasped Nell's shoulder firmly and led her away. "Forget what you saw," she said.

"What happened? Is Hettie all right? Why were you hugging her? Does Papa know you are friends?"

"We are not friends. Hettie was upset and I did what any decent human would. Please don't mention it to your father. He has enough on his mind."

"What was she upset about?"

"She didn't say." They were at the stairs now. "Did you draw anything?"

Nell beamed, the incident forgotten. "Look," she said, brandishing a sheet out of her drawing book.

Tilly took the drawing and offered some small praise. Nell was much better at writing than at drawing. It was another task that she rushed through because it wasn't easy for her. "Let's go inside," she said. "You can look up the Latin name for this and write it in."

Nell went in ahead of her. Tilly looked back towards the garden. Hettie was kneeling at the side of a garden bed, composed again, and appeared at this distance completely recovered. Tilly felt much less composed, much less recovered.

•

Later that afternoon, Tilly was taking tea in the parlor when she saw Nell walk past on the verandah. Ordinarily, Nell would be clamoring for Tilly to share tea with her, but she walked out into the long shadows instead. Tilly didn't think anything of it, then remembered Nell's interest in her exchange with Hettie earlier that day. She stood and went to the window, and could see Nell, the afternoon sun shining on her chestnut curls, hands behind her back, chatting to Hettie.

She hesitated. Should she go out and stop them talking? No, all would be well. Hettie would not reveal to Nell the things she had revealed to Tilly. They were probably talking about flowers or the weather. Tilly stood behind the window and watched, then remembered her tea and returned to the couch.

She sat, saucer in her lap, teacup in her fingers, staring into the middle distance. Hettie's story had shaken her up. Her husband had been a violent, abusive man. She had been defending herself and her children, and for that she was in prison. Tilly judged her own situation and held herself guiltier than ever. It was she who should be in prison; the world was topsy-turvy when a protective mother was locked away and Tilly, who had suffered nothing more than a cheating husband and had caused two deaths because of it, lived in freedom.

Tilly wondered if she had the courage to do what she knew she should do.

EIGHTEEN

Inside the Stockade

Tilly had no appetite for supper. She watched Sterling, his hands and wrists moving as he cut his pie, ate his vegetables. All she wanted was that sweet oblivion that had engulfed them both last night. In such a moment she knew she could forget the black thoughts crowding her mind. She craved him, and food was unnecessary, a distraction.

Nell was quiet tonight, solicitous, not letting her father stretch too far to reach for the gravy, pouring his glass of water, and offering to fetch the maid to clear the table without having to be asked.

"You need to rest, Papa," she said. "Straight to bed after dinner."

"If it's all the same with you, Nell," he said, "a glass of sherry in the parlor would make me feel much improved."

Tilly's body flushed with warmth. At last, at the end of the long day, they would be together.

Finally, Nell was off to bed and they were closing the door on the parlor. Tilly launched herself into Sterling's arms and he held her for a few moments before gently pushing her away and saying, "I need to be sensible a moment and ask for your advice."

Tilly hid her disappointment. "Go on."

Sterling went to the drinks cabinet, set up their two sherry glasses as normal. "It's about Nell." He unstopped the decanter and poured their drinks. "Life on an island . . . perhaps it's not the best thing for her."

"She is very happy here."

"Her happiness is a secondary concern to her safety. That prisoner who escaped came here to find me. What wouldn't he have done to hurt me? When he had finished with me, what would have stopped him coming inside to find Nell?"

"But that's the only time this has happened," Tilly replied. "Usually prisoners run away from the staff, not towards them. He was confused in his mind. That's what you said."

"Yes, it was random and because it was random it was more terrifying. I could not have predicted his behavior. There is nothing to say a similar thing won't happen again, but worse. I've always believed Nell was safe up here on the escarpment. But now . . . I don't know."

Tilly sipped the sherry. "What would you do then?"

"Boarding school on the mainland."

"She would hate it."

"She would be safe."

"It would stifle her spirit. She isn't made for rules."

"She'll have to learn them sooner or later."

Tilly considered Sterling by the lamplight. What she wanted to ask was what he expected would happen to her, Tilly, if Nell was shipped off to boarding school. But she tried to focus on giving good advice. "Sterling, the business with the escapee was only one night ago. You are still understandably shaken up. It may take us all some time to feel safe again. I don't think it wise to make a decision under such circumstances."

He smiled, touched her cheek. "You are wise, my Tilly."

She dropped her voice low. "Will you kiss me?" she said, putting aside her sherry glass. "I have urgent need for kisses."

"Of course I will."

∙

Tilly woke in the gray before dawn, still in Sterling's bed. Alarm lit up in her veins. They had decided they wouldn't sleep, that she would be back in her own bed long before Nell woke. She reassured herself it was still very early and rose, turned back to look at Sterling, sleeping. How divine it had been to lie, her back curled against his front, and drift off. The night enveloping them in its balmy warmth, the shushing sounds of the sea beyond the open window, the retreating passion leaving joy in its wake along her skin. She smiled—wouldn't have been able to stop herself smiling—and returned to her own cool bed.

∙

In the four months she had been on Ember Island, she had never been late to class. This morning was an exception. Her late night adventures meant a late morning, waking after breakfast, dressing quickly and pinning her hair unevenly, and arriving at the library with a growling stomach.

But Nell wasn't there.

Tilly sat and looked through the day's lesson. Now all the excitement was over, it was time to return to the lesson plan she had written in January. Today would be double Greek translation, then she allotted a few hours for Nell's creative writing, which Tilly counted as practice in rhetoric.

Still Nell didn't come. Now Tilly grew curious, prickled lightly with worry. She left the library and went out onto the verandah. The sky was churning with dark clouds. It looked like rain was about to set in. Down into the garden, looking between the rows of flowers and hedges. Then back to circle the whole verandah, eyes searching the distance. The prisoners in their white uniforms were back in the cane fields, which were bright gold against the dark gray sky. She hoped to see a flash of blue or red, Nell's favorite dress colors, but she saw nothing.

Back inside, she went to Nell's room, knocked lightly. Perhaps she was sick. "Nell?" she asked. "Nell?"

No answer. Gently, Tilly opened the door. The room was empty, the bed either made neatly or never slept in. Pangur Ban was missing from his usual place on the bedside table.

Nell was gone.

•

Tilly waited until eleven, then decided she couldn't go another moment without telling Sterling. It had started raining now, heavy mournful rain that hammered on the roof and pooled on the verandahs. She went to the office and knocked lightly. She could hear voices within: no doubt more questions and paperwork related to the escaped prisoner.

"Come in," he shouted gruffly, and it was so different from the soft loving words he had said to her last night that she caught her breath. Then she pushed the door open.

Sterling sat at his desk, Dr. Groom opposite. A warder stood at the side of the desk, clutching a sheaf of papers. Tilly had the strong sense that she had entered a men's world, where she and her news would be unwelcome.

"Tilly?" Sterling said, warmly enough that Dr. Groom gave him a suspicious glance.

"I'm so sorry. I didn't want to disturb you. But Nell's gone missing."

Sterling jumped to his feet, then winced, clutching his side. "What? When?"

"She hasn't been in the library all morning."

"Have you checked her room?"

"Of course. Her bed is either made or never slept in. I wasn't sure when to start worrying, but . . ."

"Now, we start worrying now. There are prisoners all over this island, most of them under heavy guard or in leg irons, but there are also armed warders with twitchy fingers who might shoot at a body that's not accounted for."

Tilly flushed, angry at herself for not saying anything earlier. "I'm sorry. I've left it too late."

Sterling began to pace. "If her bed wasn't slept in, she might have been out all night. She might have gone down to the mangroves and been caught in the incoming tide. She might—"

"Get yourself under control, Sterling," boomed the doctor. "That child is a handful of trouble. Two short days after a prison escape, she's going to drain all your resources searching for her. I say leave her out there. She'll come back when she gets wet or hungry."

Sterling stopped pacing, anger in check, but immovable. "Thank you for your suggestion, Dr. Groom." Then he turned to the warder and said, "Alert everybody. Prisoners should be locked down. Somebody make sure every one of them is accounted for. All staff are to be out there searching for the child. I want a team combing the mangroves particularly. Get the men up the towers too, in case she's gone in the . . ." Sterling couldn't finish and Tilly's heart squeezed tight.

"Sterling," she said, longing to touch him and comfort him, "Nell's smart enough to know not to go in the water."

"I know that," Sterling replied. "She's also smart enough to know which drawer in my office I keep the key to the boat shed. But not strong enough to row on a stormy day." He brushed past her and outside, pulling his raincoat off the hook by the door and thundering off down the stairs.

The warder ran after him. Dr. Groom stayed, gave Tilly a wry smile and a lift of the eyebrows. "Uncontrollable. You remember I told you that?"

Tilly didn't return his smile. "I'm going out to look for Nell."

She went to her room for an umbrella and headed outside. She couldn't see Sterling anymore, so she presumed he'd gone down to the stockade, where she knew she wasn't allowed. The rain fell hard on the ground and bounced up, soaking her hem. She closed her eyes and tried to think like Nell. Where would she be hiding?

Tilly opened her eyes. Her shoes were filling with water. She squelched down through the garden, searching under every hedge, up every tree. The wind rose up in a squall and turned her umbrella inside out, so she discarded it, surrendering to the heavy rain. She certainly wasn't anywhere in the garden. The white uniforms had disappeared from the fields now, blue uniforms replacing them. Tilly headed down the path and through the graveyard, around towards the mangroves to help search there.

As the path ran out and she crossed the long, muddy strip that led down to the water, the chief warder, Mr. Donaghy, was briefing a party of men. He saw Tilly and said, "You should really go inside, Miss Lejeune."

"I can't just be inside doing nothing. Please, let me help."

He smiled kindly. "You can accompany me, then. You will get muddy."

"I'm already muddy."

The men went off in different directions, and she followed Mr. Donaghy, whose sturdy boots were much more suited to this task, into the saltwater forest. The mangrove trees were dank, their roots shooting up like pointed stones through the stinking mud that sucked at her feet as she picked her way along beside Mr. Donaghy. The trees crowded close together, and would be a wonderful place to hide if the mud wasn't so thick and sour-smelling. Tilly couldn't imagine Nell being happy to hide out here, especially not in the rain.

"Is there nowhere on the island where there is shelter?" she asked Mr. Donaghy, rain streaming down her face.

"No."

"No cave or overhanging rocks?"

"No, Miss Lejeune. We know every hiding place on this island. She's probably out in the open somewhere."

She trudged after him. Was Nell really silly enough to put her father through all this, to put all the prison staff through all this, only days after they had pursued an escapee? In the rain, too? Tilly began to worry: what if something else had happened to Nell? Sterling had feared it straightaway, she could tell. What if he was right to fear it? If she was injured or kidnapped or worse . . .

"Nell!" she began to call. "Nell!"

Mr. Donaghy looked at her, curiously. They weren't used to calling out for prisoners who escaped. But then he seemed to decide it was a good strategy. "Nell!" he shouted. "Nell, where are you?"

•

Freezing, wet, and muddy, Tilly returned home late in the afternoon. She was weak and tired, hadn't eaten, hadn't found Nell. In her bedroom, she peeled off her wet clothes and dried herself off. Her fingertips were white and waterlogged. She found dry clothes in her wardrobe and dressed, then sat on the bed to think.

Had Nell run or was she taken?

What reason did she have to run? Guiltily, she thought of Sterling making love to her last night. Had they been too loud? Had Nell overheard and run off, angry with them both? No, it had been late when they'd finally felt safe enough to creep to Sterling's bedroom, and Nell wouldn't have known what to make of anything she heard in any case.

Then she remembered. Nell had spoken to Hettie that afternoon, and then in the evening she had been quiet, subdued. Had Hettie said something to her? Or had Nell, perhaps, said something to Hettie?

Tilly climbed to her feet. She would have to tell Sterling . . . but then, what would happen? Would somebody go and question Hettie and find out that Tilly had been asking about her crime? Sterling had so much on his mind already.

She could always go to the stockade herself. Tilly shivered at the thought. But she became more and more certain that Hettie knew why Nell had run, and perhaps even where she might have run to.

Tilly went down the hall to Sterling's office. Of course he wasn't there. He was somewhere on the island, looking for Nell. She moved out onto the verandah and looked down, over the treetops towards the forbidding buildings of the stockade. Dark stone, iron bars, grim and silent in the heavy rain. Would they even let her in to see Hettie?

Today they might. If she could hold her nerve.

She pulled her spine up straight and walked down the stairs. The rain had eased to a miserable drizzle, but black clouds on the horizon threatened more to come. She picked her way down the dirt road, which had turned to rutted mud, and then took the side road that led to the stockade. She had never walked this way before. She had no idea where to go to get in, but she remembered Sterling saying the female prisoners were at the far southern end of the building, so she headed in that direction.

A separate entrance stood outside the southern wing. A small yard, perhaps an exercise yard, was enclosed in iron bars. The yard was nothing but scant grass and mud. No wonder Hettie loved the garden so much. Beside the yard was an arched wooden door in a stone wall. She wondered if she was supposed to knock, but then tried the latch and found it opened on a small wood-paneled room that smelled of lye soap and lemon. A young turnkey with carroty hair sat in a chair there, legs spread wide, his finger firmly jammed in his ear, giving it a thorough clean.

He saw her and dropped his hand, jumped to his feet. "You're not supposed to be here, ma'am."

"Superintendent Holt sent me. I have to speak to prisoner 135."

"I haven't seen any orders."

"Of course you haven't. He's searching the whole island for his daughter. I'm Eleanor's governess, and the superintendent and I have good reason to believe 135 may be able to help us find Nell. I simply need to speak to her for a few minutes."

He hesitated, then said, "Wait here." He lifted a large loop of keys off his hip and unlocked a door behind him, disappeared through it. The sound of the locks going back into place. She waited. The rain intensified again, deafening on the tin roof. The clouds had blocked out any light coming through the windows, turning the little anteroom into premature nighttime. Five minutes passed, another five, then Tilly heard the door unlock again, and the red-haired turnkey was back with an older, balder man.

"You say the superintendent sent you?" he asked brusquely.

"Yes." She met his eyes, didn't blink.

"He hasn't sent any word."

"As I said to your colleague, that's because he is otherwise occupied. And the longer you hold off letting me speak to 135, the longer young Nell is going to be outside in the elements."

The older man shook his head. "I don't threaten, ma'am. I follow orders. I haven't had any orders."

Tilly steeled herself. Her plan was falling apart. "I saw Hettie speaking to the girl yesterday. She may have some clue. You must let me speak to her. This is what Sterling wants me to do."

He raised his eyebrows at her use of the superintendent's first name, but to her surprise, he didn't throw her out. "Well, then. I expect the paperwork is on the way and I wouldn't want to hold up the search for the girl. Follow me."

"Thank you," Tilly said, managing not to gasp in surprise.

"I reckon we all want to see the lass found safely," he said in a gruff voice.

The old turnkey unlocked the door and led Tilly into an office with two desks and a wooden cabinet. Everything was remarkably neat and clean. Beside the wooden cabinet was a door with a square, barred window in it. He unlocked this door too, and it opened on a dim stone corridor, with a series of doors placed close together. He walked up to the first one and unlocked it, pulled it open, and said to the person within, "Miss Lejeune is here to talk to you." Then he stood aside, and gestured Tilly through, while he waited in the hall.

Tilly could barely fit in the tiny room. Hettie sat on a hammock bed, opposite another hammock bed with another woman—a Chinese woman with gray hair at her temples—lying in it. A tiny washstand stood in the corner, a wooden bucket beneath it. A small, barred window, up very high, let in the only light and a few spits of rain. Despite the cooler weather outside, the cell was close and humid. Tilly imagined that on those very hot summer days, it would be unbearable in here. How on earth did they sleep?

"Hello," Tilly said.

"What is it?" Hettie asked, puzzled.

Tilly moved in close so the other prisoner couldn't hear, but Hettie said, "Don't worry, she hardly speaks a word of English."

"Nell's gone missing."

Hettie's eyebrows shot up. "So that's why we're locked down?"

"We think . . . we hope she's run away. It's very bad weather out there today, and we are desperate to find her safe and well."

"Why are you speaking to me, then?"

"Because I saw her yesterday, talking to you. I wondered if she said anything, or if you said anything . . . I wonder if you have any clue you can give us. Think very hard. What did you speak of?"

Hettie shook her head. "Nothing out of the ordinary. She showed me her drawings. She told me you said she hadn't taken her time with them. I said she should always take her time with things that matter, and how I did exactly that in the garden . . ." She frowned, trying to recall every detail of the conversation. "She asked if we could grow some daisies. She said she's grown fond of daisies. I said I'd see what I could do . . . Honestly, Miss Lejeune, that's all."

Tilly hung her head, sighing. "Nothing else?"

"Nothing. Only . . ."

Tilly lifted her head again. "Only what?"

"The girl always knows things she shouldn't. For instance, last year, she came out to wish me happy birthday. How did she know it was my birthday? She must have looked at a document somewhere, something she shouldn't be looking at. Perhaps she's seen or heard something she doesn't understand and it's set her off."

"Oh," said Tilly, realization sweeping over her. She had been so busy feeling guilty about her developing romance with Sterling, that she had forgotten the conversation they had conducted the previous night about Nell and boarding school. Nell must have eavesdropped, then run away in an angry fit. Perhaps run away to punish her father for even considering it.

And thinking of schools and teachers made Tilly suspect she knew where Nell was too.

"Thank you, Hettie," she said. "Thank you. You've been more help that you can imagine."

She turned, nearly knocked over the old turnkey leaving.

"Off in a hurry?"

"I need to find Sterling."

He unlocked the door for her. "He was with the search party that went down to the southern cane fields."

"Thank you!"

Finally, she was free of the grim stockade, only to emerge under a leaden sky to deepening rain. She raced along the muddy road, hard fat raindrops driving against her, until she reached the edge of the cane fields. The cane was hip height, laid out in neat rows with paths between them. She plunged in, looking left and right for somebody who could lead her to Sterling.

"Sterling!" she called. "Sterling!"

A man in blue with a bushy gray beard caught her as she was about to plow into him. "Miss Lejeune?"

"I need to find the superintendent. I think I know where Nell might be."

"This way." He hurried further into the cane field, and soon they happened upon Sterling, soaked to his skin, calling for Nell with a hoarse voice.

"Sterling!" she shouted over the rain. "Come with me!"

"You've found her?" He trudged through the field towards her.

"I hope so. Do you have the key to the chapel?"

"I have the key to everything. I don't have my daughter."

"Then come."

Sodden and hopeful, they found their way out of the cane field and began the walk down to the chapel. He was clearly exhausted, still recovering from terrible injuries and lack of sleep, so she tried not to hurry ahead. She was desperate for her hunch to be right, that Nell was where she believed she was.

"I know why she ran," Tilly told him. "She must have overheard us talking about sending her to boarding school."

"I hope that's all she overheard," he said, mouth set in a hard line. "Why are we going to the chapel? We've already checked there."

"She once told me about a secret ladder, up onto the roof. How she and another child had hidden up there from their teacher."

"Secret ladder?"

"In the ceiling."

He shook his head. "I hope you're right. I hope this isn't some silly story she made up." He redoubled his speed and Tilly noticed he was wincing every time he put a foot down. The rain was unrelenting now, blurring her vision. But a few minutes later, they were inside the chapel, dripping on the wooden floor.

A chair pulled up near the end of the chapel, where Jesus mournfully hung on his cross, gave away the location of the secret ladder.

"Will you look at that?" he breathed, gazing upwards at the hatch. "I thought I knew every inch of this island."

He was already climbing onto the chair, reaching upwards and slipping his finger through the ring in the hatch. He pulled it and the hatch opened, and a ladder slid open, narrowly missing his head.

"Nell?" he called.

Tilly stood underneath him and he wriggled through the hatch and disappeared. She followed him up and found herself in the dark space between ceiling and roof, crawling on her hands and knees. Ahead of her, Sterling crawled too, until he found an iron door that opened onto rainy daylight. By the time Tilly made it onto the flat walkway above the eaves, she could already see Sterling crouching next to Nell. The girl stood very still, her body grasped in the circle of her arms, staring out to sea. Pangur Ban had been set on the brickwork in front of her, with his face also turned to the bay. He was as impassive as ever.

"Nell!" Tilly exclaimed.

Nell didn't respond. Tilly hurried over to join them.

Sterling was berating her. "You foolish child! Do you not know you have sent all my staff on a wild-goose chase? They are exhausted. *I* am exhausted. Last night you wouldn't let me reach for the gravy myself, but today you forced me to tramp around cane fields in pain and fear."

Nell wouldn't look at him. Tilly reached out to grasp Sterling's arm. She understood that all his tension was pouring out of him as anger—anger she hadn't known him capable of—but Nell wasn't listening.

"Nell," she said. "Is this about boarding school?"

Nell turned her face to Tilly. Her lips were blue, her curls hung in sodden tendrils. She nodded.

Sterling collapsed forward onto his hands, shaking his head. "I'm not sending you to boarding school, Nell. I would have you by me, all the time until you are grown."

Nell relaxed her body, dropped her head, and began to sob. Sterling pulled her into his arms and they stood there, in the pouring rain, clinging to each other while Tilly looked on.

NINETEEN

A Single-Minded Man

That night, Sterling went to bed before dinner and didn't get up the next day. Dr. Groom was sent for, expressed concern about his injuries and exhaustion, and ordered Sterling off the island for three weeks to recover.

Sterling told Tilly this in the half hour before his boat was due to leave the next day, as he folded shirts neatly into a suitcase, avoiding meeting her eye. "I have insisted that Nell come with me," he said. "I think that will be a good thing. We haven't had a holiday since Rebecca died. Perhaps we will spend some time in the city. Lord knows she needs new clothes."

"I want you to be well again," Tilly said.

Sterling paused in his packing, and his expression as he regarded her frightened her. There was pity in it. Pity never preceded anything good. "I would make you the offer to take the time off as well and travel with us to the mainland. But we would have to part company at the wharf. Nell doesn't know about . . ."

"I know. I promise you, I am happier staying here. I will read and garden and relax." She smiled shyly. "And look forward to your return."

He focused very hard on his packing. For an instant, she was back in Guernsey with Jasper, feeling the sick embarrassment of his rebuffs.

"Sterling?" she said. "Do you regret what we have done?"

"I make it my goal not to regret anything," he said. "I will miss our conversations, but it is only three weeks. I think we will all benefit from the break."

Tilly worked hard to stop tears from pricking her eyes. "Yes," she said, "perhaps you are right."

Then Nell came in, excited but in a subdued way. She had been diffident and pouty since the running away, no doubt because Sterling had limited her freedoms and enforced a number of unpleasant punishments in the form of household chores, but also because nobody on the island spoke to her anything but sternly now. They were all still angry with what they saw as a selfish prank.

Only Tilly had sympathy for her. "Are you looking forward to your holiday, Nell?" she asked, playfully tugging one of the girl's curls.

"I am looking forward to being in a place where I don't get frowned at quite so much," she said with feigned boredom. "Don't play with my curls. I'm nearly thirteen."

"You brought the frowns upon yourself, Nell," Sterling said, distractedly, searching in the top of his wardrobe for a hat. "And you ought not to speak sharply to your governess."

Your governess. Not *Tilly.*

"What were you two talking about?" Nell asked, considering Tilly by the morning light coming in the window.

"You," Tilly said.

"None of your business," Sterling answered, at precisely the same time.

Tilly laughed lightly, but Sterling remained stern.

"Nell, you must learn your place. If you hadn't eavesdropped on my conversation with Tilly, you would never have gone off with half a conviction in your head that made you—"

"I know, I know. That made me waste time and resources on the island."

"And possibly put yourself in danger. Don't forget that," Sterling added.

Nell turned her eyes up to Tilly, tried a little smile that didn't quite reach her eyes. "You'll miss me, won't you, Tilly?"

"Of course I will. Be good to your father. He is good to you."

And then they were off, down the rutted path to the jetty, leaving her in the west wing of the house alone. Mr. Donaghy would take over the superintendent's duties in Sterling's absence, so she could expect his company for lunch daily. Apart from that, she was on her own schedule, could do whatever she pleased.

It made her feel a little empty.

•

Tilly read that day until three, when the worst of the heat had faded, then she headed out to the garden.

It wasn't until nearly nightfall that she saw Hettie, who was planting some seedlings along the far northern border of the garden. Tilly realized she hadn't thanked Hettie for her help in finding Nell, so she peeled off her dirty gardening gloves and approached.

Hettie sat back, wiping the back of her hand against her forehead.

"Mind if I join you?" Tilly asked.

"Please," Hettie said, gesturing to the grass next to her. "I think I'm done for the day. Pansies. They came on the boat this morning. They'll be so pretty."

Tilly stretched out her legs. The dusky sky was cool. The wet heat of summer was finally loosening its grip on the island. The sea breeze was almost enough to make her arms come out in gooseflesh under her sleeves. "I meant to thank you for your help finding Nell."

"I didn't help."

"You did, indirectly. You provided a different perspective. I think that's always a valuable thing."

Hettie dropped her head slightly to hide her smile. "Well. You're welcome."

"She and her father have gone off to the mainland for a few weeks, so I'm at a loose end. You might see me out in the garden a little more."

"It's always nice to see you," Hettie said. Then the rest came out in a rush, "I'm sorry about crying on you. It wasn't . . . appropriate."

Tilly's voice grew gentle. "You are a human being and so am I. There is nothing inappropriate about wanting comfort."

"I rather think the superintendent would see things differently."

"No, you'd be surprised. Sterling Holt is a forgiving man. He has a very kind nature."

Hettie looked at her for a moment, in utter bafflement.

Tilly grew curious. "You don't believe me? But he lets you maintain the garden."

"Lets me? He *makes* me."

"But you said yourself: you would have sunk into despair without it."

"Yes, I enjoy it, but it's work. I have to do a certain amount of hours a week or I get my privileges taken away. I'm not like you. I don't flit in and out when I feel like it."

Tilly stung at her words, but then Hettie softened. "I am sorry," she said. "I don't mean to be so rude to you. But today I am tired and unwell, and I would rather be resting on a nice soft bed."

"You should tell the turnkeys. They could put you in the infirmary."

"The infirmary is for male prisoners. Female prisoners are simply not allowed to get sick. Besides, I did tell the turnkeys and they prodded me in the back and told me to get to work anyway." She clasped her hands together and rested her chin on them.

"I'm sorry you're not feeling well," Tilly said. "But I promise you Sterling is a kind man."

"He is not an unkind man, I suppose," said Hettie. "But Superintendent Holt is certainly a single-minded man and I have seen the side of him that you, perhaps, have not. He adores his daughter, and so do you, so you agree on what is fundamental to him. Perhaps if you disagreed with him you would see it. There is a hardness about him, once he makes up his mind . . ." She trailed off, her eyes flicking away to the distance. "I suppose I oughtn't talk like this to you."

"If there is a blurring of an accepted etiquette between us, Hettie, that is entirely my fault." Besides, Tilly wanted to hear more about this side of Sterling she didn't know. "Do the other prisoners think the same of Sterling?"

"I only know seven other prisoners," she said. "I never speak to any of the men. But I've heard the turnkeys talking. They often say similar things. Single-minded. Stubborn. Holier than thou." Hettie stopped, perhaps reaching a point of feeling she shouldn't say more. "I know you are fond of him."

"He has been kind to me."

"I know it is more than that. You love saying his name. Your mouth savors it the way it might savor a ripe peach."

Tilly blushed, speechless.

"In the end, Miss Lejeune, he is a superintendent at a high security prison. He must be as he is, or he would be unlocking doors and setting us all free. He must believe what he believes about us, even if it's only half true."

Tilly turned this thought over in her mind as the sun fell behind the mainland in the west, a huge orange ball that turned the sky shades of amber and pink. Its last red wedge paused a moment in a gap between distant mountains, then winked out. Night had fallen.

"Do you know, I believe you shouldn't call me Miss Lejeune," Tilly said slowly.

"Why not?"

Because it's not my name. The desire to tell her everything was too great. Tilly had to clear her throat loudly. "Because we are friends. And I call you Hettie, so you should call me Tilly."

"Yes, Tilly," she said, trying out the name. "If you prefer it."

"And if you would like me to speak to the superintendent on your behalf . . ."

"No. Please don't rock the boat. He'd put me on some other awful duty to spite me."

Tilly didn't answer. She didn't believe such things of Sterling.

At least she was fairly sure she didn't.

•

The days dragged. Hours stretched out and lost their shape. Tilly missed Sterling more than she could have imagined. After their first lovemaking, she had known one taste was not enough. But she hadn't counted on a second time making the craving worse. She woke up thinking about him, went to sleep thinking about him. After the first week, the idea that two weeks still remained before she saw him again caused her such a bolt of physical pain that she gasped.

She kept busy as best she could. Her own garden plot required little work as autumn glimmered on the horizon, so she started helping Hettie out with her gardening chores. Together they pulled weeds and raked leaves and scrubbed stone features. If Mr. Donaghy walked out onto the verandah to check on Hettie, Tilly would simply walk a few paces away. Most of the time, though, they were at the back of the garden, unobserved. Now that Hettie comfortably used Tilly's name, it had unlocked a deeper intimacy between them. Hettie spoke without restraint about her family back on the mainland, about her life before prison, her difficult childhood. Tilly shared too, still careful to avoid details that might reveal who she really was. But still, it was a great relief to talk about her grief at Grandpa's passing, about her odious cousin Godfrey, about her long journey to the antipodes to build a new and independent life for herself. Almost without realizing it, in that three weeks Sterling was away, she and Hettie became friends.

In her darker moments, before sleep, she wondered if befriending Hettie might be a way for her to assuage her own guilt. To hold close to her that person who was living the life she might have lived, had she not been a few minutes ahead of the police in Chantelle Lejeune's room . . . was it a way of vicariously experiencing the punishment she thought she was due?

She resolved that, on Sterling's return, she would talk to him about Hettie's case. About whether anything could be done to reduce her sentence in light of what she had told Tilly: was there not some special plea of self-defense Hettie could make?

But then, thoughts of Sterling would take a different turn in her mind and Hettie would be forgotten in that delicious memory of pleasure.

•

Nell's voice was the first indication to Tilly that they had returned. Slamming through the front door, calling out, "Helloooo? Tilly?"

Tilly, who had been curled up in an armchair in the library reading, leapt to her feet and raced out. Nell stood there, a suitcase in each hand, smiling.

"It's me!" she declared.

Tilly gathered her in her arms. "Welcome back. Your father?"

"Right behind me. He has rather a large trunk. Do you not think I look taller? Papa bought me all new clothes." She dropped her suitcases and reached into the satchel that was slung over her shoulders, pulling out Pangur Ban and a sheaf of untidy papers. "I have been writing so much! Would you like to hear some? Let's go to the library right now."

Tilly was desperate, though, to see Sterling. "Can we wait a few moments?"

But she could see now that Mr. Donaghy stood outside on the verandah, in deep conversation presumably with Sterling. He wasn't coming in yet. For an awful moment she wondered if he was actively trying to avoid her.

"Please, Tilly? I have missed you so and wanted so much to read you this."

Tilly forced a smile. "All right, then. But let's put your suitcases away in your room first."

Nell's new chapters were as wildly imaginative and vividly described as ever. Tilly tried to relax and enjoy Nell's reading, but eventually grew restless to see and speak to Sterling.

"Enough for today, Nell," Tilly said. "I think you should go and unpack, so that tomorrow we have a clear day for your studies."

"But I'm getting to the good part."

"Save it for another day. Always leave your reader wanting more."

Nell straightened the edges of her papers and lay them on the table, then pushed back her chair—did Tilly imagine the huffiness?—and left the room.

Tilly didn't waste a moment. She went straight to Sterling's office and knocked gently, hoping hard that he was alone.

"Come in."

She opened the door. He glanced up, smiled. "Tilly."

"Sterling."

He indicated his desk, an open ledger, a pile of papers. "I am so busy."

"I will come back later, then."

"No, no. Wait. I need to speak to you."

She prickled with anticipation.

"Mr. Donaghy spoke to me at length. He said you spent a great deal of time with prisoner 135 while I was away. Is that so?"

"I . . ." Her heart thudded in her throat. "We've been working in the garden together."

"He said he saw you talking more than working."

"Is that a crime?"

He frowned. "I'd advise against it."

She spoke quickly. "Yes, I admit Hettie and I talked. A lot. Perhaps more than we should have. So I may as well tell you that I don't understand why she has such a long sentence when it's clear she acted in self-defense and—"

Sterling was half out of his seat, waving his hands in a "stop" gesture. "Tilly, Tilly, no. No. Do not say another word."

Embarrassment suffused her cheeks.

Sterling paced. "I blame myself. Perhaps I did not warn you sufficiently. We give the prisoners numbers for a reason, so that we can interact with them impartially. You ought not have befriended this woman to such a degree that you are calling her by name and speaking to her about her crime."

"But she says—"

"She is a murderer, Tilly," he said, whirling around to face her. "After I spoke to Mr. Donaghy, I checked her records. She killed her husband, the man she stood beside, in the eyes of the Lord, and promised to love and honor. She got him drunk on potent homemade whiskey and then held two pillows over his face until he stopped breathing."

Tilly paused a moment as the image sunk in. Hettie's hard, raw hands around a pillow, a slack-limbed man beneath it, growing more and more still. "Yes, but he was beating her," she said in a quiet voice.

"Is this what she has told you?"

"Yes."

"Because the court records something quite different. He had been working up in the gold fields for six months. She had taken up with another man. On her husband's return, she murdered him so that she could be with this other man. Her lover helped her dispose of the body and is currently serving a sentence for it back on the mainland."

Shock and embarrassment fought for precedence in Tilly's body. She felt cold and warm all at once. Why had the court recorded such a different version of events? Was Hettie lying? Or was the court biased against Hettie? Tilly could imagine that so easily: women were rarely afforded fair treatment in any other aspect of public life.

He must believe what he believes about us, even if it's only half true. Tilly had seen too many times how men's opinions of women were formed out of what they heard from other men, not what they had observed from the behavior of actual women.

"I can see I will have to take 135 off garden duties," he muttered, returning to his seat.

"No! Don't do that. That's unfair to her."

"She should know better than—"

"No. I'm to blame. I was too friendly. I asked her about it. If anyone should be forbidden from being in the garden, it should be me."

Sterling looked at her. Pity again. Sadness. Regret. Nothing good, nothing promising. "Very well, Tilly. Stay out of the garden. It's nearly autumn anyway. I can send one of the prisoners up to rake up leaves and pull weeds. Perhaps, in spring, we'll review the situation. But I want you nowhere near that prisoner."

Tilly nodded, feeling like a naughty schoolchild.

Sterling seemed about to say something else, but then he stopped himself.

"What is it?" she asked.

"I will need to speak to you at length tonight. About . . . other things. About us. About Nell."

Tilly's heart sank. "Your tone frightens me."

"There is nothing to be frightened of, Tilly, my dear," he said, in a gentler voice. "I am not frightened."

Still, he wasn't smiling. And Tilly feared the worst.

·

Tilly could barely concentrate on her teaching that afternoon, so she was a good match for Nell who could barely concentrate on her lessons. In the end they decided that, as the tide was low, they would walk down to the small strip of sandy beach and look for shells to draw the next day. They tied on their bonnets and took a basket and honey sandwiches for afternoon tea.

"I have so missed the sound of the sea," Nell said, sitting on a rock and removing her shoes and stockings. She jammed her toes into the sand and wriggled them energetically. "The city is very noisy. Trams rattling and horses running about."

Tilly removed her own shoes and stockings and walked down the sand to the water. She lifted her skirts and stepped in. The sea was warm, but the breeze coming off it was cool and fresh.

"I think we should give this beach a name," Nell said. "Something like Seven Yard Beach."

Tilly turned. Nell's face was in the sun. Something about her fine, pale skin made Tilly ache with affection. "Prisoners' Cove," she said.

"Shark Beach," Nell said, grinning mischievously. "Don't go out too far, now, Tilly."

Tilly laughed and kicked water at her. "I think Seaweed Beach or Jellyfish Beach would be more descriptive. There are plenty of both around."

"I like Seven Yard Beach. It sounds poetic, but I think it is only seven yards or so across. I think I might draw a map of the island this afternoon and name all the places. What about the escarpment?"

"Sterling Cliff," Tilly said, immediately.

"Ooh, yes. Sterling Cliff sounds very foreboding. With

Starwater House directly on top, looking out to Seven Yard Beach and Stockade Flats." She stood up and came down to join Tilly in the water, circling her waist with her arms. "I'll draw sea monsters all around the island."

Tilly put her arms around Nell in return. They stood like that for a few minutes, the shallow waves lapping at their feet, and Tilly closed her eyes and felt the sun in her hair and the sweet breath of contentment in her lungs. Nell loved her, and she loved Nell. Sterling's cautionary tone would melt under such a truth.

Then they stepped apart.

"Honey sandwiches?" Tilly asked.

"Let's."

They sat together on flat rocks by the sand, eating and chatting, as the afternoon shadows grew long and the tide began to turn.

•

Sterling was too busy to join them for dinner. It was nearly nine o'clock in the evening when he knocked lightly on Tilly's door.

She opened it, heart thudding. "I thought I'd never see you."

"I'm sorry. The reason I do not like to take leave is because it makes so much more work when I get back."

"Come in," she said, opening her door wide. She wore only her nightdress and dressing gown.

"No. No, I . . . Can you please get dressed and come to the parlor? I'll pour us sherry."

Tilly nodded and he closed the door.

She quickly found a housedress and changed into it, but didn't bother to pin her hair and put stockings on. She went barefoot to the parlor, where Sterling waited, gazing out the window. Two sherries sat on the low table.

Tilly cleared her throat.

He turned. His dark eyes looked sad, and the sadness instantly transferred to her. She wanted to turn and run and not hear what he had to say to her.

"Sherry?"

She wordlessly picked up her glass.

He took her free hand in his, stroked her fingers gently. "It's too soon for Nell."

"Nell loves me."

"It's too soon for me."

She had no response.

"It's too soon for everything. The circumstances of our . . . consummation were so unusual. There was wildness in the night, in the air. We did the wrong thing."

"I love you, Sterling."

"We mustn't talk of love. We must talk of care and responsibility. We are not wild animals, Tilly. I am more fond of you than I can say, but Nell's well-being is my first concern. I can't have her running off again and—"

"That was nothing to do with overhearing us talking of love, Sterling. That was her fear of being sent to boarding school. You know that."

"I do not know what else she has heard or intuited. I just know that she veers between sweetness and aggression, she is fearful and unsettled. She dreamed nearly every night of her mother while we were away. It is too soon."

Tilly fought tears. "Then what's to become of me? Am I to lose my job?"

"No, of course not. We will continue as friends for now. We will proceed slowly. Please do not interpret my words as a rejection of your affections, Tilly. You are dear to me. But now is not the time for us."

"Then when?"

"We will know when the time is right."

"When you say 'we,' I think you mean 'you.' I am not part of this decision." Her temper had been ignited. She hung on grimly to the last bough of calm in her heart.

"I hope you will see things my way as my view is very sensible."

Single-minded. Stubborn. Holier than thou. "And my way isn't sensible? Or is it simply not worth listening to?"

Still, not a spark of anger or passion in his voice, almost as though the more flammable the situation became, the slower and more reasonable his tone became. This infuriated Tilly, who was fast being positioned as the hysterical party in this exchange. "You are very young, Tilly. It is perhaps my major misgiving about our . . . relationship, especially after seeing your ill judgment with regards to prisoner 135. You are nowhere near old enough to be Nell's mother and, yes, she loves you, but not as a mother. You and Nell and I: we are not a family."

Tilly felt the ground fall away from beneath her. Not a family. But that was precisely how she'd been imagining the three of them. Now Sterling was pushing her away, with vague reassurances of "fondness" and a time in the future when there might be a chance for them to be together. Well, she was having none of it.

She threw her sherry glass on the floor. It shattered into bright pieces. "You impossible man," she shouted. "How dare you play with my heart in such a way?"

And Sterling was shocked: she could see it in the way his pupils dilated, in the way his skin turned pale. He had not seen her angry before. She had managed her temper so well for so long. "Tilly,

I never meant to play with your heart. I admit what I did was immoral—"

"No it wasn't. It was beautiful and you know it was. Don't reduce it to a sin, a shameful secret." Sobs bubbled up now. "What have I done in my life to deserve such raw treatment at the hands of men? Are you all as cruel and thoughtless as each other?"

Sterling fell silent, realizing that anything he said would become fuel on the fire. She glared at him as the broken glass glinted on the rug between them, catching the lamplight. Nothing she could do or say would change his mind; and why should he anyway? It had been doomed from the start. He knew nothing about her shameful past. *He didn't even know her real name.* Her shoulders drooped.

"I'm sorry," she muttered. "I will clean up that mess on the floor."

"Don't concern yourself," he said, not meeting her eye. "I'll get the staff to do it. Go. Find some peace and comfort on your own."

Palming tears off her face, she ran from the parlor. She should have known nothing would ever come of her feelings for Sterling. Her future would not exist until she had atoned for her past.

•

That night, her sleep was riven with nightmares. She woke again and again from fragmented sleep, in and out of images of fire and broken glass, of ghostly shapes condemning her, of Sterling and Nell on a ship receding further and further into a foggy distance while she sat upon the cold shore frozen with misery.

When dawn finally came, she lay awake, eyes on the canopy of her bed, and sifted through the terrible images. Why would she have such a night of terrible dreams? She wasn't ill. She hadn't drunk too much sherry. There could be only one reason. God was punishing her, showing her that she was not worthy of love or comfort because she had committed a terrible sin. He knew what was in her heart, even if nobody else did.

She feared the future. She feared Judgment.

Tilly knew exactly what she must do.

•

All through the next day, Tilly's mind flicked on and off her plans. She watched Nell drawing in a sunbeam that fell through the library window and stroked her hair gently, her mind wandering elsewhere. Out in the garden, in the cane fields, in the mangroves, on the bay. Afternoon came. A fresh wind from the southeast. The season was turning. Soon it would be Easter and Nell said the damp clinging heat of the wet summer would be behind them. Tilly could see the trees moving in the wind outside, the palms, green and golden, flapping madly.

"Time to finish up," Tilly said, right on the dot of four.

Nell sprang from her seat. "See you at dinner."

The nape of Tilly's neck prickled with anticipation, as if any moment a firm, hot hand would come down on it, stop her, press her down. She moved out onto the verandah, breathed the sea-salted wind. The garden, that place she was forbidden from entering, waited. She couldn't see Hettie, but she would be in there. Somewhere.

Tilly took her time, made sure that Sterling wasn't about to step out of his office, that Nell wasn't about to burst onto the verandah demanding Tilly come and read with her, that Mr. Donaghy wasn't about to walk up the stairs. But it was a quiet and empty afternoon, almost as though the world was retreating in the face of the dry, cool season that was nearly upon them.

One foot in front of the other, into the forbidden garden. Down past the roses, past the Grecian woman, past the shady magnolias, past her own tidy, colorful plot. And there was Hettie, kneeling on the grass, pulling weeds and collecting them in a wooden bucket.

Hettie glanced up and smiled. Tilly skidded to the ground next to her, adopted an urgent voice. "I'm not meant to be here."

"Why?"

"Sterling thinks we have become too close."

Hettie's forehead wrinkled in concern. "Will they take me out of the garden?"

"No, I made him forbid me from coming here instead. Listen. Carefully. I have to tell you something."

"What is it?" Hettie's gaze was fully upon her, round eyes, dark strands of hair loose and trailing across her florid cheeks. "Is it something bad?"

"No, it's something good," Tilly said. "I'm going to help you escape."

TWENTY

Fields of Fire

2012

No matter how afraid I was of Elizabeth Parrish, I had a deadline to meet. I was up and down like a roller coaster. One day I'd write seven hundred words and be unable to sleep for excitement; the next I'd delete half of them and then patrol the house, poking around skirting boards and between bricks that Joe had uncovered, desperate and unable to produce a word.

It was afternoon on a bad day when I walked down to the pay phone at the Stockade shops, intending to call Marla and tell her I was giving up. That she would have to let publishers in twenty-three countries know I couldn't do it, and I would have to sell my apartment and pay them all their money back. Then Elizabeth Parrish couldn't hurt me. I'd be free.

Fortunately, before I reached the pay phone, I ran into Lynn McKiernan, Joe's mum. She and Julian were coming out of the post office.

"Nina!" Julian shouted, racing up to me and grabbing me in a hug.

"Hello, dear," Lynn said. "What a lovely surprise to see you." Lynn, too, gave me a hug. I've not ever been a particularly huggy person, but in my current state of mind, all of this impromptu hugging was bliss.

They stood back, and Lynn said, "What brings you down here?"

"I was going to make a phone call," I said, "but now I'm not so sure it's a good time to make it."

Lynn didn't press me for further details. "Julian and I are about to sit down for afternoon tea at the café. We'd love it if you joined us."

"They make great strawberry milkshakes," Julian told me, persuasively.

I thought about Marla, the carefully rehearsed sentence I was going to say: *Marla, I'm sorry but I am leaving the publishing world and I want to cancel all my contracts*. And then I thought about having afternoon tea with Lynn and Julian and there was no contest. "That would be really nice."

The café was tiny, with a bell over the door that jingled as we went in, and four little tables crammed in front of the glass-fronted cake case. A red soft-drink fridge hummed loudly. Sounds of clattering trays and running water came from out the back.

"This is our favorite table," Julian said, dragging me to the one closest to the front window. "Nanna and I always sit here."

"I'm sure I'll like it too."

A waitress came and took our orders, then retreated behind the counter to slice cakes and make a pot of tea. Julian would have dominated the conversation, but Lynn firmly but kindly told him it was time to let the grown-ups talk. Lynn gave him her phone to play with. Within seconds we heard the sound of cartoon birds flying into brick walls.

Lynn shook her head in awe. "Children are amazing, the way they can work those technological things out. Julian fixed my video player the other day."

"It's not a video player, Nan," he said, not looking up. "It's a Blu-ray player."

"Well, whatever it is."

"Dad bought it for her last Christmas," Julian said.

"That was sweet of him," I said.

"My Jonah is a sweet lad," Lynn said proudly. "I have the best son and the best grandson in the world."

"You're very lucky."

"Lucky doesn't begin to describe it," Lynn said emphatically. "How my boy and I could have missed each other, after all those years of me longing for him." Her eyes welled. "I never did understand why I had been born with such a desire to be a mother and all the wrong insides to fulfill that desire."

Julian glanced up, made uncertain by her tears. "Nanna?"

"Oh, you know me, Julian. Always blubbing." Lynn rubbed his head. "You adorable monkey."

Julian made a monkey noise and returned his attention to the phone.

"But eventually we found each other, Jonah and I," Lynn continued. "And it was all for the best. You don't have any children, Nina?"

"No, I don't." Treading carefully now. "I still feel like a child myself. I think I'd be a rotten mother."

Julian said, "No, you wouldn't. You make great Legos."

I laughed lightly and the mood lifted. Our pot of tea arrived, and chocolate cake, too. Julian ate like a horse, then started fidgeting violently, bored by our adult conversation.

"Outside with you then," Lynn said. "I'm going to have a second cup of tea. How about you, Nina?"

"That sounds lovely."

Julian ran outside and across the street to the leafy edge of somebody's farm. Within seconds he was inside the barbed-wire fence and climbing a mango tree.

"Is he okay to be in there?" I asked, my city-girl instincts about private property firing up.

"Oh, that's fine. The barbed wire is to keep cattle in, not children out. That's Reg Byrd's farm. He couldn't care less if Julian climbed his trees. And, frankly, Julian misses out on so much stuck over here on this island, I'm loath to stop him larking about."

I stirred sugar into my second cup of tea. "You think he misses out?"

"Yes, as Joe did before him. Over on the mainland, he'd have friends, he could go swimming in a pool, skateboarding in a skate park, see a film before it came out on video . . . He's only going to be a little boy once. It seems a shame to waste it over here."

I watched out the window. Julian had started running some kind of climbing circuit. Up one tree as far as he could go, then back down again. Then to the next tree and up that one, and so on. He moved further and further down the fence line. "He doesn't look as though he's wasting his boyhood to me," I said.

Lynn turned and watched him a while too. "It was different with Joe. He was always quiet, bookish. I didn't feel quite so much that I was repressing his spirit, letting him grow up over here. It only became apparent later that we hadn't given him enough opportunities.

He was sharp as a shiny pin, that boy. Not like Dougal and me. And yet it took him so long to get going."

"He's doing a PhD. That's a big thing."

"He's thirty-four. He spent a few too many years in his twenties helping Dougal on the farm, not sure what to do with himself. I think we should have sent him to boarding school back in the city. He would have figured it all out earlier. He wouldn't have met that woman." Her mouth went into a hard line.

I presumed she was talking about Julian's mother and I said gently, "But then he wouldn't have had Julian."

She sighed, and sipped her tea. "Of course, you're right."

"Who was she?" I asked, more curious than I had a right to be about Joe's past.

"Andrea? She was the girl next door. Literally. Her father and Dougal were good mates, but I never liked her mother. Thought she was better than us. Thought Andrea could do better than Joe. She and Joe were on and off for years, then finally the little fellow came along and suddenly I was babysitting two and three nights a week because she 'needed a break.' We still thought things could work out. We paid for a wedding." She shook her head slightly, angrily. "Paid a bomb for it. Booked the little chapel down the road, made invitations. Two weeks before the wedding, she disappeared. Left a note saying it was all too much. Abandoned them both." Again, Lynn's eyes welled and I came to understand that she was a woman who wore her heart on her sleeve. "Can you imagine? Walking away from that darling little boy? Well, we all tried to give him more than enough love, so that he wouldn't die of sadness. He remembers none of it now, and I don't want her ever to come back. It would just confuse him." Lynn picked up her napkin and dabbed at her eyes, then blew her nose noisily. "On the day he was supposed to marry Andrea, we couldn't find Joe anywhere. He went down to the chapel and, even though he's not a religious man, he sat in there all day crying. Since he came out, he hasn't shed a tear. He's just got on. I'm so proud of him." Now she sat back in her chair, blushing. "Here's me rabbiting on. You can't get a word in, you poor thing. Dougal's always telling me I talk too much."

"That's not true," I said. "You talk precisely the right amount." My thoughts had got caught on one of her ideas, the way seaweed catches on a rock. The chapel.

"Oh, you're a sweetheart. No wonder our Joe likes you so much." And then, when I looked away awkwardly, she added, "Surely it's not a secret."

I looked into my teacup, deliberately avoiding her gaze. "I have a boyfriend," I said, and I knew it sounded like a lie or an excuse, or both.

"I know. The poet. You've been here quite a while now, Nina. Is the poet going to come visit you?"

I opened my mouth to tell her the truth, but it was easier simply to say, "I don't think so."

"And do you think you'll stay? Starwater's a lovely old house."

"It is," I said. "I would love to stay, but I . . ." I thought about all the work I had left to do in the three weeks remaining. All around the world, publishers were gearing up to edit, translate, print, and promote my book. "At the moment the future's pretty uncertain."

Lynn nodded. "That's good, though. It means anything could happen."

I tried a smile. "Yes," I said. "I guess you're right."

•

I went back to Eleanor's "secret confession": *I imagined myself slipping away from classes and coming here to write on the walkway, hiding my stories in the warm, dark ceiling.* Had Eleanor in fact hidden some of her papers in the ceiling of the chapel? She had owned it until the 1930s. It had sat empty all that time until she donated it to a small group who thought the island needed a church.

While I was trying to write, my mind kept returning again and again to the chapel. Was there something up there? What if Elizabeth Parrish got there first? I couldn't concentrate. At sunset I left the house.

The chapel was small and hunched next to the much larger stockade. I didn't know much about churches, but assumed that somebody would be in who might let me have a poke around. Especially if I told them I was Eleanor's great-granddaughter. The front door was closed but not locked. I pushed it open, then let it bang shut behind me. I found myself in almost darkness. Only the faint glow of the sky through the windows lit my way.

"Hello?" I called.

No answer. I advanced down the aisle, over uneven stone tiles, and found a box full of candles. *Light a candle for a prayer. $2.* I picked up a candle and put it in one of the empty iron holders, then lit it with a match from the box that lay next to it. I turned around to look.

The church had a smell like old wool and secondhand books. The pews were neat but scarred. Little leather-covered psalm books were stacked at the end of each pew. In the back corner of the church was a wooden chest overflowing with faded children's toys. Cold air reflected off the stone walls.

"Hello?" I called again. Then turned to the back of the chapel where Jesus hung on his cross. This was a new Jesus, all white and gold enamel paint. Not the one Eleanor had mentioned. I looked up at the ceiling, and could clearly see the outline of a ceiling hatch. Did anyone still use it? I supposed that electricians and termite inspectors probably did. Would they have found any papers stashed up there? Kept them? Thrown them away as rubbish? Given them to the local pastor?

I looked around for a chair or something else to stand on. There was nothing, unless I wanted to drag a pew up here. But then I realized the toy box might give me the height I needed. I walked back up the aisle and tipped the toys out. Clowns and teddies landed on the floor. A chunky plastic airplane burst into noisy life. *Zoom-zoom. Come fly with me!* My heart skipped a beat. I dragged the empty toy chest up the aisle in the flickering candlelight, dimly aware that if anyone walked in right now I would have to do some fast talking. My pulse picked up its rhythm. I positioned the chest under the hatch and climbed on top, reached up carefully to ease the hatch down. A ladder—a steel one—was bolted to the inside of the hatch. I released the latch on the side and it slid down and banged loudly on the chest.

I tested it for strength, then climbed up. I was in complete darkness now, so I eased my mobile phone out of my pocket and switched it on so that its face could give me a little light. I crouched, reaching above me to feel where the roof was. I shone the phone around. Electrical cables, insulation, rat droppings. I crawled around, poking in corners. No papers. Nowhere for them to hide.

When I came to the little door that led to the ceiling, I almost didn't bother to go out. No papers could have survived the elements out there, but the bolt slid easily and I was curious. I crawled out onto the roof, and stood up in the last light of the day on an iron walkway with a safety rail. The bay was pale silver-blue, the clouds pink and yellow over the mountains on the mainland. My heart slowed a little as I breathed the sea air. A sailing boat glided past in the distance, its sails white against the darkening sky.

I turned my phone on again and crouched down, running the light all along the corners of the walkway, just in case. Just in case.

Right at the end of the walkway, the light picked up a shape. I got on my knees and held the light close. A little painted face looked back at me from the gap between the brickwork and the iron walkway. I reached in, and pulled out a wooden cat, about the size of two fists.

And when I turned it over, I saw painted on the bottom in a childish hand *Nell Holt*.

I gasped. I had certainly found something of my great-grandmother's, and while it was not what I'd hoped for, the thrill was there nonetheless. It was as though time melted away and I was touching the past, holding it in my hand. The wooden cat looked back at me. Its white paint was moldy and it looked like rats had chewed its edges. But it had survived, protected by bricks for more than a century.

I pressed it against my chest and closed my eyes, holding on to the feeling of being connected to Eleanor.

•

I cleaned up the wooden cat and set it on my desk to watch over me, hoping some good luck might rub off it. In fact, I did write more than usual that day, and didn't hate it too much. Still, I was happy when Joe knocked on my door just before lunch.

"Hi," I said, wary as always not to smile too broadly.

"I've just finished the last wall, and I found something." He pulled up a spare chair beside my desk and offered me a handful of papers. "One's a diary entry, like the others. Eighteen ninety-two this time, so a little later. But look at this. I thought you'd appreciate it."

He unfolded a piece of paper. On it, a map of the island was drawn. I saw it and had to laugh. Nell had drawn the house, the stockade, the cane fields, the mangroves; but had surrounded the island with sea monsters and pirate ships. "I love her more and more," I said, taking it from his hands.

"We know she was calling this place Starwater from child-hood," he said, pointing at the title written over the crude drawing of the house.

"She's named everything. Sterling Cliff . . . I believe that was her father's name; we don't know much about him, except what's on the public record. Seven Yard Beach. The Swamp of Despair." I laughed out loud. "Brilliant."

"Tilly's Memorial," he read. "That's nowhere near the cemetery. I wonder who Tilly was. A pet?"

"Looks like it was out in the gardens, so perhaps." I turned the wooden cat around so it faced him. "I found this last night. It used to be Nell's."

He picked it up in awe. "Really?"

"It has her name on the bottom." I glanced through the diary, then put it aside to read later. "That's it, then. You've finished stripping all the walls. That means we've got every last thing Elea-nor wrote and kept."

"It would seem so. The diary was in pieces, so I presume there were other parts. But perhaps they didn't survive renovations or weather or people moving in and out."

The finality of knowing I wasn't going to find what I wanted to find took a while to sink in. I didn't know what was going to happen to me next. My pages, like the pages of my novel, were unwritten, blank, a mystery.

"Hey, are you okay?" Joe said. I realized his hand was under my elbow. "You look like you're going to faint."

"No, no, I'm fine," I said. He didn't move his hand. We were so close that I could feel the heat off his body. Then he withdrew and rolled his chair back in his own space, leaving me in mine.

I changed the topic. "So. Last day on the job?"

"I can still do other things for you. Whatever you need. I can still do your shopping, fix anything that needs fixing." He seemed so eager, but I couldn't encourage it. "No, I think that's it. I won't be staying much longer anyway."

"Oh," he said.

"I do need to sell the boat. Can you help?"

"Sure," he said. "How about tomorrow we pull it out of the shed and take some photos to put online?"

"That would be great. Thanks." But he felt it as much as I did. This wasn't the beginning of something as he hoped, as I had secretly hoped. This was getting close to the end.

•

May 28, 1892

It is late.

I am beside myself. I have heard that expression a thousand times, but now I understand it. I am beside myself, looking at myself, sitting in my bed with my diary on my knee, my inkwell on the sill, the curtains open but the window closed against the smoke and ash, watching the lamps swinging in the dark as they try to find her; but she will not return because she walked into that field and she did not walk out.

The girl I am looking at, the girl who is beside myself, seems almost normal. There is a twitch in her wrists, yes. Her eyes keep flicking to the window, hoping to see the shape of somebody who cannot be—who cannot ever . . .

I have sat here now for ten minutes, looking at my page, the last line I wrote. I do not know—

What has happened has happened, and there is no saving her now, so I must protect her good reputation and not mention it because Papa would—I cannot imagine how Papa might feel and he . . .

I must stop rambling. I must stop it. I must pull all my parts together and write down a true and accurate account of what I saw in case it ever matters in a court of law. But after I have written this down, I will bury it far from my father's eyes. If I can spare him from the truth about Tilly I will.

The suspicions I recorded in previous entries have been confirmed. The manner by which the act has been planned and carried out are still largely mysterious to me, so all I can record here is what I saw this afternoon, what I did about it, and how I ultimately failed to save her. If my words seem rational or cold, that is simply because to record my feelings about this terrible, terrible night would require more words than exist in the English language. Or in Greek, Latin, or French, those three other languages that she taught me so well.

We finished lessons in the morning because Tilly had complained of illness. She met with me for lunch, but by then seemed distracted and emotionally fragile. Tilly's heart is ever-present in her sweet face, whether she is blushing prettily when my father was nearby or fighting down black-eyed anger or preoccupied with some haunting thought of the past, which she never disclosed. I have come to presume that she lost a love, in awful circumstances, and that is why she moved so far from home and spoke so

*little of her past. She had called out several times for a man named Jasper,
when she was sick with a fever; but had denied any great love for him
when I questioned her. I will never forget the queasy expression—grief?
guilt?—upon her face.*

*So, today, I knew Tilly was preoccupied and I knew she was not really
ill, and I suspected it had something to do with that awful woman, whom
I now hold responsible for this evening's horrors.*

*I let her go and she went off to her bedroom and closed the door quietly.
I grew agitated, as though her anxiety were contagious, and I promised
myself that I would go into the garden later that afternoon, when 135 usually arrived, and I would find whatever way I could either to listen to their
conversation and plans or, if I could not find a good place to hide, disrupt
them. And if I saw even one more shred of evidence that Tilly were planning something too wild for my father ever to forgive her, an act that might
indeed put her in a prison, I would stop her.*

*Around four o'clock, I walked past Tilly's door and it was still closed.
I am in the very next room, so would have heard her if she'd gone into the
hallway or into the east wing to look for food. I went into the garden, looking about for 135. She wasn't there. As the weather has grown cooler and
drier, she is usually in the garden from three, so I knew she wouldn't be far
away. So I found a place in the garden beds nearest Tilly's plot, behind the
hydrangea hedges, and settled there with my skirts in the soil to wait.*

*At first I had sun on my hair, and it was pleasant. Soil and foliage have
an agreeable odour; I suppose it is the odour of the natural world, which
we are so often divorced from in our housebound lives. I know Tilly has
spoken often of how working in the garden helps her to feel less of a bird in
a cage. The way climbing a tree makes me feel.*

*Time passed, though, and the sun moved on and cool collected in the
shadows and still I heard neither Hettie nor Tilly, and I feared something
was afoot.*

But then, it is an awfully large garden and perhaps they met down on its perimeter; everybody knows I'm a terrible eavesdrop and perhaps they were being careful. So I stood and brushed off my skirts and then wandered through the garden, crunching through fallen leaves. I walked up and down the rows, all around the edges, and saw nobody.

Which was curious because Hettie works every day in the garden except Sundays.

I went back inside the house. From deep within, I could smell dinner cooking. Meat and pastry smells, and my stomach stirred with hunger. I crept down the hall to Tilly's room and listened at the door. Nothing. I knocked lightly.

Nothing.

So I opened the door. She wasn't there.

Where was she?

I left the room and closed the door quietly behind me and went back outside and down to the huge ancient fig that spread over the northern side of the house. Its bark was cool beneath my fingers as I hoisted myself up amongst its boughs and climbed as high as I could. The view was impeded by leaves and branches, but I could see the stockade, the cane fields, the cattle fields. Tilly had been wearing a dark red dress, so she would have stood out among white and blue uniforms. But I saw no flash of red.

For some reason my eyes returned to the cane field. Something was different today. Then I realised: I saw nobody down there. No prisoners in white nor warders in blue. I watched for a while. The cane was very high, so perhaps I simply couldn't see them because they were hidden behind the golden stalks. But no, nobody moved in or out of the rows, and I started to wonder if 135 had already deployed her plan, if the escape protocol was already in place and all the prisoners returned to their cells.

But no. I saw them in the other fields, around the stockade, near the entrance to the blacksmithery.

"Nell!" Papa's call broke into my train of thought. He stood on the verandah, looking left and right for me. I climbed down from the tree and

ran towards him, put my arms around him. How I wanted to tell him what I had overheard and what I suspected. But you must understand I was not perfectly sure yet—it still seems impossible that she had ever thought it a good idea—so I said nothing for fear Papa would hate me or Tilly or both of us.

"Tilly is unwell and presumably won't be at dinner tonight," he said. "Given I have a busy schedule today, would you mind eating alone in the kitchen? Just let cook know when you are hungry."

"I will." Tilly had lied to him. She wasn't unwell. She was out some-where, doing something. I didn't know where or what.

He looked around, admiring the garden in the dying light of the sun. "It's a beautiful afternoon. Be careful in that tree."

I wanted to ask him if he knew why 135 wasn't about. I should have. I should have exposed them, exposed everything I knew. "I'll be careful," I said to him. He kissed me on the top of my head and returned inside to his office, none the wiser.

I sat on the verandah with my head between my hands, thinking and thinking. Hettie was missing, Tilly was missing, I had overheard them talking about getting Hettie off the island . . . certainly neither of them had used the word "escape," but what else would that mean? I heard them yester-day, but couldn't get close enough to hear details. I did hear Tilly tell Hettie of items she had acquired, ideas that she had. What other conclusion was I to draw than that Tilly was, at this moment, helping Hettie escape? But if I reported Hettie missing, Tilly would be implicated and bad things would happen to her. I didn't want bad things to happen to her; so it was up to me to find her and stop her before events proceeded too far.

So where were they? In the mangroves? At Seven Yard Beach? In amongst the high cane? I am not three people. I could not split myself in pieces and search everywhere. I felt overwhelmed and tired, so very tired. So I climbed the tree again, as much to gather my thoughts as to keep a look-out. I imagined I might look down into the garden this time and see them, where I hadn't before: Hettie raking leaves while Tilly stood nearby, keeping a watch for father who didn't like her going in the garden any more.

I didn't see them in the garden. Above me I could see a bough, not as strong as the one I was on, but I knew it would give me a better view. I put my arms around it. Tested it. It bent but did not break, so I climbed onto it, hanging on with arms and legs as I wriggled along on my stomach to the point where the view through the foliage was clearest.

And I saw Tilly. Her grey scarf, her dark red dress. I saw her on the edge of the cane field, and then I saw her disappear inside.

I had such a shock, finally seeing her, that I almost fell off my branch. I climbed down as quickly as I could, landed with a thump on grass that was growing dewy. I began to run, down the road, dodging carts returning to the stockade. A warder called out after me, "Miss! You aren't supposed to be down here!" But by then I'd already climbed a fence over a cow paddock and was bolting towards the cane fields, to catch Tilly, to tell her to abandon whatever her mad plan was and come home to Starwater, to beef pies for dinner, to a simple, happy life.

In my blind haste, my foot landed in an enormous cow pat and I slid over and fell hard on my bottom. The pain shuddered up through me but I stopped myself from crying out because I didn't want anybody to hear me and pursue me. So I struggled to my feet and went slower, limping, towards the cane field where I had seen Tilly disappear.

The smell was the first indication. A smoky smell. Acrid and sweet.

Suddenly the empty cane fields made sense. No prisoners, no warders because tonight they were burning off the cane. I saw shadows in the dusk; men walking the perimeters of the fields, ready to set them alight with burning faggots made of dead cane leaves.

Walking the perimeters because they burn the fields from the outside in.

"No!" I cried. "No!" And I redoubled my speed to get to the field, to save Tilly from being burned alive.

With an intense, sharp crackle, the first fire surged into life. I kept running towards it, heedless of my own safety. It was the field Tilly had gone into. I pulled up sharply as the air became sucked into the fire and the flames doubled and doubled again, whooshing up towards the evening sky, racing towards the centre of the field. As fast as the flames raced in, mice and snakes raced out, skittering across my feet. The smell was burnt molasses and vinegar, acridly sweet, choking me. Orange smoke in the deep blue sky. Then, softly, black ash began to snow down on me. I stood there at the edge of the field, watching it burn and turn to a smoking mess, watching the other fires burst into life, knowing she was in there, and she would never walk out.

One of the warders found me, half an hour later. I was black with soot, sobbing on the ground.

"Miss Holt?" he said, scooping me up in meaty arms. "Are you hurt?"

I sobbed, barely able to make words come. "Miss Lejeune has been burned alive."

"What?"

"I saw her go in the field, right before they lit it up."

"Good God!" He began barking orders, noise and confusion gathered around us, men with lamps, commands to stop the burning immediately. But it was too late, it was already too late. Why didn't they understand?

The warder—whose face I cannot bring to memory: I was so lost in the black moment of my grief and shock—carried me up the hill to Starwater. Papa, who had been alerted to some disaster, was on the verandah pulling on his coat.

"Nell?" he asked, shocked, when he saw me.

The warder deposited me on the stairs where I kept sobbing.

"She says she saw Miss Lejeune walk into the field, right before it lit up."

I didn't see Papa's face because I was sobbing into my knees, but the silence was long and I heard his pain in his breathing, as he tried to find his voice. "Find her," he managed, croaking across pain so brittle it threatened to break his throat. "Get everybody out there to find her."

He yanked me to my feet, heedless of my pain in the heat of his own. "Are you sure? Are you sure?"

"I saw her from the tree. I ran down to catch her."

"The tree is a long way from the cane fields."

"I saw her red dress."

He looked at me, horrible realisation in his eyes. Then he pressed me hard against him and I sobbed into his chest.

They are still looking for her. But there will be nothing left of her to find. Papa is out there and he still believes she might be safe. I am in the house alone. I do not know what has happened to 135, but I can only presume she was hiding in the cane ahead of whatever they planned. But my heart doesn't hurt for the prisoner. I blame her. Somehow, she put Tilly under a spell. And she killed my Tilly as sure as she killed her husband.

TWENTY-ONE

Come Together, Fall Apart

I couldn't stop talking about the diary to Joe, as we unlocked the boat shed the next day.

"I mean, I've enjoyed reading all the little bits of diary, but this one was incredible. Prisoners escaping and people in burning cane fields. Like a novel, not a diary."

"Maybe she made it up," he said, pulling open one of the doors while Julian attempted to pull open the other. "Here, let me do that, mate," Joe said, securing the door on the hook in the brickwork.

"I don't know. Perhaps you're right. I couldn't sleep after reading it, though. Who was Tilly? Was she the governess? Eleanor mentioned her teaching Latin and Greek. Or was she the superintendent's girlfriend?"

"Maybe she was both."

"Oh, stop! How romantic. Like *Jane Eyre*."

He smiled at me. "Okay, can you take Julian out of the way while I hook up my car and pull the boat out?"

"Come on, Julian," I said, taking the little boy's hand. We moved over to the sandy gully, where Julian found a perfectly round rock.

"Look at this," he said, holding it perilously close to my eyes.

"It's a beauty."

"It's almost like a marble," he said. "I haven't played with my marbles for a while. Do you play marbles?"

"Ah . . . I did for a while, when I was a child."

"Maybe you could come and visit Dad and me sometime, and we could play marbles."

I smiled at his artlessness. "That could be fun."

"You like being with me and Dad, don't you?"

"Yes, I do."

He grinned back at me, and I had the distinct feeling I had passed some kind of test. Joe called me and I joined him at the boat with my phone, ready to take photos to put on a boat sales website.

"Now I haven't the faintest idea what kind of things sell boats," I said.

"Just take photos of everything and choose the most flattering ones later," he said.

"Dad!" Julian called from the boat shed. "Can I play in here?"

"Sure, mate. Just don't climb anything. It's old in there, okay?"

Julian nodded and disappeared into the shed.

"There isn't anything in there to climb, is there?" I asked.

"There's a platform, almost like a loft. Lots of old fishing nets and paddles and things stored up there." He extended his hand to me. "Here, let me have the phone for a minute."

I handed him my phone and he took some close-up photographs of the motors and the dashboard dials.

"That rip in the vinyl seat doesn't look great," he said.

"I suppose we could shoot around it."

"No, go sit on it. Look happy."

I laughed and climbed up into the boat, sat over the tear, arms extended across the back of the seat, and smiled. Joe took several photos, then helped me down.

"Is that false advertising?" I asked.

"No, we'll say in the description that it needs some minor repairs." He thumbed through the photos. "You certainly light up every picture you're in, Nina."

I watched him, his head bent as he looked through the photos, and experienced a surge of affection and longing that nearly winded me. He glanced up; I was about to say something—I don't know what, but it would have been something foolish—when we heard a loud crack, a yelp, and a horrible thud from the boat shed.

Joe went white. "Julian," he gasped, before turning on his heel and sprinting for the boatshed. "Julian! Julian! No. No no no."

I was a second behind him, out of the bright light and into the dark boat shed. In an instant, I could see what had happened. The loft that Joe had spoken of was half hanging down, the wooden beam that had supported it cracked in half. Julian lay on the ground, still and not breathing. Joe bent over him, but had lost his ability to speak or think. He said, "Oh, God, oh, God," over and over, too shocked to do anything else.

I quickly pushed in front of him. The rough wooden floor scraped my knees. I had basic first-aid training from my years working in day care, but I had never had to use it. "Call emergency," I said to Joe.

My command snapped him out of his shock. He still had my phone in his hand, and I heard him talking to an emergency operator while I checked for a pulse then went to work on Julian: breathing into his soft damp mouth, compressing his little bony chest. Adrenaline sparked through me, flushing me with intense heat. Life had become suddenly more real than usual; the edges of everything were sharper, the light brighter. "Come on, Julian," I said, pressing rhythmically on his chest. Then down again to breathe air into his lungs.

And in a moment that seemed like a miracle, he gasped and started breathing on his own.

"Oh, thank God, thank God," I said.

Joe pushed me off. "Julian? Julian? Hang on, little buddy. The helicopter's coming." His frantic fingers brushed the hair off his child's forehead as he rolled him gently on his side. "Hang on, okay? You're going to get a free ride in a helicopter."

Julian's eyelids flickered, his eyes rolled, then he closed them again. His color was coming back as his breathing resumed.

"My darling," Joe said, not for an instant taking his eyes off his little boy. His tears fell on Julian's face. "My son."

I sat back and waited for the welcome beating of the helicopter's blades.

•

My own problems were dim and small after watching Julian and Joe helicoptered off the island, while Lynn and Dougal stood beside me holding each other and crying with shock and fear. They went straight down to the jetty for the afternoon service back to the mainland. I made them promise to call me the moment there was any news, but I only realized later that they didn't have my number and my phone hardly ever worked anyway.

So I wandered around my house, from verandah to verandah, completely disengaged from my work and my worries, all my mind bent on the fate of that little boy. I couldn't stop thinking about the feeling of his ribs under my palms, about Joe's anguished voice.

Around nine at night, there was a knock on my door. I answered it with my heart in my mouth. It was Donna from the local shop.

"Oh," I said, "I hadn't expected—"

"Lynn called me and asked me to come up and see you." Outside, a light rain had moved in, and I noticed Donna's hair was damp. "She wanted to call you but she didn't have your number."

"Julian?" I asked, breathlessly.

"He's stable. He's got a couple of broken ribs and a bad concussion and they've got him in an induced coma, until some of the swelling in his brain goes down. But they say he's going to be fine. Just fine." Donna touched her hand. "You saved his life, Nina. Lynn said she didn't know how they were ever to thank you."

I started crying too. It was the first time I'd cried for a long time.

•

Life was quiet without Joe around. He was staying at the hospital until Julian was good to come home. I missed him. I missed him more than I had expected to miss him. Lynn and Dougal had been up to give me the biggest bunch of flowers I had ever seen, but I hadn't taken them up on their offer of dinner yet, and the flowers drooped and died because I forgot to change their water. I was writing. Not much, but I was writing, every day, under the watchful eye of Eleanor's wooden cat. I still had no hope of meeting my deadline, and I decided it was time to let Marla know and see what consequences would come.

I went to the pay phone in the bright noon of the week my

manuscript was due. I dialed her number and waited, my heart thudding hard in my throat. Marla's secretary answered and put me straight through.

"Nina, how are you?"

"I'm . . ." Words got stuck in my throat.

Marla sighed. "I'm not an idiot," she said. "I've already got you a stay of execution."

"You have? How long?"

"Another six weeks, but that will take us up to nearly Christmas and I doubt anybody will be looking for that manuscript before January."

Relief flooded my body. "How long have you known about this?"

"Over a month. But I didn't want to tell you because I don't want you to think this means you can cruise."

"I am not cruising," I said, hurt. "I promise you, nothing about this feels like a cruise."

Her tone became gentle. "Nina, my dear, you'll have to forgive me. A lot of publishing schedules have been disrupted and I've had to stave off some very ferocious inquiries about your fitness to produce this manuscript. I trust you. Don't let me down."

I wanted to tell her. I wanted to say, *Don't trust me*. But I didn't. I said, "I won't let you down."

"Now, I need to talk to you about something else."

I leaned my back against the glass wall of the phone booth, winding the phone cord around my fingers. "Go on."

"A journalist has been looking for you."

A little jolt to my heart. "Elizabeth Parrish?"

"Yes, her."

"Don't talk to her, please. I have nothing to say to her. I think she's getting ready to do a terrible hatchet job on me."

"You want me to take care of it?"

"Please. Fob her off. I have nothing to say to her."

"Consider it done. Now, get back to your desk, stay on the island, and *please* finish that book."

"Consider it done," I echoed, hoping and hoping that this time it would come together.

•

That afternoon, Elizabeth Parrish sent me a final text.

If you won't talk to me I will start talking to others about you.

I ignored her. We would have to have a conversation eventually, but not now. The Widow Wayland was solving a crime, and I wasn't about to stop her.

•

Then, finally, Joe came back.

I heard footsteps on the front verandah just after I'd turned the kitchen light on to start making dinner. A storm front had moved in, making evening come early. I was at the door before the knock came.

"Hi!" I said, too enthusiastically.

He smiled back at me. "Hi. Long time no see."

The rain started to fall. Thunder grumbled in the distance. "How's Julian?"

"He's at home, in the spare room at Mum's, with a *Young Avengers* comic and a packet of chips. We got back this morning."

"I'm so relieved."

"Can I come in?"

"Absolutely." I stood aside and then closed the door behind him.

"Look, I need to apologize," he said, before I could even invite him to sit down and pour him a glass of wine.

"For what?"

"That day. I didn't even say thank you. In my defense, I was out of my mind."

I touched his shoulder. "I want you to know that I have never once, in the days since the accident, thought that you should have remembered to say thank you."

I withdrew my hand, but he caught it, and rubbed my fingers softly, almost absently, as if it was the most normal thing in the world to do.

"The crazy thing is, I know how to do CPR. I could have saved him myself, but all I could think was *he's dead, he's dead*." His voice caught.

"It must have been awful for you."

He gathered himself, met my eyes. "But you were there. Thank God for you, Nina."

I smiled back at him, the moment gathered itself and intensified. The anticipation was real and thrilling. He pulled gently on my hand and I was in his embrace, my arms around his neck. The heat of him, the smell of him. And then his lips on mine, soft and firm all at once, insistent and gentle. My body bent back, his hands caught me in the curve of my spine and the warm passion flooded me.

His lips left mine and wandered to my throat. "I knew when I first saw you," he said. "You would be important to me. You can't imagine how important you are to me."

Niggling guilt.

"I love you, Nina," he said, almost casually. Naturally.

Then he was kissing me again, deeply and passionately, and I knew I loved him too but I couldn't say it out loud.

"Wait, wait," I said, pulling away. "This is . . ." I had been about to say "wrong," but looking at him in the half-light, as the rain hammered down outside, I knew there was nothing wrong about my feelings for him.

Joe smiled. Such a wicked smile, making me melt like toffee in the sun.

I caught my breath. "Never mind," I said. "Never mind."

•

The storm rattled over and passed, we ate in bed, then slept wound around each other. Tomorrow and all my other tomorrows receded away from me. No deadline, no facing up to my sins and secrets. Just Joe and me, skin against skin, in the soft morning dark.

•

Joe was up at first light, pulling his jeans on while I blinked away sleep.

"Where are you going?"

"I feel terrible. Julian's first night out of hospital and I wasn't there to put him to bed."

"It was a wild storm. You couldn't have walked home," I said, sitting up. "And your parents were there for him."

He sat down, shirtless, reached across to stroke my hair off my face. "I should still go."

I smiled at him, feeling something bright and hot swelling in my heart. I said, "Wait," before I knew I was going to say it.

He looked at me curiously.

"I can't have children. I mean, I can't get pregnant."

"So?"

So.

"It's why Cameron and I split up. And I know you want more kids one day . . ." I trailed off, feeling foolish.

"I did. But not anymore. Julian's eight. I don't want to go back to baby days. It's too hard." He leaned down and kissed me. "How long has that been on your mind?"

I laughed. "Since day one."

"Well, I'm glad you got it out. Anything else you need to tell me? Skeletons in the closet?" He made a spooky gesture with his fingers.

I kissed him back, hard.

"I have to go," he said.

After he left, I lay there a long time. Smiling and smiling. When my phone rang, I picked it up, still smiling.

"Nina, it's Marla."

"Hi, Marla. I was about to start writing. Things are really starting to move along now, so—"

"I spoke to Elizabeth Parrish."

My skin prickled. Her tone was curt, almost angry. "The journalist?"

"Yes, the journalist. When I refused her request to speak to you, she told me why she's writing about you." A moment of silence as the phone signal dropped out and then bloomed back into life. "Do you want to know?"

Heat in my heart. Something bad was about to happen. I managed to keep my voice even. "I guess . . ."

"She says she's been through the archives of Stanley and Walsh Publishers, 1926 through to 1929. She's found letters . . ."

"No," I said aloud. Or maybe I said it in my head.

"Letters between the publishers and a woman named Eleanor Holt, rejecting a series of manuscripts about a character called the Widow Wayland."

My mouth opened and closed, unable to form words.

"Please, Nina, please tell me these were just your inspiration. Please tell me you didn't plagiarize those books."

I hung up, switched the phone off, and threw it in the corner.

It had all fallen apart.

TWENTY-TWO

The Boat Shed

1892

Tilly felt guilty and fearful breaking Sterling's rule about being in the garden. Not that he was ever around to enforce it, but Nell was a little harder to get away from. One week to the day after Tilly had first made her proposal to Hettie, she found herself locking her bedroom door carefully, then climbing out her window onto the verandah. If she went the long way around, to the back of the house, she passed neither Nell's window nor Sterling's office. She took the back stairs down, behind the kitchen, then rounded the house on the north and from there plunged into the garden.

Hettie had said she needed a week to think about it. At first, Tilly had found this astonishing. Was she not aching to get out of prison? To flee from the island and into her children's arms? But Tilly told her to take her time, and then worried for the whole week that Hettie would report Tilly. Every footstep on the verandah had made her heart start: was it a warder coming to tell Sterling what she had done?

But here it was, a week later, and Hettie was waiting for her down near Tilly's plot. She turned at Tilly's footsteps on the leaves. Her face was florid and her eyes almost black.

"Hettie?"

"Yes," she said. "Yes, I will . . . we will do this. I knew I would say yes a moment after you said it. But I had to think . . . I am sorry I killed him. I am so sorry. But my babies . . ."

Tilly realized she had been hoping, deep down, that Hettie might say no. It was no small thing to help a prisoner escape; and yet it was the only thing she could do to absolve herself of her own guilt. She grasped Hettie's calloused hand. "I know you're sorry. But he deserved it." Not like Jasper. Not like Chantelle. "He might have killed you one day, or the children."

"How is it to be done, then?" Hettie said. "We must . . . plan it. So many have tried before and not succeeded."

"Because they have done it alone, with rough materials, with no resources. That's what makes this different. I can help you." Tilly lowered her voice, looked around. "I think I can get you a boat."

Hettie's eyes widened. "Really?"

"And together we will row our way across to the mainland and put this island behind us forever."

"Together?"

Tilly nodded, firm in her intention. She risked too much by staying. She was not naïve: assisting a prisoner's escape would be punishable by law. No, if she left the island, left Chantelle Lejeune's name behind there, life could resume on the mainland. She would take a job, far away where nobody cared much who she was and where she came from. Perhaps it would be safe to reclaim her old name: Matilda Kirkland. A woman from another time.

Hettie squeezed her hand. "Then let us start to prepare ourselves. We must be careful and clever."

"And we mustn't rush."

"If we wait for the cooler weather, when the sun goes down earlier . . ."

"A month from now, then?"

"A month."

•

A boat. Tilly needed a boat. Not a raft made of sticks found around the island and lashed together with a pajama belt. These were the kind of vessels escaping prisoners usually made, building them over months and leaving them stored amongst the mangroves and mud. Sterling said they routinely searched the area and found many half-made boats; none were ever seaworthy. If the escapees did make it off the island, they would sink in the dark water and be prey to sharks.

But there were boats on the island, in the boat shed. Sterling had mentioned it when Nell had gone missing, had said she knew which drawer the key to the boat shed was in. Tilly would be mad to ask Nell for help. The girl's curiosity would unbind all Tilly's plans. So she resolved instead to find the key herself.

Tilly lay in bed, awake, very late that night. She had no trouble fighting sleep. Her mind whirled. Sometimes she remembered what she had done, or what she intended to do, with a terrible jolt. She had not been bred for such things; for burning houses and helping prisoners escape. She had been bred for tea and meek conversation. And yet, these things had happened; and she needed to make peace with the fact that she was not meek. She had never been meek.

Long after midnight, when the house was quiet, and the sigh of the wind outside and the ticking clock in the parlor were the only sounds, Tilly rose and lit a candle. Her feet creaked lightly on the floor, so she moved slowly. Past Nell's room safely, through to the dining room, then to the door of Sterling's office.

The doorknob was cool in her hand. She turned it and the door opened. She slipped in, closed the door behind her. She was overwhelmed by the smell of the place. His smell. Tilly placed her candle on the desk. Shadows flickered across spines of record books, papers laid out in neat piles, inkwells and pens, across the framed map of Moreton Bay hung on the wall. On Sterling's blotting pads were doodles of seabirds: some with spread wings, others standing on rocks or in water. They were beautiful, rendered in soft pen strokes, with finesse and fine form. She was fascinated by the idea of Sterling as an artist: he always seemed such a practical man. A lover of art but not a man with time to make it. Indeed, he hadn't time to make it. These were blotting-paper doodles.

Tilly shook herself. It wasn't time for reflection, nor was it time to fall deeper in love with Sterling. This process she had set in motion would take her away from him forever; the double duty of freeing Hettie and denying herself Sterling's love would surely absolve her sins. Instead of mooning over Sterling, she should be searching drawers.

She started with the desk. She found two keys tied on a piece of narrow rope. Was it to be that easy? She laid them on the desktop and went to the next drawer. In this one she found blank sheets of paper like the ones he gave Nell. In the next drawer there were boxes with ink bottles in them, and another key; this one on a loop of metal with a paper tag on it. Nothing was written on the tag. Tilly put it with the other keys. Now she turned to the bureau behind the desk. Four drawers. In amongst empty ledgers, pencils, candles, matches, snuffers, rulers, and balls of string, she found two more sets of keys. All together, she had seven keys. She glanced around the room. No more drawers.

Tilly sat down at Sterling's office chair, considering the keys. Which one was the one to the boat shed? The only way to know was to go down there now and try them all, one by one.

She gathered them up in her palm, and returned to her room. This time she dressed, pulled on stockings and shoes, lifted the sash and climbed out her window, just as she had done that afternoon. The night was cool and she shivered a little. But the sky was clear, a million stars, and the path down to the boat shed dry.

The island appeared deserted at night. With all the prisoners counted and locked in, the warders either went to their own beds or contracted in small crews around the hulking black shape of the stockade. Tilly wore a dark dress so she wouldn't catch the eye of anyone, should they be out at this time of night; but she feared nothing from discovery while simply walking down the road. She was a free woman after all, and a late-night bout of insomnia could explain away her movements. No, it was when she was at the boat shed that she needed to be fearful, careful. So she took her time walking down there, being aware of sights and sounds. The movement of palm leaves, the white-bright sliver of moon, the shush and pull of the sea. Near the boat shed was the tall look-out tower they used when somebody had escaped. Now, it was empty, a spindly white ghost in the dark.

She had no light but the stars and the thin moon. She fumbled through the keys, telling them apart with her fingertips. The first key she came to was clearly too big for the lock. The second fit the lock but wouldn't turn. Tilly pulled it out, but it was stuck. Hot fear engulfed her. She wriggled it, looking around wildly. With a sudden jerk it slipped out. She paused a moment, walked away from the shed. Surveyed the area all around. Nobody, nothing.

The third key, the single key with the paper tag, slid in easily. She took a deep breath and turned it.

Click.

The lock gave. The handle turned. The door swung outwards.

Tilly opened it only as far as she needed to slip inside, then closed it behind her. Now she was in pitch black, cursing herself for not having brought a lamp. She stood very still, waiting for her eyes to adjust to the dark, but still could make out nothing more than a few shapes less dark than the black surrounds. So she put out her hands and gingerly felt her way forward. She bumped almost instantly into the prow of a rowboat. With her hands, she felt around its contours. It was upside down on the ground, next to another like it. She presumed there were a number of rowboats in here, but where were the oars? Shuffling on the dirt floor, careful not to kick anything and bruise her shins, she made her way further into the shed. Against the stone back wall she found oars, felt along them to see they were supported by hooks in the wall.

Satisfied that she understood where the important things were in the shed, Tilly quietly slipped out and locked the door. She knew she needed to return to the house and replace the keys, memorizing the drawer where the paper-tagged key rested, but her mind felt heavy. So she walked down to the jetty and along the wooden boards, then sat down with her legs over the side, her hands on the rough timber. Turning ideas over in her mind, plans coalescing, the future rushing up to meet her.

•

"We'll go out through the mangroves," Tilly told Hettie, after four days of wild winds that had kept her inside in the afternoons. "I will have the boat waiting for you."

"How will you get it there?" They sat together on the grass, shielded from curious eyes by the hedges.

"I'm still working that out. Do you know how often they use the boats? Count them?"

"I have no idea." Hettie crossed her knees and hunched over them. "You don't understand. I spend most of my time inside that stone box. It boils in summer and freezes in winter. I come to the garden a few hours a day and that is my life, in its entirety. I don't know what else happens on this island."

"Well, I'll find out. But it will mean you have to escape from the garden in the late afternoon, before the turnkey comes to take you back to your cell."

Hettie took a deep shuddering breath.

"It will be all right," Tilly said.

"What if somebody sees me? This prison uniform is so . . . white."

"I'll loan you one of my dresses."

Hettie's mouth twisted wryly. "I will not fit your dresses, Tilly."

Tilly turned her eyes up to the sky, thinking. A lone gull wheeled overhead, catching thermal currents under his wings. She smiled, watching it. "Do you think that gull would enjoy himself so much, if he knew he was on a prison island?"

"He's in the sky. The sky isn't a prison. Nor is the sea."

Tilly turned her attention back to Hettie. "I will get you two dresses. One to wear on the day, that looks like one of mine. Then, if somebody sees you, they will think it's me and not pursue you. And one for the onward journey."

"Where will you get these dresses?"

"That I am also still working on. I could make them, but Nell would see and ask questions . . . In any case, let me take your measurements. Have you any garden twine?"

"No. But there is some holding the lemon trees straight. Wait here."

Hettie shuffled off and Tilly waited on the grass. She might have to go to the mainland. It was a matter of asking Sterling, and he wouldn't say no. They had not spoken more than a few words to each other since the night she broke the sherry glass. He usually said something friendly over dinner; she usually answered in short, dispassionate sentences, always careful not to be so cool as to arouse Nell's suspicion.

Tilly stood when Hettie returned with a length of twine.

"Lift up your arms," she said, and then wrapped the twine around her bust, tied a little knot at the right point. Then she moved down to Hettie's thick waist, her mannish hips. She became very aware of the other woman's physical presence. Because Hettie often kept her head low and wore a deferential expression in her soft eyes, Tilly had never noticed before how powerfully built she was. She thought of Sterling's words; how Hettie had held two pillows over her husband's face. Now Tilly could imagine it too well: the force in her hands, the strength in her arms and trunk.

Tilly balled up the twine and kept it tightly in her fist. "Hettie," she ventured. "Why does the court record say nothing of your husband's violence towards you?"

"It doesn't? How do you know?" Her eyebrows turned up, her forehead furrowed.

"Sterling said that you had . . . another man, who helped you."

Hettie's eyes dropped, and she clenched and unclenched her hands. "Of course. Of course they would say that about me. I had a friend and, yes, I did love him. Yes I did wish for a life with him. But I knew it wasn't possible. I'm not a fool." Hettie lifted her head. "Look at me, Tilly. I'm not beautiful. I'm not young. I'm not you with your milky skin and bright hair and long lashes. What man would love me? No, he was a friend to me. He lived across the road and that awful night, after I had . . . defended myself. After I had been hit over the head with a cast-iron pan and he had threatened the children . . . My husband had been away a little while, and he had returned with an intent to unleash all his stored rage upon us. So that night, after I smothered my husband, I called on my friend, my neighbor, and asked him what I should do. I was desperate. He helped me take my husband's body into bushland." Hettie took a big breath, her eyes going towards the sea. "He looked so peaceful there, lying under a tree."

"Did you tell all this to the police? To the judge?"

"Of course I did. Tilly, they charged my friend too. He's in prison too, because of me. On a much shorter sentence. At least they believed me that he knew nothing about the murder until after it was done."

Tilly was silent a few moments.

"You believe me, don't you?" Hettie said, her voice desperate. "I told them. I told all of them how he had treated me, what he had done to me. I showed them my bruises."

"Yes, I believe you," Tilly said. "I've not been in this world very long, but I have seen plenty of evidence that men do not like women's tempers and seek to punish them for it. I have seen that they believe the worst of women very quickly, that a precocious girl is called uncontrollable, that we are thought to be ruled by our passions while they believe themselves rational and our judges. I believe you, Hettie Maythorpe. I believe you."

Hettie managed a smile.

"I need to go away and think about how all this is to be done," Tilly said, turning away. "I will find you when I know anything at all. You aren't to worry. I will take care of everything."

"Wait, Tilly," Hettie said. "I need to ask you something."

Tilly faced her. The cool rush of sea air lifted her hair at her nape. "Go on."

"Why are you doing this?"

Tilly couldn't speak for a long time. There were so many possible answers. In the end, she said, "Because I have to."

Hettie seemed about to ask for clarification, then changed her mind. "I will see you soon," she said.

"As soon as ever I can," Tilly reassured her.

•

It was early the next morning that Tilly arrived at Sterling's office door. She had not slept well, again, and gave a brief, vain thought for the dark shadows under her eyes. But then she reminded herself she had no claim on Sterling, no future with Sterling, so it wouldn't matter if she had grown two heads. She gave two sharp raps, and heard him say, "Come."

Tilly opened the door.

His surprise to see her was in his eyes, in his body language as he quickly put aside his work and stood to greet her. "Tilly. I hadn't thought to see you here."

"I need to speak with you before lessons start for the day," she said, keeping her voice very even. She wouldn't have him thinking her irrational. "I have come to request a short leave of absence to travel to the mainland."

"For what purpose?"

"My business is my own," she said.

Sterling nodded softly. "Of course it is," he said. He walked to his window and looked out. "It's a beautiful morning. Let us walk."

"Walk?"

"I find it helps me to think things through."

"There is nothing to think through. I want a leave of absence and I want some of the money I am owed for working here and—"

"Yes, you will have your leave. I am not arguing against it. But there are other matters I wish to discuss with you and this"—he gestured around—"is not the right place in which to speak of them."

She hesitated. All her body and heart bent towards him, to go walking with him on this clear, sunny morning. But her brain warned her against it.

"Come, Tilly. A short walk. Ten minutes. Then we will both get on with our days."

"Very well, then," she said, trying to sound cool, as though her heart wasn't thudding madly.

They descended the front stairs and walked down the road, taking the path west, away from the stockade and down towards the little strip of beach. Sterling didn't speak for a long time, maintaining a gruff bearing for any of the men they passed who called out good mornings. He walked swiftly and she had to hurry to keep up next to him, all the while sneaking glances at his face to see if she could guess what he intended to speak to her about.

"Here is a good place to sit," he said, indicating the flat rock at the beach where she and Nell often sat. He perched on the edge, but a small part of her wanted to defy him. She had walked all the way down here with him and now she wouldn't sit. She chose instead to stand on the sand, facing out to sea.

"Did you know Nell calls this Seven Yard Beach?" she said.

"She does?"

Tilly turned. "She has a map. She adds to it all the time. Everything is slowly acquiring a name." She hid a little smile. "The escarpment is Sterling Cliff. She said it was a stern enough name for the place."

Sterling leaned forward, his hands folded between his knees, his gaze going out to sea. "Stern? She thinks I'm stern?" The waves were low today, rolling softly onto the gritty sand and breaking with a quiet shush. The air was thick with the smell of seaweed.

"I don't know. It's what she said."

He shook his head. "I love that girl too much," he said.

"There is no such thing as too much love," Tilly said, her voice growing hot. "One can't measure or control it. One must simply feel it. It is the only moral thing to do."

Sterling said nothing for a long time, as her face cooled and she recomposed herself.

She watched him watching the sea. A seagull went by overhead. The sun was in Sterling's hair, the wind pushing it back off his face so she could see clearly the broad plane of his brow, the strong angle of his nose. She couldn't remember ever finding any other face so pleasing to look upon, and it began to irritate her that he wouldn't speak. As though he had brought her here just to put a spell on her with his lovely countenance.

"Why did you bring me here?" she asked. "What is it you want to speak of?"

"I am sorry, I . . ." he said, searching for words. His eyes were still on the water, squinting slightly against the glare. "I treated you ill. Last time we spoke, I realized that I had not apologized. Perhaps my apology will help you. I meant it when I said I wished to keep you as my friend. I miss our conversations, but currently you seem uninterested in conversing with me."

Tilly said nothing for fear she would cry.

This time, he looked directly at her. His eyes were sad. "As a man, as an older man, in a position of responsibility, I should have been far more careful with you, your honor, your heart," he continued. "I have said it before: living on this island feels as though we are outside society somehow. We spend so much time around people who have murdered or brutalized others, that our own behavior seems beyond reproach."

Still nothing.

"Tilly? Speak to me."

"All I have heard here is that because you are a man you are more able than I am to know what is right, to protect my honor. And that our lovemaking was ill treatment and that falling in love with each other was somehow comparable to criminal behavior," she said.

"I said none of those things."

"You said all of them."

"You are twisting my words. Why must women be so . . . ?" He stopped himself, but he had already said the thing most likely to light her fuse.

"Tilly, I miss you. But we can't be together yet. We must be patient, we must control ourselves—"

"I don't want to control myself!" she shouted at him. Then she turned and ran back towards the house, leaving him on the beach alone.

•

Nell and Sterling both stood on the jetty to see her off. Nell, blithe to the underlying passions between her father and Tilly, was bright and excited.

"Enjoy your holiday," she enthused. "Buy yourself something pretty."

There was room enough in Tilly's bag for a number of new dresses, but she wouldn't be bringing dresses back for herself.

"I will see you in a week or so," Tilly said, kissing the girl's forehead. "In the meantime, get to work on that new story."

"Good-bye, Tilly," Sterling said. The sun was in his dark hair, on his skin. She saw lines around his eyes, a few gray strands in his sideburns. She longed to touch his face, kiss his lips.

"Good-bye, Sterling," she replied.

He took Nell's hand and they stood on the jetty while Tilly walked up the gangplank of the steamer. It bobbed on the morning tide. The sun glistened off the bay, which was blue-green today. The wet season had passed and the dry season, with its crisp sun and cool air, had finally come. She left her case downstairs and went up to the top of the boat to watch the jetty. They were still there, hand in hand. Nell waved at her with Pangur Ban. Sterling lifted his hand also, as the crew untied the ropes and the boat pulled away. They waved at her as though she were family.

But they weren't family. And this trip to the mainland would ensure that they would never be. That she was moving inexorably into a future that they could not be part of.

TWENTY-THREE

A Letter from the Past

Tilly had not had time to write ahead and organize somewhere to board, though she'd lied to Sterling and told him all was taken care of. She remembered a draper and dressmaker near Mrs. Fraser's boardinghouse, where she had stayed on her arrival in Australia, and so she took the tram from the dock back to Mrs. Fraser's, hoping there would be room for her to stay. She found herself on the doorstep just past midday, ringing the bell at the tall boardinghouse, with its iron lace railings and creaking weather vane.

Footsteps inside, then the door opened.

"Yes?" asked the young woman.

"Is Mrs. Fraser in?"

"No, she's at the shops. Can I help?"

"I need a place to stay for a week. Mrs. Fraser knows me. She said she'd be happy for me to return any time."

"We are full."

Under the circumstances, small complications took on enormous proportions to Tilly. Her resolve fluttered. "Yes, but Mrs. Fraser knows me. Chantelle Lejeune. She said . . ." Tilly trailed off. If they were full, they were full. "Do you know anywhere else?" she finished limply.

"About five miles down the road on the esplanade there's a bed-and-breakfast." The young woman's eyes flicked away. "Run by a gentleman. Perhaps a single lady such as yourself will not want to stay there alone. You could head towards town . . ."

"I'm sure it will be fine," she said. Then reconsidered. Sterling had been right. The island skewed judgment of what was appropriate. Nonetheless, she needed a place to stay, so she walked down to the esplanade, where tall trees bent over the road. A horse and carriage trotted past and she jumped out of the way, narrowly avoiding a pile of horse dung. She hadn't been on this side of the bay for many months. She passed couples, families, men heading to the beach with towels and bathing caps. Nobody was dressed in white or blue uniforms. They were free to move about, to come and go to town or further. She strained her eyes across the water but wasn't sure she could see Ember Island from here. Many islands dotted the bay, and it was hard to tell one from another. Over there: prisoners and orphans and displaced natives and lepers. Over here: civilization.

At length, she reached the place the young woman at Mrs. Fraser's boardinghouse had told her about. A little wooden house with a low front verandah and an overgrown courtyard garden. She stood across the esplanade from it, considering it. It didn't even have a sign; it looked like an ordinary, small home.

Her feet were pinching from the long walk, so she crossed the road, pushed her way through vines that hung low from the arch of the gate, and knocked at the door.

A gentleman in his seventies, with white hair and a kind smile, answered. "May I help?"

"I heard you have bed-and-breakfast rooms here."

His smile turned upside down. "Yes, but only for men. You should try Mrs. Fraser—"

"Mrs. Fraser is full, and I don't want to go to town, and I simply want a place to stay."

"You are very forthright." He stroked his chin. "I've never had a young lady here before."

"I am not so delicate a young lady," she replied. "I've spent the last several months working at the prison facility on Ember Island." She wanted to say, *I hit a man so hard with a brass poker that his nose was spread across his face like butter.* But she didn't.

"How about this, then? You can stay here now because all three rooms are empty. But the bathroom is shared, so if another guest, a man, arrives, you will have to leave."

"Agreed," she said. "What is your name?"

"I am Richard Hamblyn." He opened the door wide and took her suitcase. "And you are?"

"Chantelle Lejeune. Governess to the superintendent's daughter on Ember Island." She followed him inside, removing her gloves. The foyer was clean and comfortable, with a thick rug and brightly polished brass.

"Governess? Well, then. We shall have something to talk about. I am a retired schoolteacher." He led her down a dim hallway and fumbled in his pocket for a key. A moment later, he had the door open on a tiny room looking out onto wattle trees. The window was open and the filmy white curtain caught in the light sea breeze. "Dine with me tonight and we shall talk of the best way to teach Latin grammar." His eyes twinkled.

Tilly liked him. He reminded her a little of Grandpa, with his bent back and his twinkling eyes among the folds and wrinkles. "I would like that very much. Mr. Hamblyn, do you have a copy of the newspaper?"

"I shall bring it forthwith."

An hour later, her bags unpacked, her shoes eased off her tired feet, sitting cross-legged on her bed, Tilly scoured the help wanted advertisements. Many were local. She needed to get much further away. She found positions in far northern Queensland, and in the gold fields. But they were servile positions. Cooking and cleaning. Surely there would be another family somewhere in need of a governess. Perhaps she should travel first, somewhere remote, then look for work. The thought tired her. Perhaps she was tired from the day's traveling. She lay back on her bed and closed her eyes, felt herself begin to drift off.

She was back at Lumière sur la Mer, walking along the corridor between the top of the stairs and Jasper's bedroom. She could hear the sounds of people making love: Jasper and Chantelle, just as she had heard them that night. This time she would stop them. This time she would throw open the door and shout at them to stop it, to end their affair; that way, they would stay alive. But she touched the door handle and it was searing hot. Smoke leaked from under the door.

Tilly shouldered the door hard. It flew open and she saw them on the bed, surrounded by flames. But it wasn't Chantelle, it was Hettie, dressed in her white prison gown, sitting astride a man's body. Pillows covered his face. She pushed down hard, all the meat and muscle of her thick body concentrated into her arms.

Tilly tried to move her mouth to say, "Fire! Fire!"

Hettie turned to her. An expression like thunder. Dark hair like snakes in the smoke. "He deserved it," she spat.

Tilly woke with a start. The daylight baffled her, the strange filmy curtain tangling itself into knots as the afternoon wind picked up, ruffling the newpaper pages on the bed. She rose, shook her head to clear it, and closed the window. All was still and silent again. Dread cooled in her heart, along her veins.

And she knew she was doing the right thing. Because anything that would make those nightmares stop was the right thing to do.

•

Tilly walked to the draper late that afternoon, when her feet were rested and the sun wasn't so bright. The inside of the store was cool and dim and quiet, as though all the fabrics absorbed any noise. A woman worked with a dressmaker's dummy in the light coming in the front window, pinning panels of fabric together. Bolts of cloth were arranged haphazardly across the counter and leaning on the walls. Tilly approached a bolt of red cloth, considered the price per yard. The dressmaker took the pins out of her mouth and called, "Can I help?"

Tilly approached. Under her arm she held one of her own dresses. "I need you to make a copy of this dress, in a different size, for a friend."

The dressmaker took the dress from her and unfolded it, shaking it out. "Yes, that's easy. I won't be able to match the fabric precisely, but I can get close with the color."

"I also need another dress, in a very basic fabric, in her size. What might it cost?"

The dressmaker led Tilly to the glass counter, filled with boxes of buttons and ribbons, and reached for a notepad. With a pencil, she jotted down the measurements and then added up an affordable estimate.

"Can you do it within a week?"

"No, I'll need at least ten days."

"I'm sorry, I only have a week. I'll pay you extra."

The dressmaker cocked her head, considered Tilly dispassionately. "I can move a job. You don't need to pay me extra."

"Thank you," Tilly said.

Tilly's dress lay on the counter between them. The dressmaker tapped it with her fingertips. "You'll have to leave this here."

"Yes, of course."

She smiled, her eyes curious. "And you and your friend . . . dress identically often?"

Tilly laughed, realizing it must sound an odd request. Most women couldn't bear seeing somebody in the same gown. "No, never. Just this one time. Then never again."

•

On her return to Mr. Hamblyn's house she was greeted with the smell of roasting meat. It reminded her she hadn't eaten since breakfast on the island. He emerged from within his rooms when he heard her unlock the door, and smiled. "Dinner at seven?" he asked.

"What time is it now?"

"Six."

Her stomach rumbled. "I don't suppose you can ask the cook to have it sooner? I didn't eat lunch."

"The cook? I don't have a cook. I do it all myself. If you're hungry, my dear, I will have it on the table as soon as I can. Go and wash up, and I will knock when it's ready."

Tilly went to her room, splashed her face with water, and changed into a comfortable housedress. Mr. Hamblyn knocked only a few minutes later and she followed him to a dining room set out with three small tables. One had been set with a clean but threadbare tablecloth and two places. All the bright lamps were lit. "Sit, make yourself comfortable," he said.

She did as she was told, reached for the crystal glass to sip water while he went to fetch their plates. Moments later, he laid in front of her some kind of semi-cooked meat, gray gravy, with shriveled potatoes swimming alongside.

"And why don't you employ a cook?" she asked as he sat across from her, shaking an abundance of salt onto his meal.

"I'm usually alone or I have just one guest." He tucked into his meal enthusiastically.

Tilly tried her meat gingerly. It was bland and still rather bloody. She decided to fill up on the potatoes and gravy. She found herself longing for one of the sumptuous dinners on Ember Island: fresh rolls from the bakery, baked fish caught that morning, vegetables grown yards away.

"So, Tilly, tell me how you became a teacher."

"A governess," she corrected him. "I have only one student. I learned from a governess myself, and from my grandfather, who was a very clever man. I always excelled at languages particularly. What about you?"

"Me? I simply loved children."

"And you never had any of your own?"

"No. I never married. I never had children. But I taught so many. I remember them all, the bright ones, the naughty ones, even the ones in between." His eyes took on a faraway happiness. "I hope they remember me too."

"I'm sure they do." Tilly felt warmly towards him. "I have such a special relationship with my student, Nell. It's like love."

"Do her parents mind?"

"Her mother is dead. Her father . . . I am not so sure."

"Ah, yes. Parents want you to like their children, but not for their children to like you too much." He kept shoveling food into his mouth, talking while chewing. "Teachers aren't meant to be competition."

"I'm sure her father doesn't see me as competition. At least not for him. Perhaps his late wife."

"Nonetheless, young Nell will grow up and not need a governess anymore, and you will slip out of her life as though you had never been. They go on to live their lives. I always felt a little lost when one of my pupils left, as though a little part of me had somehow gone missing." He frowned a moment, and Tilly wondered if he were remembering a particular pupil.

"Miss Lejeune, you must tell me how you came to Australia," he said, brightening now, pushing his spectacles up high onto the bridge of his nose.

"Ah. That is a little more complicated a thing to explain," she said, cutting off thin slivers of cooked meat to eat so she didn't appear ungrateful for the meal.

"Go on. I am very clever and I can follow any complicated story," he chuckled.

It had been a long time since she had rehearsed the lies about her past, so she simply told a version that skimmed over the top. "I lived with my grandfather, who died and left everything to a male cousin. I married, very unwisely. Then my husband died. I needed to put all of this behind me and I thought the best way to do that was to travel a very long way."

"So you aren't Miss Lejeune? You are Mrs. Lejeune?"

"I am . . ." Neither. She was neither. "Call me Tilly."

"Well, I am most sorry to hear about your husband's death. He must have been very young."

"Just twenty-four, sir."

"Illness?"

"Accident. I cannot speak of it. It upsets me too much."

"You loved him?"

"At first. Very much. But he was not . . . what I thought he was."

"And you are happy now? On Ember Island?"

"Yes."

"I am sorry, but I noticed the newspaper in your room was open to the help wanted pages." He spread his hands. "So perhaps you are not so happy."

Somewhere in the next room, a clock rang out the half hour. Tilly pushed her food around on her plate with her fork. "Well . . ."

"Would you like me to ask around for you? I have many friends who still teach in schools."

"Not here. I want to go somewhere more remote."

"More remote than a prison island?" He sat back, dabbing his mouth with his napkin. "That's quite an ask."

"I like remote places."

He considered her a little while by the flickering lamplight, his old hands folded in front of him. Then he said, "You are running from something."

Tilly prickled with guilt and anger. How dare he presume to know anything about her? "And what if I am? Can a woman not run from something unpleasant without having everybody interfering, to know her business, make her answerable?"

Mr. Hamblyn seemed delighted by this answer. He threw his head back and laughed. "You are running from something and you have a quick temper. Oh, you are a thrilling creature, Mrs. Lejeune. Don't worry, I do not intend to stop you. I simply never meet anyone interesting these days and I've found your company very diverting."

Tilly found herself smiling despite her irritation. "Grandpa always told me to keep my temper in check. He would be most ashamed of me speaking hotly to you, a gentleman so many years my senior."

He waved his hand in refusal. "But tempers grow worse if overly managed. I have seen it time and again with children. The harder one presses upon them, the more explosive the eventual outburst."

"I am not a child."

"We are all just grown-up children," he said. "We know only a little more than we did then, and learn a little more each year, until we die knowing about a quarter of what there is to know."

Tilly put down her knife and fork. She was done with pretending the food was edible. "I do lose my temper," she said. "And then I feel sick with guilt and push it down until it comes up again."

"One should never get sick with guilt. If there is offense, one should make amends. But often there is no real offense. I see girls, especially, like to blame themselves when everybody isn't happy." He pointed to her food. "Was it that awful?"

She looked at her plate. She had managed a single potato and a few slivers of meat. "I'm afraid so," she said.

"I have bread and apples in the kitchen."

"Thank you."

They ended up in the kitchen, sitting at an old wooden table, eating apples and bread spread with drippings. Mr. Hamblyn was full of wisdom and he made her feel at ease. He told her some of the remote places she could go in Australia—out in the western bushlands or deep in the Tasmanian wilderness—where she might find work as a teacher or a governess. She began to feel, if not positive about her future, at least not so frightened of it. All that was waiting for her, on the other side of this dark deed. She would be unfettered by love or guilt. She would be free.

•

The week passed in the good company of Mr. Hamblyn, or in
her own company walking along the esplanade or buying little
trinkets to take back for Nell. It was on her second-last morning
on the mainland, as she sat on the front verandah in the warm
sunshine drinking tea with Mr. Hamblyn, that a woman pushed
her way through the tangle of vines over the front gate and approached the stairs. Tilly recognized her as Mrs. Fraser from the
boardinghouse.

"Good morning, Mrs. Fraser," Mr. Hamblyn said. "We are having tea. Care to join us?"

"I can't stay," she said. "I actually came to find Miss Lejeune.
How are you, dear? Bessie said you had been by. I am so sorry we
couldn't offer you a room."

"I have had a good week here with Mr. Hamblyn," Tilly said.
"Please don't concern yourself."

"Well, I'm glad you're here," she said, reaching into the pocket of
her apron and pulling out a letter. "This came for you some months
ago. I hung on to it, because I wasn't sure where you'd gone next."

Tilly stood and took the letter from Mrs. Fraser, puzzled. Was
it an answer to a help wanted advertisement she had written away
for? It was addressed to Chantelle Lejeune, certainly, but she was
sure nobody owed her a letter. Then she turned it over. Her body
and blood turned to ice.

"Are you well, Tilly?" Mr. Hamblyn said, his hand under her
elbow, guiding her to her chair.

She realized her knees had given way. "I . . . I think I stood up
too suddenly," she said, pressing her palm to her forehead.

She stood again, the letter still clutched in her right hand.
"I am sorry. I feel unwell. I must go to lie down."

She nearly tripped over her chair getting away from Mrs. Fraser and Mr. Hamblyn as quickly as she could. Then into her room, locking the door, throwing herself onto the bed, reading the return address again, as though perhaps she had imagined it the first time.

Laura Mornington, Le Paradis, St. Peter Port, Guernsey.

Her past was catching up with her.

TWENTY-FOUR

Back to the Island

Tilly's room at Starwater, on Ember Island, was reassuringly familiar. She closed the door behind her—a signal to Nell to stay away—and dropped her suitcase on the floor. Somewhere in the bottom of that case was the letter from Laura Mornington. She had almost thrown it into the water on the steamer journey back to the island, but couldn't bring herself to. Should she answer it? How could she answer it? Laura had once said that Chantelle was like family to her. She understood now that it must have been shocking and sad for her when Chantelle disappeared overnight. Shocking and sad enough for Laura to track her down, through port records or shipping registers or the post office or local busybodies, all the way to Mrs. Fraser's boardinghouse.

Tilly opened the suitcase, unfolded the letter again, and read the lines on the thin pages within. She had read it many times. *... worried sick about you ... terrible fire ... Jasper and his wife were killed ... need to know you are safe and well ... forgive*

*everything you've done . . . write to me, write to me please, my dear, so
I can put my mind at rest . . .*

But Chantelle Lejeune was dead; and the person Laura had
actually tracked down was the person who had caused her death.
If Laura somehow discovered she wasn't Chantelle, then her crime
would surely be exposed.

It wasn't simply the threat of exposure that frightened Tilly. It
was that she had somehow been located when she thought she'd
disappeared. Was it even possible to disappear? How close to the
ends of the earth would she have to travel before she dissolved
into the air and could never be found by her past? She had spoken to Mr. Hamblyn about wild places she could go. Would that
conversation come back to haunt her? Would the police scour
those places for her, when Hettie escaped and she was blamed?

Tilly walked to the window and opened it, letting in the sea air.
She had no right to ponder these things. If rescuing Hettie held
no menace, meant no sacrifice, then Tilly wouldn't be redeemed.
A favor bestowed lightly or easily was not a favor at all. Tilly had
to pay for her crimes and getting Hettie off the island would balance the ledger. Yes, she might be caught and punished, but perhaps that was what she deserved.

She would not answer Laura's letter. She would not pretend to
be Chantelle Lejeune to the people who loved Chantelle Lejeune.

Tilly's hands closed over the wooden windowsill. It was warm
from the afternoon sun in the west, painted smooth. She knew
this windowsill well. She knew this room well, this house. The
people in it. The landscape beyond the verandah, the palms and
the fig trees, the broad gardens, the dirt road off the escarpment.
This had been home for many months. And yet she had to give it
up, as she had given up her last home on Guernsey, and the home
before in Dorset. Tilly had a hollow sensation in the arches of her

feet, as though she were not standing on the world but suspended a fraction of an inch above it. There was no purchase for her here, no matter how desperately she stretched out her toes. The world shifted beneath her, and she waited, helplessly, to come to rest.

•

Just on sunset, Tilly knew she had to go to the garden and make plans with Hettie. She was surprised, when stepping off the bottom stair, to see a warder standing near the garden, staring off towards the sea. Hettie worked nearby. Hettie was never usually under guard; as one of the trustee prisoners, it was assumed she needed only accompaniment to and from the stockade. Not supervision.

Tilly hesitated, took a step back. The warder turned, saw her, gave her a smile. Tilly responded with a short wave, then went back inside. She ran into Nell, coming the other way.

"Oh, there you are," Nell said, giving her a hug. "I'm so happy that you're back. I've been quite bored without you."

"Why is there a warder watching Hettie?" Tilly asked.

Nell shrugged. "I've no idea. I hadn't noticed." Nell cocked her head curiously. "That's rather an odd question to ask when you haven't seen me in over a week."

Tilly squeezed her. "I'm sorry, I'd never seen her under guard before. Now, where is your story up to?"

"Oh, it's taken quite a menacing turn. I don't know who is going to live or die. Would you like me to read you some?"

"Can we sit on the verandah? It's a lovely evening for fresh air."

So they sat on the verandah while Nell read and Tilly watched from the corner of her eye. She became convinced that the warder was shirking some other duty because he paid little attention to Hettie. He spent most of his time leaning up against the gardening shed smoking tobacco or working on a little wood carving he was making from a thick twig. So what was she to do? Ask Sterling? That would draw too much attention to her.

Tilly became aware that Hettie had seen her. Her black eyes indicated she was trying to communicate without words, but such communication was impossible. Instead, Hettie glanced at the warder, who was paying her no attention, and slipped a little further into the western end of the garden.

Tilly stood. Nell stopped in midsentence, looked at her questioningly.

"I . . ." Tilly started.

"There are still two chapters to go."

"I have . . ."

"A headache? Another one?" Nell's voice was skeptical, even angry.

Tilly made herself smile, leaned down, and touched Nell's curls. "You are a dear girl. I have an urge to walk about and think for a while alone. I was cooped up on the steamer and I need fresh air and—"

"It's fine," Nell said curtly. "Go. My story can wait."

Tilly flushed with guilt. Nell pushed back her chair and gathered her papers roughly. When she had disappeared into the house, Tilly checked on the guard—his back was half turned to her—and quietly went down the stairs and into the garden.

Her skin prickled. She expected at any moment to be called back. But then she was out of his line of sight and into the northwest corner of the garden behind a row of hedges.

Hettie saw her and joined her. They crouched down, close to each other.

"The turnkey?" Tilly asked.

"He's new. He's meant to be down in the cane fields. The cane is growing so high the prisoners are getting harder and harder to see. I've heard him lying to the head turnkey at the women's wing, saying he spent the afternoon in the fields with the men in chains, when he's actually whittling and smoking up here. Right under the superintendent's nose."

"Sterling's office faces the other way."

"Can you report him?"

Tilly shook her head. "It would draw attention to you. To us. No, we'll have to rely on his inattention."

Hettie nodded. "Well, then. If you say."

"I have the dresses. I will bring them . . . on the day."

"And when will that be?"

"Soon. When I've figured out how it is all to unfold. Try to be patient. You must trust me."

"I do trust you." Hettie reached out and grasped Tilly's hand, squeezed it.

Tilly looked down, regarded Hettie's rough hand. Strong, almost mannish. The dream she'd had returned to her, Hettie as a monster suffocating a man with her weight and strength. A faint shiver spread along her veins.

Hettie withdrew her hand. "I trust you more than I have ever trusted anyone," Hettie said. "I have lived for many years without sympathy and I came to believe that I deserved no sympathy. But you . . . you have allowed me to feel as though I belong in the human race again. I cannot ever thank you enough. For what you have done already. For what will come."

Hettie's warm words were precisely the antidote for Tilly's cool doubts. So precise that it seemed almost as though Hettie had read her mind. She refocused on the practical steps. "It is probably best if we do not try to speak too often under the circumstances," Tilly said. "Trust that I am working away at our plan and will come to find you when I need to."

"Thank you, Tilly."

Tilly stood, stretched her legs, and walked softly away. Behind her, she heard Hettie moving off in the other direction, her feet crackling over leaves.

But then there were other, lighter footsteps, ahead of her. Tilly froze, every sense alert. She hurried her steps, peering over the hedges.

And saw Nell, running fast away from her, back up the stairs, and into the house.

•

Tilly's instincts were to pound up the stairs behind the girl, grasp her roughly before she went anywhere near Sterling. How much had she heard? Anything? If not, then why run? But no, she couldn't go thundering after her. She had to appear cool, rational, she had to deny everything. Not once in the conversation had they used the word "escape." Whatever Nell had heard, she had only her imagination to interpret it. But if she alerted Sterling to the fact that Hettie and Tilly were meeting secretly to talk, then that might upset all their plans.

She went inside as calmly as she could. All was quiet. Nell was nowhere in sight. She went to Sterling's door, rapped bravely.

"Come."

She opened the door. "Have you seen Nell?"

"Ah, you're back. Good. No, I haven't seen Nell since break-fast." He frowned. "Has she done something wrong?"

"No, no. All is well. I will see you at dinner." Then she closed the door before he could say anything else to her, ask any questions about her trip. Although she longed for intimacy with him, she had to hold it as far away from her as possible.

Tilly moved down the corridor, found Nell's pages spread out on the table, but no Nell. So she tried Nell's bedroom, knocked softly.

"Go away."

"Nell, may I speak to you?"

Nell threw open the door. Her face was sulky and pink. But Tilly noticed for the first time that this wasn't the petulance of a small child; it was the genuine hurt and betrayal of a young woman.

"May I come in?" Tilly said, pulse hard in her throat.

"No, you may not."

Tilly kept her voice quiet and even, fearing that an argument would alert Sterling. "Were you eavesdropping?"

"There are no eaves in the garden," she snapped.

"Were you listening in to Hettie and me?"

"And what if I was? Do you have something to hide?"

"No."

"Then why are you worried?"

"Then why are you angry?"

Nell glared at her, then softened a little. "I don't know."

"Let me in."

Nell held the door open and Tilly slipped in. Nell closed the door and huffed down on her bed. Tilly sat next to her, studying her profile. She needed to find out what the girl knew or suspected.

"What did you hear?"

"I didn't hear anything," Nell said.

"I don't understand why you're upset."

"Because you sent me away saying you needed fresh air and

your own company, and you raced straight down the back of the garden to hide with Hettie and talk in soft voices, and I know you're not even supposed to be talking to her."

Tilly's limbs felt light with relief. So Nell's anger wasn't about suspecting an escape plot; it was that she was hurt by being spurned, told a lie.

"I know I'm not supposed to talk to her," Tilly said. "And I will understand if you feel you have to tell your father. Hettie and I are friends and we talk about things she cannot say to others. We are both grown women and . . . and you are not. So I wouldn't expect you to understand."

"I am nearly thirteen," Nell said.

"That is very young still."

"I am not a child," she snapped. Then added, "I'm sorry. I oughtn't lose my temper."

Thirteen. Nell was on the precipice of womanhood. Tilly thought about herself at that age, how her temper had become unmanageable, how every small slight grew to a monstrous insult. Grandpa had come down hard on her, insisting that she learn self-control or spend her life in her bedroom. He had shamed her, criticized her in front of friends and family for her intemperance. She had always believed it to be a flaw in her personality, but looking at Nell now, she wondered if it was simply that the swing of the hinge between childhood and womanhood was confusing and infuriating enough to make a girl sensitive. Why had she been made to feel so ashamed of it? On many occasions, anger had been precisely the right response. When Godfrey had tripped her in the garden or the man at the post office had called her freckle face or Mrs. Beaumont had gossiped to everyone who would listen about Tilly's all-too-obvious interest in Peter Ireland who worked at the bank.

Just now, it was perfectly reasonable for Nell to be angry. She was a clever young woman with a strong sense of self and justice, and Tilly had offended her on all three counts.

"No, I am sorry," she said. "And I admire you for your good sense of what acceptable behavior is and your courage to point it out." Tilly wondered how much different her life might have been, if Grandpa had ever said such a thing to her.

Nell beamed at her. "You do?"

"Absolutely. And I know your father would admire it too."

"I'm not so sure." Nell reached across to Tilly's lap and grabbed her hand. "Don't worry, I won't tell him about you and Hettie. I don't want you to be in trouble. I don't want him to send you away."

Tilly stroked Nell's hand, sadness blooming under her ribs. She was going away anyway and there would be no chance to say good-bye.

•

Tilly arrived the next morning early at the library. She was determined to make the next week or so, before she left, a special time for her and Nell. She would be more patient, spend more time listening to her stories, make time to read *Sir Gawain and the Green Knight* together.

But Nell wasn't there yet. A huge pile of her papers lay spread on the table, and Tilly approached them to tidy them before classes started.

Immediately, she saw that some had a date on the first line, like a letter or a diary.

A diary. Nell kept a diary.

Tilly glanced over her shoulder. No Nell. Just Tilly, her ticking pulse and the dust motes in the morning sun in the dim room. Nell had not indicated she suspected Tilly was involved in an escape plan with Hettie, but then Nell was very good at dissembling. Tilly flicked the page over, her eyes scanning for anything that might reveal Nell suspected her.

She skimmed. A lot of talk about Papa, about how she felt about her new book, about walking on the beach with Tilly. She flicked a few more pages.

> *Papa misses Tilly. I can see it clearly. Why can he not see it? Why can he not tell that he needs to ask her to marry him?*

Tilly's attention was arrested. She picked up the page, read on.

> *Ever since she left for the mainland, Papa is a loose end at night. He wears a faraway look in his eyes. He asks me the same question twice and doesn't listen to either answer. But when Tilly is here, his face is warm and his eyes are on her. I suspect he loves her. She, of course, loves him. There is nothing so obvious in the world as that. Tilly's face is an open book.*

"Tilly?"

Tilly spun around, shame-faced, Nell's diary page in her hand.

Nell's eyebrows were pulled down hard. She strode in and snatched the page out of Tilly's hands. "*That*," she said, "is private."

"I'm sorry. I was looking for your story, so we could read ahead this morning."

Nell pushed in front of her, arranging the pages, putting some aside and keeping others in a jealously guarded pile in front of her.

Tilly felt the prickle of anxiety; was there something in particular Nell was hiding?

Nell glared up at her. "I would rather you didn't touch my papers," she said.

Their eyes were locked like that a few moments. Nell at her desk, Tilly standing before her. Between them, mutual suspicion where there had once been guileless love. Tilly reminded herself that she was the adult here, that her own suspicions—that Nell knew something—were so far unfounded.

She forced her face to soften. "Today, we are going to take *Sir Gawain* down to the beach and read him in the sunshine all morning," she said.

Nell, sensing she was being manipulated, didn't smile. "We are?"

"Would you like me to ask the kitchen for a picnic basket?"

"Why are you being so nice to me? Are you not paid to torture me with Latin declensions?"

"I simply want to enjoy our time together. We have been rather at odds since I arrived back."

"That's because you arrived back different," Nell said.

"In what way am I different?"

"It's been coming on for a while. You're distant, preoccupied. You don't have sherry with Papa in the parlor anymore."

Tilly pulled out a chair and sat close to Nell. "And that troubles you?"

"He was happy. Now he seems . . . not as happy."

Tilly was tempted to tell Nell to have this conversation with Sterling. It was him, after all, who had put the distance between them. But there was no point now. Their relationship couldn't be fixed, and soon Sterling and Nell and Ember Island would all be behind her. "I assure you I am the same woman I always was," Tilly said.

Nell nodded, though she still seemed unconvinced. "Yes to the picnic," she said. "And yes to Gawain, but only if you promise to have sherry with Papa tonight."

Tilly shrugged. "Very well, if that's what it takes to make you happy."

"Oh, it would take much more than that," Nell said, the first glimmer of a real smile for the day on her lips. "But that is a good place to start."

.

They were halfway to the beach for their picnic when Nell changed her mind.

"I know a better place to go," she said.

"Where?"

She pointed to the chapel. "It's a glorious day. We can sit up on the roof and look for ships and nobody will see us."

"I don't know about going up there, Nell," Tilly said, remembering the hot, dusty ceiling.

"Oh, please."

Tilly relented quickly. She was eager to keep the girl happy. "Very well, then, but we must be careful on that wretched ladder."

Before long they were up on the chapel roof. Tilly leaned on the bricks and gazed out at the ships in the bay while Nell unpacked the picnic basket and set a place for herself, for Tilly and for Pangur Ban.

"This looks wonderful," Nell said, reaching into the basket for a banana.

Tilly sat with her. "It's not all play, you know. We need to read as well."

"Yes, *Gawain* is at the bottom of the basket." The sunny breeze moved in Nell's curls. "We have to eat our way through to him."

They made their way through fruit and sandwiches and tarts and a bottle of milk, and then cleared away and read for an hour, until the sun became too direct and hot and Tilly feared they would both burn.

Nell grasped her hand on the path on the way home, and Tilly had the feeling something had been mended for now.

Right at the bottom of the path up to Starwater, Nell stopped, gasped.

"What is it?" Tilly asked.

Nell threw the picnic basket on the ground and desperately went through it, pulling out dirty plates and cups and crockery. "Pangur," she said with a panic. "I think I left him up there."

"Shall we go back?"

Nell sat back on her haunches, looking wistfully down towards the chapel. "I . . . well, maybe not."

"No?"

"I am nearly thirteen. Maybe I'm too old for Pangur now."

Tilly's heart squeezed. "If you want him, I will happily go and get him for you."

But Nell was resolute. "Toys are for little children, aren't they? I'm nearly a woman."

Tilly touched her hair. "You know where he is. You can always go and find him another day."

"Yes," Nell said, picking herself up and repacking the basket. "I know where he is."

•

As the dinner plates were being cleared away, Nell kicked Tilly under the table.

Tilly remembered her promise and cleared her throat awkwardly.

Sterling, who was half out of his chair, throwing his napkin on the table, looked at her.

Nell gave her an emphatic nod of the head.

"Sterling, I wonder if we might . . . have a sherry tonight?" Tilly asked.

Sterling stood, hands clasped in front of him, then behind him. "You would . . . like that?"

"We haven't for a while."

"Then let's."

Nell beamed at both of them, then seemed to remember she should be elsewhere and bade them good night.

Tilly stood and Sterling accompanied her, careful not to touch her, to the parlor. The window was open, letting in a breeze almost too cold to bear.

She went to the window to close it while Sterling poured sherry. "It is astonishing to me how quickly I have become accustomed to the heat," she said. "Now the cooler season is upon us, I'm quite unprepared." She could see the shape of the stockade through the glass. "It must be very cold in the cells."

"Our winters are short," he said. "And nearly always dry."

Tilly turned away from the window and saw the two sherry glasses on the table. She came to sit on the sofa and he sat across from her. How she longed for his body to be closer to hers, so she could feel his heat, smell his skin. Unexpectedly, she felt tears on the way. She swallowed them back, hid her emotions by taking a large gulp of the sherry.

"So," he said. "How was your holiday?"

"It was fine. Thank you."

He waited for a moment, perhaps to see if she'd elaborate, but when she didn't, he pushed on. "Good, then."

They sat in silence. The wind rattled the panes. Would it be cold out there on the water? She didn't have a coat for Hettie. It occurred to her that she should find out about the boats in the shed, but she wasn't sure how to raise the issue without it sounding forced or suspicious.

"And was the weather fine over on the mainland?" Sterling continued.

"It was, yes. Sterling, it occurred to me that if ever I was injured or unwell and needed treatment on the mainland, I would have to wait up to two days for the steamer."

"Are you unwell?" he asked, concern on his brow.

"No, no. I'm just wondering . . ."

"We have several large rowing boats and several smaller ones. We are not completely without means to get off the island."

"I didn't know that," Tilly said. "I have never seen the boats." It wasn't a lie. The boat shed had been pitch-black inside.

"They are locked up down at the shed. Barring emergencies—escapes and injuries and so on—we only take them out once a week. One of the guards does a patrol around the island looking for suspicious activity."

Once a week. Which day? Which day? If she asked, he would grow suspicious.

"Which day?" she said, her voice small.

"What's that?"

"Is it a weekend job?" she asked.

His eyes told her he was puzzled. Whether that puzzlement would harden to suspicion depended on what happened next. Would he ask her why she wanted to know? What possible interest it had to her? Or would he assume she was simply making awkward small talk, as he had done when he had asked about the weather.

"Fridays," he said.

She laughed lightly. "I'm sorry. I feel rather awkward and I'm simply trying to make conversation."

He smiled in return. "I am feeling awkward too. Perhaps we need more sherry."

He indicated her glass and she looked down and saw it was empty. She couldn't remember drinking it that fast. On the one hand, she very much wanted more sherry to relax her. On the other hand, if she became too relaxed she might do or say something that aroused his suspicion.

It was too late. He'd taken her silence for affirmation and was filling her glass. His shirtsleeves were rolled up to reveal his forearms. She watched his strong hands stop up the bottle and put it aside.

Fridays. Her plan could not unfold on a Friday. They would see a boat missing and raise the alarm. Early in the week, then. Next Tuesday. One week from today. The decision was made. Heat flashed across her ribs and she told herself she could do it the week after or the week after that. That she didn't have to do it at all. She could leave the island and never look behind her.

But that wouldn't work, would it? Because what was behind her still haunted her.

"You look quite pale," Sterling said. "Are you well?"

She picked up the sherry and gulped it. "I am as well as can be expected," she said, dreading an evening of light chatter between them, when she had such heavy thoughts on her mind.

TWENTY-FIVE

Watching the Water

For the rest of the week and the weekend, Tilly watched and made a note of what time the sea crept up or peeled back from Seven Yard Beach. Sitting on the rocks, shoes off and bare feet in the water, she counted hours and days and decided a hundred times she wouldn't do this, and as many times that she would. Her life was already blighted by the fire; what comfort and familiarity she hung on to were simply illusions.

By now, she was sleeping only a few hours each night, as her brain ticked over her plans. Her ideas changed from day to day, then solidified. Of one thing she was certain: she did not want to be trying to steal a boat on the afternoon of the escape. That she would have to put into place earlier.

And so, at four in the morning on Monday—the day before the escape—Tilly rose in the dark after a few fitful hours of sleep. The wind from the night before had dropped, and all she could hear was the muted sound of the grandfather clock ticking in the parlor. She pulled on stockings and a dark gray dress, but did not

take the time to pin her hair or lace into underwear. Her sturdiest shoes were under the bed, and she slid her feet into them and
wiggled her toes so she could feel the floor, the world beneath her.
Then she pinned on her cloak and wrapped a blue ribbon around
her right wrist.

Tilly cracked open the door and listened carefully. Not a
sound. Not a stirring body or a fluttering eyelid. The whole world
held its breath.

She moved like a silent shadow down the hall, opened the door
to Sterling's office and closed it behind her with an almost inau-
dible click.

Tilly struck a match on the flint on his desk and lit the lantern.
She opened the drawer and a moment later had the key to the
boat shed in her hand. Taking the lantern with her, Tilly climbed
out Sterling's office window and into the cool morning air.

She hurried away from the house, throwing her cloak around
the outside of the lantern so it wouldn't draw the attention of
any early risers. The air was crisp, the sky dark and sprinkled
with stars. Dawn was still two hours away, but Tilly felt the pressure of time upon her nonetheless. She had a lot to do before
Sterling woke, before the guards and turnkeys started their daily
rounds.

Down at the boat shed, she stopped and stilled her heart. The
sea was calmly breaking against the shore; the tide was low enough
to launch the boat from the beach. She unlocked the door and
crept inside, holding the lantern aloft and sending dark shadows
into the corners. With her eyes she counted five large rowing
boats, and three small ones. She understood that a small one
would be all she could manage on her own and set down the lantern. She bent and pulled on the rope attached to the prow of the
nearest boat, dragged it with both hands out of the boat shed and

onto the grass. Then she returned for a set of oars. Her skin was alive with anticipation, fearing discovery at every second. Awkwardly, she concealed the lantern under her cloak again and made her first trip to the narrow strip of beach, with the oars curled in her free arm, tight against her body.

She perched the lantern on the rocks, left the oars in the sand, and returned for the boat, locking the door behind her. Dragging it with all her strength, walking backwards in the dark, praying not to trip or make an alarming noise or be seen. And then equally praying that somebody *would* see her; and that she would be forced to stop before she could commit this crime.

But ten minutes later she was on the beach alone. She hefted the boat over and placed the lantern in it. Took off her shoes and stockings, and put them in the boat, too, and the oars. Tilly hitched her skirts high and tied them in a knot in front of her. Her legs were white in the dark. And then pushed the boat into the water, until the cold sea came up over her knees and the boat cleared the gritty sand. The low waves slapped the wood softly. She climbed in, picked up the oars, and started to splash the oars on the water. She had never rowed a boat before and managed to instantly send the boat back into the sand.

"Curses," she muttered, climbing out of the boat and pushing it into the water again. The cold was creeping deep inside her now, the fear and the guilt intensifying it and making it icy. Once more the boat was bobbing freely. She climbed in, picked up the oars and lifted them, paddled madly for a little longer, this time somehow getting herself free of the shore and into deeper water, but still not mastering the oars.

She stopped, drifted a little while on the dark water. Breathing deeply. She thought about the sharks that frequented these waters, and it seemed to her that her mind, too, was infested by sharks.

Dark, sharp-toothed thoughts, circling. The lamplight flickered. Her hands on the oars looked like somebody else's.

"Now," she said. "Row."

Lift, drop, push. Lift, drop, push. Arrowing slowly through the water, staying close to the shoreline with her little light the only company. Already Tilly's shoulders were aching. She hoped Hettie had the strength to row them all the way to the mainland because Tilly certainly didn't.

Two weak women in a boat. The moment they knew Hettie was missing, somebody would climb up the white towers and sight them. Or they'd send out the other boats, rowed by dozens of strong men, and catch them long before they approached the mainland. Her heart fluttered. Hettie had strong hands. Strong enough to kill a man. She would surely be a strong rower.

Tilly approached the first curve of the island. If she kept going straight from here, she would eventually end up in the Coral Sea. Instead, she intended to take the boat around to the mangroves and hide it there for the escape. She had toyed with the idea of dragging the boat across the island in the dark, but the risk of discovery was greatly increased if she was on land. Besides, she was starting to get the hang of the oars and it felt good to be driving herself through the water. The dark island slipped silently past, its silhouettes made unfamiliar from this perspective. The stockade, the wide flat cane fields, the escarpment, the house where Sterling and Nell were sleeping, warm in their beds, with no idea what she was doing.

Then she passed around the tip of the island and the water grew rougher. The tide was coming back in. The dark, grotesque shadows of the mangroves waited. She rowed hard, on the dark side of the island now, and brought the boat in on the mud.

Tilly climbed out of the boat and pulled it as far up on shore as she could, her feet squelching through mud and shallow water, and bruising themselves on the spiky roots that stuck up through the ground. She fought off branches and bugs alike, breathing hard and perspiring under her warm dress, even though her bare feet were freezing. The dank smell of the mangrove forest, the moldering shadows. She rested the boat between two trees, then picked her way back down to the water's edge to find the tree that leaned out the furthest. She unwrapped the ribbon on her wrist, wading calf-deep in the water, and tied the ribbon around an extended branch. Then returned to the boat to collect her lantern and shoes, and trudge back towards the house.

A rocky cliff face separated the swamp from the house, so she had to either come around the bottom of the island or cut through the mangroves and then take a route through the cane fields. The latter was quicker, but didn't appeal to her. The mangroves were full of spiders, the cane fields full of snakes. Instead, she walked along in the cold ankle-deep water, through mud and roots, until she found the rocky shoreline that took her around past the lime kiln and the sugar mill. She extinguished her lamp then cut up through the cemetery and onto the main track. Her aching feet were caked with mud, so she stopped in the garden on her way back and washed her feet in the pond. It wouldn't do to return the lantern and the key to Sterling's office and leave a set of muddy footprints. The sky was growing light in the east, the stars paling. But she sat for a moment in the garden, waiting for her feet to dry, eyes sore from lack of sleep.

Not so long now. Today, then tomorrow's dawn, and then . . .

Dawn somewhere else. Not on Ember Island.

She dragged herself to her feet, tiptoed up onto the verandah, and let herself back into Sterling's office. Returned the lamp and the key. She stopped to consider the map of Moreton Bay Sterling kept on his wall. An idea struck her. She lit a match and held it up, studying the map. So many islands.

She studied the map so long that the match burned down to her fingers and fizzed. Alarmed, she shook it out. But her right thumb and index finger stung with the burn. She sucked on them, eyes watering, trying not to make a noise, wrapped them in her damp skirt.

The house was still quiet and still as she made her way to her bedroom, where she lit her lamp and examined her burnt fingers. Already a big welt was growing on her index fingertip. She touched it and winced.

And thought about Jasper and Chantelle . . .

She touched it again, making the pain ignite all along her nerves. Soon that debt would be cleared; then she could be free of the black-ash shadows of the past.

•

Tilly rolled the red dress as tightly as she could and tucked it under her arm. She was brutally tired from lack of sleep the night before and a full day working with Nell. Nell had asked her what plans Tilly had for schoolwork for the following week, and Tilly had not been able to answer. She had planned no life beyond the escape, as though Ember Island itself would cease to exist the moment she and Hettie rowed away.

Her heartsickness about Nell was crippling her. She had grown to love the girl, and thoughts of her now made her teary and full of dread. She tried to tell herself she was simply tired, but no matter how she viewed her weak knees and heavy heart, she was still about to commit a crime.

The garden was growing slowly now. The prevailing winds had changed; dry winds came from the west now, lifting the undersides of leaves and making them flicker white and cold. The lazy guard was there again. He saw her and offered a smile, but paid no further attention to her as she went down to the back of the garden to meet Hettie.

She was pacing, her dark head bent.

Tilly stopped a few feet from her, cleared her throat.

"You came," Hettie said, quietly but relieved.

"Of course I came."

"I keep thinking you'll change your mind."

"I won't change my mind."

"It's been days since we last spoke. I haven't been able to concentrate on anything. I keep thinking of the children and I am . . ." Her voice trembled and began to break. "I am tortured by the idea that I won't see them after all."

Tilly checked behind her. They were alone. "Here," she said, thrusting the dress into Hettie's arms.

"What is it?"

"It's a dress and scarf, identical to the ones I will wear tomorrow."

"Tomorrow?"

"The boat is in place. In the mangroves, about half a mile down from the tip of the island. There is a tree that leans over the water; I've marked it with a blue ribbon. We will meet there at sunset."

Hettie nodded, the dress clutched between desperate hands.

"The best way out is through the cane fields. If you can get changed down here, then slip by the eastern side of the house and down the steep side of the escarpment, you'll be on flat ground in no time. If anyone sees you from a distance, they'll think it's me."

"But what if they see you too?"

"I'll go through the western edge of the cane fields. It doesn't matter who sees either of us; they won't see both of us. You'll probably get to the boat first. Wait for me there. Don't panic, I will come." Tilly checked around again. "We will not row to the mainland."

"No? Then where?"

"There is another island to the north. It's uninhabited. I will fill the boat tomorrow with food, water and blankets. We will make it our home for a week or so. They will be expecting us to make for the mainland. While they are all searching to the west, we will be heading to the north."

Hettie's eyes glimmered sharply. "That is a good plan," she said, then added, "But you don't look well."

"I am tired. I was awake in the night, moving the boat into place."

"I don't know how I can thank you."

"You can thank me by living a happy life."

Hettie turned her face up to the afternoon sunshine, closed her eyes. "I will be so happy when I hold my babies in my arms. When last I saw them, they were so small. My son little more than a baby, with only a few words. I can see him in my mind's eye." She tapped her temple, then opened her eyes. "He will be different. The plumpness will have melted, his limbs grown long. My daughter, too. You cannot imagine how precious the years with them will be to me; years that I thought I had forsaken forever. I thought I might not see them again until they were grown, with no memory or care for who I was. And you have made this possible. God bless you, Tilly. God bless you."

Tilly's heart swelled. Yes, this would work. This would absolve her. She was desperate now for the plan to unfold without incident, for Hettie to be returned to the arms of her loved ones without detection. Was she naïve to think either of these things were possible? And what of her own future?

"Hide the dress under a hedge," Tilly advised. "Even if the dew falls tonight, it will have most of the day to dry out. Tomorrow I will organize the food and blankets. Everything should be in place for sunset."

Hettie clasped her hands in front of her, trembling visibly. "I will be ready."

"I will see you at the boat."

•

Tilly slept like the dead, exhausted from the previous night, and only woke when Nell knocked hard at her door.

"Tilly? Are you there?"

"Come in," Tilly croaked.

The door opened. Nell's face was pale with concern. "You weren't at breakfast and then you didn't come to class. Are you ill?"

"I . . ." Tilly realized she might need an excuse to get away early today. "I am a little. Yes. But I will dress and come to class. Go and wait for me in the library."

"Are you certain? Perhaps I should get somebody to bring you breakfast on a tray."

The thought of eating made her stomach lurch. "I have no appetite. I may feel better once I'm up and about." She offered a smile. "You may have to be gentle with me today."

"I will be so gentle," Nell said, hand on her heart. "And I'll understand entirely if you want to stay in bed."

Then Nell was gone, closing the door softly behind her.

By the time Tilly was dressed in her red dress and had arrived at the library, Nell had been to the kitchen and fetched a banana for her.

Tilly picked it up gratefully. "Thank you, dear."

"I know you're not hungry, but food may make you feel better. I stayed up late last night writing another chapter, Tilly. Would you like to hear it?"

Tilly peeled the banana and took a bite. "I certainly would," she said.

"Go and sit on the sofa. You'll be more comfortable."

So Tilly took her banana to the leather sofa beside the bookcases, and Nell came and sat on the floor next to her and read. Tilly closed her eyes and listened, allowing herself to be lost in Nell's world. The girl really was a fine writer, with a big imagination and a wonderful command of language for her age. She wondered what Nell would do in the future, how life would treat her, who would break her heart.

After an hour, Nell stopped, right at a crucial point.

Tilly opened her eyes. "Go on," she said.

"That's it. That's as far as I've written."

"But does Emmeline ever find her mother?"

Nell shrugged. "I'm not sure. You'll have to wait until I write some more."

Tilly's eyes pricked with tears and Nell noticed immediately.

"Tilly? Did I make you cry?"

"Your story is lovely," Tilly muttered, sniffing the tears back. "That's all."

Nell beamed. "Do you really think so?"

Tilly took her hand. "I really think so. You're a marvelous writer. Imagine the places you might go with it."

Nell stood and did a little twirl of delight. "Imagine the stories I might write. I don't really want to go anywhere. There couldn't be anywhere as beautiful as Ember Island, don't you think?"

Back to reality, Tilly was swamped by the things she had to get done. Her stomach twitched. "Nell, would you mind if we canceled lessons for the rest of the day? I can give you some exercises to go on with . . ."

"No, I'm going to my room to write. So I can read you some more tomorrow."

Tomorrow. The tomorrow that wouldn't come for them. "That's a wonderful idea," she murmured.

Nell was gone in a flash, brimming with excitement and imagination.

Tilly lay back again, closed her eyes. One moment of quiet before the storm of apprehension and agitation. Opened her eyes. Stood and went to the kitchen.

The big echoing room was empty. Their cook had left a large pot of soup simmering on the stove, filling the air with the salty smell of ham. Tilly found the largest picnic basket they kept, under the big wooden table in the middle of the room, and placed it on the bench. A hulking bunch of bananas sat on the table, mostly green. She put in a dozen of those, a loaf of bread, a knife. Heard footsteps come and go in the hallway and stood frozen a few moments. Then went searching for more things. Eggs, flour, matches, a small pot. She realized she was grasping things at random, but as long as they could stay alive for a week on the next island, they could eat well when they finally got to the mainland. Tilly closed the picnic basket when it was filled to the brim, piled two blankets rolled around two spare dresses on top, and went out the back door.

The cool air stirred with a wind from the sea. A sailing ship glided past in the distance, between the island and the mainland, all its sails gleaming white in the autumn sunlight. The bay was green-blue, thumping. Tilly hoped the wind would calm by this evening, that the swell would settle. She didn't relish the idea of being out there on a small boat.

She took the road down towards the beach and then came around the rocks and into the swamp. The sun fell vertically through the trees onto the dank mud. The tide was up, so she had to make her way between the trees rather than along the shore line. Her skin shrank against the bugs and creeping branches. It was slow going and she made a note to herself to leave plenty of time this afternoon. It would be better for her to arrive before Hettie, to greet her and put her at ease.

For a long time she didn't think she would see the tree with the blue ribbon. She wondered if it had blown away into the water, but the tide was up so the tree was a lot further out than she remembered, standing in the salt water with the bright ribbon rattling in the wind.

She saw the boat a moment later, as she'd left it. She made her way over, and placed the picnic basket and blankets in it. Then stood for a moment looking out through the trees at the water, catching her breath and her thoughts. The minutes and hours were buzzing past. Soon it would all come to fruition.

•

On returning to the house, Tilly's first order of business was to change into a clean dress and shoes. Mud had spattered the ones she was wearing. Nell was a curious girl and Tilly hadn't the energy for a series of plausible lies. From outside her door, she could smell food and it made her stomach rumble. She stepped out into the corridor and down to the dining room, where Nell sat alone at the dining table with a tureen of tomato soup and a plate of bread rolls in front of her. Tilly stopped in the threshhold.

"Are you feeling any better?" Nell said, her eyes revealing a hint of suspicion.

"Not much."

"Will you eat? There's more than enough. Papa has some business over at the stockade and couldn't join me and I do hate to eat alone."

Tilly wouldn't be here for dinner and food might be scarce over coming days, so she said, "Yes. Yes, I will."

She pulled out a chair and served herself some soup, dipped the warm bread into it, pushed it in her mouth. Took a moment to savor it. "Did you write?" she asked Nell.

"I only stopped because I was so hungry," Nell answered. "I have had a breakthrough. I believe I'll finish it this afternoon and can read it to you tomorrow. Provided you are well, of course."

"Who knows what tomorrow will bring?" Tilly said lightly, between mouthfuls.

Nell was quiet a few moments, then said, "Tilly?"

Tilly's skin prickled. "Yes?"

But then Nell shook her head. "Nothing. It's good soup, isn't it? Cook never makes it too salty. We once had a cook that added so much salt to everything that sometimes my tongue would feel thick after a meal."

And on she went, making small talk. Tilly nodded and made noises in the right places, all the time her mind a whirl of other, darker thoughts.

After lunch, she returned to her room and went through her belongings. While she couldn't be seen with a suitcase, she had a cotton bag that she could sling over her shoulder and take with her, so she slid her inlaid writing box into it: the last remnant of an old life that receded further and further into her memory. What would Grandpa, not quite a year dead in his grave, think of this turn of events? What shame he would feel, knowing she had fallen so low and was preparing to take such desperate steps.

"I'm sorry, Grandpa," she said, under her breath, caressing the box. Then she put the bag down near the dresser and knelt by her bed and, for the first time in many months, began to pray.

It was while she was begging for forgiveness and clarity that a knock sounded at her door. She stood, smoothed down her skirt and said, "Come in."

It was Sterling, in his dark blue vest and shirtsleeves. His familiar smell—skin, soap, leather—washed over her and she had to restrain herself from leaning towards him to take a deep breath.

"I am terribly sorry to bother you," he said, "but we've had our mail and there's a letter for you."

"For me?"

He held out the envelope. He was curious, she could tell. The handwriting was familiar and the return address was the same as the last. Laura Mornington had written again, via Mrs. Fraser's. The series of crossings-out on the envelope told her it had been passed on to Mr. Hamblyn's before being redirected here. "Thank you," she said, in a tone that was as neutral as she could manage.

"Where precisely is Guernsey?" he asked.

"It's an island in the English Channel. I lived there for a time," she added boldly. There was no point in hiding it. "Very unhappily, I might add."

"So you are no stranger to islands, then," he said gently. "Perhaps that is why you fit in so well here." His eyes lit on the dress and shoes that lay in a pool on the floor. "Is that mud?" he asked.

"I've been down to the mangrove forest," she said, heartbeat twitching in her throat.

"For fresh air?"

"I was thinking of taking Nell down there next week. For a

science lesson. I wasn't prepared for quite how muddy it was, so I turned around almost immediately."

"Don't take Nell down there, please," he said. "It's neither safe nor pleasant."

"I am unwell," she said coolly. "I won't be at dinner. And I'll be resting all afternoon and don't want to be disturbed."

He blinked rapidly, taken aback. "Of course." He gathered himself, resolved. "I'll let Nell know. Good day."

She turned away so she couldn't watch him leave. When the door had closed she said, "Good-bye, Sterling," and tears welled and spilled over. She sat on the bed with her face in her hands and let the tears fall. Tears of love and loss and fear and strain. Tilly cried for nearly half an hour, then turned to Laura's letter.

There wasn't the urgency opening it this time, for she suspected it would say much the same as the first. In fact, she almost didn't read it. It wasn't for her at all. But then she thought that a fresh stab of guilt over her crime may be necessary to get her through the evening. She tore the envelope and unfolded the pages within.

•

Dear Chantelle,

It has been some time since I last wrote, and I waited in vain for a letter from you to reassure me. I can see now why you didn't write back, and perhaps this letter will disappear into nowhere because you have already moved on, as you must, given how culpable you are.

Since my last letter, things have come to light that were not apparent to me before and I feel such a fool for trusting

*you, giving you the benefit of doubt, and even defending you
to the very woman who suspected you wanted to destroy her
happiness. Now I know you would have willingly destroyed
her happiness and destroyed her along with it.*

*After the fire, when the police came, they found love
letters between you and Jasper in your room. They found no
passport, and we all presumed Jasper had broken it off and
you had fled. No suspicion over the fire was laid upon you
because the cause was found to be simply a broken lamp in
a downstairs room. Perhaps the curtain had caught it. The
window had been left open and the curtains appeared to
be the first thing that went up. I was glad when the police
had told me all this because I had been so worried that the
timing of your leaving would cast suspicion on you. "She is
a good woman," I had told the police so many times. "She is
an orphan and I have done my best to help her."*

*And so I went on, believing you innocent of all sin,
suspecting only that you had run off with a broken heart
and didn't even know about the accidental fire at Lumière
sur la Mer. I worried for you, nearly every day. I even
kept your room for you, until it became impractical. My
daughter Maria and her child have now moved in with us,
and we needed to hire more servants. It was time to clear
out your room.*

*I had a few sad moments as I packed up your dresses
and shoes, your hair clips and toiletries. Much of it I have
thrown away or given to charity. As a servant, you had
nothing fine. Or so I thought.*

*On the final day, before the two new beds were to be
moved in to a room you had luxuriated in alone—thanks
to Jasper, and to Tilly's great dismay—I checked the dresser*

*drawers one last time. I noted that the bottom drawer
was shallower than the others, and in investigating this
irregularity, I discovered the drawer had a false bottom. When
I lifted out the flat panel of wood, I found all your secrets.*

*Not just jewelry—jewelry a woman of your station could
never afford—but the other letters, the wicked letters as
I've come to think of them. Every single one of them from
Jasper, but do not think that you are not implicated in every
wicked line.*

*Some made me blush with their lascivious details.
I wonder if you wrote such shocking and improper letters
in return. I read through them, even though they made
me ill. What I thought were fantasies on the page turned
out to be memories. The fact that you saved such lewd and
indecent writings from him says something of your character,
Chantelle.*

But there was much worse to come.

*Other letters, hidden also. The letters you wanted to save
but wanted nobody ever to find. Letters that spoke of love
and lust, but also spoke of plans for murder. When I think of
poor Tilly coming to me for comfort and how I simply told
her that husbands have affairs and it means nothing and
she should go about her life expecting happiness . . . it makes
me want to sob with guilt and anguish. That poor young
woman, played like a fool by Jasper, egged on by you, with
the goal of taking her money and then making her appear
to be going mad, and ultimately . . . would you have really
done it, Chantelle? Would you have really gone through with
poisoning her? Pushing her out a window? Drowning her in
the sea? These were all suggestions Jasper had made, and the
letters indicated that you were avidly involved in arguing*

the details of these acts with him. Would you have really stood by as Jasper spoke to the authorities of her repeated attempts to take her own life? She had no family left to speak of; I suppose you might have got away with such a lie. And then would you have set up house at Lumière sur la Mer with Jasper as though you somehow deserved it?

What a horror you are. What a ghastly last few weeks in this world poor Tilly must have experienced. Well you might run, Chantelle Lejeune. You had much to run from.

Ralph insisted I burn the letters, so you need not fear the interest of the police. His reasoning was that Tilly is dead now, and unable to be saved. That Jasper, too, will never answer for his crimes. And that he wants to think of it no more, and he doesn't want the trouble and shame of an investigation. I disagreed with him, but did as a good wife should and followed his directions. All those letters were burned in my hearthplace, and I swear they smelled of brimstone as they went up: that is how much evil was in them.

But although you need not fear the judgment of the earthly law, Chantelle, you will face the judgment of God on your final day. That gives me comfort. And writing this letter has given me a chance to express my horror and anger. I wish you only misery. I wish you an awful life.

Laura Mornington

•

Tilly refolded the letter with shaking hands.

Jasper and Chantelle were plotting to murder her. Perhaps that night was the night they intended to go through with their plans, perhaps not. Nonetheless, they were not innocent. Certainly, it was not for Tilly to decide their punishment, but she hadn't, had she? She had decided nothing.

Now that clarity was pushing through the guilty mud in her brain, she saw the fire differently. Fighting Jasper off. Him knocking the lamp over. That room full of old papers because there was no furniture left to store them in. Yes, she had locked him in, but she had feared for her own safety. The moment he was free, he had gone upstairs anyway because his lover was hidden in the house. A congregation of events, set in chain by Jasper and Chantelle and their murderous plans, that ended in their accidental deaths.

Tilly didn't kill them. She had tortured herself with guilt for months with no good reason.

And now time ticked by on her last day here, on her plan to help Hettie escape so that she could absolve herself: there was no absolution necessary. How she longed to call it all off. To stay here and resume teaching Nell and wait for Sterling to come back to her arms. She choked back a sob.

It was too late. She couldn't go and face Hettie and say, "No, we are not proceeding." Hettie's mind was already fixed on holding her children again. Besides, the matching dress was under the hedge, the boat was in place loaded with supplies. Tilly's crimes had already been committed, and she wouldn't be able to stop Hettie now. And if Hettie escaped, Tilly couldn't stay on the island.

The only way out was escape.

TWENTY-SIX

Blood and Ash

L ike a condemned woman going to the gallows, Tilly silently left the house at the appointed time and made her way down towards the cane fields. The shadows were long, the air cool, the dusky sky turning pink. She wondered how Hettie had got on, escaping from the garden in her matching dress and matching scarf tied down over her hair and low across her face. Had anybody called out to her? Waved and expected a wave back and been startled by those big rough hands?

Tilly was nauseous from anxiety. Her stomach roiled as though with seasickness. Every step felt heavy with portent. She crossed the cow paddocks, noticing for the first time that she couldn't see any movement around the cane fields. Had they all gone in early this afternoon? That would make this easier. At least she and Hettie needn't fear detection.

At the edge of the field, Tilly paused. The wind rustled through the cane. She smelled the sea and the earth. She turned, as much to check if anyone was watching her as to say good-bye. Starwater was in darkness up on the hill. Somewhere in there, Sterling was working, Nell was reading or writing or playing. Their lives would go on.

Tilly hitched her cotton bag up on her shoulder and plunged into the cane. The towering plants grew close together, crushing out the light. She couldn't see her way to the other side, so she had to rely on the compass in her head to take her directly through to the other side. She knew there were narrow rutted roads between stands of cane, so she would have to be careful not to be spotted while emerging. But now it seemed as though she'd never find the next road. She was surrounded on all sides by plants, long stalks and green leaf-like shoots that rustled against her clothes and whipped her face. The ground was uneven so it was hard going. Underfoot there would be rats and snakes. The bottom part of the cane was sometimes broken and sharp, catching on her skirt or on her skin. The strong stalks stopped her from falling, but the plants were tough and dense, and she had to plow through them, pushing with her arms and shoulders, like swimming through sticks.

She was concentrating so hard on pushing through the cane that she was surprised when she came to the first road. Only two shoulder spans across, it nevertheless gave her a moment to breathe. Tilly checked left and right. Nobody was in sight, so she bent double, caught her breath. She had studied the cane fields carefully from the back verandah of Starwater. Each massive square was divided into four neat rectangles by these roads, so she had to cross another three rectangles before finally emerging near the rocky shoreline. She looked at her hands and noticed a trickle of blood from her right palm. She sucked it. The metal tang of blood mingled with the sweet taste of sugar.

Back into the cane.

She grew more confident, pushing and plowing against the cane. A smell came to her on the wind and it took her a few moments to recognize it as smoke.

Her heart lifted into her throat.

In late autumn, they light it up.

Tilly began to run.

It's spectacular, as though half the island is on fire.

Her chest bursting, her throat raw, leaves and broken cane whipping and cutting her, she ran. Then she heard the flames, rushing up around the edge of the field. The undergrowth began to shift and slither with small animals, smelling the smoke and desperate to be free. She ran with them, hoping to find one of those narrow roads she could escape down, out of the fields.

The heat and sound of the flames grew nearer, closing in on her. Her feet burned and her chest stung and her ears rang with terror. It was suddenly clear to her that she wouldn't escape this, that she was doomed to die in this fire, as Jasper and Chantelle had died.

And then she burst through onto a road. She looked wildly left and right. Flames everywhere. She stood in one of the last few places that wasn't alight, right in the middle of the field. But if she ran down this road to the end . . .

Frozen with fear. Fire surrounding her.

She had to act. It was the only possible way she would emerge from this alive. She ran, down the long narrow road towards the flames. Beyond them, fresh air and freedom and life.

The whooshing of air being sucked into the fire was almost deafening. She could see flames in the fields that were twenty feet high. On either side of her, blackened stalks were silhouetted against the orange fire. The next ten feet she would be running directly through it, the tiny gap barely any protection against the flames. She pulled her scarf over her mouth, put her head down, and found the last burst of speed she had in her body.

The bag over her shoulder grew too hot. She had to fling it off, Grandpa's wooden writing box tumbling in amongst the embers. Stinging pain pressed onto her shoulders. She could smell her own hair burning.

Then she was free, stumbling to the ground, landing facedown in the dirt. She lay there a moment, coughing against the smoke.

Get up, you have to get up.

She climbed to her feet and cut across the cow paddock, fearful of what had happened to her body. Her shoulders were raw with pain. She ran as fast as she could, made her way over the cow fence and then down onto the rocks. Without thinking, she plunged into the cold water.

Relief. The edge of the pain wore down. She lifted her shoulder and upper arm out of the water and considered them in the light of the fire reflected in the water. Her dress had burned right through and her skin was raw and dark pink. She would need a medical salve, dressings. On the next island there would be none of those things.

Had Hettie made it through the cane field?

Tilly stood in the water, her face working hard as she sobbed openly to the evening air. Pain and fear. Her throat burned.

But she had to keep moving, in the twilight, to meet Hettie.

•

Tilly waded, stumbling, crying in pain. Her shoes were heavy and clumsy with water but she daren't take them off lest she cut her feet on rocks. The salt water in the little scratches on her legs stung. Up past the cane fields which, one by one, went up in an orange blaze as the sky darkened to velvety blue from the east. How she longed to be sitting on the verandah with Nell, watching the burn-off comfortably, enjoying the soft evening and the hard, sweet smell of the smoke. Softly, ash began to patter down. Tiny, light flakes that dissolved on her skin. Black snow. She pushed on, got herself back up on shore once past the fires, and then picked her way over rocks to the swamp.

The last of the light was disappearing over the mainland, an amber blush in the west. The sea was pewter. The low tide meant she didn't need to wade through murky water anymore, so she made her way along the mud, frightened by the pain in her burnt skin and wondering if she would be able to survive even a night without medical treatment, let alone a week. She pushed on, beyond endurance because there was no turning back.

The blue ribbon was barely visible in the twilight, but Tilly didn't need to see it. Hettie was already there. She'd untied the boat and was pulling it down to the water.

"Hettie!" Tilly called, and it came out as a guttural gasp.

Hettie looked around, her face half in shadows, eyebrows lowered. Then she went back to the task at hand.

"Hettie, wait. I'm injured." She stumbled forward. "Did you get caught in the fire?"

"No, I went down the back way. Down the cliff. The idiot who was minding me stood right where I wanted to go."

"You climbed down the cliff?"

"Of course I did. I want to escape. Here, help me with this." She hauled on the rope and together they got the boat into the water. Hettie jumped in and the boat swayed a moment, then became still. Tilly stood thigh-deep in the swampy water, helping Hettie straighten out the oars. The boat was floating away from her.

"Here, help me in," Tilly said, extending her hand. "I can barely move I'm in so much pain."

Hettie said nothing. Her facial expression was neutral. She picked up the first oar.

"Hettie? Please. I can't climb in by myself."

With sudden brutal force, Hettie picked up the oar and struck Tilly around the head with it. She started to go down, ears ringing, and grasped desperately at the side of the boat. Hettie stood, making the boat rock unevenly, and this time smacked the oar across her ribs. The pain was unbelievable. Her hands started to slip, but then Hettie hit them too. Peeled her fingers off the side of the boat, pushed her into the water.

And rowed as fast as she could, away.

Tilly fought to stand up, fought to get her face above the water. Salt water in her wounds, her head spinning and thundering, her ribs pinching her so she could barely catch her breath. She would drown if she didn't stand up. Mustering every last reserve of strength she pushed herself to her feet.

"Hettie!" she called, but her voice was a wheeze. The boat grew distant, Hettie's dark shape disappearing.

The betrayal might have been the worst pain of all.

•

Stumbling, splashing, falling, catching herself. Black covering her eyes and lifting again by force of will. The ten feet between where she had been thrown off the boat and the shore might as well have been ten miles. Finally, finally, skirts waterlogged and dragging behind her, she collapsed on the mud. The pain overwhelmed her, sending her spinning into the dark.

●

Flashes of consciousness. The tide lapping at her feet. The memory of Hettie's betrayal. The soft ash raining on her. But every time, her tortured body took her down again.

But then there was light, flickering between the black branches. She tried to take a breath to call out, but the sharp pain in her ribs prevented her from doing anything more than gasping.

Closer they came, three or four men: her addled mind couldn't make out the numbers. Then Sterling's voice. "I found her! Over here! I found her!"

She tried to make her tongue move, but it wouldn't. Her ears began to ring again. She stayed conscious long enough to feel his strong arms close around her, but then the pain of him moving her made everything go black.

Tilly was aware of being jolted along, every movement an agony. Then she was somewhere soft and dry, flickering lights all around her. She heard Dr. Groom's voice, felt her sodden clothes being stripped from her body. She heard him say words like "burns" and "broken ribs." She heard Nell sobbing and wanted to reach out and tell her not to worry. She heard Sterling saying, "Do what you must." And then a cloth, with a sweet gluey smell, was pressed lightly against her nose and mouth.

"Breathe, Tilly," Dr. Groom said.

She breathed. Once, twice, three times. Began to grow dizzy, felt her blood pressure falling, her hearing fading out.

Then merciful freedom from pain and fear.

•

Tilly woke to grainy dawn light and a body that felt battered. As her eyes flickered, she took in the scene. She was in her own room, the curtains were open, her body felt stiff, and one small wriggle told her she was bandaged in many places. She gingerly turned her head, and saw Nell sitting next to her bed in an armchair she had hauled in. The girl was asleep.

"Nell?" Tilly managed.

Nell's eyes flew open. "Tilly! How do you feel? Are you going to die?"

"I hope not," Tilly said, but laughing or smiling were out of the question. "I feel as though perhaps I won't."

"Oh, I wish I could hug you. But I cannot touch you. Dr. Groom said you are most terribly injured, but that you will make a full recovery now your wounds are all clean and dressed. And Tilly. Your hair."

Tilly lifted a hand to touch her hair, only to feel stinging pain in her shoulders and a thunderous ache in her ribs.

"Some of it has burned off," Nell said. "Your beautiful red hair." And Nell began to sob, pent-up emotion released by this small symbol of Tilly's bodily trauma.

"Shhh, now," Tilly said, all of the events of the evening flooding back to her. "I have many questions to ask before your father or Dr. Groom come."

Nell sniffed and wiped her cheeks. "You will not be in any trouble."

"How do you . . . Do they know . . . ?"

"I knew. I suspected and . . . I knew and I told them that it was me that gave the boat to Hettie and that you had gone down to stop her to save me."

Tilly shook her head as gently as she could. "No, Nell."

"And I'm to be sent to boarding school for my sins, but I don't care if it protects you."

"I can't let you do that, Nell."

"You must let me do it." Her face was flushed with desperation. "You must."

The door cracked open, and Sterling, wrapped tightly in a deep-red dressing gown, peered through. "Tilly? You're awake?"

"I did it," Tilly blurted, before Nell could pounce on him. She would not have more guilt in her past. To go forward meant to tell the truth. "It wasn't Nell. She's lying to protect me. I did it for reasons that were stupid and . . . seemed important and . . ." Tilly fought tears. "I did it so she could be with her children again because I couldn't bear the thought of her being apart from them."

Sterling stood shocked and silent for long seconds.

"No, Papa, no! Don't listen to her." Nell threw herself at him, clung to him around his middle.

He put her aside firmly but gently and approached the bed, knelt beside it.

"Tilly. Tilly, say it's not true."

She took a deep breath and the pain in her ribs arrowed through her. She winced and Nell cried, "See what you're doing to her? Leave her be."

But Tilly talked over the top of her. "I cannot say it's not true, for it is true. Nell did nothing. I was going to run away at the same time as Hettie, but she pushed me out of the boat and I don't know why. I am a fool, and I know I will be punished, and I deserve to be punished. I cannot let this child take the blame for me."

Sterling bowed his head, pinching the bridge of his nose. How she longed to reach out her fingers and touch his shoulders, run her hand through his hair. But she was in too much pain and all of that was over. Gone, never to return. Like Hettie.

Sterling lifted his head and gently took Tilly's hand. "This is the last softness I can offer you," he said in a low voice, his thumb smoothing over the back of her hand. His eyes were filled with pain and sadness and horrible resignation. "Tilly, Hettie has no children."

Tilly began to cry in earnest, great heaving sobs that shuddered through her body, making her injured ribs stab with pain. Sterling released her hand, slowly, and then stood, his face growing carefully neutral. "You will have to be under guard until I work out how to proceed. Nell, you aren't to be here with Miss Lejeune. Leave immediately."

Nell cried, open-mouthed like a baby. "No. Papa, no! Don't do it. Don't!"

Thunderclouds gathered on Sterling's brow. "Get out of here this instant!" he roared, and Nell scurried away sobbing, slamming the door behind her.

"My name isn't Chantelle Lejeune," Tilly said boldly.

Sterling turned, eyebrows shooting up. "Then who are you?"

"My name is Matilda Dellafore, formerly Matilda Kirkland. There is much I haven't told you."

Sterling hesitated a moment, torn between duty and curiosity. Finally, he sat in the armchair that Nell had vacated, folded his hands in his lap, and said, "Then tell me now, for it is the last chance you will have."

Tilly told him everything.

•

It was nearly three weeks before Tilly could get out of bed and move about, and she was instructed that she was to go on the very next steamer back to the mainland. In a piece of unexpected mercy, Sterling had decided she was a victim rather than a perpetrator. He demanded her immediate departure from the island rather than pressing any charges, provided she answered any and all questions he had that might help in Hettie's recapture.

Of course they hadn't recaptured her. Hettie would have known Tilly would tell them to look to the next island to the north, and gone in another direction entirely. All they had to go on was a description of a boat and a red dress. Tilly thought about the level of strategy and cunning that Hettie must have employed from the moment they met, even from before that, when she managed to convince Sterling that she should be a trustee prisoner. And she knew they would never find Hettie.

Sterling probably knew that too.

Tilly packed her bag slowly, with her last remaining things. Inconsequential things such as dresses and hairbrushes. Nothing to show for more than twenty years in the world.

A soft knock at the door. She looked up. "Nell? You're not supposed to be here."

Nell held her finger over her lips in a "shh" gesture and beckoned her. Tilly followed, fearful of discovery and Sterling's ire, as Nell led her into the garden.

The grass was dewy, the air cool and brisk. Nell took her down one of the greenways. Tilly hadn't been in the garden since the escape and found she could barely tolerate the smell of earth and flowers. It reminded her so strongly of her foolishness.

"Here," Nell said, at last. On the ground was a flat rock, and painted on it was a green band with a bow in it.

"What is it?" Tilly asked.

"This is from Seven Yard Beach. One of the rocks from down

where we used to sit. I brought it up here myself and painted it. Do you know what this green thing is?"

Tilly shook her head.

"It's Gawain's green baldric. When he came back from his failure in the court of the Green Knight, the baldric was the symbol of his weakness. And everyone in Arthur's court put a green baldric on, to show they loved him and to share in his weakness. For we are all weak, Tilly. We all make mistakes, we all lose our tempers, we say foolish things and make foolish decisions. When you are gone . . ." The girl's face started to work against sobs. "When you are gone I will come here every day and remember you, and remember that I didn't save you when I could have."

"You couldn't have saved me."

"I could have. I knew you were planning something."

Tilly gathered the girl against her. "I will miss you more than I can say."

Nell sobbed against her chest for a few minutes, then stood back and took both Tilly's hands. "He won't be happy without you."

"He won't be happy with me either, Nell. I have let him down so sorely. If there was any love there . . . I am sure it is gone."

Then footsteps crunching across the leaves alerted them they were not alone. The chief warder, Mr. Donaghy, was there, clearing his throat and indicating they should step apart. He had Tilly's trunk by his side. She was to be led under guard to the jetty, but once she was on the steamer she would be a free woman. Somehow she was to make a life over on the mainland and put this part of her life behind her. She longed to see Sterling again, to read in his expression his love for her, his sense of loss. But he had carefully transformed himself into a closed book around her, dealing with her in the cool, neutral tones he used for people he cared little for or despised.

Tilly joined Mr. Donaghy, who indicated her trunk. "Is there anything else?"

"No," she said, "that's it."

She followed him out of the garden and down the road towards the jetty. She turned for a last glimpse of Starwater behind her in the distance. The palms were rattling, the sun in the clear sky shone on the tin roof. Sterling stood on the verandah, watching them. She lifted her hand to wave good-bye, but he turned and went inside.

Tilly paused a moment. Closed her eyes.

"Miss Lejeune," Mr. Donaghy said. "Are you ready to go?"

"No," she said, her heart aching dully. "But I will go, nonetheless."

TWENTY-SEVEN

The Truth Fixes Everything

2012

The knock was unexpected but not surprising. I'd been avoiding all calls for days. I shuffled to the door in my robe and bare feet, and opened the door.

"Stacy?"

"You look like shit."

"Thanks."

Stacy held up the roughly written note I had pinned to my door. It said, *I have gone back to the mainland. Sorry for inconvenience.* "Who is this for?"

"Everybody. Mostly Joe."

She crumpled it up. "And you don't answer your phone anymore?"

"It doesn't work over here."

"Yes it does. It works enough. I usually have no problem getting you, even if it takes a few hours." She pushed her way in, dropping her suitcase by the door. "I'm here because you've clearly crashed and burned if you're not answering me. And those who have crashed and burned need friends."

I put my head in my hands. "Oh, Stace. You have no idea how badly I've screwed up *everything*."

Stacy put her arms around my shoulders and hugged me tight enough to bruise me. "And you thought the best way to handle this was to cut off all contact with the world?"

I nodded, afraid that if I spoke I would cry.

"Okay, Nina, listen. I'm going to make tea and you are going to tell me everything. And you aren't going to do your usual thing where you only tell me half of everything because you think you'll bore me or burden me or make me hate you. Everything." She let me go and I stood back.

"All right," I said, "as long as I can do it from bed."

Stacy made tea and brought it to my bedroom, where I was back between the sheets curled into a fetal position as I had been since Marla called.

"Sit up," she said. "That's a start."

I sat up and took the mug of tea she offered.

"First things first, why did you leave that note for Joe?"

"I slept with him."

To my surprise, Stacy started laughing. "'Sorry for the *inconvenience*'? That's how you tell somebody you wish you hadn't slept with them? I will have to try that."

Her laughter cheered me a little. "That's not why I'm hiding."

"Then why are you hiding?"

"It's big. I have a . . . big secret. And when you hear it, or if Joe heard it, then you'll know why . . ." I trailed off, feeling lightheaded and out of breath.

Stacy settled on the bed, her feet pulled up under her. "I'm listening."

I had never told anybody this before. I had a superstition that somehow the act of taking the horrid truth out of my head and saying it in the world was going to kill me. My ribs shook. "Okay. Here goes. Seven years ago, when I was going through Eleanor Holt's papers, I found a manuscript of a story. A novel. About a crime-solving widow in the fourteenth century."

Stacy nodded, keeping her face deliberately impassive. I had been expecting pity or anger, so wasn't sure how to proceed.

"Go on," she said. "Everything."

"I read it, and I really liked it. I thought, you know, this ought to be published. But it was written so long ago, it was kind of . . . old fashioned. The characters said things like 'oh, bother,' and sometimes instead of shouting their lines, they 'ejaculated' them. Can you imagine? The Widow Wayland ejaculating all over the place?"

Stacy was laughing again.

"So I started retyping them, changing things. It became apparent it wasn't just little things, it was big things too. The story was so slow to start, so I cut out five thousand words from the front and started it with the first body. But it's her story. The first novel was Eleanor's: the premise, the characters, all the research, even the title. A friend gave me Marla's name and address, and I sent it off to her because I thought she might appraise it and tell me if it was publishable." I sipped my tea, then put it back down on the bedside table. "I had no expectations at all, but then Marla got back to me and she already had a publisher interested. I know now that I should have said right then that I didn't write it, but I was swept up in the moment, and by then I'd found another two manuscripts and was thinking about how I'd reorganize and rewrite those. It seemed such a little mistruth, to say I'd written them, simply because I thought maybe ten people would buy the book and I'd be able to point to it and say to Mum, 'Look, I did something of value.'" I shrugged, feeling foolish and guilty. "I had no idea how successful they'd be. Marla had warned me, I'd talked to other writers: the market was flat, most writers earn nothing, it was a tough industry. I had no idea. Marla had no idea. And then the first book came out and . . . boom."

"Indeed," Stacy said.

"But then I was out of manuscripts."

"Hence the writer's block."

"It's more like typist's block. I'm not a writer."

Stacy tipped her head to the side. "See, that's not what I'm hearing. I'm hearing very much *cowriter*. The books weren't publishable in the form you found them in. Certainly you didn't create the widow, but you have written half a book about her on your own, haven't you?"

"It's rough. It's rubbish. I don't know anywhere near enough about the Middle Ages."

"Then hire somebody who does. And give it a good edit. Nina, I'm sorry, but I did something naughty last time I was here. You were sleeping in after a bad night, and I went into your computer and had a scan through what you've written so far."

I was both aghast and grateful. "And?"

"It's fine. Nobody will know the difference, once you've polished it up. I think your voice is probably more a part of the Widow Wayland stories than you realize."

The relief that flooded my limbs made me feel light. "Really?"

"Really."

"But I still have to live with the knowledge that I stole the ideas."

"Do you still have the manuscripts?"

I looked down guiltily. "No, I burned them. I became so worried somebody would find them and expose me."

"Good," Stacy said. "Very wise. So, the only people who know are you and me?"

"That's right."

"And you're not going to tell anyone and I'm not going to tell anyone . . . so . . ."

"The journalist. The one that was trying to get access to my papers. She found copies of letters from the publishers to Eleanor, saying we don't want to publish your Widow Wayland books."

Stacy stroked her chin. "That's still not proof of anything beyond the fact you might have borrowed the name."

"Are you saying I should lie?"

"When we can't expect people to do the right thing with the truth, I don't see why we should give it to them. This journalist, if I'm guessing rightly, wants to take you down? You're rich and pretty and young. Giving her the truth would be irresponsible. So you cowrote a few of the books with your great-grandmother? That sounds like a family matter to me. It's nowhere near a copyright infringement."

I turned Stacy's words over in my mind. Cowritten? Is that what they were? And was that why this one was so difficult? My cowriter hadn't shown up for work.

"Nina, let me offer you some advice," Stacy said. "If you find writing alone too difficult, then get out now. Don't keep banging your head against it. You will be fine. You can sell that ridiculously overpriced apartment and come live with me for as long as you need, and I'll help you sort out your contractual obligations and repayments. But if you think you can do it, then put this behind you, never speak of it again, and keep writing."

I sank back against my pillow. "I'm so tired."

"I'm led to believe writing is hard work for most. Lord knows I couldn't do it. Being tired is not a reason to stop. It's not a reason to switch off your phone and put ridiculous notes on your door for sexy marine biologists."

I put my face in my hands again. "Why is life so complicated?"

"Because you're a grown-up. But you get lots of benefits. You get to drive and buy your own shoes."

I dropped my hands and smiled at her. "Thank you for coming. Will you stay and help me sort this out?"

"Of course I will."

•

Joe showed up after lunch. I was dressed by now, for the first time in many days, in one of Stacy's dresses. I hadn't bothered with laundry in a while.

"You're back," he said.

"I never left," I replied.

"Yeah, I guessed that. But the note's gone, so . . ."

"I'm sorry. I had a . . . meltdown of sorts."

"To do with me?"

I shook my head.

"Well," he replied. "I want you to see something."

Stacy was at my shoulder now, all fluttery eyelashes. "Hi, Joe."

"Do you want to come down to the boat shed with us?" he asked her. "I was fixing the damage that Julian caused when I found it."

"Found what?" I asked.

He turned his gaze back to me. "A box full of papers. Eleanor's papers."

My heart jumped. "Why didn't you bring them?"

"It's a big box and the bottom is falling out of it. Have you got a laundry basket or something similar?"

I raced to the laundry, tipped out my dirty washing, and followed Joe and Stacy down to the boat shed.

They chatted ahead of me, no awkwardness between them. I thought about how Joe had said he loved me. I wondered how different he'd feel if I told him the truth about the Widow Wayland. What if he saw it differently from Stacy? I thought of the admiration he'd expressed for my creativity. He would be disappointed; he might even think I'm a liar.

The boat shed was dark and musty. I could see the new beams Joe had nailed in.

"You know you didn't have to do this," I said.

"Yes, I did," he replied. "Julian broke the old ones." He smiled. "It was supposed to be a surprise."

"Consider me surprised."

"The box is up in the back corner of the loft. I'll go up and hand down the papers for you to put in the basket. Okay?"

"Okay," Stacy said.

We watched Joe climb up on the new beams and haul himself into the loft.

"Be careful," I said. "No more accidents in here."

He came to the edge of the loft with the first handful of papers. "I've reinforced it," he said.

Joe kept passing down handfuls of papers and we piled the papers as neatly as we could in the laundry basket, then took them back up to the house.

At the door, Joe hesitated, clearly hoping for an invitation to come in.

"Thanks, Joe," I said, outside the door, my hand on the doorknob, my body barring the way in. "I didn't even think of looking in the boat shed for more papers. Largely because I only recently found out I had a boat shed."

Stacy, Joe, and I stood there for a moment in awkward silence, then Stacy slipped past me with the laundry basket. "I'll leave you to it," she said.

When she was gone, I closed the door behind her, leaving Joe and me alone on the verandah. Joe smiled at me sadly. "So," he said.

"So," I replied.

"So you've been avoiding me and now you're not going to invite me in?"

"I don't think it can work," I blurted.

"You still love Cameron?"

I nearly laughed. There was no way I loved Cameron, and my feelings for Joe were burning a hole in my ribs. "I don't think it can work," I said, with more conviction this time because it felt so true. I didn't want him to know the truth about me, so I had to let him go.

He smiled tightly and, without a word, turned and left.

I took a moment to gather myself and went inside.

Stacy had the laundry basket on the floor of the living room. She'd moved the coffee table up against the wall and was slowly sorting. "You broke up with him?" she asked, her head bent over the box.

"There was nothing to break up." I knelt next to her. "You know what I'm hoping to find, don't you?"

"I'm half hoping you won't find it," she said.

We dived in.

•

Letters and short stories and poems and essays. We sifted through them all. They appeared to be in no order, as though the pages had been dropped, regathered haphazardly, and thrown in the box.

It was Stacy who found it.

"Widow Wayland!" she shrieked, snatching up a sheaf of papers.

I could see immediately it wasn't a full manuscript, but I took them from her hands anyway.

"*Dark Horses*, a Widow Wayland Mystery," I read from the front page. My hands shook.

"Go on," she said, leaning into my shoulder.

"It's not a full novel." I already had the front half of a novel. I didn't need this; I couldn't use this.

"The rest might be somewhere else."

But I went to the last page in the bundle and read the last paragraph aloud to Stacy. "And then the Widow Wayland became disillusioned because no man would publish—nor even read without some prejudiced idea of 'women's stories'—her manuscripts and so she ran off to Havana with a handsome young man and lived happily ever after. THE END."

"What does that mean?" Stacy said. "Does that happen in the story?"

"Of course not. That was Eleanor, angry that she had been rejected."

Stacy picked up a manila envelope, stuffed with folded papers. "Oh yes, she was rejected. There are dozens of letters in here, telling her to take her manuscript elsewhere."

"And no doubt a copy of one of those letters is what has that nosy journalist interested," I said. I read the last lines over and over. She gave up. Eleanor gave up.

Stacy touched my shoulder. "Are you all right?"

"I'm going to have to write this book, aren't I?"

Stacy looked at me, waited for me to finish.

"This is it. She stopped. She gave up, Stacy. But I'm not going to. I am absolutely not going to give up. Eleanor was writing at a time when it was so difficult for women. Everything's been easy for me and all I do is whine. I have to finish this book, and then write another and another. For Eleanor. Because she couldn't."

Stacy leaned in to hug me. "She would have been so proud."

"Except for the part where I plagiarized her," I said, through a mouthful of Stacy's dark hair.

"You mean the part where you took her unpublishable manuscript and made millions of people read about the Widow Wayland and see her on the television?" Stacy sat back. "Don't tell me she wouldn't have been pleased."

I felt a smile curl the corner of my lip. "Maybe you're right."

•

I called the journalist myself. I wasn't going to hide behind Marla anymore. Down at the pay phone, with Stacy hovering in the background patting a dog tied up outside the coffee shop. The warm sea breeze and the smell of seaweed that had become familiar to me. Like home.

"Elizabeth Parrish speaking," she said.

"Hello, Elizabeth. It's Nina Jones. Sorry I've been a bit hard to catch. I'm on an island with no Internet and very poor phone reception."

I could hear her roughly and quickly gathering papers. "Nina. Thanks for calling me. Do you mind if I record our—"

"There will be nothing to record." I launched into the little speech that Stacy had drilled into me. "I'll be sending you a photocopy of a partial manuscript my great-grandmother wrote about the Widow Wayland. As you will see, it bears no resemblance to any of my books and she never finished it. I took the title character from her and that was all. If you want to write an article about how difficult it was for women to be published in the early twentieth century, I think that would be a fine thing for a journalist like you to do. Aside from that, I have nothing else to say to you."

"Wait, I just want to ask—"

But I hung up the phone, my heart thudding. I bent over and grasped my knees. Stacy was behind me, rubbing my back. "Well, that's done."

"Then why do I feel so unhappy?" I said, straightening up and pushing my hair out of my eyes.

"I expect it's because you still have to write the book," she said.

But it wasn't that. I had an extension of my deadline and, now I wasn't holding out for another of Eleanor's manuscripts to rewrite, I believed I might stop second-guessing myself and finally get on with it.

I was unhappy because I was in love with Joe.

•

Stacy walked me down there that evening, to Joe's shed. I could see muted lights on at his parents' house, behind pale blue curtains. But Joe's place appeared to be all in darkness.

"I don't think he's home," I said, hesitating on the road.

"I can see a flicker of light. Maybe he's watching television," she said. She poked me in the ribs. "Go on."

"This is a bad idea. He's going to hate me."

"If he hates you, then he wasn't worth having, dear." She dragged me to the door and knocked on it hard.

"Stacy!" I hissed.

But then Joe opened the door. I could see Julian on the floor with his PlayStation controller, with another controller lying beside him. The sound of explosions came from the television.

"Hi," Joe said curiously.

"I've come at a bad time. You're busy."

Joe glanced over his shoulder to Julian, who was completely absorbed in the video game, then back at me. "I'm playing a video game. I'm not busy."

Something blew up and Julian rolled over groaning. "Dad, come back. We are getting owned by these aliens."

Stacy stepped in. "Will you show me how to play, Julian?" she asked, and even the eight-year-old boy was captivated by her eyelashes.

He sat up and offered her a controller and started showing her the buttons.

"Come for a walk?" I said to Joe.

He turned to Julian. "I'm off for a little while, mate. You okay with Stacy?"

"Sure."

"If he gets worried, my mum and dad are next door," Joe said.

"I'll be fine," Julian said, getting comfortably cross-legged and mashing the keys on his controller. "I bet Stacy is a better space marine than you."

Joe turned back to me. "Let's go," he said.

"Down to Seven Yard Beach," I said. "I need to tell you something."

The last blush of dusk was in the east, over the lights of the mainland. The sea breeze cooled off the land, and palm fronds rattled all along the road. We walked down to the beach in silence, then sat on the sand side by side but not too close. I wrapped my arms around my knees and looked out at the waves, breaking softly on the shore.

"What do you need to tell me?" he said at last. "I don't mean to hurry you, but I have an inkling Stacy's not going to be such a great space marine after all."

I turned to him, the wind tangling my hair. His eyes were almost black in the evening dark. "I have lied to everybody."

He frowned. "About what?"

So I told him everything, the raw truth without tidying it or polishing it, as quickly and as simply as I could.

When I finished he said, "And that's it?"

"That's a lot," I said. "I've presented myself to you as some creative genius with a big international career."

"No you haven't," he said. "We've barely talked about your career. And since we met you've told me repeatedly how you are anything *but* a creative genius. Nina, I don't care about what you do, how many books or babies you can or can't produce. I care about who you are."

I was momentarily speechless.

"I love you, Nina. The woman sitting here in front of me. The woman with the golden-brown hair and the silky skin and the gentle hands. The woman you are, Nina. The real you."

"Wow," I said at last. "I was sure you wouldn't want anything to do with me."

"Then you don't know me very well," he said, pulling me against him. "And I'm looking forward to you getting to know me better. A lot better."

I turned my face up to kiss him and dissolved against him, warm with happiness. Tomorrow I would sort out the book. Tonight was about the summer breeze, the fresh smell of the sea, and the giddy thrill of new love.

TWENTY-EIGHT

Finding Tilly

1893

Sterling stood outside the little schoolhouse, the sun in his hair and a swell of apprehension under his ribs. He told himself he didn't have to walk up the front path, he didn't have to knock. But it had taken him many weeks to track her down; he couldn't possibly walk away now.

This little house, which had once been a bed-and-breakfast, had been converted into a school for local children in a bequest when its owner had died. Mr. Richard Hamblyn had been a friend of Tilly's and had charged her with setting up and running the school.

Sterling knew all this because the man he had paid to find Tilly had told him. He still remembered the prickle of surprise and delight at knowing that, all along, she had been just across the water.

He straightened his collar, took off his tall hat, and made his way up the path. If Nell knew what he was doing . . . ah, well, she would find out soon enough if things went as he hoped they would. Hardly a day passed when his little girl didn't talk of Tilly. Little girl? No, she was a young woman now. He often wondered if Nell spoke about Tilly so often because she somehow knew Sterling loved her.

He loved her. He had never stopped loving her. The business with the escaped prisoner was fading from the institution's memory. Hettie Maythorpe had never been found and eventually they had stopped looking. And with a change of chief warder and visiting surgeon, the gossip about Tilly's role in the escape had long stopped spreading.

And still he loved her. Every morning he woke up expecting himself to be cured of it. Instead, he woke up with the same cold pebble in his heart, the same bruising ache.

Thus, the only practical course of action became finding Tilly. Sterling had expected it to take much longer.

He rang the bell and waited, his pulse hard in his throat. The door opened and a matronly woman with gray hair stood there.

"Can I help you?" she said.

"I am here to call on Miss . . ." He couldn't finish the sentence. What did she call herself now? Miss Lejeune? Miss Kirkland? Mrs. Dellafore? "Tilly," he managed. "Is she in?"

"Miss Kirkland is taking a class," the woman said. "But she will be finished in a few minutes if you'd like to wait here on the verandah."

Sterling hesitated. He could go. He could run away from this and never have to face the possibility of her rejection. It had been nearly a year since she left. Was there any chance at all she still loved him? He had treated her so ill. He burned with shame for it. He didn't deserve her love . . .

"Sir?"

Sterling shook himself. The woman had asked him a question. "I'm sorry," he said.

"Would you like tea?" she repeated.

"No. Thank you," he said. "I will wait here for her."

"Your name?"

"Sterling Holt."

"Very good, sir. She'll be along shortly. Please take a seat." The woman went back inside and closed the door behind her.

Sterling didn't want to sit; couldn't sit. He needed to keep moving so he descended the stairs into the front garden. The neat garden beds had him wondering if Tilly had planted and tended them. On reflection, he could trace the moment he'd started falling in love with her to her asking for a chance to work in the garden. A woman as pretty and accomplished as Tilly would ordinarily recoil from soiling her hands. But there had always been something charmingly natural about her.

The sun filtered through the leaves and made patterns on the grass as the wind moved in the treetops. He paced the garden, certain that hours had passed when his pocket watch told him it had only been minutes.

Then the sound of the door bursting open. He looked up and she stood there. Her red hair catching the sunlight, her pale eyes frantic, her mouth a little *O* of surprise.

He told himself to be courageous.

"Tilly?" he said, and all of his fears and hopes were compressed into the question he had made of her name.

"Sterling!" she gasped, and ran down the stairs to his waiting arms.

ACKNOWLEDGMENTS

A s I wrote this book in something of a white heat, I can only assume that I will forget to thank somebody. But never before have I been more aware of the fact that writing a book requires the support of so many people.

My Sisters, who are the best writing group in the world. My agent, Selwa Anthony, who represents both business acumen and love. My dear friend, Mary-Rose, who helps me see the world clearly. My incredible, tireless, intelligent, priceless research assistant, Heather Gammage, without whom this book would be full of holes and errors. (If there are errors, they aren't her fault. Sometimes I gleefully ignored her good advice for the sake of a good story.) Julie and Karen Hinchliffe: thank you for sharing early memories of sugarcane fields. Thanks too for those who responded on social media with your burning cane memories: the black snow is down to you. I want to acknowledge those who gave invaluable editorial input: Vanessa Radnidge, Jody Lee, Kate Ballard, Heather Lazare, and Paula Ellery. I continue to benefit greatly from the resources and generosity of the University of Queensland, its libraries, staff, and students, but especially my colleagues in the School of English, Media Studies, and Art History.

This book was researched and written in part on St. Helena Island and Moreton Island, the islands on which Ember Island is based. They are both wonderful places, for different reasons, and Moreton Bay is a fabulous location for a holiday if you feel so inclined.

My personal life is held together by seven lovely mammals who share my space: Ollie, Luka, Astrid, Petra, Nyxi, Wiglaf, and Sigrun. As always, I want to thank my mother, who still lets me lay my head in her lap so she can stroke my hair. The longer I'm alive, the more I love you, Mum.

Ember Island

Ember Island tells the mesmerizing story of two women, separated by a century, who discover long-buried secrets in an Australian manor house.

In 1876, Tilly, a recently married young Englishwoman, is reeling with shock and guilt after her tempestuous marriage ends in horrific circumstances on the remote Channel Islands. Determined to get as far from England as she can, she takes on a new identity and gets a job on Ember Island in Moreton Bay, Australia, where she becomes the governess to a prison superintendent's young daughter, Nell. As Tilly fights her attraction to the superintendent, Sterling Holt, she befriends one of the few female inmates, and a dangerous relationship develops. Meanwhile, her precocious charge, Nell, is watching her every move and writing it all down, hiding tiny journals all over Starwater, her rambling manor home.

More than a hundred years later, bestselling novelist Nina Jones is struggling with writer's block and a disappointing personal life. Her poet boyfriend has recently broken up with her, and a reporter is digging into the past of Nina's great-grandmother, Nell, making Nina realize that there are some secrets she may no longer be able to hide. Retreating to Starwater, she discovers Nell's diary pages hidden in the old walls and becomes determined to solve the mystery. Though Tilly and Nina are separated by more than a century, Starwater House will change both their lives.

Deeply affecting and beautifully written, *Ember Island* is a sweeping novel of secrets, second chances, and learning to trust your heart.

TOPICS AND QUESTIONS FOR DISCUSSION

1. Nina tells Joe that her great-grandmother, Nell Holt, was "legendary in our family. . . . She was a wild nonconformist. . . . She was fierce" (p. 8). What were your initial impressions of Nell? Do you think her reputation as "fierce" is justly deserved? Why or why not? What, if any, examples of Nell's fierceness did you observe?

2. Nina's friend Stacy says, "The nineteenth century wasn't a great time to be a woman" (p. 178). Do you think she's right? How does Tilly's experience bear out this statement? Since Tilly will not inherit her grandfather's property after his death, what options are available to her?

3. Why is Starwater House so important to Tilly, Nell, and Nina? Nina gives several explanations for her decision to stay at Starwater House longer than she initially planned. Do you think her explanations differ from why she's actually staying?

4. Laura, an acquaintance of Tilly's, tells Tilly, "Expectations are the enemy of happiness" (p. 126). What does she mean by this statement, and how does it apply to Tilly's current situation? Do you think Nina's expectations have gotten in the way of her happiness, particularly with Joe? How?

5. At Tilly's wedding, before her husband "registered that she was regarding him, she saw something that made her stomach prickle with doubt" (p. 2). How does this foreshadow their life? What were your initial impressions of Jasper? Did your feelings about him change? If so, how? Why did Tilly marry Jasper originally? Why do you think she stays after his true character is revealed?

6. Tilly's grandfather leaves her a box of banknotes along with a short message that reads, "This is for you and nobody else. A woman should have at least something in the world" (p. 55). In what ways does Tilly's grandfather try to protect her? Do you think that Tilly is right to keep the banknotes after she gives Jasper her other possessions? Why or why not?

7. Nina says "one thing I hated more than anything was being asked to speak about my historical research" (p. 19). Why does Nina hate speaking about her writing process? Were you surprised to learn where many of Nina's ideas came from? How does Stacy react to Nina's disclosure? Do you agree with Stacy's viewpoint?

8. After the accident at Lumière sur la Mer, Tilly feels immense guilt because "[t]he punishment was immeasurably out of

equivalence with the crime" (p. 144). Do you agree? What were Jasper and Chantelle's crimes? Discuss Laura's final letter to Chantelle on pages 396-99. Do you think that Chantelle was as guilty as Jasper in the crime against Tilly? If so, explain why.

9. Nell's diary is interwoven through the narrative, connecting the past and the present. Discuss the ways it helps give insight into the events at Starwater House during both Tilly's and Nina's time. Did reading Nell's diary help you see her differently? Compare how Nell presents herself in her diary to the way other characters perceive her.

10. When Joe's father asks Nina if she is in a relationship, she lies, rationalizing her decision to do so by saying, "Joe had to know I was unavailable and it wasn't as though I could easily tell him why. I wouldn't be on the island for long; it didn't matter if I lied" (p. 161). Why does Nina assume a relationship with Joe wouldn't work out? Do you agree with her assumption and her decision to lie? How does Stacy react to her decision?

11. Fire is an important conceit throughout *Ember Island* and, although the thought of fire "made [Tilly's] stomach turn to ice" (p. 196), she is deeply connected to it. How does the author help establish this connection in her descriptions of Tilly? There are two significant fires in the book. Describe the effect that each has on Tilly's life and the lives of those around her. How did Ember Island get its name? Discuss the ways in which the name of the island alludes to both the events that occur on it and Tilly's life in Guernsey.

12. Discuss Tilly's relationship with Hettie. In what ways are the two women alike? When Tilly decides to help Hettie, she believes that "[s]he could erase her actions of the past with her actions of the present" (p. 271). Why does Tilly think that helping Hettie will absolve her of her guilt over what happened with Jasper? Do you agree with her logic? Were you surprised when Tilly decided to help Hettie? Why?

13. In *Ember Island*, islands are described as "places in between; places neither here nor there, but rather places on the way somewhere" (p. 82). How does this statement apply to both Tilly and Nina? How does each woman end up at Ember Island? Do you think it's a temporary stop for them? Explain your reasoning.

14. After speaking with Sterling about Mr. Burton's accusations, Tilly mutters, "The truth fixes nothing. . . . The truth is a great burden" (p. 254). Do you agree with Tilly, or do you think Sterling is correct that "the truth fixes everything"? Does being truthful hurt or hinder Tilly and Nina? After each woman decides to be truthful, what are the results?

ENHANCE YOUR BOOK CLUB

1. Nina says of the reporter Elizabeth Parrish, "Maybe I had been angry with Elizabeth Parrish because she revealed the truth: I wasn't an artist. I'd always known that" (p. 23). Discuss what art is with your book club. Do you think that Nina's bestselling Widow Wayland series can be classified as art?

2. After reading Nell's diary, Nina thinks, "These were my ancestors. This was my family history. . . . Do we honor the past by projecting ourselves forward into the future? By carrying on genes and traits and family stories?" (pp. 169-70). Discuss Nina's statement. How do you honor your own family history? Share your own photos and stories with your book club.

3. Nell is fascinated with *Sir Gawain and the Green Knight*. Read it with your book club and discuss why you think the story appeals to Nell.

4. Nell's companion is her wooden cat, Pangur Ban, whose name is taken from an Old Irish poem. Read "Pangur Ban" as a book club. What does the poem say about writing and inspiration? Discuss how it relates to Nina's writing or your own creative process.

5. To learn more about Kimberley Freeman or *Ember Island*, read her blog at http://kimberleyfreeman.com.

ABOUT THE AUTHOR

Kimberley was born in London and her family moved back to Australia when she was three years old. She grew up in Queensland, where she currently lives.

Kimberley has written for as long as she can remember and is proud to write in many genres. She is an award-winning writer in children's, historical, and speculative fiction under her birth name, Kim Wilkins. She adopted the pen name Kimberley Freeman for her commercial women's fiction novels, *Duet*, *Gold Dust*, *Wildflower Hill*, and *Lighthouse Bay*, to honor her maternal grandmother and to try to capture the spirit of the page-turning novels she has always loved to read. Kim has an honors degree, a masters degree, and a Ph.D. from The University of Queensland, where she is also a lecturer.

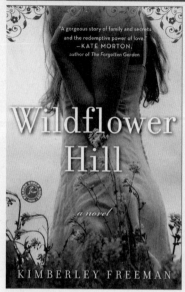
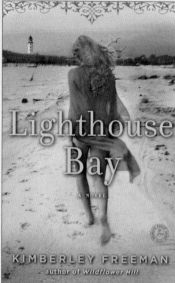